MORE HIGH PRAISE FOR COLLEEN THOMPSON!

HEAT LIGHTNING (cont'd)

"This nicely complicated tale has plenty of edge-of-your-seat suspense. The villain is quite violent and evil, and the mystery moves along at a good pace."

—*Romantic Times BOOKreviews*

THE DEADLIEST DENIAL

"Captivating...Thompson, a RITA finalist, is skilled at building suspense."   —*Publishers Weekly*

"Thompson's style is gritty, and that works well with her flawed and driven characters....High family drama mixes with deadly suspense."   —*Romantic Times BOOKreviews*

"*The Deadliest Denial* is a spellbinding read with a gripping, intrigue-filled plot. There are twists and turns around every corner....This is a great read. Ms. Thompson has gifted us with another all-nighter."   —Fresh Fiction

FADE THE HEAT

"RITA finalist Thompson takes the reader on a roller-coaster ride full of surprising twists and turns in this exceptional novel of romantic suspense."

—*Publishers Weekly* (Starred Review)

"The precise details of Thompson's novel give it a rich, edgy texture that's enthralling....For keen characters, emotional richness and a satisfying story that doesn't fade away, read Thompson's latest."   —*Romantic Times BOOKreviews*

FATAL ERROR

"Fast-paced, chilling, and sexy...[with] chemistry that shimmers."   —*Library Journal*

"Thompson has written a first-class work of romantic suspense."   —*Booklist*

FRAMING THE SHOT

"About the other day, I'm sorry. Sorry I shook you up like that. I came off a little—"

"You came down on me like a tornado, the way I remember it." She offered a wan smile. "And you had every right to. Listen, Zeke, I had an idea that you wouldn't want me taking that picture. But from the moment I saw you there and framed the shot, I knew it would be the best I've ever taken. Could be the best I ever *will* take. So, yes, I buried it deep in that proof stack in the hope you wouldn't see it. That wasn't right, and I *am* sorry I misled you. But I won't ever be anything but proud of that photo."

In her voice, he heard an echo of his own passion for his work; in her eyes, he saw a reflection of the same fears he kept buried. Fears that the ugliness of the past would overtake him, that he was helpless to outrun it no matter how many miles or years might pass. It was not pity, though, but the core of strength that drew him to her, that had him gripping her thin shoulders and leaning in to claim a kiss.

TRIPLE EXPOSURE

Colleen Thompson

LEISURE BOOKS NEW YORK CITY

*To all those who dare to soar,
whether it's in the cockpit of a plane,
the pages of a book,
or the limitless skies of the imagination.*

A LEISURE BOOK®

August 2008

Published by

Dorchester Publishing Co., Inc.
200 Madison Avenue
New York, NY 10016

ISBN 10: 0-8439-6143-0
ISBN 13: 978-0-8439-6143-0

The name "Leisure Books" and the stylized "L" with design are trademarks of Dorchester Publishing Co., Inc.

Printed in the United States of America.

10 9 8 7 6 5 4 3 2 1

Visit us on the web at www.dorchesterpub.com.

ACKNOWLEDGMENTS

I have very much enjoyed my visits to the beautiful little town of Marfa, Texas, home of the mysterious Marfa lights, setting of James Dean's final movie, *Giant*, and—thanks to the artist Donald Judd and those who followed—a fabulous destination for art lovers. The Marfa of *Triple Exposure* is based upon this desert gem, but various changes, exaggerations, and flights of fancy have altered the geographic, business, and social landscape where needed to serve the story.

I'd like to thank Burt Compton of Marfa Gliders (which differs significantly from the glider business described in the book) for sharing his expertise on soaring the high country. If you're ever in West Texas, be sure to look him up for a one-of-a-kind experience. Mona Garcia, owner of the lovely Arcon Inn, was kind enough to take me on a tour of old Fort Russell, which is becoming something new and wonderful thanks to the efforts of the International Woman's Foundation. Thanks, too, to John Boors of Alternate Pest Control in Alpine, who answered questions on the local insects.

My research on gliders also led me to visit the Soaring Club of Houston, located in Waller, Texas. Thanks to the many club members who tirelessly answered questions and especially to pilots Douglas R. Courville, David Martin, Miguel Lavalla, Ed Toohey, and Anne Berry. Thanks to pilot Sylvia Szafarczyk for helping me brainstorm ways to make a relatively safe pastime dangerously exciting and most of all, to Glenn Giddens for sharing his expertise and taking me on my maiden glider flight.

ACKNOWLEDGMENTS (cont'd)

I'd like to express my appreciation to my agent Karen Solem, along with Jennifer Schober, also of Spencerhill Associates, for their encouragement and assistance. Thanks to editor extraordinaire Alicia Condon, along with the other members of the Dorchester Publishing family, for everything they do to put my books into the hands of readers.

I want to thank, too, first readers Barbara "Bobbi" Sissel, Joni Rodgers, and Jo Anne Banker for their invaluable assistance, as well as other members of my critique group, The Midwives: T.J. Bennett, Wanda Dionne, and Anna Slade. I couldn't do without your insightful comments and suggestions, along with the support of my many RWA friends.

Last but never least, thanks to the folks at home, Mike and Andrew, for their loving support. And thanks to furry folks at home, Zippy and Jewel, who are always up for a romp or a snuggle, at least when they're not inspiring me with canine mischief.

TRIPLE
EXPOSURE

CHAPTER ONE

Before the beginning of years
There came to the making of man
Time, with a gift of tears;
Grief, with a glass that ran;
Pleasure, with a pain for leaven;
Summer, with flowers that fell;
Remembrance fallen from heaven,
And madness risen from hell;
Strength without hands to smite;
Love that endures for a breath;
Night, the shadow of light,
And life, the shadow of death.

—*Algernon Charles Swinburne,*
from Atalanta in Calydon, *chorus, stanza 1*

The inky blackness spawned light, as it did so often on the high desert plain surrounding tiny Marfa, Texas.

Ghost lights, mystery lights—the local population claimed they'd been there since the native people roamed the land. Some supposed they were the spectral campfires of long-vanished tribes. Another contingent subscribed to the alien spacecraft theory, while still others wove explanations from the strands of science—citing weather phenomena, refracted, distant headlights and jackrabbits dusted with naturally occurring phosphorescence. Because no one could say for certain, the mystery had for decades drawn the curious, the eccentric, even the mad, and this particular night was no exception.

The telescope brought it in closer: a glowing greenish glob that first hovered and then bobbed along the dark horizon. As a great owl hooted nearby, the light seemed to trace the foothills bordering the Chinati Mountains, themselves obscured beneath the velvet cloak of night.

Green shifted into violet and then brightened to white before the glob split into twin orbs. Split, like the observer's attention, diverted by word of a troubling new arrival. A disturbing new spark that burned into awareness, smoldering like an ember on a woolen rug.

A threat to be extinguished quickly, before the spark burst into a wild blaze, consuming everything held dear. A threat that could be beaten out or drowned or smothered. The method didn't matter, as long as it—as long as *she*—was killed.

In the shadow of the mountains, one of the two lights winked out while the other grew and strengthened. Head buzzing, the observer breathed more quickly, taking this as confirmation.

The Spirit Guides had sent a message, one that could not be ignored.

Tuesday, February 5

With one last glance at the bruised silhouette of Mount Livermore looming in the distance, Rachel Copeland slipped through the glass door and out of the chill wind that had followed her from Philadelphia. She raked back the red-brown bangs that had blown across her eyes and took in a sight that had her sighing in relief, forgetting how eagerly she had once plotted her escape. Forgetting everything but the familiar post-lunch-rush scents. Grilled burgers and tacos. Onion rings and fries. A lingering trace of cigarette smoke, and the pine-scented aroma of the liquid used for cleanup. She sniffed deeply, as if she'd pressed her nose to a bouquet of rare blooms instead of the surgeon general's worst nightmare.

"I told your dad you'd turn up sooner or later." From behind the café's counter, Patsy Copeland's moon face smiled, not in welcome but with the satisfaction of being right.

Never physically attractive, with her broad-beamed build, her serviceable smocks worn over stretch pants, and her white-streaked hair pinned tightly behind her head, she had also never made a pretense of replacing Rachel's mother. Nor had she called her stepdaughter since the events that had changed her life last winter.

Rachel tried not to hold it against her stepmother. Tried even harder to keep the quiver in her knees from escalating into shaking she'd be powerless to hide. Instead, she reminded herself of an early lesson that her dad had taught her: *Never pass up a rough landing site without a better one on the horizon.*

Since the acquittal had ensured she wouldn't be a guest of the Commonwealth of Pennsylvania and her attorneys' fees had ensured she wouldn't be solvent in the next millennium, she was fresh out of better options. Best to remember that before she popped off a response she'd regret.

"Good to see you, too." She hoped her expression looked more like a smile than indigestion. Prayed that Patsy wouldn't simply tell her to get back in her rust bucket of a van and keep driving.

Easing the worn strap of her duffel bag off a shoulder aching with fatigue, Rachel slid its weight onto the black-and-white tiled floor. Other than the two of them, the place was empty, with every crumb swept, each surface gleaming, and all the photos of framed gliders—or sailplanes, as enthusiasts called them—hanging straight against the sky-blue walls. Patsy kept a clean place, a tiny grill known as The Roost, not only in honor of the fliers who stopped in for a quick bite at the little airfield's edge, but as a nod to the huge owls that couldn't be dissuaded from nesting behind its rooftop sign. Rachel had seen one on her way inside, an enormous great horned specimen that had peered at her through sleepy, golden eyes.

She guessed one killer didn't get overly excited upon seeing another.

Patsy gave her a once-over, taking in the travel-creased jeans and long-sleeved, ivory T-shirt Rachel wore beneath her leather jacket. "You look like you could use a good feed. How about a pizza-burger? You always used to like those."

Rachel released the breath she had been holding at this sign that Patsy wasn't about to send her packing. Though her stomach growled, she answered, "Thanks, but do you know where—? I have to see my dad." One of his bear hugs was what she needed, more than any other kind of sustenance. He'd come out to stay with her for a week before the trial started but couldn't be away long from either his business or his frail, eighty-six-year-old mother, who'd been shielded from the news of Rachel's "troubles."

"He's up in the tow plane still, I 'magine. He's putting a big group of gliders in the air. Gettin' ready for a competition this weekend."

"And Bobby?" A close family friend for years, the pilot-mechanic felt more like an uncle than the down-on-his-luck stray her father had taken under his wing years before.

"You know Bobby." A trace of a smile drifted across Patsy's features before dissipating in an instant. "If that man doesn't have his head in somebody's engine, it's up in the clouds."

Patsy slapped a frosty round onto the sizzling grill, reminding Rachel that she had never credited her stepdaughter with the sense to eat when it was needful. *Smart as a whip when it comes to staying one step ahead of trouble, but not so much in the horse sense department,* Patsy had observed not long after she had married Walter Copeland when Rachel was sixteen.

Though that was seventeen years past, Rachel still remembered the shock of the pair's Vegas "getaway" and the rings they had returned with. As far as she'd been concerned, her dad should still have been grieving for her mother, who had died suddenly a mere ten months earlier.

It still made Rachel cringe to think of the way her father's ruddy face had split in a wide grin as he'd broken the news, his head wagging excitedly as he'd said, *"And now we'll all be a family. Isn't that great?"*

That was the day he'd hit an all-time high score on the

old Clueless Meter and opened a chasm of awkwardness neither his daughter nor his new wife could find a way to bridge. Instead of bonding as he'd hoped, the two had toughed out two long, awkward years until Rachel—with Patsy's loving guidance—had enrolled in the most distant of several liberal arts colleges to offer her a scholarship.

Rachel's father had harbored hopes that she would return to work at his side, but she had her own dreams, even if they'd eventually imploded like an old Vegas resort. Yet what echoed through her memory was not the boom of demolition, but the clean crack of the little .38 revolver she had grown desperate enough to buy for self-defense.

The odor of the cooking burger turned her stomach, overlaid as it was by the acrid smell of gun smoke. But she said nothing, instead sitting at the counter while Patsy prepared the bun with pizza sauce and mozzarella cheese, tearing a few fragrant, fresh basil leaves for good measure. That last addition meant she was taking special pains.

Considering the money issue that lay between them, Rachel figured the sandwich was the closest thing to a welcome she would get. Besides, she had decided that part of retaking control of her life was going to involve regaining at least a portion of the twenty pounds she'd dropped since last December. And Patsy, Griller of Red Meat, Maker of Milk Shakes, and Fryer of Damned Near Anything That Didn't Get Out of the Way Fast Enough, was just the woman to help her put it back on. *If* the two of them could peacefully coexist.

Rachel eyed the broad back that was turned to her as Patsy flipped the burger, and said doubtfully, "Listen, this— this situation, with me staying, it isn't going to last forever."

Patsy peered over her shoulder. "No. One of us would for damn sure kill the other—"

She cut herself off, her round face flushing and her watery, blue eyes bulging. As she stammered an apology, saying she hadn't meant it that way, Rachel found herself doing the last thing she would have expected.

For the first time in over a year, she laughed. So hard she couldn't catch her breath. Waving off her stepmother's contrition, she finally managed, "Sorry. I shouldn't—shouldn't have laughed, but that had to be the most un-Patsy-like thing I've ever heard you say."

Patsy laughed, too—a little, though caution lingered in her eyes. As she busied herself plating the burger and grabbing an ice-cold Dr Pepper from the cooler, a light flush bloomed against her winter-pale skin, and perspiration beaded her upper lip and forehead.

"Was just a figure of speech, that's all." As Patsy set the meal on the counter, the words snapped out, hard as broken bits of plastic. "Wasn't trying to make light of—well, you know."

Rachel sobered, recalling how much her father's wife hated feeling embarrassed. Remembering the methods she had of serving everyone else a share of her discomfort.

Even a hard landing beats no landing at all.

"It's probably good we got this out of the way right off," Rachel said. "We both know what happened is too big an elephant to tiptoe around for very long.

"A—a man died," she went on, though her conscience echoed with the doleful tones of the prosecutor's summation: *A nineteen-year-old is not a man. Not yet. And because of Rachel Copeland's actions, now he never will be.* "It's not something we can pretend away, no matter how much we'd like to."

"I prayed for you, I truly did." Patsy snatched a bag of jalapeño chips out of the rack and dropped it next to Rachel's elbow. "Every night. That you'd get what you deserved."

Rachel swallowed back the need to demand, *What the hell is that supposed to mean?* Instead, she sucked in a calming breath and answered, "I did. Thanks." *For not stepping forward as a character witness, anyway.*

Patsy smiled, and Rachel bit into her pizza-burger and chewed slowly, willing herself to taste it. Flavor had eluded her since That Night, with the exception of the sour essence of her own stomach acid.

"The basil's a nice addition. Really brings out the tomato," she said as a peace offering. In reality, the sandwich might as well have been made of cardboard.

Patsy puffed a little. "Started growing my own herbs, in the bay window your dad built onto the kitchen."

"You got him to build out the window?" For years, her father had promised Rachel's mom he would do it, just as he had promised to take her to Las Vegas. But instead, year after year, he'd put off his vows, making excuses to spend more time with her greatest rival, his planes.

Patsy turned to scrape the grill and said over her shoulder, "I didn't exactly twist his arm. He surprised me with it for my birthday."

Rachel choked down another bite of burger, along with her resentment. So what if her dad had learned from his mistakes with her mom? *Good* for him. For both of them. It wasn't any skin off her nose.

Patsy frowned, looking as if she had more to say. But the jangling phone spared them both for the moment.

Moving with her typical efficiency, Patsy caught it on the second ring. At the same moment, Rachel heard the distant but familiar drone of a small plane's engine. Her dad's Piper Pawnee tow plane, from the sound. Though it had been overhauled since she'd last flown it, she would know the music of that engine anywhere.

Before Rachel could hurry to the window, Patsy speared her with a look and raised a finger. Cautioning her to silence, Rachel thought.

"No, she's *not* here, and we haven't heard from her." Her voice was a blunt wall of resistance, without a single foothold. "I told you before, quit calling."

Rachel's heart thumped, and she pushed away the plate containing her half-eaten burger. Was it a reporter, or one of the same lunatics who'd called her apartment until she'd figured it was time to depart the City of Brotherly Love while she still could? One particularly crazy-sounding woman had somehow gotten her cell phone number, too, before Rachel had ditched it. She had thought of Marfa as a safe place, a refuge so remote that only the most determined would find her, and so small that outsiders easily stood out.

"She's no murderer—the jury said so," Patsy argued. "And they've got laws against harassment. Sheriff's department's tracing this call now."

A moment later, she added, "Threats are only digging you in deeper, lady. Hope you've set aside enough for a good lawyer."

Rachel held her breath. The woman again—she'd been the worst and most persistent. But at least she was two thousand miles away, back in Philadelphia.

A smug smile stretched Patsy's colorless, thin lips. "Well, now. She hung up."

And you protected me. Rachel felt both amazed and grateful. "Have you really contacted the sheriff?"

Patsy shook her head. "Harlan Castillo? Fat chance I'd call him if I was being held at gunpoint naked."

Harlan Castillo—a deputy last time Rachel had heard—must have gotten himself elected to the top job. Patsy had been married to him years before. Rachel didn't know what had caused their breakup, but she'd heard Patsy tell one of her few friends, *"I wouldn't cross the street to piddle on that man if he was on fire."*

"So who's been calling?" Rachel asked.

Before Patsy could answer, the belled door jingled as it opened. Rachel jumped to her feet in alarm, elbowing over her forgotten soda in her hurry.

When the woman recoiled at the sight of him, Zeke Pike knew his run was over.

Zeke, who after all this time had come to think of himself by that name, was used to people noticing him. Tall for his age since childhood, he was the kid who could never get away with anything, the one adults in authority felt compelled to make an example of and guys his own age needed to prove themselves against in fights. No avoiding it, nor the attention of what too often turned out to be the wrong kind of woman.

Six-three and over two hundred ten pounds, with green eyes that drew too many comments, he'd had to work damned hard at blending in here, recasting his once gregarious nature into something so sullen and aloof that other people soon considered him one particularly hard-shelled desert tortoise. On those occasions he ventured into town, they said hello, and over time, they'd grown more and more inclined to recommend his hand-crafted furniture to well-heeled out-of-towners. But for the most part, they respected his desire to be left in peace.

And they sure as hell didn't jerk away like they were wasp-stung when he walked into a café. Which meant, he was almost certain, that the rail-thin woman staring at him with huge, brown eyes knew who he was, knew all about Willie Tyler. His pulse thundering in his ears, he almost ran out before he noticed Patsy Copeland's head shaking.

"It's okay. He's fine," she assured the younger woman. "This is Zeke Pike, Rachel. He comes in every afternoon about this time. I've known him—what's it been, Zeke? Twelve years, or is it fourteen?"

Frozen to the spot, he nodded, struggling to make sense of the situation. And then the name registered. *Rachel.*

Of course. This must be Walter's daughter, the one who'd been the subject of so much talk that even a recluse couldn't help but hear it—and form his own opinion.

From what he'd overheard, Zeke figured that unlike Willie, Rachel's so-called victim—the dumb son of a bitch—had no one but himself to blame for ending up on the wrong side of the grass. Out here in West Texas, such a case would never have gone to trial. But folks said the boy had come from some high-dollar family with all kinds of connections, and Zeke had learned the hard way how such factors reshuffled the deck.

Rachel Copeland eyed him carefully before nodding. "Oh—sorry. I thought—I took you for someone else."

He wondered if the kid she'd shot had been big, too. Or if, in light of her experience, she was spooked by men in general. Too bad, if that was the case, because she was a pretty thing, early thirties, maybe, with a coltish build and big, doe eyes partly hidden by long bangs. The rest of her dark, reddish hair was sleeked back in a careless ponytail that hung straight and glossy along her axle-stiff spine.

"I can go," he suggested.

She shook her head, her face flushing. "Don't leave, please. Come inside and have your lunch."

Her voice triggered something in him, made him imagine himself undoing her hair, running his hands through the silken river of it, or tangling it as he laid her back and—

"Maybe that'd be best," he said, aggravated with the direction of his thoughts. He'd been mostly celibate—with a few occasions off for bad behavior—for a lot of years now, but instead of forgetting about sex, he spent way too much time thinking on it. Made him wonder about priests and monks—how the hell they stood it, when here he was, picturing this scrawny, scared, stray kitten of a woman naked.

Patsy said, "Let me get your sandwich started. And this one's on the house."

He gave a dismissive snort. "Like hell it is."

She shrugged. "Suit yourself. The chicken salad?"

He took another step inside, then cracked a rare smile. "It's still Tuesday, isn't it?"

He and Patsy had it all worked out. He'd show up some time after the lunch rush and have a different meal each weekday, for which he paid on Friday afternoons, in cash. Cheeseburger and fries on Mondays. Chicken salad on whole wheat with barbecue chips Tuesdays. BLT, more chips, on Wednesdays. Salad plate with cold cuts Thursdays, and chicken-fried steak Fridays to reward himself for eating something green, other than his usual dill spear, the day before. Each meal was followed by a slice of whatever fresh-baked pie Patsy had on hand—Zeke had never met one of her homemade pies he didn't favor—and then he'd get up and walk the mile and a half down the highway and long, private road leading back to his place, where he would work well into the night.

No muss, no fuss, and only the bare minimum of interaction. And better yet, he didn't have to eat his own cooking, which wouldn't pass muster in a Third World prison.

He glanced over at his usual seat, a table near the window, as far from the possibility of conversation as a man could get. But for the first time he could remember, he didn't immediately head to it, put his back to those present, and stare out the window to watch graceful, long-winged aircraft pulled like kites into the sky.

Though he couldn't bring himself to make eye contact with Rachel—he was losing the knack for it—he felt words squeezing loose, working their way out of him like embedded cactus spines. He would have stopped himself if he were able, but instead, he cleared his throat and said, "What you did—they should've given you a medal. Most feel the same around here."

"Glad to know I meet with your approval." She shaded the words with equal parts relief, sarcasm, and defiance.

He liked that, liked that what she'd been through hadn't melted down the mental toughness that had prompted her to kill rather than allow herself to become a victim. He'd been wrong earlier, when he'd thought of a starved kitten. This was a little lioness, fallen on hard times.

"You'll be all right." He nodded, feeling yet another smile—*two*, in one day—pulling at one corner of his mouth. Then he turned back to his spot and sat to face the window, where he watched Walter Copeland turn on a dime and waggle his little plane's wings for sheer joy before buzzing around to make his landing.

Zeke heard light steps behind him and felt, rather than saw, Rachel Copeland's nearness as she bent to peer out, too. She smelled nice, like a lemon drop shot through with honey. He wondered if it was just her shampoo, or if the whole of her smelled so good. He shifted slightly, figuring she'd either scream or shoot him if she caught sight of what was going on beneath the table's edge.

"That father of mine—the man never changes."

He envied her for the affection bubbling through her words, for the ease with which she spun away and hurried out through the door. He watched her glide past a beat-up gold van with Pennsylvania plates, break into a trot, and then run toward the airstrip. Fluid, graceful—bliss suffused her movement. The joy of her homecoming, her reunion with a parent who would always take her back, no questions asked.

Zeke had no patience for self-pity, and until that moment, he would have said—if he'd had anyone other than his horses to confide in—that he'd rooted out and vanquished the last traces from his soul. But it must be like his sex drive, something a man could fight off but never truly conquer, for at the moment, grief lanced through him, sharp and bitter and unutterably painful.

Grief that left him reeling with awareness of the price paid for his choice.

CHAPTER TWO

*There shall the great owl make her nest, and lay, and hatch,
and gather under her shadow . . .*
                        —The Holy Bible *(King James version)*
                                        Isaiah 34:15

Finally alone. It was all Mary Alice had wanted in the dark
wake of her husband's funeral. And all she'd been denied
for what had seemed like ten eternities. First, she'd had to
suffer through the clumsy platitudes of the mourners who
had swarmed her house after the service. She had wanted to
scream at each one: *Don't you remember, you said that same
thing the last time? Don't you remember how it didn't help at all?*

But her grown daughters, Marlene and Kathy, must have
seen an outburst coming, for they'd hustled her off to the
kitchen, where they'd plied her with herbal tea and hugs.
Mary Alice didn't want their coddling either, didn't want
anyone's comfort but their brother's, the lost son that her
husband had unfairly been allowed to join ahead of her.

She hated Jim for that, God help her, and hated him for
leaving her the object of so much useless sympathy. What
she really needed wasn't pity but a crowbar, to pry open the
single, locked room in the upstairs hallway.

As she slipped out her back door and made her way
around the edge of the pool, she wondered why her two
surviving children didn't turn their backs on her. Despite
the way she had virtually ignored them for so long, her
daughters still felt the need to comfort her. Or maybe they
themselves were seeking comfort, as both seemed shaken by
their father's sudden death. As well they might, for ever
since the family's first loss, he was the only parent who ac-
knowledged *their* grief, *their* existence.

A few fat snowflakes fluttered past, but Mary Alice, dressed only in a gray silk blouse and black slacks, noticed neither the flurry nor the blue norther's biting cold. She knew she should feel guilt for her part in her family's dissolution, just as she should feel pain for the loss of the man she'd slept beside for decades. But those emotions were beyond her and had been since the terrible day her son had been taken from her.

The day her precious baby boy was *murdered*.

Her eyelids pinched shut, and colors swirled. Crimson and obsidian: the stark flash of police lights against the blackness of that night. The keening of a siren and her own stricken wailing formed the soundtrack to the memory, as always.

Trembling less from cold than pain, she came to the neatly painted back shed and frowned to find that her chronically forgetful husband had locked it as securely as he had her son's bedroom door. Like that key, this one was missing, but since her Jim had loved to putter with his roses and camellias back here, she suspected he would have a copy hidden nearby.

"And this time, you aren't here to stop me," she told the man she had just buried. The man who'd always thought he knew best for her.

"You're going to have to put this thing behind you," she heard him say, as he'd been saying since a few months after their son's death. At first he'd advised her gently. Then firmly. And finally, he had dragged her to a variety of counselors, psychologists, and then a shrink who'd prescribed all sorts of medications.

She'd flushed every pill. Because she didn't want to dull the edges of the only feelings left to her. If she lost touch with the pain, the rage, and the glowing, molten ball of her hatred, what would she have left except a featureless, gray void?

She would die in that drugged blankness. Die without her dark dreams of revenge, the shocking fantasies that featured the hot spurt of blood against her clean skin, the scent and taste of flesh as her teeth tore it, the surge of power flooding through her as she smashed a killer's heart beneath her heels.

On her knees now—her good wool slacks would be ruined—she found the key beneath a clay pot as a few more snowflakes spiraled past. Her husband had never been very imaginative, not even in his choice of hiding places, she thought as a sting of tears surprised her.

She let herself into the shed. And found the tools she would need to pry open the long-locked door to her son's room.

Tonight, she would sleep among bedclothes that might yet hold a trace of *his* scent and rest her head upon *his* pillow. Tonight, she would sleep deeply, while her darkest dreams held court.

As he hopped down from a bright yellow, single-prop crop duster and walked toward his daughter, Walter Copeland gave no sign of recognition. But the moment she called, "Dad," his face flushed with elation. He ran toward her, shouting her name and throwing his arms wide.

But that was Rachel's father. For better or worse, he had always worn his feelings with all the subtlety of a tie-dyed T-shirt, right out in the open, for everyone to see. When he loved, he loved lavishly, without apology. When he felt hurt or anger, those internal maelstroms, too, were visible as a toddler's.

Rachel loved him for it, though he had caused her nearly fatal humiliation throughout the years she had struggled to fit in with her peer group. For a long time, she had blamed her failure to be accepted on her father, who was slyly mocked for his geeky fixation on all things airborne, his never-changing aviator glasses worn with sky-blue coveralls, his brush-cut red hair, and the effusive hugs he'd give her in front of anyone.

It was not until much later that she realized her obsession with her camera and one infamous plane stunt she'd pulled as a sophomore were in and of themselves enough to forever bar her from the inner circle. While other kids might have cheered the daring of a football jock who'd sent upperclassmen scurrying as he buzzed the senior picnic, they'd been far less amused when the same exploit was undertaken by a gawky late bloomer with braces, bad skin, and allergies that often left her red-nosed.

Whether it was her ill-considered attempt at humor, her appearance, or some combination of the two, she had remained a dateless wonder until college. In the years since, she'd changed enough to attract plenty of male attention, but Rachel still tended to think of herself as the nerdy type. Consequently, she'd been first bewildered—and then sickened— by the news coverage that categorized her as some sort of hot-bod femme fatale. *Her.*

She ran into the embrace of the one man who had always thought her pretty. "Dad . . . It's—it's so . . . good to see you."

Rachel felt stupid, falling apart right then and there for anyone to see. For all she knew, not only the gold-eyed owl but that stranger from The Roost was watching, a plainspoken man who had startled her with his sheer *presence.* But she'd had to hold things together for so damned long, she was helpless to keep back her pent-up tears.

Her dad was crying, too, hugging her for dear life and saying, "It's all right now. It's gonna be fine, Rusty."

Though his use of her childhood nickname made it harder, Rachel pulled herself together, still mindful of the mountain man at his place by the window.

"So, uh—" She glanced upward, desperately seeking a distraction, and found it in a jet-black pair of vultures rising on a thermal. Close by, three sailplanes formed a gaggle, all spiraling higher on the same column of rising air. "Looks like a great day for soaring."

Taking his cue, her father pulled away and smiled, staring as if he couldn't get enough of her face. The crinkles around his eyes had deepened, and his red hair had faded, with snowy patches appearing at his temples. He looked smaller, too, somehow, diminished by this past year, just as she had been. Perhaps he'd had it even tougher, being forced to stay at home to tend to his mother and his business while his heart was under siege some two thousand miles north and east.

His suffering was another cost Rachel could add to Kyle Underwood's tally. Or maybe her own.

But instead of speaking of it, her father cleared his throat and regrouped. "Cloud ceiling's good and high, too. They could stay up for hours."

She nodded and fell gratefully into a conversation about thermals and ridge lifts and the outrageous impurity—in her father's view—of optional engines in a sailplane.

"What's next? Helicopter rotors planted on top?" he asked, head shaking.

She smiled at the thought that nothing here had changed, that they could simply pick up where they'd left off when she had gone away to college at eighteen. In Marfa, she could start her whole life again, and maybe this time, her dreams wouldn't land her in the realm of nightmares.

"You can't pretend away the past." Dr. Thomas's gentle admonition floated through her memory. She shoved the thought aside, taking cover in a fantasy so beautiful that she could only listen, for her throat was too clogged with tears to speak.

Eventually, however, she picked up on the concern in her dad's face. "Did you hear a word I just said?" he asked.

She shook her head and swallowed. "Sorry. I was trying to take it all in—being back here, talking soaring with you. It feels just like old times."

As if nothing ever happened.

His face lit up. "Make you want to climb back into the cockpit and take the Pawnee for a spin?"

She closed her eyes a moment, bowled over by a wave of longing for the days when she'd done just that. "You know I can't," she told him.

He waved off her protest. "It's like riding a bike. You don't forget. Hell, you practically grew up in the air."

"It wouldn't be legal." She'd long since quit worrying

about her biennial flight reviews and the medical certifica-
tion required to keep her current as a pilot in command. It
hadn't seemed relevant in Philadelphia. Flying was something she'd done because she was Walter Copeland's daughter, an expectation, not a passion. The only times she ever
missed it were during rare, brief visits home to see her dad
and grandma.

"Since when were you so concerned about flight regula-
tions? I can remember when you used to—"

Before he could wax nostalgic over the same craziness for
which she'd once been grounded, she said, "That was before
I figured out that gravity applied to me personally. And that
even an accusation of wrongdoing can wreck a person's life."

He looked down. "Don't worry, Rusty. We'll get you up-
to-date. I'll help you study the rule changes, practice with
you—"

"It's been a long time," she said uncertainly.

"You'll be back in the air before you know it. You're a
natural. Always were. And I could use the help. Aside from
the glider business, I've been using the Cessna as an air
taxi—ferrying folks out here from the big airports."

Averting her gaze, she looked out over the various metal
hangars. Squinting at the nearest, she said, "Is that another
bizjet?"

Her father nodded.

"Cessna's not fancy enough or large enough to suit the
big boys or haul all their luggage, so the place's been drowning in the damned things." He peered over his shoulder to
make certain no one could be listening.

Rachel understood. While its population dwindled,
Marfa had clung to life for decades, a struggling, high
desert nowhere-ville desperately clutching to its mystery
lights and its place in cinematic history—iconic rebel
James Dean had performed his final leading movie role in
Giant, filmed here over fifty years before. Sailplane pilots
loved the area for its vast, unbroken vistas, its year-round
flying weather, and its thermals, but the niche hobby

couldn't support more than her father and a couple of part-time employees.

More recently, the high desert light and scores of run-down but charming adobe houses had made Marfa a mecca for the culturati, rich outsiders who had bought up half the town on the cheap. In time, they drove up home prices beyond long-term residents' modest means and replaced the mom-and-pop stores people had relied upon for years with upscale wine bars and pretentious restaurants. A lot of the locals wished the newcomers would haul their liposuctioned asses off to Aspen, Taos, and all the other small towns they'd "ruined" by making them into chichi playgrounds.

However they might feel, though, few natives could afford to turn down the money the art people brought in. Including Walter Copeland, who had contributed most of his life's savings to his only daughter's fight to stay out of prison.

"Speak of the devil," he said as a silver Range Rover turned into the airport and rolled directly toward them. "That'll be Antoinette Gallinardi. She's been pestering me all week to talk to you."

"Who?" Rachel asked.

After he repeated the name, her father grumbled, "I thought she'd at least let you get settled in and give me a chance to broach the subject."

"Broach what subject?"

"Ms. Gallinardi's the director of the Blank Canvas Foundation. It's a group dedicated to keeping Starbucks, Wal-Mart, and other—what's it they call 'em? Oh, yes, and other 'tasteless relics of suburban blight' out of Marfa."

"Oh, the horror," Rachel said dryly. She would *love* a nice chai latte right about now.

Her father frowned. "They claim they want to preserve the town's uniqueness."

"They want to cast it in Lucite, like one of their museum pieces."

Her dad nodded. "Gallinardi and her league of art snobs would probably think that's a wonderful idea. But they do have a point about the changes—if they can ever get the locals on their side. People come to Marfa to escape all the sameness out there. And as many pictures as you've snapped of the place and people, I'd think you'd appreciate that."

"Oh, I do. I'm just feeling contrary, that's all." And maybe a little bit caffeine deprived, despite the Dr Pepper. "To tell you the truth, my needle's pushed past Contrary and is dropping fast toward Wiped Out."

"Can't blame you," Rachel's dad said. "You must've really pushed it to get here in—what—two and a half days?"

The journey was already fading to a bright blur in her memory: two thousand miles of mostly interstate, punctuated by fast-food pit stops and far too little sleep.

At her nod, he added, "I can ask Ms. Gallinardi to come back another time. Just try to be polite, for my sake. This lady knows *everybody* in the high rent circles."

"I don't get it," said Rachel. "What would she want with me?" Since the trial, the only people who had sought her out had been vultures interested in getting the inside dirt on . . . *Oh, hell. Don't let this be about the trial.*

The Range Rover slowed as it approached them. Inside, Rachel made out two forms, but could only discern the features of the passenger, a narrow-faced woman with a raven's wing of jet hair cut in an aggressively angled bob.

The SUV came to a stop, raising puffs of dust from its four tires. Inside the vehicle, a scrawny scrap of an animal—Rachel was undecided between dog and rat—bounced wildly. A moment later, the tall, slender passenger edged out, scolding, "No, Coco. Bad Coco," before shoving the fawn-colored creature back inside and closing the door.

She drew in a deep breath as if to regroup before turning, perfectly balanced on the three-inch heels of her black boots. Otherwise, her elegant form was swathed in charcoal gray, a beautifully tailored riding jacket over a matching wool sweater and a long skirt. Her face had an ageless, airbrushed quality, marred only by her frown at the yapping and window-scrabbling going on behind her.

She extended a slender hand that wouldn't have looked out of place in a cocktail glove, or holding a cigarette at the end of a slim, jeweled holder. "You must be Rachel Copeland. I'm Antoinette Gallinardi. It's such a pleasure to meet you."

The crème brûlée smoothness of her voice had Rachel mentally rechristening her "Art Deco Woman." The kind of woman mortal females tended to despise on sight. Rachel, however, reserved judgment.

"As always, it's nice to see you, ma'am, but my daughter just got in," her father explained. "She's tired, hungry."

Gallinardi withdrew her hand from Rachel's. "Please forgive me. I was so eager to meet you that the moment my assistant told me you'd been seen driving through town, I asked her to bring me straight over."

Disturbed that the woman's assistant would recognize her—how closely had people here followed the media coverage from Philadelphia?—Rachel glanced at the figure still seated in the vehicle. She was unpleasantly surprised to recognize Terri Parton, who had been just a year ahead of her in school. Which wasn't nearly far enough for Rachel's taste. Though Terri had put on weight with the years, she'd kept her trademark blonde locks, which were even longer and more silvery than they'd been when she had run the cheerleading squad like her own petty fiefdom. She shot Rachel a look that said time hadn't softened her opinion of the geek-girl she and her friends had considered far beneath their notice. Or maybe she was remembering the day Rachel had buzzed the picnic, an act that drew attention to the private party Terri had been conducting in the backseat of her Chevy with the soon-to-be-*ex* band director.

Surely, Terri would have moved past the fallout from that old scandal by this time. . . .

"I believe the two of you went to school together," Gallinardi said. "Terri Parton-Zavala?"

"Sure, I remember her." Rachel guessed that Terri must have married Cristo Zavala, a trombone player—a self-styled ladies' man who had liked to run around asking girls if they'd enjoy the honor of blowing his horn. If those two had hooked up, they deserved each other.

"But I don't understand," Rachel added. "Why would you rush over here to meet me?"

Dumb question, she thought bitterly. For months, she had been fending off not only anonymous callers and obnoxious reporters, but acquaintances eager to pick the story's bones. Had she really gone to her apartment with Kyle Underwood a few, short weeks before his murder, as witnesses had testified despite Rachel's denial? Had there been more to those pictures of the two of them than the salacious details that came out during the trial?

Whether Terri had put Gallinardi up to it or she'd come of her own accord, Rachel couldn't allow that garbage to get a foothold here in Marfa—even if it meant cutting off Art Deco Woman at the knees.

Gallinardi looked at Walter, her sleek black brows arching in surprise. "You haven't told her?"

He grimaced. "I haven't had the chance yet."

Splashes of pink suffused fashionably gaunt cheeks. "I see I've made a mess of things, Ms. Copeland. But please, let me assure you, it's your talent that's made me overeager. The work you did for *Nouveau West*—the images of the Marfa of your childhood were breathtaking."

Terri Parton slipped out of the vehicle but took care not to let the frantic dog escape. "Rachel," she said with an unenthusiastic nod.

Rachel returned it and lied, "Nice to see you, Terri," though her head was spinning with Art Deco Woman's words. *Talent. Overeager. Breathtaking.*

"You saw my . . . photos?" Rachel had given up on anyone from the art world noticing her work by the time the magazine had bought the rights to print her Marfa series. For years, she'd had an online gallery featuring images she had taken before leaving and on her infrequent visits home, along with a great deal more work she'd done along the

East Coast. For years, her sales were barely enough to cover the cost of maintaining the online storefront and camera supplies. To survive, she'd turned to bridal portraiture— never her favorite—and teaching classes at a community college just outside of Philadelphia. Which had put her squarely in the path of a student named Kyle Underwood.

The crack of her old handgun reverberated through her mind, and her throat closed at the memory of hot spray against her chill skin. Along with her stark-naked stalker, her burgeoning career had died that night, too. Or so Rachel had thought.

Art Deco Woman nodded. "Oh, yes. Everyone in the foundation agrees you have a very fine eye."

When Terri—who'd grown even heavier than Rachel had first realized—reddened and pursed her lips, Rachel was fairly sure she'd gone from hell to heaven.

"Those photos form an extraordinary chronicle of how art has changed, perhaps even *saved*, this community," Gallinardi went on.

Rachel resisted the urge to argue about her choice of words. For one thing, Gallinardi was at least partly correct that the attention of the art world had saved Marfa. But even more importantly, Rachel was soaking up every drop of praise like a parched desert drinking in the rain. Pathetic, yes, but after the year she'd had, it was all she could do not to wag and whimper at the woman's feet. If Terri weren't there bearing witness, Rachel probably would have slobbered just a little. Instead, she managed, "Thank you," trying to sound modest but not unused to such praise.

Stick *that* up your megaphone, Terri "Let's Make Geek-Girl's Life a Living Hell" Parton.

Terri, for her part, affected boredom by averting her eyes and sliding her tongue against the inside of her cheek, a habit Rachel remembered from their years in grade school.

"We were hoping," Art Deco Woman went on, raising her voice to be heard over her dog's noise, "that you might allow us to license some of your earlier images for our campaign and that you'd consider photographing some of Marfa's local artists at their work."

Terri's sly smile forced Rachel to slow down and consider.

"What sort of campaign is it?" she asked.

"We'll be sending press releases, with copies of your images, to various news outlets, along with art and travel magazines. We'll use them to promote a showing of works produced by other local artists and offered up for sale. And we'd very much like for you to be the featured artist at the exhibition."

Rachel barely caught her jaw before it swung open like a loose hinge. This was . . . this was beyond imagining. A well-publicized showing, for a pariah like her? Sure, she'd had a few successes, from commercial gigs to the *Nouveau West* series to acceptance of her work in a couple of prestigious art photography shows, but never before had she achieved the kind of . . .

Never before had she been notorious: a woman accused of sleeping with a very young—almost criminally young— man. A woman who had been tried for killing him. Quite a curiosity . . . and Terri's amused look confirmed that there was something beyond the foundation members' admiration in play.

Was the wreckage of her life the honey sweetening this deal, forming the newsworthy "hook" this Blank Canvas group was seeking to publicize its goals? Rachel's face burned at the thought, igniting the short fuse of her temper. Even worse was the idea that Terri might have been the one to suggest this appeal to Geek-Girl's vanity.

"And of course, there'll be remuneration," Gallinardi added, darting a frown over her shoulder toward the small dog's histrionics. "Or should I discuss your fees with your agent?"

The flame sparked ever closer toward detonation. Sure, Rachel could expect to be compensated for the work used to illustrate articles or publicize the event, but this wasn't a real art show. If it were, she'd be expected to pay a jury fee even to be considered. Competition for display in such shows was fierce, not so much for the modest prizes of a few hundred or perhaps a thousand dollars, but for the prestige of winning and the boost it would give one's studio. Rachel knew she was good, but she was honest enough to know her work was not so special or well-known that she could expect to circumvent the rules.

Apparently annoyed by her hesitation, Terri interjected, "Oh, come on, Rachel. Don't play coy. You can't *possibly* be mulling better offers."

The ice-blonde woman's employer shot a stern look in her direction. "Perhaps you could go back and see to Coco, before she chews her way through my upholstery."

"Uh, yes, ma'am. I'll do that." With a look of pure resentment, Terri stalked off to do her boss's bidding.

The moment the SUV's door slammed, Art Deco Woman's expression shifted from angry to contrite. "Please accept my apologies. I can promise you, I will speak to her about that display of rudeness."

"What's this about, Ms. Gallinardi?" Rachel asked her. "And I mean *really*, not whatever cover story you and Terri have trumped up."

"Rusty," her father warned before he looked pleadingly at the gaping woman. "Please forgive my daughter. She's not herself right now. The long drive—and then, the other thing. She's been under a great deal of stress."

Gallinardi blanched, teetering on her spiked boot heels. "I'm aware there have been . . . difficulties, and my assistant's comment was unfortunate. But clearly, my timing has been—"

"No *coincidence*?" Rachel finished for her, which earned her another alarmed look from her father.

She closed her eyes and dragged in a deep breath to clear her head. These art people brought in business for her dad, and more than that, they'd become a real presence in this town. If they chose, they could make her father's life incredibly unpleasant. For his sake, she could at least pretend to think about the woman's offer.

"I—I'm sorry I snapped," Rachel managed. "It's just— this is a little overwhelming."

Gallinardi visibly relaxed.

"I was wondering," Rachel asked Art Deco Woman, "do you have a card? I'd like to call—to have my representative call you to discuss this. But it's been very nice to meet you."

Gallinardi smiled, nodding, and produced an elegant, dove-gray card from a stylish black purse. "Certainly, Ms. Copeland. And I sincerely hope we'll have the chance to work with you. There's a bit more to it than we've discussed, but we can talk about the details later."

Once Gallinardi climbed back inside her Range Rover and headed for the exit, Rachel's father said, "Nice recovery. You had me worried for a minute."

"Sorry," she said simply, not wanting to alarm him with her suspicions until she had a better handle on the offer.

"And I didn't know you had an agent for your photos," he added.

Her dad looked so impressed that she couldn't help smiling. His idea of a photographer was still the department store guy who distracted howling babies with rattles long enough to snap a few shots.

"I don't," she said, "but I know where I can hustle up a reasonable facsimile in short order."

"And here I was, worrying they'd knocked all the starch out of you this past year." He gently popped the side of her arm. "That's my Rusty. That's the girl who always knew how to set this town on its ear."

Rachel's mood darkened as she thought, *Unfortunately, Marfa's always had a way of setting me on my ass in return.*

CHAPTER THREE

Man, like a light in the night, is kindled and put out.
                                                    —Heraclitus

Monday, February 11

Zeke spotted her first as he rode in off the desert: a lean woman in faded jeans and a brown leather jacket standing by his paddock. As he watched, she reached across the fence to stroke the new mare's thin neck. Though the horse, a brown-and-white pinto fuzzy with her winter coat, looked pleased with the attention, Zeke felt only irritation. A glance in the direction of the shrouded sun told him it was maybe eight thirty or nine, no later. Too damned early in the morning to have to talk to customers.

He puffed out a breath that rose like dragon smoke on the cold air. Dealing with people shattered the calm he'd built by seeking out wood, an early-morning ritual in which he imagined the twisted, skeletal forms of dead trees expressed as chairs and tables, headboards and smaller pieces that followed nature's lines. Today had been a good day; amid a powdered-sugar swirl of snow flurries, he'd found some particularly high-quality mesquite, a hard, durable, and ancient specimen in a deadfall he'd somehow missed on earlier forays. Before he'd finished cutting it and loading Gus, his pack mule, the flurries ended without chilling either man or beast too badly.

Leading Gus, Zeke nudged his oversized mount, Cholla, into a jog. Pricking his ears forward, the buckskin clattered over hard-packed soil with big, shod hooves as black as his long stockings. When the pinto whinnied a greeting to her two pasture mates, the woman turned in his direction, jolting him with recognition. Rachel Copeland waved and smiled, though he hadn't seen her face-to-face since their first meeting in the café almost a week earlier. This morning, her unbound hair flamed redder in the sunlight, so he hadn't recognized her from behind.

Which was pretty damned ironic considering that he had dreamed of her just last night—a dream from which he had awakened cursing and questioning his reasons for remaining celibate.

Too dangerous, getting close to anyone, let alone a woman. Too unfair to pull her into something I can't risk explaining.

Zeke's breath caught, the jagged edge of his attraction slicing deep. He needed to steer clear of this woman even more than most. Lust was one thing. He could deal with that. But her presence, considering her recent troubles, had stirred up old memories, sleeping dogs that rose, snarling, with their glittering teeth bared.

She gave the mare a final pat and said, "Hi there. I was worried I might miss you. Patsy told me you go out riding in the morning, but she didn't know the time."

He couldn't guess how Patsy had gleaned even that much information. He barely spoke to her, at least no more than he had to. When people talked, they let their guard down. They let things slip that ought to be kept private.

He swung down from his horse's back and led the buckskin to the hitching post.

"What do you need?" His words came out blunter than he had intended. But instead of apologizing, he let the question ride.

"Relax. I didn't come for small talk." She smiled, as if she found him amusing. No flinching today; the little lioness had recovered. Gesturing toward her camera case, she added, "Just a few photos, if you're willing."

His turn to spook now, taken aback by the idea.

"No." The word came out clipped and pebble-hard, but curiosity got the better of him. "Why?"

Her brows rose. "No one explained it to you?"

He shook his head and then turned to unhitch Gus from the loaded travois he'd been dragging. Two more bundles of wood lay across the mule's back, carefully padded by a thick horse blanket. Since Zeke's equines were his workforce, he took their care seriously. Since they were also the closest thing to company he had, he went out of his way to keep them comfortable as well as healthy.

"Do you want what they told me, or would you rather have the truth?" she asked.

"I'm a big fan of cutting to the chase."

"There's a shocker." A hint of a smile bubbled through her words. "The Blank Canvas Foundation is throwing some crumbs to the natives. Took me a few days to figure that out and a couple more to decide it's a good deal. They're putting together a special showing for area artists, letting us sell our work to help them publicize their views. The event will be well advertised and should draw some serious collectors, so we'll all profit from—"

He turned to look at her, indicating his derision with a reflexive snort. "I'm no artist. I just make furniture out of useless scrub wood. So why tell me about this?"

"I've been waiting for a while, and you left your workshop door unlocked." She jerked a nod in the direction of the long, low, concrete building, which in a bygone day had been a candelilla factory, where the spiky desert plants were once processed for their wax. "I went in and looked at your stuff, and I'm afraid I have bad news . . ."

She drew it out with a grave nod. "You're definitely an artist. Your work—it's fantastic and utterly unique. I've never seen anything like it in my—"

"You walked inside my *home*?" He lived on one end, which he'd restored and refinished to create a rudimentary apartment. On the end opposite was his showroom, an informal space where he displayed and sold his finished pieces.

She raised her palms in surrender. "I didn't go anywhere other than your workspace, but I'm sorry. You can quit glaring at me, Mr. Pike."

"It's Zeke," he said as he removed the mule's packs. "Just Zeke. And I'm not glaring."

When he glanced her way, her pretty nose scrunched. "Maybe you should check that theory in your mirror sometime. Or lock your door when you aren't in the mood for visitors. Even a Keep Out sign would suffice."

He didn't take to mockery, wouldn't put up with it. "Or I could take a page from your book. Shoot unwelcome callers."

Her mood turned on a dime, the lightly teasing smile vanishing. Soft brown eyes went ironwood-hard as she stepped nearer, thrusting her chin toward him. "Screw you, then, *Just Zeke.* If you don't want me taking pictures, bringing in more business for you, say so, by all means. But don't you dare take potshots at me about a situation you don't understand at all."

Zeke felt a rush of heat, along with a swift kick from his conscience. There was a fine line between unfriendliness and cruelty, and he'd just stepped across it. "You're right. I was out of line."

"You sure as hell were." Fair as she was, the color that rose to her face made her appear sunburned.

He knew he should make amends, but he wasn't sure how. So instead, he asked, "Those snooty art folks pay you for the pictures?"

"Yes, if it's any of your business—"

"Then take as many as you want. Anything in the workshop or the showroom." He pointed to the far end. "Long as you steer clear of my apartment."

Or more importantly, of the secret stashed inside. He should have burned it by now, every last trace of the man he'd once been. But he couldn't bring himself to destroy the letter. *Her* letter, and his last, remaining link.

Never try to come back, she had begged him, *and don't risk sending me more money. Because they'll find you and they'll kill you, one way or another, just the way that they killed him. And I can't live through it again. I won't. . . .*

He forced himself to put the past aside, to live solely in

the present, dealing with life moment by moment as it un-folded. It was the only way for him to stay sane, to keep his lungs working and his heart beating. Because he owed his mother that much.

"Don't worry," Rachel said sullenly. "Your bedroom's the last place on this planet I have any interest in exploring."

He turned back to the task of unsaddling his mount. Best to ignore her, he decided. But as he checked both animals' hooves for stones and turned Cholla and Gus loose with the pinto, Zeke couldn't stop picturing the way her face had closed. Couldn't stop thinking of how she had bared her claws at his insult.

From the time he'd been a kid, his mouth had always got-ten him in trouble. He'd thought he had learned better than to use it.

He was moving the mesquite and trying to forget her when she came out of the workshop, her head shaking.

"Camera battery's gone bad." Her forehead creased as she frowned. "It's not holding a charge worth anything, and I left my spare back at the casita."

Patsy had mentioned Rachel was staying in one of the two tiny guesthouses she and Walter usually reserved for visiting pilots. He'd never understood why The Roost's owner felt the need to try and chitchat, but instead of ask-ing, it was easier to simply listen as he watched the planes and tiny gliders mount the sky.

"You can come back," he said, bothered that Rachel wasn't meeting his eye. "Anytime you like."

She stared long enough for him to see her indecision. Probably debating whether he was worth the aggravation.

Decision made, she nodded. "All right. I'll stop by. I need to take my grandma to see her doctor in Alpine, so it prob-ably won't be until this afternoon."

As Rachel neared the fence-line, the pinto mare thrust her head across to nudge Rachel's arm. Pausing to scratch her spotted neck, Rachel took a deep breath, then said, "Look, it's probably not my business, but this horse . . ."

She trailed off, her face flushing.

"What?"

"Well, she's sweet as anything, but she could really use to put on some weight."

"You're right." He allowed himself to relax into a smile. "It's none of your business."

She opened her mouth to speak, but he kept going.

"It was none of mine either when I found her starving in some overgrazed patch of nothing that was supposed to be a pasture. There was another horse there with her— buzzards were eating what was left of it."

"You saved her." Some new emotion dawned in Rachel's expression, but it had been so long since Zeke had seen approval, he didn't know how to react.

"Listen, I'm no bleeding heart, but I know potential when I see it. And this mare's got potential. What she needs is time and care and good feed." *Like you,* it came into his mind to say, but he bit down on such foolishness.

"So you bought her?"

He shook his head. "Had a talk with the ignorant fool who owned her. Made him see the wisdom of giving her to me. Unless he wanted to hear from the law about that dead horse."

"*You* are a nice man. But don't worry." When she smiled, her nose crinkled again, and this time he made out a faint smattering of freckles across the bridge. "We'll keep it our secret."

As she turned and walked back toward her van, his gaze lingered on the sweet sway of slim hips and the flutter of her red-brown hair in the cool breeze.

And something in him was resurrected—something that would better remain dead and buried until his body shared its dusty grave.

"Don't know why you'd want to drive this awful thing," Rachel's grandmother, Benita Copeland, complained. "A person needs a ladder to climb up into this monstrosity."

As they'd headed east on Highway 90, it hadn't taken long to leave tiny Marfa in the rearview. Once they crossed the currently dry Alamito Creek, the wintry-dull desert plain rolled out ahead, bounded only by the knobbed silhouette of Cathedral Mountain in the distance.

"I knew I was moving, and it held most of my stuff." Rachel didn't bother explaining that after her Mini Cooper had been repossessed, a friend with an uncle in the car business had given her the ugly gold van, with its peeling "wood grain" panels. She'd been grateful to have any mode of transportation, particularly one that could haul all her photography equipment—and serve as temporary housing in a pinch. "You're just put out because you've been scheming with your canasta buddies to sneak out late at night and go joyriding in that zippy little car I used to drive."

Her grandma, who had given up her driver's license years before, laughed and waved aside such nonsense in a gesture that sent upper-arm flab swaying dangerously. Always a heavy woman, she wore a deep purple pantsuit that made her look a little like an eggplant, along with square-framed, thick-lensed bifocals. On sunnier days, she donned enormous sunglasses that fit right over the top of her regular pair. Today's heavy, low clouds nixed that fashion statement, just as it had grounded all the sailplanes.

"That's probably for the best." She sighed. "If I got down inside one of those little jobbies, you'd probably need a forklift and a team of chiropractors to get me out again. It just seems a girl your age should have a spiffier set of wheels, that's all. Back when I was young, I had this bright red-and-white T-bird. You know, the ones with the big fins? It was a convertible, but no matter how my mama scolded, I never covered my hair with a scarf. I just let it stream out, blonde and beautiful, and drove the menfolk wild."

"Sounds like a lot of fun." Rachel smiled, knowing from family photos that her grandmother had kept a tight cap of perm-fried, brown curls close to her head throughout her younger years, curls that had stood the test of time, though they had long since silvered. Rachel suspected, too, that Benita, who had never had much—nor liked to part with—money, was speaking of a car she'd seen in advertisements instead of anything she'd really owned. Since Rachel's last, brief visit two years earlier, either her grandma was growing more inclined toward exaggeration, or problems with her memory were painting her younger years a rosier hue.

Over dinner last night, Patsy had cast her vote for something more serious. *"I'm afraid it could be a problem. With her living on her own much longer, I mean. She's a diabetic, Walter, and keeping her blood sugar stable is a tough balancing act, especially with her vision the way it is."*

But Rachel's father had been adamant. Anger flashing in his eyes, he'd snapped, *"She's been managing for twenty years. She knows what she's doing. Sure, she forgets little things now and then, the same as anybody, and she has to use a magnifying glass to read the labels. But I gave her my word she'd live out her life in the house Dad built her, and there's no way, no way in hell, I'm going to break that promise."*

When Patsy had carefully raised the subject of the medication mix-up that had sent Benita to the hospital the month before, Rachel's father had accused his wife of wanting to stick his mother in a nursing home so the two of them could travel. Clearly furious, Patsy had dumped her dinner in the trash and left the house for a long walk.

Rachel grimaced, considering the first fault line in a marriage that had until now appeared rock solid. Despite her ambivalence toward her father's wife—who had been quick to insist Rachel would be more "comfortable" in one of their Spartan and poorly heated guest casitas—it made her stomach hurt to witness the two of them squabbling.

She had volunteered to drive her grandma to the ophthalmologist today, partly to get a handle on her physical and mental state, but mostly to relieve Rachel's own tension. It occurred to her that before That Night, she could have coped with such a skirmish easily—could have told her dad to chill out and listen to what sounded like a legitimate concern. She and her father might have even raised their voices at each other, both of them secure enough in their relationship that it felt safe to do so.

She wondered if her dad or Patsy had noticed the ways she'd changed. No one had mentioned anything, not even her grandmother, who didn't know about the trial. Presumably.

"Still boycotting the TV news?" Rachel asked. A few years back, her grandmother had sworn off it, saying she'd lived through enough heartache for one lifetime without taking on the whole world's. Interfered with her appetite, she'd claimed, and kept her from sleeping. Had turned her into a door-locker, too—an aberration in a town with almost no crime.

"You betcha. Stopped the paper, too, while I was at it."

Rachel understood the attraction of her grandmother's decision to insulate herself from others' pain. To remain oblivious to terror's black moths chewing holes in the world's fabric. To live in ignorance of the cruelest of murders, rapes . . . and trials. "Doesn't it make you feel sort of . . . disconnected?"

Her grandmother shot her a surprisingly shrewd look. "If you're fishing around to find out if I know about your trouble, the answer is yes. Of course I do, in spite of your father's ridiculous attempts to shield me. I might have my struggles with small print these days, but I'm for doggone sure not blind."

"You—you've *known*? For how long?" Rachel glanced over at her. "Why haven't you said anything?"

Her grandmother's look turned pouty. "When I first heard over at the Hair House, I was madder than a wet hen. I'm an old woman, not a child, and I've weathered tougher things than you can imagine. Buried a husband and my first son, when he was just a tiny baby. Watched boys go off to wars they hardly understood, some of 'em never to come home. Grew up poor enough to know hunger on a first-name basis. Lost both my sisters in the last five years. I know how to stand things, Rachel, and I might have had a thing or two to say to you about it. But no one wanted an old woman's opinion. So I kept it to myself."

No wonder her grandma hadn't invited her to stay at her house. Rachel winced as moisture blurred the green splotches of juniper among the dry, gold grasses and rocky soil that lined both sides of the road.

"I never meant to hurt you." Rachel wished she'd considered how the woman who'd stood by her after her mother's sudden stroke would take being "spared" her granddaughter's pain. "I'm—I'm so sorry, Grandma. I just didn't know how—how to say the words. And Dad thought—"

"You know your daddy." A smile softened her grandmother's expression. "He could tell you anything you'd want to know about those contraptions he's always zooming around in and not a durned thing worth knowing about how a woman's mind works. But you, Rachel . . . You might have—"

"I was so ashamed." Rachel blinked hard to clear her vision. "You had such high hopes for me. Without you, I don't think I'd have ever imagined seeing my photographs in galleries, or making a living doing what I love. You've always meant so much to me—especially after Mom died."

"This—this boy that ended up killed. Was there anything to those stories he was spreading to his buddies?"

As worn, tan mountains rose before them, Rachel struggled against starkly ugly memories. Explicit voice mail messages and e-mails, the disgusting discovery of a used condom hanging on her doorknob—made worse because the culprit had removed the bulb from the security light above. She remembered it all in horrifying detail—everything except the evening at the restaurant that had supposedly set it all in motion.

That's because nothing happened worth recalling, she reminded herself, *nothing but a perfectly forgettable outing with my students.* No matter what a few liars claimed or her own psychologist had suggested.

"No, Grandma," Rachel insisted. "I would *never* do that.

Not with anybody I was teaching and especially not with—
He was just a big kid to me, that's all." Before he'd become
a monster, anyway. "A little more polished than some—I
understand he'd been kicked out of the finest prep schools.
But still, he was my student, just an overgrown boy I
thought had talent. The rest—"

Her grandmother shook her head. "I got into quite a
fight with Tally Sue Ryan, over at the Hair House. Told her
I wouldn't believe you'd do a thing like that and if she
meant to argue, her stylist was going to have to tease that
fuzz of hers over a couple of new bald spots."

Rachel's tension dissolved into laughter at the image. "I
am Grandma, hear me roar. So, you *didn't* believe the gossip."

"That boy wouldn't be the first to run bragging to his
friends about escapades he made up. The same thing used to
happen back when I was in school. That sort doesn't think
about the girl's reputation, only his own."

Rachel lapsed back into silence, thinking how far beyond
mere boasting the tall and model-handsome Kyle had gone.
How he'd used skills learned in her class to graft her face
onto pornographic photos, how he'd added his own image
to make it look as if she were on her knees before him,
open-mouthed for his erect . . .

How those photos had been so skillfully manipulated, it
had taken the defense's own set of experts to discern the
trickery, a finding that had proved false those disgusting
messages Kyle had sent her—messages whose contents in-
tersected with the yawning gap in her own memory.

Pain twisted through her midsection, so overwhelming
she had no choice except to pull the van onto the stony
shoulder. She bailed out without looking, barely noticed the
blare of a semi's horn at her flung-wide door or the swirl of
her loose hair in the chill wind of the truck's passage.

In an instant, she lost the breakfast Patsy had insisted on
feeding her that morning. A short time later, she heard the
crunch of orthopedic shoes on gravel and felt her grandma's
hand, a warm and steady presence at her back.

"It's all right," she crooned, her voice soft and comforting as faded denim. "It's all right, Cora. *I'll* drive."

Her grandmother's slip of the tongue pulled Rachel back from the brink of another round of sickness. Great Aunt Cora, Grandma's older sister, had died four years before.

But it was the offer to drive that most concerned Rachel, as her grandmother, who hadn't been behind the wheel in years, attempted to tug the keys from her hand.

"We'd better get going." Rachel led her back to the passenger side. "Wouldn't want to be late for your eye doctor appointment."

"But the baby's making you sick. You should let me drive you, Cora."

Rachel stared at her, heart sinking, wondering if Patsy had seen this confusion. And if her father had refused to.

"I'm okay. I promise, Grandma."

But as she helped her grandmother back inside the old van, Rachel wondered if either one of them would ever be all right again.

CHAPTER FOUR

Grief fills the room up of my absent child,
Lies in his bed, walks up and down with me . . .
— William Shakespeare,
from King John

"She's back to sleeping in his bedroom, Kathy." Marlene's younger sister lived in Phoenix, but the two of them talked by phone once or twice a week. Though both had husbands and families of their own, they had mothered each other for so long, the sibling bond had grown as strong as steel.

Marlene recognized the clunk of her sister's coffee mug as she set it on the counter.

"I *knew* it," Kathy burst out. "I offered to stay after the funeral, but she practically shoved me out the door—"

"It wouldn't have made any difference. As soon as we turned our backs, she'd have been inside. She's . . . she's sleeping in that bed again. *His* bed." Marlene was not referring to their father.

"Lord. Probably hasn't even washed the sheets."

Marlene made what her sons laughingly called her Primzy-Prude face. "Or dusted—"

"But those could be *his* actual skin cells." Though Marlene was the one who most closely resembled their mother, Kathy could do an impression of her that was so dead-on, it raised gooseflesh. "You can't think I'd just allow the maid to *dust* them up. Or *vacuum*."

Despite the chill zinging up her spine, Marlene laughed. They both did, though it felt a little on the mean side. But laughter helped, more than either the therapy or the anti-anxiety medication Marlene had tried, more even than the massage sessions her husband, Dan, had paid for—bless his heart—to ease the tension knotted in her neck and shoulders.

"We're going to have to do something," Marlene said anxiously. "It isn't right, letting her live like that."

"Who cares how she lives?" Kathy's voice went bitter, but Marlene heard hurt there, too. Since Kathy had been tiny, she'd done her best to cover her pain with anger.

"It's not like she worries over how *we're* doing—or gives a damn about poor Daddy," Kathy accused. "Do you think she ever said she loved him? After she called for the ambulance, when he was sprawled there, dying, on the bedroom floor? Do you think she held his hand then, even for an instant?"

A tear broke free, but Marlene couldn't let herself be drawn into that conversation. Couldn't allow herself to think about their father's final minutes. "But she's our *mother*, Kathy. What will people say if we don't take care—"

"You know what? I don't give a shit what people have to say about it."

Marlene thought that was easy for her sister, who had moved so far away. Kathy didn't have to face the family friends, the neighbors—everyone who knew what excellent care their father had taken of their mother since the baby of the family had been murdered. She could simply leave it all to Marlene, the way she had so often.

Stupid of her to get mad over it again, when she'd been certain they'd gotten past the longstanding issue. But that was the way of old squabbles between Marlene and her sister. They always squeezed out under pressure.

"What would Daddy say about it?" she couldn't stop herself from demanding. "I promised him, we both did, that we'd see to her if he was the first to go."

Marlene heard her sister's indrawn breath, felt her vacillation. When she finally answered, Kathy's voice held a strength that Marlene both envied and resented.

"Our father was a loving man. So loving, he couldn't imagine a woman drained of everything that made her human.

So he made excuses for her, babied her instead of demanding that she stop this nonsense and get back to her old self."

"You can't *force* a person to get better. You can't just demand that she snap out of it."

"I'm finished with her, Marlene. My own kids need me here now, and my boss—I could get fired for taking off more time after coming back."

"Fired? I thought things were going so much better at this new place." Marlene, who had worked in the same office more than ten years, had lost track of how many times her sister had changed jobs. She was beginning to suspect that Kathy herself was the problem, not the "crazy bosses" and "bitchy co-workers" she blamed.

"Well, I didn't mention it," said Kathy, "but I took off kind of a lot back when Bryce and I were separated. So between that and the funeral, I'm going to have to work through my vacation to catch up on the backlog. Besides, the price of flights is ridiculous on short notice."

"What if I helped you with the ticket?" Marlene knew her husband wouldn't like it, but she had some money squirreled away toward a new sofa and recliners for the family room.

"It's not just the cost. It's—it's Mother. After all this time, all her rejection, I'm finished pretending I feel something for her when I don't."

Her sister still cared. Marlene knew it. But there was nothing to be gained by arguing. Once Kathy dropped into Mule Mode, nothing short of dynamite could move her. "So I'm on my own in this?"

"I'm really sorry. If I could do it for anyone, Marl, it would be for you. But I can't. I just—*can't*."

Marlene's temper flared as she wished that, for once in their lives, *she* had the luxury of refusing. "You mean you won't."

She banged down the phone in a rare display of temper, but the two sisters' estrangement didn't last long.

Only a few short hours later, Marlene called Kathy from

the house where both of them, along with their dead brother, had grown up.

The place stood empty, every door and window open. Only a few things were missing. The bedclothes, stripped from one bare mattress. A photo album, and a macabre collection of news clippings. A purse, cosmetic bag, and a few articles of clothing.

And the woman herself, their mother, who had left without her Cadillac . . . or a word to anyone to explain where she had gone.

The morning's clouds had long since rolled back by the time Rachel returned to Zeke Pike's place. She parked behind his pickup, a dust-covered blue Chevy even older than her van, then climbed out, leaving her leather jacket tossed across the passenger seat. For a minute, she stood beside the corral in the late afternoon sunshine, allowing it to warm her through her cotton blouse and jeans. Or maybe she was stalling, dreading another meeting with a man as jarringly abrupt as his name.

He might have startled her at first, in the wake of the unexpected phone threat, but Rachel suspected Mr. Personality was more afraid of her—of everyone—than she was of him. Despite his attempts to alienate her, she found herself wondering what would drive such a man to a solitary life on the high desert.

As the pinto mare nickered and stretched her neck forward, Rachel figured that, gruff or not, Zeke didn't lack for offers of companionship. She rubbed the mare's neck while her mind conjured a green-eyed man whose thick hair was dark, wavy, and just long enough to look disreputable, and whose skin had been bronzed and weathered by the elements. A man like that with a build like his could have his choice of women.

If women were his choice. She considered, then immediately discarded any other possibility. Zeke Pike was definitely a hair-on-the-chest, beef-in-the-belly, scratch-where-it-itches sort. Which probably meant his antisocial tendencies were the only factor keeping him alone.

With a final pat for the mare, Rachel said, "Anybody who would save a bag of bones like you *has* to be more bark than bite, right?"

Since the pinto gave no answer, Rachel told herself to quit being a wimp and go to Zeke's workshop to get her pictures. Taking a deep breath, she strode toward the building. This time she noticed that its concrete-block sides still bore the faded outline of the words *Superior Wax Co., Candelilla Unit No. 1.* Barely visible was the shadowy image of a burro, looking ecstatic beneath an enormous load of bundled sticks. Or more likely, it was gritting its teeth instead of grinning.

Gritting her own, she made for the center of the building, where someone, probably Zeke, had installed a modern garage door. It was halfway up now to let in both air and a measure of late sunlight, rich and golden. In return, the workshop issued the canned music of cheap speakers, which bleated a twangy, old-time instrumental that made her itch to move her feet.

Yet she stood rooted to the spot, for inside, working on a piece of furniture, was a sight to make a nun weep. Even Rachel, who would rather have a root canal than a naked man in her life at the moment, gaped dry-mouthed as she watched the shirtless Zeke lean forward to oil a heavy tabletop. As the sun's rays gilded him in profile, the cloth in his hand glided like a lover's over curves and natural imperfections. While muscles moved beneath the surface of his skin like restless spirits, he expertly stroked the brilliance from the reddish wood.

Knowing she could never reproduce this moment—that the instant he saw her, he would don his shirt and growl another warning to stay clear of his private rooms—she lifted her camera and clicked away, losing herself in the play of light and shadow filling her frame.

Even as she took the photos, she knew they would be special. Just as she sensed that Zeke Pike would pitch a fit if he had any inkling she was photographing him and not his work.

He did say you could take pictures of anything inside the workshop or the showroom. Lame or not, the excuse got her through to the moment she recapped her camera lens and cleared her throat loudly to be heard over Johnny Cash's "Ring of Fire."

Sure enough, everything changed as soon as Zeke looked up. Grabbing a denim shirt off his workbench, he said, "Sorry. Gettin' a little hot in here."

You ain't whistlin' Dixie, she thought, but instead of confessing to her stealth photo session, she dropped her gaze to the table's central base as she moved closer. "You used the tree's stump for the base."

He shrugged into the shirt. "Liked the way it twisted, so I buffed it some and attached it underneath."

"It's perfect," she said, resisting the urge to skim her palms over the table's polished surface, to lose herself in the swirls and faint eyes hidden in the wood's grain. Natural flaws formed narrow rivers he had inlaid with some beautifully striated blue and copper stone. "This is *amazing,* Zeke. Just gorgeous. If I had a pile of money, I'd buy it out from under whatever rich customer commissioned it."

"Be better if I made one just for you. Something you'd want, in particular."

"But I want *this* one, in particular." Smiling, she laid her fingertip on the heavy wood, where she imagined she felt the lingering warmth of his touch. "Too bad I don't have a dining room to put it in. Or a house. Or that pile of money."

"First two're strictly optional. You come up with the last one, then we'll talk." Zeke's eyes smiled, though otherwise, he kept a straight face.

And what a face it was, with those light green eyes set off by the thick, seal-brown brows above them. It occurred to her that she could be falling into lust with something far more problematic than a piece of handcrafted furniture.

He shut off the radio and jerked a nod in the direction of an interior door. She'd noticed it this morning but hadn't gone snooping. Maybe she'd been put off by its red paint, a less than subtle warning that danger lay behind it.

"I'll be in my room," Zeke said, "until you're done taking pictures."

What kind of furnishings had he made for his own use? She tamped down the image of an immense bed, carved with the lines of wind and flowing water and covered with striped Mexican blankets.

"I—um, I don't need quiet for my work."

He shrugged again, looking as remote and unassailable as the sheer face of a mountain. "Well, *I* need it, so just honk your horn to let me know you're leaving."

He went inside without a backward glance, a dismissal so abrupt, she grumbled, "Maybe you *don't* bite, Mr. Zeke Pike, but I've had just about enough of being barked at."

The Spirit Guides had grown impatient, and the lights had ways of making their disapproval known. By refusing to appear, for one thing, and depriving the observer of their wisdom.

Over the years, the lights had come at strange times and even stranger places. Not only to the viewing area where the freaks and tourists went to gawk each night or among the shadowed plains at the feet of the Chinati Mountains, but to private places where they revealed their true selves to the observer.

The first time, it had been a crawl space, hot and filthy beneath a trailer. It stank of cat piss and writhed with centipedes, spiders and a nest of buzzing, stinging wasps, but The Child didn't dare cry out, and leaving—leaving was unthinkable. Sent there for some long-forgotten transgression—most likely stealing food meant for The Others, The Child was forgotten, left all night.

Until the Spirit Guides slipped in through a crack in the rusted metal skirting, then danced about the space as they

flashed blue, then white, then yellow. Terrified, The Child
finally succumbed to the need to cry out, weeping while
scrambling into the darkest corner, breaking tiny fingernails
in blind desperation to dig free.

The twin lights followed, blinking out a pattern beyond
human comprehension. But The Child, looking up through
tears at first, decided they seemed friendly. And over the
years, as the glowing visitors returned to darkened bed-
rooms, closets, and even once, the bottom of a dry cistern
still echoing with high-pitched screams of panic, their code
revealed itself, along with the messages they brought.

Messages of hope, imparting wisdom that helped The
Child understand that sniveling and screaming would never
stop The Others, for sniveling and screaming had been what
they wanted all along.

When The Child listened, things grew a little better. So
when the lights flashed dark instruction, they were eagerly
attended.

Even on those occasions when they called for a death.

Occasions such as their last visitation, after which the observer had allowed witnesses, logistics—and pure cowardice—
to heap on delay after delay.

So now the lights had vanished, leaving loneliness and
panic rising like a flood tide in their wake.

The Spirit Guides must be restored—and quickly.

Even if that meant carnage at the airfield, where a brazen
killer was preparing to take wing.

CHAPTER FIVE

The first historical record of [the Marfa lights] recalls that in 1883 a young cowhand, Robert Reed Ellison, saw a flickering light while he was driving cattle through Paisano Pass and wondered if it was the campfire of Apache Indians. He was told by other settlers that they often saw the lights, but when they investigated they found no ashes or other evidence of a campsite. Joe and Sally Humphreys, also early settlers, reported their first sighting of the lights in 1885. Cowboys herding cattle on the prairies noticed the lights and in the summer of 1919 rode over the mountains looking for the source, but found nothing. World War I observers feared that the lights were intended to guide an invasion. During World War II pilots training at the nearby Midland Army Air Field outside Marfa looked for the source of the elusive lights from the air, again with no success.

—Julia Cauble Smith,
from The Handbook of Texas Online

Friday, February 15

Startled by the ringing telephone, Rachel jerked out of a sound sleep to both darkness and confusion. By the second ring, she remembered she was in the tiny rental casita, her temporary home. Just two days before, her dad had gotten her this cell phone, and so far as she knew, he was the only person who had the new number.

Something's wrong with Grandma . . . Rachel fumbled until she found the phone where she had left it on the nightstand, beside the glowing red numbers that read 4:18. With her thoughts focused on her family, she didn't even glance at the caller ID window before she answered.

"Dad? Is something—"

"I know where you are, killer. *Murderess*." The woman's voice formed a fragile skin of hatred over an icy lake of malice.

Not again, not here, too. Rachel's eyes stung with frustration. The woman sounded different this time, raspier and more unbalanced than she had when the calls had started, back during the trial in Philadelphia. Was this even the same person? It must be, for Rachel's most persistent—and frustratingly anonymous—tormentor had a knack for getting private numbers. Still, how had she found this one so damned quickly?

"You are one sick bitch," Rachel snapped, her fury outrunning her better judgment. Responding to this nut case only encouraged her. "Get some help and get a life."

"I have one, but you won't soon. Because I'm coming for you, *Raaaachel*. You can't run far enough or fast enough. I'll always know where you hide—"

Rachel's trembling fingers found and pushed the power button. From hard experience, she'd learned this was the only way to stop the harrassment. If she simply hung up, Psycho Bitch would merely hit redial and start back up where she'd left off. Invariably, the woman blocked her number, and the phone company's attempts to trace her hadn't helped, since she was using—and frequently changing—disposable, prepaid cell phones.

As Rachel burrowed deep beneath her covers, her pulse pounded and her ears strained for the slightest sound. And not just any sound, but those that ruled her nightmares: the turning of the closet doorknob, the quiet footsteps of an intruder who had stripped off all his clothing and hidden there in darkness until he'd thought she was asleep. The casita might be chilly, but she felt sweat trickling from her temples. Despite the fact that she had checked and rechecked both the closet and the door's locks earlier, she could almost swear she heard the quick scrape of someone's breathing—*Kyle's breathing*—and see the featureless, black silhouette looming above her that last instant before she reached the gun.

Flinging back the blankets, Rachel rubbed her prickling arms and clicked on the bedside lamp. As light flooded the two-room cottage, she peered at the closet door she had left open—and sighed to see that it was empty of all but her clothing and her fears. Even so, it infuriated her, that one whacko hounding her from Pennsylvania had so much power over her that she had had to look.

Like mother, like son, Rachel couldn't help suspecting. For the longest time, she had blamed a few unbalanced fans of Kyle's mother, a popular news anchor and Philadelphia morning talk show host, for taking it upon themselves to avenge the famously personable blonde's all-too-public grief. Most of the callers had admitted that much, but this woman, this incredibly persistent head case . . . could the Psycho Bitch be Mrs. Underwood herself?

Heaven only knew the woman had been rocked off her foundation. Rachel had sympathized with the tearful break-down that had been played and replayed on the news, had even tried to reach out to tell the woman how sorry she was for her loss. But Kyle's mother had flipped out on her, then gone public with accusations that Rachel had seduced her "baby" and shot him down when he tried to end their sleazy, secret sex. The grand jurors had been sympathetic— enough to hand down the indictment that Rachel's lawyer had been certain wouldn't happen.

But whoever her tormentor was, Rachel wasn't about to let the woman push her back into the habit of self-medicating. After Rachel had been charged, her attorney insisted she meet with a clinical psychologist who worked with victims of vio-lent crime. Not only had Dr. Damien Thomas later testified on her behalf, he'd helped her wean herself off the sleeping pills she had used to get through each long night after the shoot-ing. It had been hard, harrowing work with the pressure of the trial looming, but she hadn't fought to save her life from her attacker only to end up as an addict . . . or a suicide.

Reclaiming your life's the best revenge. Dr. Thomas had been right about that, Rachel reminded herself, even though he was wrong—dead wrong—about the evening she'd forgotten.

From outside, she heard gentle hooting, the soft call of a nearby owl to her mate. It was a sound she remembered from her childhood, something as familiar to her as the drone of an airplane or the sweep of winter winds down from the mountains. But not even the owl's serenade could lull her back to sleep now. A little after five, she gave up and crawled from the bed, then used the coffeemaker to heat water from the bathroom. While her tea brewed, she pulled on sweats with fuzzy slippers and switched on the radio. She needed friendly chatter but had to settle for the country tunes that had already been relics in the days her mother had enjoyed them. Still, it was something else familiar, something more to pull her back to the years before she'd first heard the name Underwood.

Soon, Rachel was sitting at the room's small writing table with a mug of hot tea and reaching for the prints she'd created using her laptop and a high-end printer. Though she hadn't finished tweaking values or yet printed onto acid-free archival paper, the proofs convinced her she'd been right about the shots of Zeke Pike at his work.

Especially about the one shot she was holding, where soft light gilded sweat-beaded biceps and highlighted a strong man's absolute absorption in his work. He was at once humility and pride and the embodiment of power, captured at a moment she felt privileged to have witnessed.

Yet there was something more as well, an undercurrent of sexuality that made her ask herself—would probably make any living woman ask—what it would be like to be the object of such total focus. Rachel wrapped her hands around her mug and shivered, at once deeply attracted and repulsed by the idea.

She had already been the object of one man's total focus—a focus that had sharpened into sick obsession. She'd had enough of male attention to last her for two lifetimes. Her reaction, she decided, had nothing to do with Zeke Pike, and everything to do with the most perfect photograph she'd ever taken.

The trouble was that no one else would see it. Because once Zeke Pike saw the proofs, he'd never sign the release that she needed to use a photo with his likeness. The image was so personal, so revealing of the man behind the misanthrope, she felt certain he'd demand that she destroy it.

And that would be a crime, every bit as much a crime as if she took a blowtorch to the gorgeous table he'd created. Both were art, and art counted for something more than the stubbornness of one of its components.

So what are you going to do about it, Rachel?

She worried at the edges of the question for a long while, until the earthenware mug grew cool between her hands. Finally, she put her tea down and pulled one print from her stack.

By the time she parked beside The Roost a half hour later, the small airport had already sprung to life. A mechanic tinkered with the innards of a small plane, and a uniformed pilot was giving one of the Learjets a preflight check. A curl of fragrant smoke rose from the café, a sign that Patsy had started serving breakfast.

Rachel climbed out and zipped her jacket, then paused and decided her meal could wait until she dealt with the contents of the envelope she was holding. As she made her way back toward the gold van, she raised a hand in greeting to her father and his two assistants, who were pulling a fifties-era German sailplane—a restoration project—from its hangar. Both Lili Vega, a tiny twenty-something whose shoulder-length, dark hair bore a fresh streak of magenta, and the more experienced Bobby Bauer waved back, but Rachel's father stopped what he was doing, jumped on a golf cart used to tow the gliders, and made a beeline for her, irritation written on his ruddy face.

Uh-oh. Her father didn't get mad very often, but when he

did, he was no subtler about it than any other of his emotions.

"What's the matter with that phone of yours, Rusty?" he asked before the cart stopped. "I tried you three or four times this morning, and it kept going straight to voice mail. Or didn't you want to be bothered talking to me?"

She pulled it from her purse and feigned surprise. "Sorry, Dad. I—uh—I guess I must've accidentally switched it off when I meant to hang up last night. I'm still figuring out which button does what on this new phone."

She regretted the lie but decided there was no need to worry him by explaining the real reason for her actions. With the young day bright and blue around her, Rachel felt light years away from her tormentor. "What'd you need?"

His expression eased, assuring her he'd accepted her explanation at face value. "I wanted to let you know this afternoon looks perfect for us to take up a sailplane. Weather's great, and Lili tells me the schedule is wide open."

Since Rachel had been home, she'd noticed that her father relied more and more on his assistants—especially Lili—to take care of the scheduling and nearly all the office work. Apparently, he'd finally learned the art of delegating those tasks he least enjoyed.

"I thought you told me earlier it would be too busy for us to fly today."

Little by little, he was dragging her back in the direction of the family business. Every evening, they had been reviewing flight rules at his kitchen table, where her dad rattled off regulation after regulation from memory. And yesterday, he'd insisted on flying her to El Paso for her physical. Though she wanted to be a help around the airfield— heaven only knew she owed him that much—she still felt ambivalent, even a little queasy, about returning to the skies.

He shook his head. "That group coming in from Reno canceled, and Lili says she'll take care of any tourists who show up."

"So Bobby's available to fly the tow plane?" When she

was still a girl, he'd started hanging around the airfield, taking flying lessons. People had talked, since only a few years before, a fatal drunk driving wreck had cost him his own wife's love and his career as a Border Patrol agent, to say nothing of the guilt he carried over the death of a young father in the accident. More than a few thought Walter Copeland insanely soft-hearted to give such a man a second chance. But over the years, Bobby had repaid Rachel's father's faith by becoming a top-notch aviator and a respected mechanic, not to mention a close friend.

Since he'd always had a soft spot for her, was in fact the only other person she allowed to call her Rusty, maybe she could talk him into having something else to do today. . . .

As quickly as the thought popped into Rachel's mind, she dismissed it as unworthy. But was it any more dishonest than what she planned to do this morning?

"This afternoon will be fine," she promised her father. "I have a couple of errands to run now, photography-related errands."

It was important to remind him she had work of her own. Not a whole lot at the moment, but she was praying that the photo of Zeke Pike was going to change that. She was hoping that with the publicity related to the showing, she could once more become capable of financially standing on her own feet, maybe starting to repay some of the money her dad and Patsy had put out. Though neither one had said a word about it, Rachel needed to pay them back, not only for her family but for herself.

Her conscience nudged her once more. As important as her goals were, did she really mean to achieve them by deception?

"Your stepmother will have something to say about it if you don't let her feed you." With a shrug of his sky-blue coveralls, her father flashed a grin. "And since I'll be the one who'll have to hear her grousing, I'd count it as a personal favor if you'd—"

"All right, already. I'll stop to say hello and grab a muffin,"

Rachel told him. Afterward, she had to run back to the casita and add one photograph, *the* photo, to the stack of proofs she meant to take to Zeke. Because as much as she wanted his permission to display it, she wasn't going to jump-start her new life with what amounted to a lie.

"Damned pain-in-the-butt conscience," she muttered under her breath as her father drove the cart back toward his work.

Zeke was leaning forward, cleaning one of Cholla's big hooves, when he heard the crunch of approaching tires on the gravel. Rachel Copeland's tires, he suspected, for who else would come by so early in the morning?

"What's she want now?" he grumbled, bothered by the unexpected—and plain stupid—pinch of pleasure at the thought that she'd come back.

The buckskin gelding used his owner's moment of distraction to snatch free his rear leg and stamp down hard on Zeke's booted foot. When Zeke swore in pain, Cholla squealed and pulled against the lead rope that tied him to a stout rail. Eyes rolling with terror, the outsized animal threw himself backward until the rail groaned and the halter attached to the rope snapped. Off balance and suddenly free, the horse threw a shoulder against Zeke, flinging him onto his back.

For one terrifying instant, Zeke was sure Cholla would fall on him. But somehow the buckskin recovered his balance, then clattered past the corral and out onto open range.

Behind him, a vehicle's door opened, and Rachel cried, "Oh, God, Zeke. Don't move. Let me call the paramedics."

"Don't do that. Shit. I'm all right," he insisted, though he wasn't quite sure yet. As he pushed his aching body into a seated position, his gaze followed the cloud of dust that marked the buckskin's flight. The pinto mare and the mule both raced around their enclosure, whinnying, braying, and bucking in excitement.

"I'm so sorry," Rachel said. "I must've startled him when I drove up. Are you sure you're all right?"

"Yeah." He nodded, more certain of his answer this time. At least until he stood and put weight on the foot Cholla had stomped. He winced and shifted, then saw Rachel looking out after his horse.

"Do you think he'll be all right? Can I help you catch him?"

Zeke's first impulse was to tell her he'd had enough of her damned help this morning, but her contrition seemed as real as her concern. Besides, his shouting had caused enough trouble already.

Shaking his head, he gestured toward the loose horse. "Look. He's slowing down. He'll turn around and trot back this way as soon as I toss some hay in the corral. But let's give him a few minutes to settle."

"I really am sorry," she repeated.

"Was my fault more than yours." Zeke shrugged. "I yelled when he came down on my foot and it spooked him. Bastard that owned him before I did used to beat him pretty bad—you can still see scars on his neck. So he's always on edge when I have to tie him. That isn't the first halter or lead rope Cholla's broken."

That look came over her again, the softening of her brown eyes as she imagined him as someone noble, some soft-hearted animal crusader. He wanted to argue that she had it wrong, that he was simply a man with an eye for decent horseflesh, a man who saved himself a bundle by rehabilitating others' castoffs. But instead of saying so, he looked down at the small paper bag she was holding, a brown bag dotted with several small grease stains.

With a sheepish look, she held it out in his direction. "Oh, I—uh—I brought you breakfast, a couple of cranberry-walnut muffins from The Roost. They're pretty good. I was just nibbling one before all hell broke loose here."

Accepting it, he smiled at the crumbs clinging beneath the curve of her lip. "I can see that."

An old reflex—a foolish reflex—had him lifting his hand to brush those crumbs free. He stopped himself from touching her, but not before she stiffened and jerked back, her eyes flaring as if she'd thought he might hit her.

"You know how it is with my animals." He shrugged and set the bag down on the flat top of a post. "Whatever else you think of me, I'd never hit a woman either."

His words shimmered in the space between them. Their gazes locked, hers gleaming with moisture.

"Especially the kind that brings me breakfast," he added quickly, discomfited by the hard tug of attraction.

The spell broken, she turned away and swore.

"I *hate* Kyle Underwood." She stared toward the faint bruising of distant mountains against the blue horizon. "I hate him for making me afraid of everything from ringing telephones to my damned closet to someone reaching out to—"

"It's okay, Rachel. A thing like what you went through, it's bound to take some time to get over."

When her head swung back in his direction, he saw that the lioness was back. "I'm not one of your damaged horses. I don't want to be soothed and petted, and I especially don't need anybody's pity. I just needed you to know I hate that sorry shit. And no matter what I told reporters, I don't regret that he's dead."

Zeke understood what it was to lose everything of value, to be left with nothing but a battered façade of pride. When Rachel had flinched at his movement, she had undermined that final bulwark, so she'd tried to prop it up with harsh words.

He nodded. "You might not be sorry he got himself killed . . . but are you sorry you had to be the one to do it?"

She hesitated before nodding and admitting, "That's what makes me hate him most of all."

Her expression shifted from defiance to concern. "Um, you're favoring that left foot. You need to get off it. Can I bring you some ice?"

A plea shadowed the words, a plea to let the discussion of her recent history drop. Zeke had no trouble empathizing, considering how very far he'd gone to avoid speaking of his own past.

"He's not breathing." The panicked whisper skated across the surface of a memory. An image formed like a phantasm: Willie's limp, pale body, shaken like a rag doll. Shaken, but completely unresponsive. *"Holy shit. What now?"*

Zeke forced it down, as he had forced down so many others.

"Let me drop some hay into the corral first," he said, "and maybe shake some grain around a bucket. See if Cholla has a change of heart."

His first pained step shot off starbursts in his vision.

"You're limping," Rachel pointed out. "Why don't you just let me help—"

"I'm fine." He blinked to clear his head. "Just need to walk it off."

"You keep telling yourself that—" There was a smile in her voice as she called after him. "—maybe it'll come true."

By the time she'd helped him to lure back, console, and corral the prodigal, Zeke was hobbling worse than ever. His left foot throbbed inside the boot.

"Hate to say this," he admitted, "but you might've been right about that ice and elevation. Could probably stand to have a little of your help with that."

Sleek reddish eyebrows lifted. "Before, I was merely notorious. But today, my name passes into legend."

"What?" He couldn't help grinning at her mock-sincerity.

"You know," she said with an offhand shrug, "getting you to talk, smile, and accept help, *all in the same day*."

He laughed at that, then nodded in agreement. "And it's still early. Hate to think what you could get me doing if you hung around much longer."

Another of those charged silences descended, with Zeke thinking of what he'd like to do and Rachel flushing as if she'd read his mind. And this time, it was more than physical attraction. It was the realization that the millstone weighing down his spirit lightened in her presence, evaporated with her smile.

But nothing would come of the attraction. God help him, nothing could. So he cleared his throat and turned away from her, then hobbled through his workshop. When he reached the red door to his private rooms, he stopped and glanced over his shoulder, only to find her hanging back.

"You don't have to come in if you don't want—if I make you nervous . . ."

He hadn't meant it as a challenge, but something sparked in her eyes, and her chin rose slightly.

"I'm not afraid of you, Zeke Pike." She strode toward him, past him, and across the threshold, the bag containing his breakfast clutched so tightly that her knuckles were white.

Once inside, she didn't bother hiding her curiosity but turned and looked over the tiny built-in kitchenette with a pair of folding chairs beside an old card table, where a dog-eared copy of the John Graves ode to solitude, *Goodbye to a River*, lay open, facedown, its spine strained by the unwarranted abuse. Beyond the pass-through counter, her gaze glanced off an old hospital bed with white paint peeling from its iron frame. Beside it, a warped and faded cupboard held his clothing, and an ancient woodstove claimed a corner.

He kept the place neat, everything except the book precisely where it should be, but for the first time ever, he saw the way it must look through her eyes, with its concrete floor and cast-off furnishings, without a spot of color in the whole place, save for the door.

"All those gorgeous things you make," she whispered, "and you haven't kept a single one. . . ."

She shook her head, then set the muffins on the table. "Talk about restraint. I'd hog all the good stuff for myself."

"Then you'd go hungry."

"But my avaricious soul would be well fed," she said with a dismissive gesture before pulling out the chair. "Now, sit yourself down and let me get you some ice."

Grateful to get off his feet, he did as she asked and

pointed out the drawer where she could find a plastic bag. It was a struggle to pull off the boot, but by gritting his teeth, he managed to do it without shouting.

"Hurt, didn't it?" she asked him before adding, "Your face is getting red."

"That's from holding in about a thousand cuss words." Cautiously, he peeled off the sock and hissed through his teeth at the violent patch of black, dark brown, and purple discoloring the base of his toes.

"Owww," Rachel said for him. "That looks like it could be broken."

"Don't think so." No way in hell was he going to the hospital in Alpine, or even the local clinic. "If it was, I couldn't have walked on it so far."

"You sure you don't want me to drive you somewhere for X-rays?"

"I'm sure. And I'm starving. You want one of these muffins?"

"No thanks." She spoke over the sound of cracking as she pulled the metal handle of his old-fashioned ice-cube tray.

The paper bag rattled as he opened it. Before he stuck a hand inside, he hesitated, then pushed himself back to his feet and staggered to the sink to wash up. Mostly because he worried what she'd think about him if he didn't.

Once he'd made it back to his chair with a paper towel, a thought occurred to him. "You didn't drive out here this morning just to feed me."

She passed him the bag of ice. "True. And I didn't come to scare your horse off or help you catch him, either. I brought some proofs for you to look at—the pictures I shot when I was here last. I'll need your signature on a release form before I do anything with them."

"Thought I already gave you my permission. It's not like I changed my mind."

As she turned away to refill the ice tray, he noticed the way her shoulders rose and stiffened. Was she worried about something?

"I need it in writing," she said.

"So go and get your paper. I'll sign."

A nod. A hesitation, then a puff of breath as she exhaled. "I'll be right back with the proofs and the form."

By the time she returned, he thought he'd figured out her problem. She was nervous, worried that he wouldn't like her work. Patsy had once mentioned—with a degree of pride—that Rachel was into art photography, so maybe she had an artist's insecurity about it. Truth was, she needn't fret. As far as he was concerned, a picture was a picture, unless somebody's thumb had covered half the lens.

By the time she came back inside, he was finishing the breakfast she'd brought him.

"Thought you'd taken off or something," he said by way of greeting.

"Here you go." She laid the envelope on the table, her eyes avoiding his, her posture radiating tension.

As he wiped his hands, he decided this was more evidence that he was just a simple craftsman, not an artist. If people liked his work, fine. He didn't give a damn about the ones who didn't, and when others ran a piece down in an attempt to talk him into lowering his price, he took their criticism as some kind of "let's haggle with the natives" bullshit and sent them on their way. He'd heard that it had given him a reputation for being temperamental. Suited him just fine and kept the socializing to a minimum.

After putting aside the form on top, he flipped through the first few photos and found himself impressed. Clear and vivid, each showed one of the pieces he'd created to its best advantage.

"These're good," he said as he reached for the release form. He'd seen enough to know the photos would be sure to bring in business.

She passed him a pen. "You don't want to . . . ?"

"Want to what?" He shook his head, taken aback at her sudden pallor, the way she looked as if she might explode out of her skin. Was it just the photos making her so nervous, or had she noticed the glances he kept sliding her way? Could she be nervous about being in his apartment with his bed in plain view?

Had *"You don't want to . . . ?"* referred to something more than photos? His libido took notice, though he told himself he was being ridiculous. Face heating with his foolishness, he signed the form and passed her back both the photos and the paper.

"Never—never mind," she said as she shoved the stack and release back into the envelope. "Listen, I'd better get going. I'm flying with my dad today. He's got a sailplane reserved."

He wondered at her sudden haste. As if she'd read his thoughts—his foolish fantasies about her.

He tried to stall her with a little conversation. "What's that like? I've watched 'em plenty, but—going up without an engine to rely on . . . Seems like that could get a little scary."

Relaxing visibly, she smiled. "I grew up around gliding, so I've never thought about it that way. But I've always liked the challenge of it, finding lift and riding thermals, soaring like the raptors. If the conditions are right and you're good at reading them, you can stay aloft for hours on end. Whereas anybody can keep a powered airplane in the sky."

He shook his head. "Not me." *I've never even been inside a plane.*

"You could learn it, easy. I've seen the way you watch those planes."

He shrugged in an attempt to look indifferent. "Just something to pass the time while I eat my lunch."

"I'll take you up sometime, once I'm flying on my own again. Is there anything else you need now? Looks to me like you'll be off your feet for a few days."

"I'll get by," he said. "Truck's out there, for one thing, and there's a pair of crutches handy. Got myself bit by a desert recluse a few years back. Damned leg swelled like a melon."

"A spider bit *you*?" She stood at the door, her brows

raised and her smile teasing. "You'd think he'd offer you professional courtesy, one recluse to another."

With the van idling, Rachel lingered. She had gotten what she wanted, needed. She'd handed him every shot she'd taken, given him every opportunity to voice his objections. So why did she feel as if she had just stolen from Zeke Pike?

The trouble was, he was starting to grow on her. Blunt and irascible as he could be, there was something refreshing in his honesty. She found that she preferred it to the way people tiptoed carefully around her, making her feel as dangerously explosive as a flask of nitroglycerin.

The cell phone she'd left in her purse rang. Mindful of her father's annoyance with her earlier, she pulled it out and checked the caller ID window.

It was Patsy calling from The Roost. Or maybe her dad had stopped for breakfast and was using the phone there.

"Hello?" she answered.

"I need you to get over to your grandma's, quick as you can." Silverware clattered in the background, and Patsy sounded both worried and distracted. "One of the neighbors called me, said that dog of hers has gotten into his trash. He knocked on her door, but she didn't answer."

"Could she be out? Maybe she went to breakfast with one of her canasta buddies."

"Most of her friends have died off or moved to be near their children. Besides, she's never out and about this early in the day. I tried to reach her on her phone, but I can't get any answer. I'd run by if I had time, but I've got customers and there's no one here to cover for me."

Rachel fired up the engine. "Does Dad know?"

"He's not answering his phone—probably up to his elbows in that restoration. Besides, he'd just tell me she's napping or caught up in one of her game shows again. I swear, the man's stone blind when it comes to his mama. After last month, when she got her medications confused . . . She might not be *my* mother, but she's the closest thing I've ever—I've been concerned about her."

Rachel thought first of the lapse she'd witnessed on the way to Alpine and then of her father and Patsy's recent argument. She still wanted no part of that squabble, but she was worried about her grandma, too.

"I'll be there in five minutes," Rachel promised, "and I'll call and let you know what's going on." If everything was all right, at least she could appease the neighbor by capturing her grandmother's trash-eating Boston terrier and cleaning up his mess.

"Thanks." Patsy quit rattling dishes and lowered her voice. "One other thing, real quick. Some woman stopped by earlier. Looking for you. Blonde with big sunglasses—I didn't recognize her, so I didn't tell her anything. When I asked her name and business, she took off in a hurry."

Rachel's throat tightened at the memory of last night's disturbing call. *I'm coming for you, Raaaachel. You can't run far enough or fast enough. I'll always know where you hide. . . .*

But there wasn't time to worry about that at the moment, so she swept it out of her mind, along with her last lingering doubts about the photographic release.

"I'll call you as soon as I can," Rachel promised. After ending the call, she turned the van around and drove toward the little, cinnamon-toast adobe house where Benita Copeland had happily lived alone for decades.

With a shiver, Rachel pressed down harder on the old van's accelerator. What if they'd been wrong to take her grandmother's health for granted? What if, right this moment, she was lying on her tiled floor, helpless and alone?

CHAPTER SIX

In the Mexican oral tradition of South Texas, the people speak of una bruja, a witch, who appears in owl form. La Lechuza, as they call her, perches upon rooftops and cries out in the darkness, seeking to lure the unsuspecting from their homes.

Those foolish few who heed her call are never seen again. . . .

—Professor Elizabeth Farnum, PhD,
from "Curious Customs of the Lone Star State"

"I know you don't want to hear this," Marlene's husband, Dan, said, "but for once, I think Kathy's right. Your mother doesn't *want* help, and she sure as hell won't thank you even if you actually do find her."

Marlene looked up from her packing to see that not only Dan, but also their two sons, had come into the bedroom. It was bad enough she'd had to listen to her sister's ragging; now Team Testosterone was ganging up on her as well.

"He's right, Mom. Besides, you shouldn't be traveling alone," the older boy said. Though Taylor, a high school sophomore, was savvy enough to claim a manly concern about her welfare, he was probably more worried she'd be unavailable to ferry him to basketball or run him to the mall.

"You aren't going to bring her back *here*, are you?" twelve-year-old Josh whined. "I don't want to have to give up my room and bunk with Taylor. He leaves his smelly socks all over, and he talks half the night on the phone when we're supposed to be asleep."

"Shut up, you little douche bag—"

"Taylor," warned his father at the same time Marlene said, "That's enough."

When Josh opened his mouth again, she pointed at him. "Shut it down. Right now. Both of you."

Her gaze flicked from the younger to the older, and then up to Dan, who had clearly been the mastermind behind this "stealth" operation. If they weren't so damned annoying, they'd be cute. "Listen, you three. I know this is an inconvenience. And I also know that Grandma, well Grandma's had some issues for quite a while now. Ever since . . . She loved my little brother, really loved him, the way that I love you. When he died, it hurt something in her. But the thing is, she's still my mother, and I promised Grandpa I would—"

"Of course she's still your mother," Dan said, "and no one could ever say you haven't done your best to help her. But you've turned over every scrap of information the police asked for, even more than they requested."

"A few old photographs and credit card numbers won't make her matter to them. Not the way she does to me." The way she did to Kathy, too, whether or not her sister would admit it.

"Come on, Marlene, isn't it time to step aside and leave finding her to the professionals? Maybe if you headed back to work, got back to your routine, it would take your mind off things a little. Then, before you know it—"

"Do you honestly think I can set appointments and hassle with insurance companies with this looming over me?" she snapped and wondered if this was really about money. Since her dad's death, she had lost touch with the family budget . . . and so many of the things she used to think important. "I understand you just want—that all three of you want—everything to go back to normal. But things won't be normal, *can't* be normal, until I get her back and fix this."

When Dan's blue eyes met hers, Marlene's heart fluttered, reminded of the boy who'd captured it so very long ago.

"Some things can't be fixed," he told her gently, "and neither can some people."

He'd never understand, no matter what words she used to explain it. Frowning, Marlene zipped up her suitcase and placed one hand on her hip. "Are you going to drive me to the airport, or do I have to call one of my friends for a ride?"

James Dean strutted down the center of a mostly residential street, his tongue lolling and his black-and-white face stained with the evidence of his most recent crime spree.

"And I'll bet you reek now, too, you little heathen," Rachel grumbled as she slowed the van and opened her door. When she whistled for the Boston terrier, he stopped and cocked his round head. Probably wondering what was in it for him should he decide to listen.

"Come on, boy. Let's go for a ride, J.D." She tried to make it sound exciting, but the small dog must have detected "imminent bath" in her tone, for he turned his stubby tail and bolted between a neighbor's bungalow and an older, pink adobe.

More concerned for her grandmother, Rachel pulled into the empty carport beside the well-kept, little spice-brown house. "Please, God," she whispered as she hurried over to the side door, "I know you and I haven't been on great terms for a while, but please let her be napping, or maybe in the bathroom."

She knocked several times, then stood on tiptoe to peer through the window in the upper portion of the door. Seeing no one, she bounced on the balls of her feet a few more seconds before trying the door. When she found it locked, she pounded hard enough to bruise her knuckles and called out, "Grandma? Can you hear me?"

She paused to listen for an answer and thought she heard the blare of the ancient cabinet television from the living room. After running around to the front porch, she found the front door locked as well, and no one responded to her knocking or shouting. Maybe her grandma *was* out. She could have thrown on her jacket and walked the two blocks to the little store for fresh bread, a temptation she should— but rarely managed to—resist.

That must be it, thought Rachel as she scooted behind the

chain-hung porch swing to peer through the front window . . .

And saw her grandmother apparently dozing in an overstuffed recliner, an afghan draped over her inert form. Heart in her throat, Rachel rapped hard at the window.

"Please don't be—Oh, thank you, God. I owe you." For Rachel saw movement as her grandmother's head turned. Though her eyes didn't open, she lifted a hand to rub her face.

"It's me, Grandma. It's Rachel. I need you to get up and let me in."

"Is she in there?" a man called from behind her.

A few days before, Rachel had met the neighbor, Mr. Morgan, a retired accountant out of Lubbock. A smallish man with wire-rimmed glasses and gray hair that wreathed a bald pate, he seemed nice enough, in spite of his understandable dislike of James Dean's trash can mayhem.

"Please hurry—call an ambulance," Rachel told him. "I saw her move a little, but she's not responding. She used to keep a key around back. Let me see if I can find it."

"I'll call your mother, too."

Stepmother, Rachel thought, but she didn't slow down to correct him. When she couldn't find the key, she took one of the rocks bordering the garden and smashed out part of a rear window. Reaching her arm through, she unlatched it, then slid it open and climbed through. Feet crunching on the shattered glass, she ran for the living room, where she found her grandma staring, her plump face flushed.

"Rachellll," she slurred, "I nee—I need some . . ." Her lids fluttered, sliding down to shutter soft, brown eyes.

"You need glucose," Rachel realized. Once, while still a teenager, she'd seen her grandmother when her sugar level dipped too low. She'd looked and sounded drunk then, too. Her breath even smelled a little like it, though she never touched alcohol. "Where are your glucose pills, Grandma?"

When her grandmother didn't answer, she raced back through the door into the little kitchen and rattled through the clutch of prescription bottles on the counter near the glucose meter. There had to be at least a dozen—far too many medications to be juggling—but Rachel couldn't find the one she wanted. So instead, she went to the refrigerator and saw exactly what she needed, a small juice box with a smiling apple on its front. Pulling free the attached straw, Rachel tore off the wrapper and stabbed it through the top of the container.

Seconds later, she knelt beside her grandmother, who roused enough to sip and swallow. Rachel held her hand and kissed her temple. "Don't worry, don't worry. This sugar's going to help, and the ambulance is coming. You're going to be all right."

By the time the ambulance showed up, Benita Copeland was far more alert and responsive. As her vitals were checked, she called Rachel "Cora" once or twice, then caught herself and said, "I'm sorry, Rachel. Of course, I know who you are. It's just that you look so much like her . . . the way I remember her . . ."

The paramedic, a clean-cut, dark-haired man whose name tag read "Alvarez," nodded in approval. "Heart rate, BP, and respirations all look good, but blood glucose is still a little on the low side. Just to be safe, you might want to have her transported and checked out in Alpine."

"I don't need to go to Alpine," Rachel's grandmother protested. "I'll make an appointment at the clinic here."

"That could take a while," Alvarez said. "Your sugar needs to be stabilized today."

"But an ambulance ride—that costs—"

"Let Medicare worry about that," Rachel interrupted.

"But they don't cover the half of—"

"Forget about it, Grandma. You scared the hell—heck—out of me this morning, and you're going to the hospital right now."

Benita was still arguing that she wasn't so old she couldn't make her own decisions when Rachel's father and Patsy arrived.

"You're going, Mama," Walter Copeland insisted. "If the

doctors give you a clean bill of health, you don't have to stay overnight, but you need to get checked out—for our sake."

"They'll give me a bill, all right. Like as not, a huge one." Benita gave a petulant frown, which on her round face looked strangely childlike.

"Please, Grandma," Rachel pleaded.

"Fine. If that's what you all want," she said before she gave them the silent treatment.

As the paramedic's partner shut the ambulance door and climbed into the cab, Rachel noticed a woman in dark glasses sitting in a black sedan with rental plates, parked behind her father's pickup. Rachel sucked in a breath, then let it go as she realized the blonde wasn't Kyle's mother.

So who was she, and why did she keep darting glances in Rachel's direction before looking away?

Rachel caught Patsy by the elbow. "Look. Is she the one who was asking for me earlier?"

Never one for subtlety, Patsy whipped around to shoot the woman a hard stare. "What the—She must have followed us. Walter, you need to go talk to that person. Find out what she wants."

"Her voice—was she the same woman who's been calling the café?" Rachel asked Patsy.

But the blonde was already opening the car door, unfolding her long, lean legs and striding toward them. No older than her late twenties, she wore a funky, fringed, pink sweater over tight, black leggings and carried a business-sized envelope. She didn't look particularly dangerous, thought Rachel, just determined.

"Not sure. Don't think so," Patsy said before raising her voice and edging in front of Rachel. "I don't know who you are, but you're intruding. Can't you see a family member's ill?"

The blonde looked over Patsy's shoulder. "Are you Rachel Copeland?"

She sounded somewhat nervous, but behind the gray translucence of her lenses, her gaze bored into Rachel's.

Rachel's father stepped beside his wife. "What do you want with my daughter?"

Embarrassed by the human barricade, Rachel edged into the open. The blonde's lilting Southern accent sounded nothing like the Psycho Bitch, and she looked sane enough. And soft enough to send packing if she turned out to be some on-the-make reporter out for a follow-up story. "What can I do for you? I'm Rachel."

"Good," the stranger said, sounding relieved and breathless as she handed off her envelope. "I'm just here to tell you, Rachel Copeland, you've been served."

"What?" Rachel demanded. This was impossible. The nightmare was all over. Her lawyer had explained that since she'd been acquitted, prosecutors could never come after her again.

Head tilting, the blonde shrugged and said, "Sorry, Ms. Copeland . . . nothing personal. Toodeloo, y'all."

With a ripple of pink, polished fingers, she spun on her high heels and scuttled back to her black car.

Rachel felt like waving back, using fewer fingers. But still stunned—and unwilling to make a scene in front of the neighbors with the gesture—she tore into the letter instead . . .

Then cursed like a trucker as the disaster unfolded in her mind. Civil lawsuit. Wrongful death. Ten million dollars— *ten million* dollars—for the "reckless behavior" that had led to the death of Kyle Underwood.

His bereaved, berserk blonde mother had found one last, legal avenue for her revenge.

CHAPTER SEVEN

I never found the companion that was so companionable as solitude. We are for the most part more lonely when we go abroad among men than when we stay in our chambers.

—Henry David Thoreau,
from Walden, *Chapter V: Solitude*

Monday, February 18

Three days later, Rachel met Antoinette Gallinardi at the old Army barracks, which had been closed by the government after World War II. Terri Parton-Zavala followed them through the installation, a sour, silent counterpoint to the lapdog that pranced happily at her employer's side.

"You've done an amazing job renovating this place." Rachel's words echoed from freshly replastered white walls, where ceiling-mounted swivel lights stood ready to illuminate displays. "It's the perfect location to hold showings."

Art Deco Woman smiled. "We're so pleased, and we're hoping this spring's event will help us raise the money we need to complete our work here—and continue promoting ordinances to keep Marfa the charming oasis that it is."

"Do you really think it's possible," asked Rachel, "to keep progress at bay?"

"I'm not certain, but I truly hope so." Gallinardi looked directly at her as she spoke, her dark eyes misting with sincerity. Earlier, she'd explained how she had fled here from a busy life as a fundraiser for a Manhattan museum, how the relentless pace and pressure of it had damaged her health and destroyed two marriages.

Rachel nodded, liking her. "I hope so, too, Antoinette."

"Unfortunately, it won't happen unless we find a way to bridge the gap between the newcomers from the art community and the longtime locals. We're well aware they look on us as unwelcome outsiders. And interfering nuisances at times."

"Which is where I come in," Rachel guessed, "as an artist who was born and raised here."

Gallinardi nodded. "That's certainly one of the factors that first drew our attention to you. That and your teaching background."

"My teaching background?" Rachel echoed.

"We've been hoping to find someone to coordinate a series of after-school workshops open to high school students and their parents. Monthly offerings featuring various artists, as a gesture of goodwill to the community."

Gallinardi must be seriously out of touch with Old Marfa's conservative streak if she thought locals would allow someone with her recent history anywhere near a classroom. But Rachel decided to cross that bridge another time and instead focus on the business that had brought her here this morning. "I—I have something I'd like you to see. I— I'd like your opinion on a proof of one of the shots you commissioned, one of the area's artists."

She swallowed past a knot of tension and pulled an envelope from the leather portfolio she carried. Though Rachel had enjoyed touring the facility, she'd come this morning specifically to see if someone else would recognize the magic in Zeke's image. If Gallinardi didn't, Rachel had promised herself she would pull his photo from the series— or at the very least, go back to his place and come clean with him about it.

Handling the proof by its edges, she passed it to Gallinardi and waited, heart in throat, for what seemed like an eternity. Terri edged closer, attempting to look indifferent while she peered over the taller woman's shoulder.

"Oh. Oh, my." Antoinette's perfectly polished nails

trembled against her neck. While she gaped, her little dog slipped like a wraith between her slender ankles.

Terri pointedly looked away, arms crossed over her over-flowing bosom.

"This is—it's amazing, Rachel, astonishing." Gallinardi went on, "We knew, of course, that you're an extraordinary talent. But this . . . Why, even Annie Leibowitz would be proud to claim this. And I have to admit, I'm not only incredibly impressed, I'm relieved. A few of the foundation's board members have had . . . some reservations about honoring your invitation. It's been pointed out our reputation could be damaged if people start whispering that we're capitalizing on a tragedy. Especially considering our plans to offer a program at the school."

Terri's venomous glance left Rachel with no doubt whatsoever as to who was working to undermine her with the board. So there was no way, no way in the world, she could refuse Gallinardi's breathless excitement. Enchanted by the shot, she looked through the other proofs, gushing over some beautiful images of a local glassblower plying his craft in a restored adobe workshop, an old weaver creating intricate designs from carefully sorted, colored grasses while a cataract of gray hair spilled over one thin arm, and the profane, acid-tongued sculptor conducting light and metal in a symphony that both astonished and appalled.

"You were good before," Gallinardi told her, pulling the shot of Zeke from the stack to look at it again, "but this work proves you've truly come into your own—and I promise you, I mean to use every contact at my disposal to see your genius is recognized. And rewarded as it should be."

"Thank you, Antoinette. I can't tell you what this means to me. I . . ." Rachel hesitated, on the verge of admitting there was a problem with the permission form Zeke Pike had signed. But at the thought of the lawsuit and all the money she owed her father, she hesitated until Gallinardi mentioned an appointment.

Rachel nodded guiltily and let the moment pass.

Thursday, February 28

Hampered by his healing foot, Zeke was forced to take things slowly over the next two weeks. He tended his animals and worked on crafting smaller pieces he could manage while seated, and after driving to The Roost for lunches, he lingered longer than usual.

He was resting, that was all. Resting and healing, not hoping to catch a glimpse of Rachel, or maybe share a meal with her if she wandered in while he was eating. But it seemed that since he'd seen her last, she'd ripped a page out of his playbook. Most times when he spotted her, it was at a distance, usually while she was working as ground crew for the gliders. On those few occasions he did manage eye contact—as he had several minutes ago, when she had run inside the café to snag a bottled water—she barely gave a tight nod and a "How's the foot?" before saying "Gotta run."

What the hell had happened to the smiles, the friendly banter, her offer to take him flying? Over at his place on that chilly morning with the horses, he'd felt something— some connection. Hadn't he?

It occurred to him, as he dutifully polished off his weekly salad, that maybe he'd misread the signals, or worse yet, whipped some pathetic fantasy out of a mirage. When it came to anything more subtle than the blunt offers he rebuffed from time to time, he was seriously out of practice. Or had he said something wrong, something unintended before she'd left? Once more, he struggled to recall his side of their last real conversation. Had he remembered to thank her for her help that day or for the pictures that would be used to publicize his work? He'd gotten bad at that, he knew. Gotten to the point where each word cost him.

Patsy looked up from the table she was wiping. "Ready for that pie yet? Pecan today."

Probably trying to move him along, he thought, so she could finish her day. The Roost had never served dinner, and lately, she'd taken to closing earlier. Checking on her mother-in-law, she'd told him, until Rachel got home to her. Apparently, Rachel had moved out of the guest casita she'd been using and into the older Mrs. Copeland's house.

He shook his head. "I'll just get out of your hair."

She paused to stare at him, her broad face disbelieving. "Made with genuine Fort Davis pecans, the way you like. I could box a slice up for you to take home."

Manners wouldn't kill him. He'd been taught once, hadn't he? So there was no damned reason he couldn't teach himself again.

"No, thanks." He gave his stomach a pat. "Foot's better, but all that sitting's caught up with me."

Patsy squinted, offered a scant smile. "Not so I can see. Sure there isn't something else the matter? Something—or somebody—who's out there motioning the tow plane to take up slack?"

On the nearest landing strip, the plane rolled slowly forward until Rachel spread her arms to indicate that it should stop. Turning back to the glider, she lifted the towrope for the pilot's inspection. When he signaled his approval, she moved alongside the sailplane to lift and level its wing before making a circular motion with one arm.

The tow plane pilot—Zeke thought it was the relentlessly flirtatious Lili Vega—buzzed its engine louder and started down the runway. Pulled behind, the glider followed, but Zeke's gaze clung to Rachel as she trotted along for a few steps before slowing to watch both planes take off.

She wore faded jeans with a light denim jacket, and her russet hair was falling messily from where she'd tucked it up beneath a blue "Soar Marfa" cap. But her focus was complete, her movements graceful as those of the pronghorns that grazed the pale, golden grasses outside the airfield, and he could barely tear his eyes away from her.

Patsy must have noticed, for she pulled out a chair at the next table and sat near him. "I've seen the way you watch, the way you've changed since she showed up here—"

"Don't have any idea what you mean," he said.

"I'm telling you," she went on as if he hadn't spoken, "you don't need that kind of trouble in your life."

"You don't know what you're talking about." He *didn't* need Rachel Copeland. *Wanted* her, maybe, and dreamed about her often, but as for needing her—or any woman—he couldn't. Damned well wouldn't.

"I've known you a long time," she said. "Almost as long as I've known that girl. Tell you the truth, we get on better. You and I, that is."

He looked at Patsy, saw the disappointment, the frustration twisting her mouth.

"She's always had a way of stirring things up. And now she's finally poked one hornet's nest that won't die down."

"You're blaming her for that mess? Jury said she's—"

"Walter always did encourage her. Thought that willful streak of hers was cute or, what did he call it, *high-spirited* or something. Went easy on her when she could have used a swift kick, time to time." Patsy held up her hands. "Not literally, I don't mean, but just a wake up. A little taste of consequences."

It seemed to Zeke that Rachel had faced a lot of consequences lately. Thinking about it, he felt guilty for the twenty years he had avoided his. Had it really been for his mother's sake, or had simple cowardice kept him rooted to this speck on the Texas roadmap?

"What do we do?" An anguished, young voice rose from the distant past. *"We can't let anyone—oh, goddammit. My scholarship—my dad'll kill me."*

Zeke forced back the memory.

"Rachel's being sued, you know that?" Patsy flicked her cloth across a tiny salt spill at the table's center. "Civil court, for damages. Ten million, by the mother. That boy's mama, she'll destroy us. Destroy everything we've worked for, everything we'll ever have. Bad enough, coming up with bail and keeping Rachel out of prison. But now we have to—"

"I don't understand." He shook his head in confusion. "Can they come after you, too?"

But he was thinking about Rachel, who had come here to regroup, recover. Rachel, who had helped him catch his horse and made him laugh.

Patsy gave a snort. "Course not, but that doesn't matter. She hasn't got a pot to pee in, but she still needs defending. And her father's hired a new lawyer to file a response, since the old one says civil courts aren't his 'specialty.' What's Walter's is Rachel's, he tells me—which means what's *ours* is hers, too, including the business I've worked at like a damned dog all these years, every bit of it on my own dime and my own steam. And I'm supposed to just put it on the table? Use it for collateral, all for a girl who can hardly stand to be in the same state with me?"

Patsy's resentment made sense to Zeke. Day after day, he'd watched her work like a rented mule to run this place on her own, a business she'd built years before she'd married Walter Copeland. Still, he felt the need to put in, "I've never heard her say a word against you."

"Doesn't mean she hasn't thought 'em. Rachel's never seen me as any more than a piss-poor substitute for the mama she lost. Pretty mama, and oh so perfect—one hell of a lot better than Plain Patsy from the café."

Zeke had no idea what to say to that, but Patsy expected no comment. He was a sounding board and no more. It was all he had to offer any woman, even a woman who'd been the closest thing he'd had to a friend for all these years.

Another glider swooped gracefully and landed. It was Walter Copeland with what Zeke thought was a student pilot. Patsy glanced at Rachel jogging in her father's direction, then looked back at Zeke, her expression sour. *Jealous,* he thought, and wishing her stepdaughter had remained back East where she belonged.

"For your own sake," Patsy said, "you ought to head home and go on about your business. You don't want to get tied up in this. You don't want to end up hurt for a girl who's

itching to run off to some big city the second she's able.
She'll do it, too, when she's wrung everything she can from
Marfa. And from us."

Zeke stood and pushed in his chair.

"Guess I'd better get back to it. Lunch was good," he
managed. More words than usual for him, but fewer than
the flock that flapped around his head. Questions, mostly.
Had Rachel withdrawn from him because she was upset
about the lawsuit? Or was the friction within her family
getting to her?

Stay the hell out of it, he warned himself as he climbed
back into the old pickup. He'd survived this long by keeping his life simple, clear of the complications that came with
other people. Besides, now that he was getting around better, it was time to get back to work in earnest. The kind of
hard, physical labor that would take his mind off the gnaw-
ing frustrations that took root in idleness. Maybe he'd trailer
the horses to the Davis Mountains and ride out today, take
an axe and break up some more wood. His mind recalled
the twisted, desert deadfall he'd spotted on his last trip out
there. It would make a fine headboard. Maybe he could fill
in the mesquite's natural gaps with some more of the
turquoise inlay that had caught Rachel's eye.

Under the spell of the bed he envisioned, Zeke was jolted
by the sight of the access gate to his place standing open.
Which, damn it all, meant customers, who would look and
talk and eat into his day like termites and at the end of things,
might easily drive away "to think about" an acquisition.

But it was a necessary evil. Since he and his animals all
liked to eat and the skinny pinto's vet care had set him back
more than he'd planned, he steeled himself to deal with a
tourist, or maybe a couple . . .

Which left him completely unprepared for the half-
dozen expensive vehicles parked around the building and
the well-dressed men and women strolling about the place.
Every mother's son among them looked toward him eagerly
as he pulled up by the corral.

"What the hell?" he asked, his brain struggling to catch up with the reality of this group, this *crowd*, at his place. Sure, he occasionally found people waiting; he even had a hand-lettered sign on his gate inviting customers to come in (Daylight Hours Only). Other locals, who ran the hotel, the bed-and-breakfasts, or rented casitas to the tourists, sometimes sent guests his way after giving them a rundown of his stipulations. If the workshop door was closed, wait outside. Don't waste time with a lot of chitchat. And whatever price he set *was* his price, not a starting point for some drawn-out negotiation.

As his reputation slowly grew, many of his visitors started tiptoeing around him, their eyes alight with the novelty—or maybe it was the sport—of appeasing a prickly-tempered craftsman who really didn't give a damn whether or not he got their business.

But today's crowd didn't tiptoe; instead, it all but mobbed him as he walked to his display room.

"I just *love* your work," one woman gushed. "Tell me, do you have another table like that one from the photo essay?"

"Could you make me one, too?" a small man in tight, black leather jeans asked him. "Only I'd adore one with coral in place of the turquoise. It would go *perrrfectly* in my loft."

With the ice broken, the other customers bombarded him with questions, picked up smaller items without invitation, and filled the echoing space with so much happy chatter, Zeke couldn't help remembering the family gatherings—the noisy, boisterous, joyful celebrations—he had long since left behind.

The thought started an ache, a sick throb that slid from head to stomach like a raw egg. But he couldn't heed it, not now, could only take the tourists, one by one, or in pairs, and help them so they'd leave him to his work.

As he did so, there were excited murmurs such as "trend in the making" and "new must-have," so many that he began to regret giving Rachel Copeland permission to take and use her pictures after all.

But later in the afternoon, when he realized he had pulled in several thousand needed dollars, he decided it had been worth a few short, uncomfortable hours away from the work that he enjoyed. What he didn't know—and would have sent him fleeing for the mountains had he guessed it— was that this afternoon was only the beginning of an on-slaught far beyond anything he could imagine or control.

Tuesday, March 4

The day began deceptively well, with Rachel submerged in a neon-bright dream where Antoinette Gallinardi and her fellow art groupies stood around the planned May opening and applauded Rachel's brilliance while Terri Parton-Zavala scowled from nearby, acid green. Caught up in their enthusiasm, the art lovers spontaneously took up a collec-tion to buy Rachel's way out of the lawsuit so she could fo-cus her full attention on her work.

From there, things went downhill. First off, Rachel woke up. If that wasn't bad enough, her mind insisted on replay-ing last week's horrifying conversation with her newly hired attorney, who had told her an investigator working for the plaintiff had uncovered, in an online storage vault Kyle had been using, a new batch of photos of the two of them "together." Only *these* photos supposedly looked dif-ferent. Rachel pushed back welling nausea, along with a memory of the testimony of one of her other students, part of a small group she had joined for dinner after they had all attended a fine art photography show one evening. Though she'd ordered nothing stronger than a diet cola, her behavior that night had supposedly been "reckless" and "provocative." Rachel had wept to hear what she'd sworn had been lies—vile lies from a male student who had been a friend of Kyle's—but no matter how she tried, she couldn't remember a damned thing about that night, other than starting to feel as if she'd been coming down with something, maybe the flu. She certainly didn't recall going *anywhere* with the youngest member of her class. But what if . . .

No. I would never do that. Dr. Thomas has it all wrong. Besides, the experts proved the last pictures were fakes. They'll do the same with these.

Fear drew a dark curtain, one she opened her eyes to escape. Only to be greeted by the sight of James Dean lifting a leg and watering the pair of jeans she'd left hanging from her laundry bag.

"Demon spawn!" Other problems instantly forgotten, she tossed a pillow to distract him. The little round head turned her way, its expression a study of contempt in black-and-white.

Her grandmother's head poked in the door he had apparently pawed open. "Is Grandma's little angel being naughty?"

"Just paying me back for that last bath." Taking a deep breath, Rachel struggled to put the dog's act into perspective. She'd wash the jeans, a far easier task than wrestling the scratching, snapping Boston *terror* anywhere near water. Glaring at the enemy, she said, "If you'd just stay in the yard and out of people's garbage, we wouldn't have to go through that ordeal so often."

J.D. laid back his ears and bared a set of crooked teeth.

"And you have a hideous underbite, too," Rachel added.

"Well, *someone* needs her caffeine." Her grandma crossed chunky arms over the thick, pink terry of her bathrobe. "Shall we start you an IV drip?"

Rachel smiled. "No, thanks. I promised I'd stop by The Roost this morning."

"After checking my medications," the old woman said peevishly, "so you can give a full report to your spymaster."

"Oh, Grandma." Rachel climbed from bed and went to her, though she had to dodge a snarling J.D. Wrapping her grandmother in a hug, she said, "We worry about your health because everyone wants you around forever. Because we love you, Grandma. *I* love you."

Her grandmother cupped her cheek with stubby fingers. "I know you do. I know, and Walter and Patsy both think they're doing right, too. It's just that I've taken care of myself for a lot of years."

"And now I'm helping out just a tiny bit, so you can take care of me right back." At the sound of a soft growl, Rachel looked down. "And your sweet angel J.D., too. Which reminds me, how'd you like me to run him by the vet's this week and see about that neutering?"

She'd suggested the procedure in an attempt to curb his wandering, be a responsible pet owner, and even reduce the dog's chances of getting testicular cancer in the future. But Rachel had to admit there was a smidgeon of payback mixed into the equation, too. Especially since he had just peed on her favorite pair of jeans.

"James Dean struttin' around this town without his nuggets?" Her grandma smiled and shook her head. "Now I know I've lived entirely too long."

After leaving her grandmother's house, Rachel ended up eating at The Roost with Lili Vega, who felt the need to fill her in on every detail of her recent love life. Or lust life, since it seemed to be comprised of a slew of hot flirtations, some periodic quick gropes, and an occasional sweaty tumble with the odd cowboy or pilot. With the emphasis on *odd*. . . .

"And after the bar closed, he took me out to the viewing area," Lili went on, referring to the park where visitors watched for lights, "but the only mysteries he was looking for were the ones under my sweater. Such a naughty boy, and such a dirty talker—"

"Better get to work now." Rachel's stomach curled as Lili's words nudged memories of courtroom testimony and ugly late-night phone calls. She bussed the table herself and said, "Thanks for the great omelet, Patsy. That ought to keep me going all day."

When Patsy didn't look up from the pancakes she was cooking, Rachel wondered if she'd been heard. But Patsy had ignored her enough of late that she didn't push her luck by repeating herself.

As she and Lili left, they heard a soft *WHO-who-WHO* from the rooftop. Though Rachel ignored it, the younger woman shuddered.

"What is it?" Rachel asked her.

"Oh, nothing." Lili glanced over her shoulder, toward the pair of owls, and a flush blossomed, deepening the color of her flawless olive skin. "Just one of my *abuelita's* silly superstitions."

Rachel smiled, gaze fixed on sleepy yellow eyes. Huge as they were, the horned owls looked frowsy and rumpled at this hour, misleadingly harmless for a pair that picked the area clean of everything from small rodents to jackrabbits. "My grandma's just as full of those old wives' tales. Guess it's an occupational hazard for old wives."

Lili twirled the tip of one short pigtail, streaked a vibrant pinkish color against the silky seal brown. Her nails were badly bitten, the polish sadly chipped. "Then let's you and I don't ever get old. Deal?"

"Deal," Rachel agreed, though stress already had her feeling decades more mature than Lili, who claimed to be twenty-six and not eighteen as she appeared.

As they walked toward the Copeland Gliders office, Lili continued chattering. Though Rachel had come to agree with her dad's assessment of Lili as a skillful pilot, her "girl talk" had all the depth of a gentlemen's club billboard.

Near the fuel pumps, Lili stopped and grinned a challenge. "Seems to me you've paid enough dues doing ground crew grunt work. Don't you think it's time to find your wings? Up there on your own, where you can really get into it?"

"I don't know if I'm quite ready. My allergies have been acting up again and—" With a shake of her head, Rachel put the brakes on her knee-jerk hesitation. She'd been medically cleared and drilled extensively, then checked both by her dad and an FAA designated pilot examiner. But all the tandem flying in the world had not restored her confidence. Or was she dragging her heels on flying solo for other reasons?

She sucked in a deep breath. "You're right—even if I suspect you'd really like me to get comfortable so you can take a day off now and then."

Lili mugged a wounded pout. "It's Bobby who's wanting more time off lately. His brother and his family moved back to the area—I forget where, exactly—and they're making up for lost time."

"Really?" Rachel was thrilled to hear it, knowing what this chance to reconnect with any family member must mean to Bobby. The tragedy he'd caused twenty years before was terrible. Beyond terrible, but he had suffered so much in the years since. Suffered and worked like hell to rebuild his shattered life from scratch. Facing the wreckage of her own life, Rachel took his progress as a sign that she, too, could work her way back from the brink. "I'd be happy to pitch in if it'll help him."

"You should have known I wasn't asking for myself." Lili sounded hurt. "I tend bar two or three nights a week over at the Psychedelic Scorpion—a girl's got to pay the bills—but the airfield's the spot for meeting the most gorgeous specimens. Speaking of which, what's Tall, Dark, and Silent doing here so early?"

Rachel turned her head toward the slamming of a truck door near The Roost. But instead of heading inside, Zeke shaded his eyes with a hand and scanned the area—until he spotted the two of them.

"Oh, my God, he's coming this way," Lili whispered. "He's never set foot on the airfield. I've done everything but strip naked and spread out in front of his lunch, but he's never taken any kind of notice. Whoa, he doesn't look too happy, does he?"

"Oh, boy." Rachel felt the blood drain from her face. *He knows about the photo.* She could see it in the tightness of her shoulders, the ruthless efficiency of his stride. "This could be the day I make good on that promise not to get old. Because he's going to *kill* me."

Lili shot her an alarmed look. "What do you mean, 'kill you'? What did you *do* to him?"

Rachel nearly choked on a hard swallow. Or maybe it was guilt. "You might want to have your ear protection handy. Because there's about to be a lot of shouting. Very loud and very soon."

Head down, Zeke came close enough that she could see the tension in his jaw, the redness of his face. Rachel's heart pounded with a memory of a male silhouette looming above her. Of the Big Bang that took one life and shattered hers forever.

Lili stammered, "I—uh—I promised your dad I'd check the schedule, then call him at home to let him know what we have going for the day."

"Maybe you should see if Bobby's somewhere handy." Rachel glanced at the mountain of muscle bearing down on them before adding, "Or the state militia."

Lili backed away, looking nervous, and spoke loudly enough for Zeke to hear. "I think I should probably stay out of this business. I, uh, I'll just step inside the office, give you two some privacy."

"Lili," Rachel ground out through tightly clenched teeth. She could have strangled the younger pilot, but there was no stopping Lili, who was already heading for the office door.

"Now it's official," Rachel told Zeke. "You're intimidating children." *And women, too—or this one.* But she didn't mention that, even though her body's shaking telegraphed her fear.

He reached out, quick as thought, and grasped her elbow before half-dragging her around the corner of the nearest hangar, out of sight of both the office and The Roost.

"Hey," she yelped. "What the hell? Get your hands off me. You have no right—"

"Did you have any *right* to take this?" He let go of her to pull a Sunday newspaper supplement from his pocket. Unfurling it, he thrust the photo in her face. "Do you have any damned idea what you've done?"

Something more than fury—could it be fear?—flashed over his expression. But Rachel had all she could to master her own terror—and the intermingling of past and present. *Zeke doesn't hurt women. He isn't Kyle Underwood, and the kind of candid photos I took weren't anything like . . .*

Her own anger blasted to the surface. Anger that she'd been reduced to a quivering, speechless victim by Zeke Pike's size and booming voice. She thought of her dad's concern that this past year had "knocked all the starch" out of her. Thought of how she had allowed her fears to keep her grounded.

"Get out of my face and we'll discuss this," she said with every bit of courage she could scrape together. "*Calmly*, or there's not going to be a conversation."

"You damned well owe me an explanation." Zeke's green eyes sparked with barely contained rage, and he was shaking, too, with the raw power of it. "If I'd known—if I'd had any damned idea this would be about the area's 'artists' more than the work, I never would've—I've been *overrun* this week. Strangers, even some woman who owns a gallery in Dallas, buying every scrap I had to offer. There were a lot of whispers, lots of strange looks—even from—from certain *men*."

He looked so disturbed about that, Rachel might have laughed—if she had dared.

"But I never understood," he went on, shaking his head, "until some giggling lady and her boy-toy pulled this out and asked for my *fucking autograph*."

"Soooo . . . business has been good?" Rachel smiled hopefully, desperate to spin something positive out of the situation.

"You couldn't've missed the damned point any better if you'd been spun around blindfolded."

"Look, I'm sorry you're upset, but I asked you to look

through all of the photos before you signed the release form. And besides, what the heck are you so afraid of? If you don't want people bugging you, just lock your gate."

"You're full of it and you know it. You were supposed to be photographing the things I make, not me. And I sure as hell had no idea you were sneaking around my place spying on me, shooting pictures when I wasn't looking."

"I wasn't *sneaking* around, Zeke," she said. His words echoed through her brain, as jarring as the clank of the jail-cell door the day she had been booked, as horrifying as the idea of photos shot while *she* had been incapable of protest. After swallowing hard, she mumbled lamely, "You told me to come back that day."

"But you *knew*—you damned well knew what I meant. And you've talked to me enough to know how I feel about my privacy. Hell, I don't even have a decent sign to bring in business. If it weren't for the bed-and-breakfast and the hotel people talking—"

"That photo, Zeke . . . Can't you see—"

"*You're* the one who can't see, or maybe you're so self-absorbed you don't want to. I guess Patsy was right about you after all."

She stepped back as if he'd struck a blow. So Patsy had talked to him about her? Her father's wife was running her down in front of customers? This piece of news shouldn't have stung her. She'd always known that Patsy didn't like her, known she was far friendlier when Rachel's sporadic visits remained brief.

Discomfort banked a little of the anger in his eyes. With a shake of his head, he said, "The hell with this. And the hell with you, too, if you're just going to stand there crying—"

"I'm *not* crying," she shot back. "It's bright out, and I left my sunglasses—"

"Just forget it. The damage is done now. You couldn't do a thing about it even if you gave a damn."

"I do," she said. "I do."

But he had already turned his back to her to stalk past Walter Copeland, who looked flushed and ready to defend her, though he was nearly a head shorter than Zeke Pike.

"Everything all right here?" he asked, and Rachel felt a surge of love for the one man who would always defend her.

Even when you're dead wrong, she realized.

CHAPTER EIGHT

*The cradle rocks above an abyss, and common sense tells us
that our existence is but a brief crack of light between two
eternities of darkness.*

—*Vladimir Nabokov,
from* Speak, Memory: An Autobiography Revisited

Thursday, March 6

The patchy predawn fog helped deaden the sound of the
observer's footsteps and the screech of metal as the hangar
door rolled open. More fortunate still, there was no one else
around yet, no one to remark upon the odd timing of this
visit . . . or to connect it with the tragedy destined to take
place later.

Such a long wait for this day, the day Rachel Copeland
would finally fly solo. A rechristening to be remembered as
she took the newly restored German glider on its maiden
voyage. *He* had insisted on it as a way to show them, rub it
in everyone's noses that she was the boss's daughter, no matter that she'd killed or forced too many others to pay the
price for her sins.

For the last few weeks, the observer had kept an eye on
her progress. Desperate, almost frantic, for an opportunity.
Still deprived of further counsel, of any glimpse of the
lights that offered guidance. Farther than ever from success,
but drifting in the dangerous direction of memories of The
Child.

Stop thinking of it. Stop remembering. The observer sucked a
breath through clenched jaws, then ground flexed knuckles
into throbbing temples in a desperate bid to make the
buzzing stop. But time ricocheted like stones hurled against

the sides of a rusted trailer. Flew back to strike the thrower right between the eyes.

That child had had nothing, less than nothing. Like a vacuum sucking at the dried teat of the world. Food was scarce, attention scarcer, and when it came down to a choice between buying booze or fixing fractures, The Child was merely sent beneath the trailer where its mewling whimpers couldn't be heard.

Never again. Never hurt and hungry and banished to the darkness, bereft of even the cold consolation of the lights. Better dead than that . . . better to disintegrate into bones and ashes than face the terrifying void alone.

Only one way to bring the lights back, that one way shirked far too long. So the observer went to work inside the hangar, a metal shell so reminiscent of a trailer that it gripped the heart with icy fingers and the soul with timeless dread.

Rachel and her father each took a wing to push the German glider from the hangar. Once they had it in the morning sunlight, her father was all smiles.

"Hell of a lot of work," he said of his restoration project. "I can't even count the hours. But this is what it's all about. Those classic lines, that incredible . . ."

Once she would have been embarrassed by the way her dad choked up, hazel eyes welling, over some old sailplane. But since high school, she'd learned there were far worse things than a father with an enduring passion for his work.

As she looked over the glider, she saw all the love he'd put into it. He'd rewired rudders, replaced gauges, and then re-skinned the deteriorated sections before repainting the old bird a vibrant red and yellow, with hand-painted "Flying Tiger" eyes and mouth beneath the single-seater's nose and canopy. The freehand-drawn mouth, she noticed, was slightly lopsided, but Rachel thought its imperfection added to its charm.

"I think I've found another undiscovered Marfa artist."

Smiling, she pushed her hair behind her ears, then pulled the compact digital camera she often carried from a pocket. "I'll have to get some pictures for my showing."

Her father crowed happily at her assessment. "You just do that, Rusty, and I'll pose next to this beauty with my beret and palette."

Rachel took several shots of her father hamming it up next to what Patsy called his "other woman." Father and daughter both laughed at their foolishness, but Rachel couldn't help comparing his reaction with Zeke Pike's. She could still see the huge man shouting, could still hear the booming echo of his question: *Do you have any damned idea what you've done?*

"As a matter of fact," she mumbled, "I *don't*." She could have understood his explosion had the photograph been unflattering or overly revealing, or if it had depicted something that would hurt his business. But every time she looked at it, she could only think, how perfect, how beautiful and sensual and . . .

She had even dreamed about the damned thing, or about Zeke working her body with the same feverish attention he devoted to his craft. And her body—the foolish traitor—responded to the moment she had captured, a moment as personal and private as the man she'd photographed.

"Were you listening, Rusty?" Her father waved a hand in front of her face. "I asked, are you getting excited about your solo flight this afternoon?"

Her toes curled inside her boots. "You sure you want me to do the honors? I mean, you've worked on this for two years. And what about Bobby and Lili? They've put in a lot of time, too. Won't they be hurt, maybe mad if I—"

"I want *you* to do it, Rusty." His stance widened, as if he were preparing to dig in for a fight. "You're family—and the future of this outfit."

"Dad, I—" She cut herself off, not knowing how to argue. Both Bobby and Lili were far more experienced pilots, and their hearts were in the business. Yet how could she refuse her father, who had just last week taken out a second mortgage to pay for a new lawyer? Rachel damned well owed her dad more than money, even if it meant she'd have to burn the candle at both ends to work at her photography in the evenings and rare days off from the airfield.

It hurt to think of pushing what she thought of as her "real" work onto the back burner. But at least a jam-packed schedule would distract her from her lackluster—make that nonexistent—social life, where any free hours were spent playing board games with her grandma or struggling to keep J.D. from anointing any more of her belongings, an effort he had only stepped up since his "nuggets" had gone missing.

"I've talked to Bobby and Liliana," said her father. "They're okay with this, I promise. And they both need to understand you'll be stepping into my shoes when the time comes."

"Dad, your eighty-six-year-old *mother* still kicks my butt at Scrabble." Although Rachel suspected she was making up a few more new words with every round. . . . "You'll be running the show out here for twenty years yet, maybe longer."

Her father turned away, ears reddening, to regard the sailplane once again. "Don't you just love the way those wings are raked back? I could stand here and stare at her forever . . . but I have a couple of lessons scheduled for this morning."

She wondered at the change of subject, but before she could say anything, Bobby Bauer trotted toward them. One glance at the pilot, who was slim and fit for his late forties, told Rachel he was upset.

"What's wrong?" she asked. "If it's about the test flight, I don't mind letting someone else—"

"The office answering machine was blinking this morning—lots of messages." He skimmed his palm over the top of his short, sandy-colored hair.

"Customers?" her dad asked, apparently not noticing his employee's obvious discomfort.

"Um, no. It was—" A muscle twitched in his jaw. "Hate to be the one to tell you, but it's reporters. Reporters wanting a comment about—was there some kind of lawsuit filed?"

Her father's color deepened, and Rachel felt her own face heating. They had tried to keep this new disaster quiet, and she had dared to hope that Kyle's mother would choose to do the same. Since no one outside the family other than Zeke had mentioned it, Rachel had harbored the hope that Patsy hadn't cried on any other shoulders. But clearly, the news had leaked out somehow. Had Kyle's photogenic mother wept her way through a TV interview or even a press conference? Did she believe another public play for sympathy would bolster her case against Rachel? Or had she cracked completely beneath the burden of her grief?

Rachel's heart dropped like a stone. As badly as the thought of facing more reporters scared her, she was more troubled by the idea that other crazies could be stirred up by the woman's show of grief. And nervous as hell over what the experts would have to say about those newly discovered photos.

"Just what I need," she said. "And yes, I'm being sued. For wrongful death, and for a pile of money."

The sunglasses hiding Bobby's eyes did little to conceal his stricken look. "And the tough breaks just keep coming. I'm really sorry, Rachel. I know your dad here and Mrs. Copeland have your back, but if there's anything you need, anything at all I can do to make things better—"

"She'll be fine," her father cut in. "The judge will see this is bullshit, persecuting an innocent girl for defending herself against—Sick son of a bitch would have—my God, he was naked—naked when he went for her. Would have killed her, probably, after he was done. We ought to countersue those bastards, sue the estate for—"

"No. We won't," said Rachel. Quietly, emphatically, as sure of this decision as she'd been unsure of so many others lately. "That woman's not only lost her son, she's been so distraught she can't work."

And if she had been making threatening phone calls, she needed serious counseling, not the added fuel of a retaliatory lawsuit.

"If she'd raised that asshole any better—"

"I've been angry, too, Dad, but don't you see? It doesn't help. Besides, from the testimony I heard, Kyle was given every advantage, including all the love a child could want. His parents tried to get him help, too, after he hurt those boys at his prep school."

Bobby frowned and shook his head. "Spoiled, rich punk. A parent can ruin a kid by giving him too much, too."

"My—uh—" Rachel started, "a psychologist I met told me Kyle's history suggested he was probably a sociopath. Glib, manipulative, with no regard for other people's feelings. No remorse for any harm he brought about. Kids can be born without a conscience, and nothing you can do will really fix it."

"*You* fixed it," Bobby told her. "Best way to fix it there is, and now you're getting shafted. It's not right."

"What I did didn't fix anything. But it's sure as hell broken lots of lives. Mine, my family's, Kyle's family. Sometimes I wish I'd never gotten scared enough to buy that handgun." Rachel's words tasted bitter as she thought of the days after her lost evening. About the phone calls and the e-mails insinuating that something had—She clamped down on the thought. "Definitely I wish I'd never pulled the trigger."

"Rusty, don't." Her father clapped a hand over her shoulder. "Don't doubt your instincts on this. It was either him or you, and I'm glad—"

"I'm sorry any of it had to happen in the first place."

Because no matter how she or anybody justified it, Rachel couldn't erase the knowledge that she had killed another human being. If she had had any idea of the scar it would leave on her soul, the damage it would wreak on her life and the lives of others, she would have found some other way. After he started to harass her, she would have found some way to make the police take it more seriously. Or she would have borrowed the money to put in a *real* security system instead of settling for the dead bolt that her landlord installed. She would have even *moved*, if she had only seen the train wreck headed her way.

"Shhh, it's all right." Her father's strong arms pulled her to him, but she remained fiercely rigid, angry at herself for falling back into the trap of second-guessing. In the months after the shooting, she had wasted so much time wondering what she'd done to encourage Kyle. Had her praise of his talent been inappropriate in some way? Had her smiles been suggestive? Had the sweaters she had worn to class been too tight or the fit of her jeans too provocative? Dr. Thomas had given her hell for buying into the notion that the target of a sick, sexual obsession bore any of the responsibility.

Rachel knew he was right, but it didn't stop her from occasionally backsliding into faulty thinking. Which made her furious at herself—and even angrier with Kyle, who was too damned dead to care how she felt.

Bobby hooked a thumb in the direction of a nearby hangar. "I—ah—I've got to go and do some . . . Yesterday, I heard a rattle on the Cessna. Better check it out before I have to fly that fella to Odessa later."

Rachel wasn't surprised by his disappearing act, nor did she blame him. After disentangling herself from her father's embrace, she said, "If you ever expect Bobby or Lili or anybody else to believe I'm capable of running all this, you have to stop treating me like I'm a fussing infant that needs coddling."

Her father let his arms drop, looking so hurt by her rejection that guilt struck her like a slap. Why had she lashed out at him when she was upset with herself?

"I'm sorry, baby," he said. "It's just—I can't stand thinking how I could've lost you. Can't stop wishing I'd been the one to keep you safe."

"I'm the one who's sorry," she said as the red-and-yellow sailplane blurred in her vision. "Sorry I snapped, and sorry that I brought this garbage into your life—"

He moved in a step and opened his mouth as if to argue.

She shook her head to stop him, "I can't do this. Cannot afford to have this conversation or take the time to fall apart now. I have to keep myself together and get over to the office. Because if I don't start returning calls and telling them 'no comment,' those reporters will be out here. Out here and sticking their damned microphones in my face for an answer."

What else would they stick in her face? The photographs she hadn't seen yet? More damning testimony?

"That's a good idea, facing this instead of running." He nodded, a look of fierce approval straightening his spine and lighting his eyes. "And you know what else you're going to do? You're going to fly today like we planned. Because that's the way to show them you're not going to let this beat you."

His faith and pride shone on her like spotlights, so for her father's sake, she laid her hand upon the glider and made a solemn promise. She *would* fly today, as scheduled. Because she would be damned if she—along with the father and grandmother who believed she could survive this—was going to go down in defeat.

Perched atop the central cupola gracing the Presidio County Courthouse, the Goddess of Justice presided over Marfa's downtown, as she had since 1886. But not *precisely* as she had, Zeke knew, for he had heard the legend that years before, a furious cowboy defendant had shot the scales from her hand on the grounds that there was no true justice here.

Zeke understood the sentiment, though he could have told the cowboy the problem wasn't limited to this corner of West Texas. And besides, no one gave a damn how raw a deal a man got, as long as it wasn't someone with money or connections. Someone like the privileged assholes he'd once mistaken for his friends.

Out of the dark haze of the past, little Willie's smile burned its way to the surface. *"You wanna be my buddy?"*

Zeke shuddered, relieved that today, like most days, he wouldn't have to venture near the pretty downtown square, with its galleries and its restored hotel, its fancy eateries and custom-roasted gourmet coffee. Instead, he avoided both the tourists and his fellow locals by resuming his habit of walking his mile-long private driveway, followed by another half-mile along a desolate stretch of Highway 17.

He refused to give up the daily ritual despite the growing backlog of custom orders he'd agreed to fill. Months' worth, by his reckoning, but few batted an eye when he mentioned the delay, nor had anyone balked when he raised his prices for the first time in many years. Finally, desperate to slow down the avalanche of interest, he had put a new, hand-lettered sign up on his front gate before he locked it.

INVENTORY SOLD OUT—NO NEW ORDERS TILL FURTHER NOTICE. He'd paused and looked at the words for several minutes, then went back to get his brush and paint and added one word: *SORRY*.

Freed of constant interruptions, at least he'd have the peace to finish the huge mouthful of work he'd bitten off—and the leisure to consider whether he was insane to keep living as he had instead of pulling up stakes and lighting out one step ahead of Lady Justice. Safer that way, he knew, with his likeness and his address floating around God only knew where.

But did he really need to? He had studied the photo carefully, memorized every detail, and measured the sum against his recollection of the very young man he'd once been. Was it possible that anyone would recognize him, with his face turned in profile and his body so very different from the still-gangly boy who'd run, shedding everything that should have mattered to him? Would his own mother—and God, how it still hurt to think about the woman who'd raised three sons on her own—know him if she flipped past his photo in her local paper's travel section? Or had he been locked in the same vault of painful memory—of painful *failure*—as his long-dead father?

As Zeke was walking from the edge of his drive toward The Roost, he stopped dead in his tracks, heart pounding, then shrugged and pulled up his collar as he heard a vehicle's approach. As a truck laden with hydroponically grown tomatoes rattled past him, he shuddered in the sand-strewn breeze of its wake. Not so much at the chill of it, for the afternoon had warmed up nicely, but at the idea that its driver had come up on him unaware.

Just the way his past might, thanks to the photo Rachel Copeland had had no damned business taking. He swore, an outburst loud enough to send a distant band of pronghorns bounding through the scrub, their gold-and-white hides blending with the yellow grasses.

"Now it's official," he said bitterly. "I'm scaring the damned wildlife, too."

While the shadows of clouds slid across the high desert plain, a trio of vultures soared above, clearly unimpressed by his tirade. A sign, he thought, that the world's gears turned without him, that his family had gone on turning, too, along with those who wanted him dead or in prison.

No one would recognize him. No one would remember. Because twenty years was a damned long time for a man to disappear.

Let it be long enough, he prayed, *for her sake if not mine.*

Thirty minutes later, Patsy had just brought him a generous slice of peach pie dotted with whipped cream when the door jingled with her stepdaughter's arrival. He glanced up at Rachel, then looked away only a split second after she did. In that instant, he decided that she hadn't been aware of the time, or she would have avoided the awkwardness of this encounter. But to her credit, she didn't turn around and walk out. Instead, she acted as if he weren't there.

He'd like to do the same, but attraction coiled like a snake inside him, rattling its tail in warning. Furious as he'd been—and still was—with her, the low buzz cautioned that his body hadn't gotten the memo on his outrage, that it still had impossible ideas about the woman who had stirred its lust.

"Have they been calling here, too?" she asked Patsy.

"Yes." Her stepmother looked up from the large, glass bowl she was drying. "Started up this morning, right off."

"What did you tell them . . . Oh."

When Zeke furtively looked up, he saw that the café's phone was off its hook.

"Damned reporters." Clean utensils chimed and clattered as Patsy dumped them into drawers. "I'm not about to talk to any of those lying scavengers."

"Nice to know—" Rachel looked pointedly at him before returning a hard stare at her stepmother "—you're drawing the line *somewhere*."

Patsy's thin lips whitened as she pushed them together. Turning her back to her stepdaughter, she returned to banging dishes so hard that Zeke was almost sure something would crack. He didn't look forward to the next time Patsy got him alone, when he figured she would lay into him about betraying her confidence to Rachel. It was no more than he deserved for losing his temper and running his mouth like a fool.

All regrets aside, he wondered why reporters would be troubling Rachel now. He didn't want them poking around here, where maybe one or two would get bored enough to start digging into the background of the newfound "celebrity" created by Rachel's photo. It wouldn't take much searching to find out that as far as records were concerned, Zeke Pike had not existed until the day he'd dragged his weary ass into this outpost some fourteen years before.

There had been other identities in the six years prior, and a slew of other towns. But he'd gotten so dog-sick of running, he'd sworn that Marfa would be his last stop. And he hadn't had cause to question that decision until Rachel Copeland came along.

She stood looking defiant with her hand on her hip before shaking her head and gusting out a sigh. After hanging up the phone, she went to the refrigerator and pulled out a plastic-wrapped chef's salad with a small container of ranch dressing.

"Thanks for saving this for me," she said to Patsy's stiff back, a step toward reconciliation that apparently fell upon deaf ears.

As Patsy continued to ignore her, tension rippled between the two like heat waves rising from hot tar. The silence was so complete that Zeke could make out the whistle of a train as it passed through town, three miles to the south.

Before he could finish his pie and escape, the phone shattered the tense stillness. Patsy turned and reached for it, but Rachel, who was closer, shook her head. "I'll deal with it. Hello?"

As a second mournful note rose in the distance, Zeke took his empty plate and glass over to the counter. He wanted to say something, maybe offer Patsy a preemptive apology, but no way was he doing it with Rachel standing there. Tomorrow, he decided.

As he turned to leave, he caught sight of Rachel's widened eyes as she listened to the caller. Zeke froze, unable to look away from where she stood breathing hard, holding the receiver in a death grip.

"Hey, Patsy," he called quietly, an instinctive warning. Because whatever this was, it looked bad, worse than reporter-bad. Maybe Old Lady Copeland, Walter's mother—hadn't Patsy mentioned she'd been ill?

"Wh-where *are* you? Are you—?" Rachel asked the caller. "I'm—I'm calling the authorities. Do you hear that? You come near me and I'm—Don't you dare hang up."

But it was clear enough the caller had, for Rachel did the same. Eyes closing, she touched her fingers to her temples and rubbed shaky circles.

"Who was that?" Patsy looked concerned now, her annoyance apparently forgotten. "Was it that crazy woman, Rachel? Thought she'd given up by now—"

Rachel shook her head. "She's never going to give up. She'll keep hounding me and hounding me 'til one of us is dead."

With that, she turned and walked out of the café, her

forgotten lunch still sitting on the counter. Patsy sighed and reached for the door pull, on the verge of following. But at the last, critical moment, she hesitated, then let her hand drop to her side.

"She's not going to want me." She frowned, as if the fact grieved her. "She'll be off to her father, just like always."

Zeke nodded. "I—uh—I didn't mean to throw you in the grease with her about what you said. Should've kept my mouth shut, but she and I had words, you see, and—"

Patsy waved off his explanation. "When I saw that picture she took, I could've told her you'd hate it. Not that she'd have listened. And don't worry about what you said. It couldn't have been news to her that I'm upset about the lawsuit."

"But it was a confidence, and I—I'm sorry." He glanced through the glassed, top portion of the door, trying to spot Rachel. He didn't see her in the grassy stretch between the building and the hangars. Had she climbed into her van to leave?

"Apology accepted."

He should go then, shouldn't he? Get clear of Copeland family business and refocus on his own. But instead, he lingered, picturing Rachel's distress. "Somebody threatening her?"

"I don't know as they're making threats, exactly. But there've been a few calls here and at the house. Crazy people—one lady in particular calling quite a bit. She'd tapered off." Patsy shrugged. "Must've gotten stirred up again about that lawsuit. Story about it just broke. That's what's started the reporters calling."

Zeke shook his head. "That's bad news, all right."

And Rachel didn't deserve it, not after she'd stood her ground and fought the charges, which took a brand of courage he had lacked. Hurt to admit it to himself, but it was true. He'd jackrabbited away from trouble as much for his own sake as his mother's.

"Work's waiting," he reminded himself. "Better get back to it."

He meant to do just that. Meant to take Patsy's earlier advice and steer clear of Rachel Copeland and her problems. But when he spotted her sitting on top of an old, forgotten picnic bench behind the café, she looked so pale and shaken, so defeated, that his feet refused to listen to his better judgment.

"You all right?" he ventured as he walked toward her. He half-expected her to demand that he leave her alone, but instead, she looked up, brown eyes shining.

"She told me she was coming for me. She told me and told me. But I never thought she'd really—"

"How many phone calls?" He moved closer.

"Plenty of them, back East. After the acquittal, every station showed his mother sobbing, breaking to pieces on the courthouse steps. It got a lot of press—she spent her whole career in Philly TV, and she's incredibly well-liked there. A lot of people thought of her as their best girlfriend or big sister."

He shook his head. "Never understood that, why people see some talking head on TV and get to think they know the person."

"The more her breakdown was replayed, the more some of her fans felt like her 'injustice' had happened to them personally. Never mind the true facts of the case, which didn't play as well in sound bites. Too long, too dry, and I was no one famous, just some evil slut—practically a child predator—pretending to teach photography so I could seduce my students."

"Can't imagine anyone buying that, even for a moment."

"Not everybody did, and thank God the jury saw through it, but some nut cases dug up my number—" She shook her head. "Back here, I thought it would finally be over. I thought I could come home and take a second stab at my life. Thought that photo exhibit might be the chance I needed."

"You can do it," he said, wanting to believe she had a future. "You will. This suit'll be dismissed—"

"From your lips to God's ears."

"And the nuts'll all get tired of running up their long-distance bills."

"Not long distance." She pulled sunglasses from her pocket and slipped them on to hide her misery. "That's what shook me, in there."

"What do you mean?"

"I mean that woman's *here*. In Marfa. The Psycho Bitch who always, always manages to get my number."

"She told you she's here?"

Rachel shook her head. "Didn't have to. I heard the whistle in the background, loud and clear. The same train I could hear from town."

"Are you sure?" He sat down on the tabletop beside her so she wouldn't have to crane her neck to look up. The conversation paused as a small plane buzzed up the runway for takeoff.

"I—I think so. I mean, I was sure at first, but maybe . . ."

"I heard the whistle, too, in town while you were talking. I think you should call the sheriff, like you said. That woman has to be crazy to follow you all the way out here—what's it take from the East Coast? Two separate flights and a three-hour car ride from El Paso?" Marfa might be popular with tourists, but it was a long way from accessible. Thank God. "If she'd go to all that trouble, she could be nuts enough to do worse."

"I'll call Harlan as soon as I finish my solo. Otherwise, I'll have to wait around for him and screw up everybody's schedule."

Instinctively, Zeke glanced up, took in the band of puffy clouds. In the distance, he made out a couple of hawks floating lazily toward heaven. He tried to put himself in their place, tried to envision their domain as they would perceive it. To the south, the quaint clutter of Marfa's buildings, laid upon the fragile grid of its streets, a town surrounded by vast stretches of dry plain that rolled toward distant mountains. A silence broken only by the wind's breath through feathered wings. . . .

And such a long, long fall should the sky grow weary of
their weight.

"Maybe you should make that call first."

"What do you care, *Just Zeke?*" Her forehead crinkled,
but her voice remained mild. "Last I heard, I'd ruined your
life."

He looked down at the hands he'd braced on his knees.
"Maybe it's not so bad as all that. And about the other
day, I'm sorry. Sorry I shook you up like that. I came off a
little—"

"You came down on me like a tornado, the way I remember it." She offered a wan smile. "And you had every
right to. Listen, Zeke, I had an idea that you wouldn't want
me taking that picture. But from the moment I saw you
there and framed the shot, I knew it would be the best I've
ever taken. Could be the best I ever *will* take. So, yes, I
buried it deep in that proof stack in the hope you wouldn't
see it. That wasn't right, and I *am* sorry I misled you. But I
won't ever be anything but proud of that photo."

In her voice, he heard an echo of his own passion for his
work; in her eyes, he saw a reflection of the same fears he
kept buried. Fears that the ugliness of the past would overtake him, that he was helpless to outrun it no matter how
many miles or years might pass. It was not pity, though, but
the core of strength that drew him to her, that had him
gripping her thin shoulders and leaning in to claim a kiss.

He felt the shock of it rush through her, felt the charge
slingshot through his own nerve endings as she pushed
against him, *into* him, as if she felt the same need, the same
affinity, that soared through his every cell. It had been so
long since his hard-won control had snapped—so long since
he'd felt the lush heat of a woman's mouth opening to his
tongue. One hand slid greedily down her back while the
other traced the curve of her waist. He felt her nails on his
back, beneath the tail of his untucked shirt.

When she murmured deep in her throat and thrust a hip
against his hard length, Zeke pushed a hand between them

to squeeze the softness of one of her small breasts. But it wasn't enough—not nearly—and he ached to push her back right there, to spread her out on the table and tear his way through her clothing. He needed to taste the swell that he was holding, to feel her smooth skin beneath his body, to take her fast and rough and—

He jerked back, a hairsbreadth from the point of no return. Flushed and trembling, she pushed her hair behind her ears and stared, her breathing rapid.

"We can't," she said.

"Not here," he agreed. Bad enough that someone could have seen the red-hot kiss they'd shared. If things had progressed a minute longer, they might have caused Patsy to douse them with a bucket of ice water.

"Not *anywhere*." She shook her head, her eyes round behind the lenses that had slid down to the end of her nose. "This was—it can't be."

Worried, he thought. Frightened. He had scared her, coming at her with all the finesse of some slobbering horndog. Raking his hand through his hair, he tried to sort his tangle of emotions into words.

Before he could manage, she was turning, then jogging toward the airstrip. Retreating to the comfort of her father after all.

He followed at a distance, telling himself he only did it for her safety, in case the woman who had threatened her was even closer than imagined. And maybe, maybe Rachel would look back to see him. Maybe send a smile ghosting his way to let him know she was all right.

She never turned or slowed, but instead made a beeline to where her dad and Lili Vega were checking out a red-and-yellow glider at the runway's end. Nearby sat the tow plane, in position to pull the gleaming dragonfly aloft, and Zeke spotted several others watching, from a pair of men in coveralls who were working on a small plane to a lone man smoking outside a hangar that housed a private jet.

They were waiting to watch Rachel, Zeke realized, so she

must be flying right away. At the thought familiar yearning deepened into an envy that surprised him. *What would it be like?*

She was safe here, with all these people, and soon she'd be beyond the reach of even the most determined stalker. With a deep breath, he turned away and started toward the highway that would take him back where he belonged.

He had only made it as far as the picnic table when he heard the tow plane's engine. He hesitated, willing himself to keep going, then abruptly turned around and said, "To hell with it."

The glider's rudder waggled, and tiny Lili waved her arm, signaling the pilot—Walter must be flying—that his daughter had given the all clear to proceed. Breath held, Zeke sank down onto the table's top as the tow plane started to roll along the runway.

Behind him, keys jingled, and Patsy said, "Thought you went back to work."

He glanced her way long enough to take in her bland expression. Clearly, she hadn't seen what he'd been doing with her stepdaughter in this very spot not ten minutes earlier. Grateful, Zeke returned his attention to the red-and-yellow glider as it picked up speed behind the powered plane.

He shrugged. "As many lunch breaks as I've spent watching them work on that thing, seems only right that I should see it fly."

The glider's longer wings lifted it before the tow plane's wheels first left the tarmac. Together, the two aircraft ascended, the former crop duster pulling the old glider into a wide spiral that kept both circling higher yet still easily in sight. Using a hand to shade his eyes, he tracked them.

"Guess that relic can fly after all." Patsy's keys tinkled once again, but her tone had flatlined with disinterest. For all the time she spent in the company of pilots, her feet were firmly rooted to the ground. "I'm heading back to town now, but I could swing you by your place if you'd like a ride."

He shook his head and remained planted. "Thanks, but I'd just as soon walk. As soon as my lunch has finished settling."

"You don't need to make excuses," she said. "You're watching out for Rachel, aren't you? Making sure she's all right after that phone call. Never realized you were such a gentleman at heart."

He smiled, recalling his recent, less-than-civilized behavior. "I try to keep it quiet. Otherwise, the ladies wouldn't give me any peace."

She laughed, a sound much like a rusty door hinge. Behind The Roost's sign, one of the owls groused noisily at the disturbance to its sleep.

"You don't like the noise, *move*," Patsy called to her unwelcome tenants. "And take your nasty leavings with you."

When Zeke looked at her, she said, "Every morning I have to pick up those disgusting packs of hair and bones they cough up."

He nodded, understanding owls and their gruesome litter.

"You have yourself a good day," she said.

Moments after she drove off in her gray Impala, he looked up to see the tow plane and the glider. As the red-and-yellow craft shrank from his vantage point, he told himself that there was no sense dawdling, that Rachel would be fine now.

That she had left her problems—him included—far below.

CHAPTER NINE

Oh! I have slipped the surly bonds of earth,
And danced the skies on laughter-silvered wings;
Sunward I've climbed, and joined the tumbling mirth
Of sun-split clouds,—and done a hundred things
You have not dreamed of . . .

—From "High Flight,"
by Pilot Officer John Gillespie Magee, Jr., RCAF,
shortly before the occasion of his death, at age 19

Rachel released the towrope and then smiled at the perfect separation. As the Pawnee wheeled to the right and downward, its engine noises fell away, leaving only the rushing of the air she sliced through. She pushed open the sliding window to her left and stuck her cupped hand outside the canopy to allow the cool wind to push it upward like a tiny, auxiliary wing.

Her father and his assistants had done a fine job on the restoration. The sailplane responded with elegant efficiency as she turned beneath a thick cloud where large birds circled. Her heart leapt eagerly as the glider's long wings caught the thermal. Gaze flicking to the merry upward spin of the altimeter, she allowed the events of the past hour to fall away beneath her. The tense silences with Patsy, the threat of the phone call, the combustion of an unexpected and spectacularly reckless kiss: she left it all behind to think of later.

For now, she soared with a pair of red-tailed hawks tumbling playfully beside her. Below, the blue shadows of huge clouds slid across the desert landscape, offering her details missed in the bright, reflected sunlight.

And in that instant, she understood that this vantage, this

play in contrasts had informed the vision she applied to terrestrial camera shots. Slipping through the skies, as much as countless classes and the years she had apprenticed with others had made her the photographer she was.

It was an unexpected realization, since flying was the thing she'd always taken for granted, the life she had returned to by default. She'd come reluctantly this time, troubled by the idea that every minute she spent in the air took her a minute farther from her dreams of succeeding in her chosen field.

But it didn't have to be an either/or proposition. She would sharpen her photography skills by reclaiming her place beside her father. And it was no betrayal if she loved her time spent airborne almost as much as he did.

Buoyed by the thought, she looked forward to an afternoon of soaring—a plan she altered when a spark of distant lightning caught her eye. Though still miles off, the storm was clearly moving her way.

She was sorry to end the flight so quickly, but long ago, her dad had made her promise never to risk a tangle with a tempest. An experienced glider pilot friend of his—a man Rachel had met a few times—had misjudged the weather and been sucked into a thunder cell, where his fragile craft was snapped to pieces by its winds. It had taken days to find the wood-and-cloth wreckage in the desert, weeks more to find the broken body where it had landed miles away.

Rachel remembered having nightmares in the months after the crash took place. Tumbling through space, through stinging hail and bursts of lightning, she'd awakened in a cold sweat, time and time again.

Yet she knew this storm was still miles off, so she felt no panic or particular hurry as she reduced airspeed and guided the sailplane toward the landing strip. Once again, the old German glider responded dutifully, and she knew a moment's selfish pleasure that she had been the first to fly the phoenix since its resurrection.

It was the last conscious thought she had, less than fifty

feet above the runway, before a loud *crack* gave her a split second's warning. Her canopy snapped up and back, some piece flying from it to slam into her face. The shock of the blow knocked her head to the right and eclipsed her vision with a splash of red-and-black pain. Blinded, she felt the glider's nose drop like a rock.

Panic slicing through her, she hauled back on the stick. A wingtip was first to touch the tarmac, first to snap and spin the craft to the left. Yet instead of flipping, the glider's wheels struck hard and slid sideways, bumping roughly as something on the underside gave way with a crunch.

With the sound of splintering, the sailplane shuddered, snagged, and jerked to an abrupt halt. Rachel sat stunned, her pulse roaring in her ears, her surprise at her survival so overwhelming she couldn't think, react, or feel pain. Until she reached up to clear the hair and blood from her eyes and touched—oh, God, what *was* that—on her forehead.

Screaming, she fought to get out, forgetting the harness that strapped her into her seat. Screaming for what felt like an eternity before she heard someone shout her name.

Zeke joined all those running, pounding toward the spot where Rachel's sailplane had come to rest. Panic careened through him as her shrill cries reached his ears, but screaming meant she was alive. Meant that at least the impact hadn't killed her. Zeke passed several other people as his long legs picked up speed, but he noticed one man, the man who had been smoking outside the jet hangar, running in the opposite direction. Probably going to call an ambulance.

Zeke saw the twisted canopy, saw the snapped wingtip propping up the damaged plane. Spotted Rachel's father bending over her, with Lili Vega pale and panting right beside him.

Rachel's screams faded to groans, and Zeke caught his first glimpse of her face, masked in streaming blood from a deep gash on her forehead. The sight drew him up short and slammed his heart against his ribs.

Walter Copeland handed Rachel a folded cloth out of his pocket and put it in her hand. "Press this to that cut, Rusty, and tell me where else it hurts."

"There was a crack," she cried, "and then the canopy just flipped back. Something flew off. Hit me in the face. I couldn't see, but—Why on earth would it fail like that?"

"Forget about that now." Despite the emergency, his voice was firm and calm. "Just settle down and think a minute. Does your back hurt? What about your neck?"

"No. No. Just here." With her free hand, she gestured toward the wound that she was blotting while Lili stepped aside to take a call on her cell phone. "Help me get out, will you? Could you unhook the harness?"

"Hang on a minute," said her father.

Lili snapped her phone shut. "Bobby's called an ambulance. Maybe you shouldn't move until they get—"

But Rachel was already struggling free, assisted by her father. Trembling violently, she swayed on her feet—with Walter's steadying hand on her arm—as she turned to survey the damage to the sailplane. "It's wrecked, Dad. All that time and work, and it's—"

"I don't care about the damned plane," Walter told her. "Planes can be restored, replaced. Not daughters."

"You're *alive*, Rach," Lili stressed. "It's a miracle you and the plane both didn't end up smashed to pieces. If you hadn't leveled it at the last second—"

Rachel took a step or two before sinking to the runway, her left hand still pressing the cloth to her forehead. "I could really use something for a headache right now."

"Maybe you should lie down," her father suggested. "Lie still until the paramedics come to check you out."

"I—I'll be all right," she told him. "Just give me a few minutes."

"Might have a concussion." Though Zeke hadn't meant to speak up, the concerned comment slipped out before being echoed by several others who had shown up.

But Rachel, hearing Zeke's voice, looked up at him, a

question mingling with the pain in her eyes. Was she surprised that he'd come running with the others? Did she still believe—even after the kiss they'd shared at the table—that he felt nothing toward her except anger over the photograph she'd taken?

They didn't talk—there were too many people around for him to call attention to himself with conversation. But he stayed anyway until the ambulance arrived and two men checked her vitals.

"Can you tell me what today is?" asked a heavyset paramedic whose name tag read *Garza*.

Rachel correctly answered two or three such questions before losing patience. "Can't you just give me some aspirin?"

"You're going to need a few stitches, minimum, to close up that cut," Garza pointed out, "and after what you've been through, I'd strongly advise a thorough examination at the hospital. But it's up to you. If you don't want to go—"

"She's going," said her father.

Rachel blinked rapidly, and beneath the streaks of blood, her pallor stood out. Either she was feeling worse, thought Zeke, or she had the good sense to realize arguing would do her no good.

"You stay awake," said Garza's partner, a blond kid who looked only a year or two past high school. But he sounded concerned as he said, "Don't go passing out—or puking in the ambulance if you can help it."

Zeke edged closer, unable to keep his distance. "Take care of yourself," he said.

"I'll try," Rachel murmured as she was loaded for the half-hour drive to Alpine.

Before the ambulance doors closed, Walter Copeland covered the receiver of the cell phone he'd been using and said, "Patsy's on her way. Soon as she gets here, we'll meet you at the emergency room."

"She doesn't have to come." Rachel's voice was strained. "I've put her out enough lately."

Walter grimaced. "She *wants* to, Rachel. She was pretty upset when she heard."

"About the hospital bill, most likely," Rachel answered before the ambulance doors swung shut.

"Hell of a way to get the last word, Rusty," Walter groused as the vehicle rolled away, lights flashing. Turning, he brushed past Zeke on his way to join Lili. Bobby appeared from a nearby hangar to meet him.

By this time, thicker clouds had rolled in and thunder rumbled uneasily around them. As the first chill raindrops plunked down, the remaining onlookers dispersed, save for Zeke, who lingered, as Walter and his employees looked over the wreckage.

The wind carried snatches of their conversation to him.

"I know we checked those canopy hinges and the latch—I checked and double-checked them personally." Bobby spoke quickly, clearly agitated. "How the hell could have worked loose on that short flight?"

"Never seen anything like this before," said Lili. "Never even heard of it."

"Don't touch anything," Walter told them. "The NTSB will be sending a team to try to figure out what happened, whether it was a parts failure—"

"Or their usual 'pilot error' bullshit." As the rain picked up, it popped against the glider's fuselage and partly obscured Bobby's irritation. "She was ready for this, Walter. I've watched out for her same as you have, and she was—"

Reluctant as he felt, Zeke made himself step forward. "Someone threatened her today. At The Roost, she picked up the phone. Rachel said it was a woman who's been calling her."

Walter looked up, jaw gaping, apparently surprised to see him still there, or possibly to hear him, since in all the years the two men had lived in the same town, they had only passed a few words. "One of those damned cranks from Philadelphia?"

"Rachel thinks she's here now, in Marfa. She heard a

train over the phone, and we could hear it at the same time from town."

Lili looked skeptical. "You're not suggesting—?"

"You know, I saw a stranger around earlier," said Walter. "A fellow I've never seen before, hanging out over there." He cocked his head in the direction of the jet hangar.

"I saw him there, too," Zeke offered. "Leaving the area while everybody else was rushing this way. I figured he was calling for an ambulance."

"Could it have been a woman?" Lili's voice rose with excitement. "Could she have just been posing as a man?"

Bobby narrowed his blue eyes, looking murderous. "What did this guy look like?"

Zeke thought for a moment. "White and in his forties, I think. Brown hair with hardly any gray, a little longer than yours. On the thin side, like a runner's build, but definitely male. Hard to say about the height. Maybe five-ten or six feet or so. Wearing—um—nothing that stood out much. Dark jeans, I think, with a blue shirt."

Walter wiped the rain from his face. "He was smoking when I saw him."

Lili's eyes flared and she snapped her fingers. "I remember seeing him, too. I thought he must be one of the bizjet people, since he didn't wave when I did. But I didn't think anything of it because he had this look, like he belonged."

"More than likely, he did," Bobby said. "Lots of people come and go around here. Place might be small, but we don't know all the new folks."

"If he called for an ambulance, maybe he left his name," Walter suggested. "I'll check into it later. But there's Patsy, with the car. I need to go and see about my daughter. If you two—" he glanced from Bobby to Lili "—could put a tarp over the cockpit before it gets soaked and get the Transportation Board to send a Go Team, I'd appreciate it."

"Just let us know how she is." Bobby clapped his boss's shoulder. "And tell her she's in our prayers. I'll cancel the Odessa flight. I'll be here if you need me."

Lili opted for a tight hug. "She's going to be all right, Walter. But you call us the minute you know anything."

Zeke wished he had a phone—or enough of a claim on Rachel to warrant being kept informed. He reminded himself that he'd set up his life as a loner on purpose—the lust-spawned kiss they'd shared entitled him to nothing. Less than nothing.

But it wouldn't stop him from worrying about her or from wondering if her *accident* had been an accident—or the work of either the stranger at the airport or the anonymous female caller, who had traveled all the way to Marfa to threaten Rachel's life.

CHAPTER TEN

To: Deputy Leo Varajas
From: Sheriff Harlan Castillo

In the matter of the phone harassment complaint by Rachel Copeland, please follow up on these items:

1. Contact Philadelphia P.D. Det. Daniel Howell regarding any records of threats from friends/family members of Kyle Underwood. Can Howell check whereabouts of poss. suspects?
2. Question Patsy and Walter Copeland—domestic stress over Rachel's reappearance? Any concern over finances?
3. Because of widely circulated porn images allegedly of Rachel Copeland, question Presidio County sex offenders w/Web access and history of stalking.
4. Routine background check—Zeke Pike. Previous addresses? Prior complaints, esp. those involving females?
5. Check w/National Transportation Safety Board investigators re. final determination of the cause of glider incident.

Saturday, March 8

"I heard you'd been in an accident, and I wanted to check on you." Even on the telephone, Dr. Damien Thomas's rich baritone reminded Rachel of a grandfatherly James Earl Jones.

But today she wasn't in the mood for soothing. She turned away from the bright window, resenting the pathologically chipper volunteer who had earlier opened the blinds as a "surefire cure" for her gloom.

"I'm doing a lot better, should be released today. But how did you find out about it?" She couldn't imagine that her father would have called him.

"Marianne Greenberg, your new attorney, mentioned it while we were discussing that ridiculous lawsuit."

Rachel's stomach spasmed. Ten million freaking dollars, and here she was, still in the hospital running up bills after two full days.

"She called you about that?" Rachel had spoken briefly to Greenberg yesterday, but the Philadelphia-based attorney hadn't brought up Dr. Thomas. Probably, Greenberg planned to call the psychologist as a witness, as had Rachel's previous lawyer in the criminal case. The psychologist was both well respected in the community and an advocate for violent crime survivors—Thomas wouldn't tolerate the word "victim."

"She wanted to discuss this latest set of photos. Rachel, I think we ought to talk about—"

"I told Ms. Greenberg I don't want to talk about those pictures. They're fakes just like the others. They have to be."

"I sincerely hope you're right about that," he said gently, in a tone that warned her he meant to once more broach the subject of what had happened after the dinner with her students, an evening she had forgotten. She told herself it must have been the flu, the same illness that had left her sick for days afterward, nauseated with a pounding headache, her muscles aching. So what if those same symptoms corresponded with the side effects he'd mentioned, of a drug sometimes slipped into the drinks of the unsuspecting? Lots of things could cause a person to feel lousy, and anyone could pick up a few unexplained bruises.

Her mouth went dry and a fresh throb hammered at her temples. She didn't want to think about this.

"But, Rachel, if these turn out to—"

"I'm not feeling well, Dr. Thomas. I appreciate your concern, but I don't think I should be on the phone now."

A long pause followed, weighted by almost-paternal disappointment. When finally he spoke again, his voice was firm. "I'm very concerned for you at this point. Your accident—is it possible you were distracted, upset about being forced to face this situation?"

"No. The trial won't be for months and months. Ms. Greenberg told me that much. And besides, I don't see what my distraction could have to do with the canopy popping open."

"What if you didn't latch it properly? Worry takes a lot of mental energy; it's fatiguing. And denial, even more so."

"I'm damned well not in denial, Dr. Thomas," she said through gritted teeth.

"I've seen those photos. Your eyes are never open. Your limbs are—"

"You mean the porno chick's limbs," Rachel insisted, though she had refused to look at the photos herself. Bad enough she'd had to face the last lot in the courtroom—to see what others had imagined was her. "I'm telling you, Kyle grafted my face on all those—"

"The arms and legs are slack in every shot. As if you—or I should say, the person photographed—was unconscious."

Tears threatened, burning her eyes. "I won't have this conversation. I came out here to get away from what happened in Philadelphia." *To get away from all of it.*

"And how's that working for you?" he asked, but the question was infused with kindness.

When she refused to answer, he left her his contact numbers—including his home phone for after hours. She pretended to take them down, then told him she would call him back when she was feeling better. . . .

Or when hell froze over, whichever came first.

She ended the call and turned her frustration to buzzing the nurses' station and demanding to know why Dr. Franconi hadn't shown up to discharge her.

"It *is* the weekend, Ms. Copeland." The woman sounded tired—probably worn down from answering the same question Rachel had already asked at least four times. "I'm sure he'll be along soon. Now if you don't mind, I need to deliver afternoon meds to other patients."

Rachel fumed, wondering what it would all cost: the hospitalization, the ambulance ride, the visit to the ER. Why would no one tell her the price of things when she asked? Her father had told her she was as bad as her grandmother. *"Quit fussing,"* he'd ordered, *"and help me rest easier by staying until the doctor gives you the all clear."*

Whatever her problems with Patsy, Rachel didn't want her father jeopardizing his marriage to bail her out again, nor did she want to throw up her hands and declare bankruptcy.

You're running out of other options. The flurry of interest in her photos had begun to generate some income, but she sensed it would be far too little, too late.

Mrs. Mary Dixon, this morning's volunteer, knocked, then swept into the room, a Pollyanna smile dimpling her apple cheeks. With her bottle blonde French-braided hair and the arrangement clutched before her, she looked like a sixty-year-old cheerleader or a slightly addled bridesmaid. "Look what I've brought for my number-one patient," she chirped as she set the vase down on the bedside table. "Somebody's sent flowers. Now where would you like me to put these?"

Though Mrs. Dixon's voice was worsening Rachel's headache, she resisted the first answer that sprang to mind. "Are you sure those are for me?"

Earlier, she'd been surprised to receive a huge fruit basket from Antoinette Gallinardi, which included a message expressing her—but not Terri's—best wishes, and Lili had brought her a hilarious get-well card, which she and Bobby had both signed. Who else would send her anything, especially so soon?

At the volunteer's nod, Rachel added, "My family's really not the flower type."

Her father might be sweet, but he'd be more likely to buy

her a subscription to *Plane & Pilot* than a bouquet, while
Grandma thought cut flowers an extravagant waste of
money for something doomed to die. And as for Patsy . . .
Rachel eyed the pure white mix of lilies, irises, and roses,
but didn't spot a single stem of poison ivy, though the lack
of color *did* put her in mind of funerals.

"Here's the card with your name." Mrs. Dixon plucked it
from the greenery to pass it to her. "Perhaps you have a
gentleman admirer."

Zeke Pike's name skated across Rachel's mind, but she
couldn't picture him sending flowers, either. After pulling
out a little card printed subtly with fern leaves, Rachel decided the volunteer's eager hovering was too much.
"Thanks for bringing these, Mrs. Dixon. But I wouldn't
want to keep you from your duties."

Once the volunteer left, Rachel flipped open the card.
And stared, forgetting how to breathe or swallow. *"Looking
forward to seeing you again soon"* was not the problem. It was
the *"Love & kisses, Kyle"* that had her climbing from her bed
and shouting down the hallway for the woman she'd just
sent out.

Concern replaced the cheerfulness of the volunteer's expression. "Shall I call the nurse? You're white as paper."

"No nurse," said Rachel as Mrs. Dixon escorted her back
to bed. "I'm not sick. I just have to know, who gave you
that arrangement to bring in here?"

"What's wrong? Did he forget to sign the card?"

"It's signed, all right, but . . ." The volunteer might be
annoying, but Rachel didn't want to scare her half to death
by telling her that her "gentleman admirer" was the young
man she'd shot, naked, in her bedroom one dark, cold night.
The same pervert who'd put her face on some poor, limp
woman to stoke his porn-fueled fantasies. "It's kind of embarrassing, but back home, I—uh—I dated two guys with
this same first name, so I'm not quite sure which—Could be
pretty awkward to call and thank the wrong one."

Since she was rumored to be some kind of femme fatale, she might as well use the reputation to her advantage.

Mary Dixon—who clearly had no idea of her past—laughed with delight and clapped her hands together. "Say no more, dear. I'll look into it for you. The flowers came from a shop right down the street, and I used to be great friends with the gal who owns it."

Once she'd left, Rachel sat up in the inclined bed and scrutinized the handwritten note more carefully. It was a woman's script—it had to be, with those loopy little letters and the empty-circle dots. Girlish handwriting, thought Rachel, but that didn't mean the sender had been female. For all she knew, the flowers had been ordered on the Internet or by phone. But that would require a credit card—a card that could offer her best chance to track the sender.

Was it the same woman who had called from Marfa, the woman whose desperation for revenge had warped both voice and mind? Rachel thought back again to the last threatening call, received so eerily close to the crash that could have killed her. But so far, the National Transportation Safety Board investigators had given no indication that the canopy failure had been anything other than an accident.

It was a stretch to believe the timing to be anything more than a disturbing coincidence. How could someone—especially an unhinged woman freshly arrived from Philadelphia—sneak inside the hangar and commit an undetectable act of sabotage?

Her train of thought was derailed by an authoritative knock that made her think of the deep-voiced, silver-haired doctor who had promised he would come by to spring her hours earlier.

"About time you finally made it," she said, unable to contain her annoyance. But her visitor was the last person she'd expected. "Zeke Pike. What brings you—"

"Needed a part for one of my tools." Wearing jeans and a

clean but worn khaki shirt, he looked uncomfortable, too big for the small and antiseptic space. "Would have set me back some, work-wise, to wait for a delivery."

Her headache ebbed, even if he wanted to let her know he hadn't made the drive specifically to see her. She inhaled, enjoying the new scents that had entered with him. Of good, clean man and outdoors . . . and maybe just a whiff of hope.

"I suppose they sell these parts right down in the gift shop?" She gestured toward the plain brown paper bag he was clutching. "That's handy."

He glanced down at the bag as if he had forgotten its existence, then colored. "Well, no. They don't sell drill bits at the hospital, exactly. But the store's in the neighborhood, so I thought, while I was this close, I might—might as well . . ."

When he wound down like an old watch, she looked at him, saying nothing. She had the odd sense that if she spoke, he would wheel around and bound off like a startled mule deer. A far cry from the man who had lit up her body like the Vegas Strip at the picnic table two days earlier. Though she'd had no business kissing anybody, she had to admit she'd enjoyed his take-no-prisoners approach.

But this version of Zeke Pike—hesitant, almost shy— touched her on another level. What could have cost this powerful, incredibly attractive man his confidence?

"Aw, hell," he said. "How are you, Rachel? I've been—I guess you could say I've been worried. Patsy said you'd be all right, but—that was a hell of a lot of blood, the other day, and—"

"Facial wounds bleed a lot. Looked worse than it was. It just needed a few stitches."

"But you have a concussion, don't you?"

Since nodding had unpredictable results—from nausea to dizziness and more pain—she simply said, "So they tell me, but I'm doing a lot better. Besides, as many people would attest, from my father to my teachers to—first and foremost—my stepmother, I'm the proud owner of one hard head."

"So they tell *me*." His smile lifted her spirits.

"I'm glad you stopped by," she said. "I need the distraction. I'm so irritated that the doctor hasn't shown up to release me, I was considering tossing the poor volunteer out my window for excessive perkiness."

He glanced out the window, toward well-tended landscaping. "We're on the ground floor, Rachel."

With a shrug, she said, "Causes too much trouble, killing people. From this point forward, I'm settling for minor mayhem. Though if you start getting all perky on me, I can't make any promises."

Though her irreverence would have shocked her family, Zeke laughed, a rich, deep sound that set her tingling in places she'd been trying steadfastly to ignore. Her mind flashed to the way he'd touched her, the heat of their mouths as the two of them explored.

What would it be like to feel that heat on her breasts, to let those big hands run free over her body? But the thought took her uncomfortably close to possibilities she didn't want to contemplate, so she shivered and buried the idea deep in her subconscious.

"Here," he said, thrusting the bag toward her. "This is—I had some scraps and such around. Odds and ends really, and I—I thought that you might like—Well, you can have it if you . . ."

The rest of his words were lost in the rattling of the paper bag and her exclamation of delight. "Zeke. This is—This is incredible. No one's ever . . . I can't believe you made this for me."

It was a wooden box. Simple, elegant, its planes a rich, red-gold that seemed to glow with the late sun's rays. In the center of its top, he'd embedded an oval silver concha set with a single, large turquoise. To her untrained eye, the stone was stunning, its brilliant blue-green overlaid with delicate black webbing. Rather than shining brightly, the embossed metal looked worn, like an old nickel.

"This part looks like an antique," she said, fingering the concha.

"Old Pawn," he said, "from a Navajo trader in New Mexico. It used to be a part of someone's belt, years back, on the reservation."

"So you drive there to do business?"

"Now and again, when the mood strikes. I like taking something old and broken, making it new and useful again. Pleasing."

"The way you do with your horses," she said.

He shrugged. "It's not for everyone. If you'd rather have something all new, I could—"

When he reached for it, she held fast. "I love it, Zeke, and I love that you went through all the trouble to make it for me."

"It wasn't any trouble. Like I said, I just had a few odds and ends around, so I thought I might as well—"

She touched his hand and waited for him to look her in the eye. "It's okay, Zeke. I like you, too. One heck of a lot better than the people I knew back in Philadelphia. Bunch of suck-ups pretending they were concerned while, behind my back, it was a completely different story."

She had supposed that she'd had good friends. Fun people, artsy types, who shared laughter along with the struggles to establish themselves in a world that all too often turned its back on talent. But when the going got tough, every one of them had disappeared from her life, vanished like so many puffs of smoke fanned by a breeze. A boyfriend, a sweet-natured math teacher she'd started dating a few short weeks before the shooting, had bailed on her, too, scared off by the negative publicity—and his own doubts once he had seen the photos.

"People'll hurt you," Zeke said, "disappoint you every time."

"Not all of them." Rachel knew instinctively that Zeke

was formed of something tougher. Something as solid and enduring as the furniture he crafted.

He looked at her so intently, a thrill slipped down her spine. Fear her words would scare him off; fear they'd bring him closer. The memory of the image she had photographed was overlaid with an image of his fury when he had learned the picture had been published.

"Do you have any damned idea what you've done?"

She'd wondered about that, wondered, could the man be hiding, living as he did in Marfa with no phone or computer, no credit cards, and very little human contact? According to Patsy, no one knew his hometown or what he'd done before buying the site of the old candelilla factory. No one knew anything about his former life.

But in small-town Texas, that hadn't kept people from imagining—and discussing in detail—his history. Some figured he'd ducked out on paying child support or was one of those mad-bomber-type weirdoes with an axe to grind against the government. Others, mainly women intent on becoming the antidote to heartbreak, guessed he'd washed up on shore here following the wreckage of a love affair.

None of these possibilities appealed to Rachel, but whatever his problems, she had far too many of her own to get involved. Yet she couldn't look away from his face, couldn't do anything but sigh in gratitude when he finally, *finally* bent to kiss her.

He moved slowly this time, so much more cautiously than the cataclysmic kiss before her crash. Not wanting to scare her as he feared he had before, he lingered in the soft pliancy of her lips, the sweet earnestness of her response. With callused fingers, he feathered touches from her temple to her jaw, then allowed his hand to drift downward along her slender neck.

As his fingertips traced the gentle inclination of her collarbone, he felt the stony fist inside him loosen, offering him a fleeting look at the man he'd hoped to be, the same

man he sometimes caught in sidelong glimpses as he rode
into the desert or shaped weather-hardened mesquite into
something lasting. Usually, he turned away, devastated by
the lost potential, but when he saw it in her warm, brown
eyes and heard it in her sweet voice, gratitude welled up
inside him.

And maybe something more. Something he had given up
the right to when he had stepped away from his past so
many years before. He thought he had made his peace with
it, thought he knew better than to hope for the possibilities
that he'd abandoned, but touching Rachel, kissing Rachel,
tore through all the layers of scar tissue and made the old
wound drip bright blood. . . .

*Blood that took him back to that night, to the boy sprawled
bleeding, dying in the old goat pasture where they'd gathered. He
could hear the labored breathing, hear those he'd thought of as
friends saying, "Langley did it. Was Langley hit him so hard, it
laid him out like that."*

Shivering and sweating, Zeke jerked back abruptly, his elbow catching the vase beside the bed. Green ceramic shattered, amid a watery puddle and a blizzard of white petals.

"Damned clumsy," he said. "I'm sorry for it—"

He was skewered on her sharp gaze.

"What's wrong?" she asked. "It was so nice, and then—"

"I've got no business fooling with you." He squatted,
picking up the larger shards of broken vase. "No right."

"You'll cut your hand. Please leave it. Just tell me what
you're thinking. Why you pulled back from me."

Not knowing how to answer, he went on picking up the
pieces—and wishing he could pick up what had been shattered long before.

The door whooshed open, and a blonde woman with a
pin reading *Volunteers Care!* swept inside. "I just got off the
phone with—Oh, dear." She glanced down at Zeke. "Sorry,
I didn't see you come in. I didn't mean to interrupt."

"Had a little accident," Zeke said.

"I'll have someone come to clean it. You wouldn't—"

The volunteer flicked a look at Rachel before returning it to him. "—You wouldn't happen to be a *Kyle*, would you?"

"Kyle?" Zeke glared, suspecting her of deliberate cruelty.

"Oh." The woman flushed bright pink. Then, to Rachel, she stage-whispered, "I'll be back to tell you later."

"Please stay, Mrs. Dixon," Rachel pleaded. Turning to Zeke, she explained, "Those flowers have a card in them. It says that they're from Kyle."

So this was someone else's malice. "Another threat?" he asked.

Rachel frowned. "If you can find it in that mess, you're welcome to read the message for yourself."

Returning her attention to the volunteer, she added, "Please tell me, what did the florist say?"

As he picked among the broken foliage, Mrs. Dixon shook her head. "A *threat*? My friend, Glory, would never pass along that sort of message."

"It wasn't a threat, exactly," Rachel clarified. "So are you saying she took the message? Was it a telephone order?"

"She said it came through a national service. It's a toll-free number that collects the orders and then uses local florists to fulfill them."

Zeke found the card and stood to read it. Though spotted with water from the vase, the words were clearly legible. And a less than subtle threat, but one that wouldn't alarm anyone unfamiliar with Rachel Copeland's history.

"Then the customer must have used a credit card," said Rachel.

The blonde woman nodded. "Yes, but Glory doesn't have access to that part, since the person paying opted to remain anonymous."

"If the order came through the computer, then why's the card handwritten?" Rachel pressed.

"I asked her that, too. She said her printer's so low on toner, the note wasn't legible, so she recopied the message onto the card for you. I also asked her if there was any way she could call the 800 number people and find out for you which Kyle really sent the flowers."

"Thank you," Rachel said with far more patience than Zeke was feeling. "What did she say?"

The volunteer smiled apologetically and blushed. "That you should keep your boyfriends straight. She said she wasn't bothering them about such a trivial—"

His tolerance at its end, Zeke burst out, "This isn't about any boyfriend. Someone's playing games with Ms. Copeland, trying to scare her with a message from a—"

"That's enough, Zeke," Rachel interrupted before looking at the clearly startled volunteer. "You've given me a place to start, and I appreciate that."

Worry lines creased the woman's forehead. "You'll be calling the law then, won't you, dear?"

"I'm living in Marfa, so I'll contact the sheriff there once I'm home. Speaking of which, is Dr. Franconi ever going to get here so I can leave? My dad's been waiting all afternoon for the call to pick me up."

"I'll take you if you're ready," Zeke offered. "If the doctor doesn't show, we'll just leave. This isn't a prison, is it?"

The volunteer looked nervous about this suggested breach of protocol. "I just saw Dr. Franconi at the nurses' station checking charts on my way in. So I expect he'll be here any minute. I'll go and find out for you."

Mrs. Dixon swept out, her blue skirt swirling behind her.

Zeke lifted the card. "Why didn't you tell me about this as soon as I came in?"

Rachel sighed. "I've been living with worse threats than flowers for a long time. The police in Philadelphia didn't take me seriously when I reported them, and I can't imagine Sheriff Castillo getting too excited either. For one thing, the crime—if there's even really been a crime—probably took place outside his jurisdiction."

"That call you got in the café. You thought it came from Marfa."

"True."

"And your glider crashed inside the county, too."

"That was an accident, a faulty latch—or at least that's what everyone thinks. The official word hasn't come down yet."

"The least Castillo could do is make a few calls, try to track down the name of the customer who sent the flowers," Zeke suggested.

Rachel shrugged her shoulders. "So far, I haven't seen much evidence of the law working in my favor. Back in Philadelphia, the only thing anyone cared about was those awful—those photographs of me with Kyle. The detectives investigating, and then the assistant prosecutor were all convinced I'd—"

"I heard some talk about those pictures," Zeke admitted. Now that he knew her, it made him sick to think back to what those men in the barbershop had said about them. About what Rachel had been doing with Kyle Underwood.

She flushed deeply. "Those were faked. You know that, don't you? My experts proved it. And they'll prove it with these new ones."

"I know they're fakes," he assured her. Yet still, the thought of such trash drifting around the Internet, where anyone could see it, made him want to smash all the computers in the world on her behalf. "And I know, too, that Marfa isn't Philadelphia. You have family looking after you, and a lot more folks who've got no argument with a woman protecting herself with firepower. And you've got at least one friend, right here."

She laid a hand on the gift he'd brought her before flashing a smile that sliced straight through his self-delusion. "So we're friends, is that it?"

He nodded, sensing she was asking, *Is that* all?

"Best I can do," he said. *No matter how much I wish things could be different.*

She reached for his hand and lifted it to her mouth, where she kissed it reverently. Looking up through lowered lashes, she whispered words that vibrated in the narrow space between them. "That's another gift, Zeke, one I'll tuck inside this treasure box and guard like the crown jewels."

By the time Zeke dropped Rachel at her grandmother's house, the new moon visible at twilight had dissolved into the black of a night sky lit with a myriad of stars.

Walter Copeland opened the front door and hugged his daughter before stepping back to shake Zeke's hand. "Come on in, Mr. Pike—"

"It's Zeke," he said.

"*Just* Zeke." Rachel flashed a grin before blocking the charge of a barking, black-and-white dog. "Oh, no you don't, J.D. You're staying in tonight. And hush."

"Don't you worry about his noise." A gray-haired older woman, comfortably plump and wearing thick, square glasses, came to the entryway to kiss Rachel on the cheek. "James Dean's always been partial to men."

"And here I thought that was an ugly rumor," Rachel quipped.

"Now you hush, too, child," her grandmother scolded, affection brightening her eyes. "Aren't you going to introduce me to your handsome friend?"

"Oops, sorry," Rachel said. "Grandma, this is Zeke Pike. Zeke, say hello to my grandmother."

"Good evening, Mrs. Copeland." Zeke had seen her a couple of times at The Roost, had nodded hello at the post office, but he wasn't surprised at the lack of recognition in her eyes.

"Benita's fine, and pleased to meet you," she said. "Please come in, Zeke. Before my angel decides to make a break for the neighbors' trash cans after all."

"Thanks, ma'am, but I'd better go."

Patsy propped open a door and stuck her head out of the kitchen. "Come on in and join us. I made some bison chili and jalapeño corn bread, and there's plenty."

"Seems like the least we can do is feed you for saving us a drive." Rachel's father's smile was relaxed and friendly.

The elder Mrs. Copeland lit up, "And you can play a round of Scrabble with us later. We can do teams. It'll be fun."

Rachel touched his elbow and whispered, "Don't worry. It's not quite as horrifying as it seems."

To Zeke, it sounded like a taste of heaven, a rich stew of family bonds and laughter spiced with subtle conflicts that had evolved over the years. It would be easy, far too easy, to let his guard down in such a situation. Ignoring the ache in his chest—and his stomach's growl of hunger at the aromas drifting from the kitchen, he set Rachel's overnight bag inside the door. "Thanks for the invitation, but I can't stay. I've got animals that need their dinner, and if I don't get to it, one of 'em will take a notion to kick down the feed shed door."

Before he'd left for Alpine, he had given the mule and horses extra hay to tide them over, but he needed an excuse, and livestock was as good as any.

"Hang on a minute, then," Patsy called. "Let me at least pack you some dinner."

He stepped inside to wait, his gaze taking in the framed family photos that hung on yellow walls and decorated every available flat surface. In a number of them, he recognized Rachel's budding talent, but the one that captured his attention was a candid shot taken of her as a young teen, her hand half-hiding the tinsel glitter of her braces, her freckles far more obvious than they were now. She was a little shy of pretty, but those big, brown eyes had held promise. Promise she'd grown into beautifully.

"Thanks again," Rachel told him as she bent to grab her overnight case.

"Hand that over, Rusty." Her dad swooped in to take it from her. "I'll put it on your bed. Put you to bed, too, if you're still feeling puny."

"I'm better," she protested.

After fluttering a wave in Zeke's direction, Rachel followed her father down the hallway, words trailing behind her. "There's something packed in there I have to show you. Zeke made me a get-well present."

Zeke felt heat rise to his face. When Patsy came out to hand him a plastic container with the chili and a foil-wrapped square that must have been the corn bread, her expression told him she'd heard what Rachel had said, too. And she wasn't pleased about it.

"What on earth are you playing at?" she asked through clenched teeth, keeping her voice low so Rachel's grandmother, who had drifted toward a game show on the TV, wouldn't hear.

"Nothing," he said. "It's just, I had an errand to run today in Alpine anyhow, and—"

"You took Rachel a *gift*, Zeke. And you hung around the other day to watch her."

"I had some scrap material around, and—and, yeah, I felt bad about her getting hurt the way she did. Just a friendly gesture, that's all."

"When's the last time you made anybody else a 'friendly gesture,' Zeke Pike?" Sarcasm smoldered in the depths of her blue eyes. "I can see what's going on, and I have to tell you I don't like it. That girl's got trouble enough on her plate without some man adding to it. Especially some man who likes to keep to himself the way you do."

"And here I thought you were warning me off for my own good." He tried a smile.

She thrust the food toward him. "If you have any sense, you'd think of that, too. But I know men get stupid around pretty women. I might not be one, but that doesn't mean I don't know it when I see it."

"Thanks for the dinner." He left, wondering if part of Patsy's problem with her stepdaughter was the fact that Rachel had grown into a face and body that commanded the type of male attention Patsy had never had. Though she was in general nearly as tight-lipped as Zeke about her background, over the years she'd dropped a few hints about a rough, hardscrabble childhood, followed by a brief marriage to the current sheriff, a man half the county knew had ditched her in favor of a former Miss Teen West Texas runner-up. She'd been securely married to Walter Copeland for as long as Zeke had known her, but he wondered if those early experiences had left her bitter. Or maybe he was imagining such things because of the toll his own youth had taken on his life.

"Like father, like son," he remembered hearing a teacher say after he'd been caught fighting in the halls. Fighting because some shit-for-brains punk had made the mistake of spreading it around school that his dad was buried in a pauper's grave outside the prison because they lacked the money to bring Joe Langley home.

That happened in another life, Zeke told himself. *To another person.* Because that boy had been snuffed out as surely as his father.

But as his truck slipped through the quiet streets, Zeke felt a restless melancholy overtake him, a growing dissatisfaction with the thought of returning to a place that felt cold and hollow compared to the warmth and fullness of the little, brown adobe where the Copeland family were gathered. For the first time in a long time—years, maybe— he couldn't bear the thought of going home, so instead he turned his pickup to the one place where he knew he could eat in peace within earshot of other human voices.

Nine miles east of town, he found it, the viewing area where locals and visitors alike could wait in the communal darkness for the famous mystery lights to put in an appearance. As he'd suspected, there were several vehicles in the parking area on this clear, Saturday evening.

After digging a wrapped plastic spoon—a relic from a fast food stop during one of his supply trips—from his glove box, Zeke walked up the rise to reach the viewing platform. Once there, he settled on a section of stone wall some distance from the spots staked out by ten or eleven visitors, some in pairs or groups of three, some apparently alone as he was. Whether sitting and talking or standing in silence, each stared across a dark plain obstructed by nothing but low scrub brush.

A good night for viewing, Zeke thought, not too chilly and plenty dark without the moon's glow. Not a half-bad night for brooding either, with the soft murmur of conversations taking place around him. Balancing his bowl, he sat there eating, enjoying the flavors of ground bison and black beans and jalapeños and the corn bread and struggling to pretend this no-strings companionship could fill the empty spot within him.

"Look, there's one." A middle-aged man with a long ponytail pointed excitedly in the direction of the distant mountains, where a glowing ball of brilliance bobbed a slow path to the west.

"I see it," a teenaged girl cried and flipped on—rather pointlessly—the flashlight she was holding.

Another man yelled, "Turn that damned thing off, you moron. You're blinding me, for one thing."

The harshness of his voice had Zeke glancing his way. He found himself looking at the profile of the same man he'd seen leaving the hangar area after Rachel's crash.

"Hey," Zeke called, putting down his food and rising as he pointed. "I need to talk to you a minute about what happened Thursday."

Perhaps he'd moved too abruptly, or perhaps the man perceived the edge in Zeke's voice as a threat. Whatever it was, he leapt over the wall and took off running . . . disappearing into a darkness lit only by the indifferent stars and the pale, receding light.

CHAPTER ELEVEN

At the door of life, by the gate of breath,
There are worse things waiting for men than death.
　　　　　　—*Algernon Charles Swinburne,*
　　　　　　from "The Triumph of Time"

"Where're they going?" The blonde girl shone her flashlight after Zeke and the man he chased, but all too soon, both passed beyond the limits of its illumination.

Zeke squinted, struggling to spot movement, and strained to hear the sound of the man's progress.

Shouts from the viewing area drifted toward him, from "Don't run that way" to the warning, "You'll get lost out there."

Zeke knew they were right. Only a fool went blundering into the desert after nightfall, with its rocks and thorny scrub brush hidden among dry grasses, its cactus and its deceptively uneven ground. At least the rattlesnakes would be inactive during the cool evening, but the nocturnal scorpions and tarantulas, though not fatal, could be damned unpleasant if a man happened to come down on one as he fell.

And fall he would, if he continued running blindly. So Zeke pulled up short, breathing hard.

Cursing, he turned back toward the low, stone wall that rimmed the platform, where people eyed him with suspicion. Several of them had turned on flashlights they'd brought with them.

"Why'd you chase him?" a balding man called.

Uncomfortable with the attention, Zeke shook his head. "Didn't want him to hurt himself out there, that's all. Mighty nervous fella."

"Did you know him?" someone else asked. "You said something to him."

"Thought he looked familiar, that's all. But no, I don't know him."

A woman with long, brown curls spiraling from the bottom of a knit hat pulled a cell phone from her bag. "Should we call the authorities?"

Zeke wasn't certain how to answer. Now more than ever, he wanted to speak to the man about the day Rachel had been injured. But the idea of involving the law—of speaking personally to the sheriff—was disturbing. Surely, Harlan Castillo would have long ago come calling if he'd guessed Zeke's past. But there was no sense tempting fate if he could help it.

"It's no crime—only stupid—to go running out there," Zeke said. "Besides, he has to come back. He must've left a car or truck here. Unless one of you brought him?"

No one present would admit to having done so.

"Someone ought to wait around to see he makes it back here," said the woman with the cell phone, "but I'm starting to get chilly, so I'm packing it in for the night."

She didn't want to be involved, Zeke figured, or responsible. And judging from the exodus that followed, she wasn't alone. Within twenty minutes, they had all departed, leaving Zeke to clean up the remnants of his dinner and then check the parking area.

His own pickup was the last vehicle remaining.

"So how the hell did he get way out here?" Zeke asked himself. But the desert returned no answers, only the subtle glow of yet another mystery light.

Through a slim, white telescope, the observer watched and wondered. How hard could it be to scare off a man who acted spooked by everything and everyone already? A man who spoke to few and trusted fewer shouldn't require a whole lot of persuading to understand he was better off keeping his mind on his own concerns.

With the lights' return—thank God they had come back, despite the failure that had taken place two days before—it was simple to see clearly. Easy to see how little it would take to discourage Zeke Pike's interference. A broken windshield, maybe, or, a few items smashed in a workshop that was often left untended.

One of the lights returned then, venomous green and blinking a staccato message that chilled the observer to the marrow. A message that whispered much more would be required—enough to slash through the thorny tendrils of whatever attachment Pike thought that he felt for Rachel Copeland.

The light warned he would be stubborn, as man is on the scent of woman, and that Pike wouldn't hesitate to use his muscle to get answers, or to punish where he saw fit.

No more punishments, The Child whimpered. Locked down in the darkness, it picked at scabs from wounds that festered, wounds that never healed. In the cold crawlspace beneath the trailer, it rocked itself for consolation, trying not to whimper when the wasps flew near.

But there had been no peace until the lights came.

And the lights, for all their blessings, at times demanded blood.

No use staying out here any longer, Zeke decided. Either the man he'd sought had hiked someplace up the road or he was lying low, squatting behind some bush and waiting for Zeke to go away. Either a cold hike or a cold wait, since there was no shelter within walking distance and the few drivers who might happen by on their way to or from Alpine wouldn't be likely to pick up a hitchhiker at this hour. But they might well notify the sheriff of his presence. In such rough and empty country, people tended to look out even for strangers.

Zeke, on the other hand, was annoyed enough, after an hour's wait, to hope the jackass froze his ass off out here. Why the hell was the man hiding? Could he really have something to do with Rachel's supposedly accidental crash, or had he seen something that day at the airport—something he was terrified to divulge for some reason?

But Zeke couldn't rule out other reasons for the man's flight. Zeke's size and the suddenness of his approach could have seemed a physical threat. Or maybe he was involved in something illegal, something such as smuggling drugs or Mexican nationals into the country—though the latter seemed highly unlikely, considering the large number of Border Patrol agents who made their home in Marfa.

Or what if the man was a fugitive from elsewhere, hiding out from a past as dangerous as Zeke's own? Zeke shivered—from the cold, he assured himself—as he imagined a dark reflection of his own life played out on this same desert. He felt the stirring of compassion, too, a visceral connection to the bone-deep fear, the base, animal instinct for self-preservation that could push such a man to unimagined risks.

"Listen, I'm not looking to hurt you or to poke my nose in your business," he shouted into the empty darkness. "I only have some questions, a few questions about what I think you might've seen. Then if you want, I'll drop you someplace. Buy you some hot coffee if you need it."

The only answer was the high yipping of coyotes that echoed from somewhere in the foothills. . . .

And the shot that splintered the still night as Zeke opened his truck door to climb inside.

CHAPTER TWELVE

*But wild beasts of the desert shall lie there; and their houses
shall be full of doleful creatures; and owls shall dwell there,
and satyrs shall dance there.*

—The Holy Bible *(King James version),*
Isaiah 13:21

Zeke dove across the old truck's seat. Behind him, the driver's side window shattered, spraying him with glass, and he heard a metallic ping—a bullet perforating the pickup's side.

Reaching behind him, he pulled the door shut before he ended up getting ventilated, too. Two more shots came in quick succession, causing him to curse the stupidity of his compassion. If he got out of this in one piece, he wouldn't make the same mistake again.

Eager to put distance between himself and the shooter, he reached into his pocket for his key, window glass raining from him with each movement. He didn't find it, so he plunged a hand into his other pocket—even as it occurred to him that he had had the key in hand when he'd heard the first shot.

His heart constricted as he realized that he must have dropped it on the ground outside the pickup. Where the shooter waited.

"Of all the damned stupid . . ." But he lost interest in swearing as his mind replayed the gunfire. How many shots—at least three. No four, or had it been five or six?

"Goddammit." He couldn't think, with his brain revving and his pulse pounding. He thought it was possible his attacker had run out—or was about to run out—of ammunition. But that assumed he didn't have spare bullets, or another clip.

It was one hell of an assumption, one hell of a gamble. Discounting it, Zeke struggled to focus on his alternatives. He could lie here waiting for the shooter to decide to walk up to the truck and head-shoot him through the shattered window. Or he could leave his questionable cover to try to find the key so he could put some distance between himself and this ass-wipe. Alone and unarmed, he had no other choices, though neither of the two he'd thought of sounded like a good bet.

But every moment he delayed left him vulnerable, unless his attacker had decided to settle for taking a few potshots before running off. Zeke decided not to count on it, that it was at least as likely this jackass might be desperate enough to try to kill him for his truck.

Another good reason to get the hell down the road while he still could—*if* he didn't get shot reaching for the key.

Wishing he'd paid attention when a "friend" had once tried to teach him how to hot-wire an ignition, Zeke sat up, his head ducked as low as possible, then threw open the door and looked down where the light spilled out onto the sand.

He saw it—the worn truck key gleaming like the proverbial brass ring. Reaching down—heart slamming against his chest—he snagged it, then yanked the door shut. In his hurry, he fumbled to jam the key into the ignition—and jumped at the sound of another bullet punching metal.

The engine caught, and he jammed it into reverse and spun out onto the highway, his shoulders hunched and his right foot smashing down against the floorboard. The old truck had edged up to ninety before he realized he'd driven out of range of any further bullets.

Yet he didn't slow until he'd nearly reached the sheriff's office in the heart of town. At that point, his habitual caution finally overcame his adrenaline. Should he let this go for fear of eliciting the sheriff's curiosity?

No, hell no, he decided as he parked. His truck—a relic he cared for as meticulously as any of his equines—had been damaged, and he'd nearly gotten himself shot. The shooting added weight, too, to the argument that the stranger might have something to do with Rachel's plane crash. And if nothing else, the presence of an armed man in the vicinity of the visitor's center could pose a lethal danger to the next person to pull in.

So Zeke gathered his courage and walked into the sheriff's office, prepared to make a statement, as any responsible and law-abiding citizen would do.

CHAPTER THIRTEEN

Some inward trouble suddenly
Broke from the Matron's strong black eye—
A remnant of uneasy light,
A flash of something over-bright!

—William Wordsworth,
from Memorials of a Tour in Scotland, *XIII:*
"The Matron of Jedborough and Her Husband"

Sunday, March 9

Marlene's breath rushed from her, an explosion of relief. Finally, they had a location. A real, confirmed location where her mother had been. And better yet, it was right here in Albuquerque, where Marlene had spent the past few days searching fruitlessly. She'd been almost ready to pack up and leave, frustrated beyond measure with her mother, who appeared intent upon remaining missing.

"Marlene, honey, are you *crying*?" Dan asked over the cell phone.

"No, no." She wiped her face and gripped the steering wheel of an SUV she could no longer remember renting and struggled to recall the smell of him, the warmth and solidity of his arms wrapped around her. "I'm just a little overwhelmed, that's all. I've spent three weeks chasing shadows."

Or chasing *ghosts*, she thought with a shudder. From Wilmington, Delaware to Tulsa, Oklahoma, she'd been stunned to find her brother's former "friends" as dead as he was. Surely, it must be coincidental. It *had* to be, for the last of the group, the one now residing in this city was very much alive, working as a construction manager for a builder of suburban custom homes. On the pretext of talking over old times, she'd convinced him, during a brief phone call, to meet her for coffee this morning near his work site. She only hoped he'd tell her that he'd neither seen nor heard from her mother.

"Three long weeks," Dan said, his voice reminding her he wasn't happy about running the household and tending both boys on his own. Though he'd made a valiant effort not to dwell on it too much, he'd dropped hints that he would have to work a lot of overtime to pay the mounting bills.

Marlene—who had long since lost track of the days— glanced down at the address she had jotted in the white border at the masthead of today's *Albuquerque Journal*. Her stomach knotted, and a rush of adrenaline quickened her pulse. "So the police are sure it's really her?"

"Oh, yeah. The detectives brought over a surveillance photo from the ATM. It was grainy, but it sure looked like your mother."

She breathed again, and Dan reported, "She stopped by around eight thirty yesterday morning, got a cash advance on one of her credit cards."

"Her first mistake." The newspaper slipped from Marlene's trembling hands and collapsed into a jumble at her knees. Up to this point, her mother's debit and credit cards had not been used. "So how did she look?"

"Hard to tell. Those images—they're only black and white, and this one was kind of fuzzy, like the camera lens was grimy. No other people in the photo, so she's probably traveling alone."

"That's what that clerk back near Tulsa told me." The motel had been of the sleazy variety, an old motor court built off a highway whose prominence had given way to a more modern freeway years before. The kind of down-on-its-luck, mom-and-pop place where no one minded cash customers, whether they stayed for an hour or a week. Or three days, in the case of Mary Alice. Marlene had been a

week behind her—until the police had brought Dan the
news of this break. Though it seemed clear Mary Alice had
left of her own volition, the authorities had taken her disappearance seriously. Not because of *who* she was, they had
been careful to emphasize, but because she was considered
at risk due to what they were calling a "mental defect."

"How was she dressed?" Marlene asked next. Though
she'd expected warmer weather, it was still cold in Albuquerque, a bitter cold that rode the gritty wind. "Was she
wearing a jacket? Did she look upset, disheveled?"

She left the most important question unasked. *Does she look
completely unhinged? Maybe even homicidal?*

"I'm sorry, Marlene. I don't really remember, except she
had on some kind of floppy hat—maybe that one you gave
her last Christmas."

"The gray one? Kathy sent that," Marlene corrected automatically as she mentally filed the detail.

"Listen, honey, I know this news is encouraging, but your
mother may have been picking up more cash because she
was about to leave town again. Which reminds me . . . In
the background of the surveillance photo, you could see the
back end of a vehicle. Something big and dark and boxy.
Definitely an SUV."

Leave it to Dan, a mechanic at a luxury car dealership, to
notice the vehicle, yet recall almost nothing of her mother's
facial expressions, clothes, or grooming.

"I'm pretty sure it was some sort of Jeep," he added,
"probably an oh-six or seven Commander."

Oh, God. The Jeep. Marlene's head throbbed as she thought
of the murdered man in Tulsa. According to the newspapers,
the police suspected a carjacking. His Jeep Commander—a
dark green 2007 model—hadn't been recovered. But Marlene couldn't bring herself to voice the suspicion that was
now becoming certainty. How could she do that to her
mother, who so clearly needed help? Not incarceration or,
even worse, a chase that might end in tragedy.

Marlene had to find her quickly. Stop her, and get her declared incompetent so she could legally take charge of her mother's treatment.

"The Albuquerque Police Department's been notified," Dan told her. "Maybe we should let them take over from this point."

"No," Marlene snapped. "I'm driving to the ATM address right now. I—I'll show people her photo at convenience stores and gas stations in the area, then look around for the kind of motels she's been staying in—"

"Surely, the police are better equipped to investigate this—"

"I said *no*, Dan. The police here don't know my mom, and I can't imagine she'd be much of a priority. But she's a priority to me. I know you don't understand that, the way she's been for so long."

"I understand," he said gently. "But I'm starting to get scared, Mar. Scared about you running all over the country, talking to people in bad neighborhoods and staying in seedy hotels to save money."

"I'm not—"

"You are and we both know it. Probably living off cheap fast food, too, and feeling terrible by this time."

He was right on all counts, but she wasn't about to admit it.

"I'm worried about your safety," he went on. "I'm worried about your health. But most of all, I'm worried . . ."

"What, Dan?" she prompted, afraid he was going to bring up their financial situation, or twist her guilt about "abandoning" their boys. Nervously, she picked up the paper and straightened crumpled pages.

"I'm worried—and Kathy's called twice. We're concerned that this search is starting to turn into some sort of crusade. That you're in danger of slipping into the same type of obsession that's destroyed your mother's life. Don't let it destroy ours, too."

"I'm not her, Dan. I'm not. And for someone whose life

has more drama than the TV listings, my sister has a heck of a lot of nerve criticizing *my* behavior." Marlene was still aggravated by Kathy's refusal to accept any responsibility for their mother.

Marlene blew out a soft breath, missing her family so much that it felt like a blade twisting deep inside her. Were Dan and Kathy right? Was she, like her mother before her, turning her back on those remaining in favor of the one person who had forever slipped beyond her reach?

It's not the same. She's not dead. At least not yet. And Marlene's father, her dear father—how could she let him down by giving up when she was so close to where her mother was, or had been?

"A few more days," she assured her husband. "If I haven't found her by then, I promise I'll come home."

"Sure, Marlene." The disappointment in his voice reminded her she had made the same promise last week. "You let me know when, because I don't want to get the boys' hopes up again, not until it's certain."

She ended the call, telling him she had to drive to Rio Rancho, a suburb to the north, to meet a man who might have seen her mother.

When he didn't show, she tried to call him at his office but only got a voice mail. But the recorded message at least gave her the name of his construction company. By asking around, she was able to find the nearby neighborhood where he was working.

Which was how Marlene came to find his body, crumpled near the blood and hair-encrusted front end of a dark green Jeep Commander with Oklahoma plates.

Wednesday, March 12

When her cell phone's ringing woke her, Rachel hesitated, mentally bracing herself for another ugly onslaught from her favorite psycho stalker. But the pearled sliver of sky showing through the window shutters announced that it was morning, and the clock read 6:58 AM. Since the psycho had never called at this hour, Rachel figured it was probably her dad with another of his get-right-back-on-the-horse-that-threw-you pep talks about flying. Lately, he'd started tossing off statistics citing the rarity of glider mishaps as compared to powered aircraft.

She'd almost rather start her day with Nut Case Woman. But when she glanced at the lit screen, she saw it was Harlan Castillo calling.

She'd gone to see him about her phone calls and found him still the same fireplug of a specimen she'd remembered, with his short limbs and barrel chest. At one time he'd been into weightlifting, and he still looked it, though the years had threaded silver through his black hair and deposited a slight paunch around his middle. Like a majority of the local residents, he prided himself—and had probably been elected sheriff—on his Mexican surname. But both his English and his blue eyes put that heritage several generations in the past.

"Morning, Sheriff," she said. "You're up and at 'em early."

"I don't believe the woman harassing you is here in Marfa," he said without preamble.

Stretching, she pushed her sleep-tossed hair from her eyes. "You're sure about that?"

"I've been asking around all week. Checking out hotels, the inn, anyone who rents a casita. Talked to people at the cafés, the bookstore, even at the grocery store," he said. "No one's seen anybody suspicious. Especially not a lone female who can't be accounted for."

Rachel was grateful he'd taken her complaint seriously enough to check around. She'd heard Patsy make a number of disparaging comments about her ex through the years, but to Rachel, he seemed both competent and genuinely concerned. Troubled by the timing of her crash, he'd been quick to talk to the NTSB investigators, who felt that her hard landing was probably related to a defective canopy latch and not to carelessness as Dr. Thomas had implied. Every time she thought about him saying, *Worry takes a lot of mental energy; it's fatiguing. And denial, even more so,* she wanted to call him back to shout, *"I told you so!"*

But to do that, she'd have to talk to him, and it wasn't worth the aggravation. Nor the cold pit that opened in her stomach each time she remembered what else he'd had to say.

"Did you check the RV park?" she asked the sheriff. "And what about the lodges outside of town, like the hot springs down near—"

"Have you heard from her again since last week?"

"Not another word," Rachel admitted as she grabbed the brush she'd left on the dresser and pulled it through her hair. Or tried to.

"Maybe she thinks she scared you into crashing," he suggested, "so she's left town to go on about her twisted little life."

"That's a charming thought." Holding the phone with her chin, Rachel worked to separate a tangle with her fingers. "But I could live with it if I thought she'd stay away."

"It's also possible she was never in the area in the first place."

"What about the train whistle?" Rachel winced as she pulled too hard and tore free several hairs. "Surely, you're not telling me that was some kind of coincidence. That wherever she was calling from, there was a train at the same time."

"That wasn't what I had in mind. I was thinking, Ms. Copeland—"

"Rachel," she automatically corrected, reverting to West Texas informality.

"I was thinking," Harlan went on, "stress can warp the way we see things. Or hear or smell or—"

"I get your drift." A paranoid suspicion, blasted through her consciousness. *Impossible.* "You're thinking I imagined the whole conversation."

"I'm not saying that. Patsy—" There was a sudden shift in his voice, a tension that made Rachel glad she hadn't been there when Patsy and Harlan spoke for what might have been the first time in twenty years. "—*Mrs.* Copeland corroborated that a woman's been harassing you by phone. But it might be possible that the whistle you *thought* you heard—"

"I *heard* it," Rachel insisted.

"You said you were upset when you recognized the voice, right? Probably a little scared, too—I know I would be."

"I was *angry*, mainly," she said before admitting, "and yes, I was upset. So I'll admit it's possible I might have imagined that train whistle coming from the phone when I was really only hearing the one here. But you'll have to admit I could be right about it, too."

"You might be," said Harlan. "Now I want you to promise to call me if you hear or see anything suspicious. And I'm serious as a heart attack about that. Your stepmother says she'll have my cojones if I cost her another child—"

The brush flipped out of Rachel's hand and clattered to the wood floor. She didn't know which shocked her more, the idea that Patsy considered her her child, or the possibility that she'd once had another. Unable to contain herself, Rachel stammered, "You—you mean that you and Patsy had a—?"

She cut herself off, appalled by what she'd blurted out. "I'm sorry. I'm sure that wasn't any of my business."

"Patsy and I were never blessed with children." Regret hung like a pall over Harlan's voice, though Rachel knew he had three strapping sons—all talented football players at the high school—by his second wife. "As for the rest, it's all old business. I shouldn't have brought it up. And if you're thinking of asking Patsy—I wouldn't poke that particular anthill. She was always the type to keep the past in the past and her private troubles private."

Rachel couldn't disagree with his assessment, but the longer she said nothing, the more disloyal she felt. Finally, the dam burst. "She's been a good stepmother to me."

"I always knew she would be." In the background, a radio squawked, and he excused himself abruptly—but not so quickly that Rachel didn't hear his regret.

She didn't bother trying to go back to sleep. Six days after her accident, she'd had all the recuperation time she could handle. For one thing, resting gave her too much time to worry about the logistics of the lawsuit against her and wonder if Psycho Bitch was lingering just outside her window. For another, her grandma had been using Rachel's convalescence as a daily excuse to purchase fresh-baked pastries from a local coffee shop. Though the frosted *pan de huevo* and mouth-watering pumpkin empanadas were ostensibly meant for her granddaughter, Benita was sampling enough that it was playing hell with her blood sugar. Today, Rachel determined, her grandma was going to start back on the right track.

Forty minutes later, Rachel, now dressed after a quick shower, carried a steaming tray into Benita's bedroom—a mushroom omelet with heart-healthy whole wheat toast and a mug of strong black coffee, along with a small paper cup containing her morning medications. As Rachel set it on the bedside table, she gently touched the rounded hump of blanket-shrouded shoulder. "Here you go, Grandma. I brought you a surprise."

James Dean—sleeping on a towel beside her grandmother—rolled onto his side and raised his nose to sniff. Slightly slower to react, Benita blinked sleepily at Rachel. "What's this?"

"Breakfast in bed. You've taken such good care of me this past week, I figured you deserve it."

"What about you?"

"I'll grab something from The Roost on my way to the airfield." If she didn't put in an appearance now and again, Patsy assumed her stepdaughter was anorexic, in spite of the eight pounds Rachel had gained since her return home. Slowly, her appetite was returning. Food even tasted good, especially if she didn't try to eat alone.

Her grandmother pursed her lips, forming crinkled spokes around a central hub. "You're going back to work already? Didn't the doctor say you needed bed rest?"

Rachel shook her head. "He didn't call for bed rest. Remember what we talked about?" She distinctly recalled repeating the instructions last night. "He just asked me to take it easy until the headaches stopped. They've been gone for two days, so I'm more than ready to start earning my keep again."

As Benita struggled to sit up, Rachel tucked an extra pillow behind her back. Next, she folded a light throw that had slid off the bed during the night and fetched Benita's blue-rimmed glasses from the dresser. Though Rachel would do anything for the grandmother who had done so much for her, their new relationship felt strange, almost parental, with their roles reversed. Now and again, her grandmother perceived the change, too—and resented it enough to bristle, becoming as ornery as the little dog that eyed her breakfast.

This morning, however, she merely looked unfocused. Wrinkling her brow, Benita complained, "You know I don't like mushrooms, Cora. I bought them for you. Remember? You were telling me you had a craving."

Slowly, Rachel bent her knees until she was at her grandmother's eye level. Since the questions that came to mind—*What year is it? Can you tell me the name of the president?*—would insult and infuriate her grandmother, Rachel opted for the gentlest of smiles. "If you keep insinuating I'm pregnant, Grandma, I'm going to get a complex about this weight I'm gaining."

Behind the big, square lenses, Benita blinked, confusion swimming in her brown eyes. And Rachel felt fear quickening inside her.

Then Benita blinked again and shook her head in obvious amusement. After pinching off a corner of her toast for J.D., she gave an oddly girl-like cackle. "Goodness, Rachel. I certainly don't think you're . . . *in a family way*. Why, you're not even married yet—and if you don't mind me offering a little advice on that front, men don't like a girl so skinny. A strapping fellow like your Mr. Pike might be afraid he'd snap you right in two."

Rachel breathed again, happy to have stumbled back in familiar, if exasperating, territory. "He's not *my* Mr. Pike. Remember what I told you? He's just a regular customer of Patsy's, so he decided to do her and Dad a favor while he was in Alpine anyway."

Her grandmother laughed. "My goodness, Rachel. Isn't thirty-two a little old to be so naïve?"

The Roost was packed this morning, every table occupied. Patsy was scrambling, so busy that Rachel pitched in for a time to help her.

With the dozen or so diners served, Patsy stuck out her lower lip and blew a stray strand of gray hair off her forehead. "Didn't plan on putting you to work," she said, "but thanks for lending me a hand. How 'bout I fix you some pancakes, now that we're caught up."

Would you have been happier with kids of your own? Would it have been easier, more natural to love them? "Maybe just a scrambled egg, if you don't mind."

Patsy nodded, and then set to work as Rachel poured hot water over a tea bag she'd dropped into a mug. Lili waved her over from the small corner table where she was finishing her meal.

"Hey, girlfriend." Lili looked up from her coffee. "It's good to see you back in action. Feeling better?"

Rachel pulled up the only unoccupied chair and sat down, though Lili's plate was empty. "Loads better, thanks. You need me to top off that coffee?"

"I'm good." Lili studied her intently.

"What?" asked Rachel. "Did I grow an extra nostril, or are you trying to figure out how to get me to take your flights today?"

"Nothing like that." Lili slid a glance at Patsy, who was

looking their way, before returning her full attention to Rachel. "I was wondering something, that's all."

Rachel fixed her tea and waited for Lili to continue. "Are you going to ask me, or do I have to forcibly drag it out of you?"

Lili's shoulders sagged, and she sighed. "I was just wondering if you're ever going to dish about what's up with you and Zeke Pike. I tell you all about my love life, but you—you're holding out on me, sister."

From girlfriend to sister, all in the course of one short conversation. Shaking her head, Rachel answered, "I didn't tell you anything because there's nothing *to* tell."

"Really? What about that day he stormed over looking mad enough to strangle you? Man doesn't get that mad at a woman unless there's sex involved."

Leave it to Lili to assume that. "I took a picture of him, that's all. For the May showing on Marfa artists."

Confusion rippled Lili's normally smooth forehead. "I remember you saying something about that, but why would—"

"He was angry it's been published in a lot of papers. He didn't know about it, and it's gotten him way more attention—*personal* attention—than he's comfortable dealing with."

Lili grinned and waggled dark brows. "So was he naked or something in this picture? And where can I get a copy blown up to poster size?"

Rachel tried for a smile, though the thought of photographing someone nude without his consent made her queasy. "No, he wasn't naked." *Only half.* "But I have to admit, he looks pretty sizzling in it."

"And he's *complaining* about that? Most guys would think that was the best thing since online porn." Lili shook her head. "But one thing's for sure. Zeke Pike isn't most men. If he so obviously *weren't*, I'd think he was gay. For one thing, it would help my self-esteem, after all the times I've tried to interest him in—"

"Sorry, but he's definitely not gay."

Lili's stare sliced, razor-sharp. "So there *is* something going on between you. I knew it."

Rachel set down her tea. "Before you get upset, you should know—"

"I'm not upset." The words were clipped and brittle. "Why would you think that?"

Rachel could point out the angry little vee that had etched itself between Lili's eyebrows, but instead she merely stared back.

"I'm just worried, that's all," Lili snapped. "Here's this strange man. Nobody knows where he's from, what his background is, who his family might be. For all we know, he could be some kind of perv, or maybe on the run from—"

"Aren't you the same person who told me you'd tried everything but stripping naked to distract him from his lunch?" Rachel started, then raised a hand when Lili reddened, rising from her seat. "You have to admit, it seems a little . . . *off*, you warning me about a man you've been gunning for yourself."

"Only a little harmless flirting, that's all." Lili's voice rose, loud inside a space that had suddenly fallen quiet. "What *you're* doing—that's dangerous, with a man like that."

In no mood for such dramatics, Rachel said, "Oh, come on."

Patsy maneuvered among chairs and tables, one broad hip leading like the prow of a great ship. As she set down a plate heaped with Rachel's breakfast—two eggs sunny side up, along with a short stack, home fries, and a fruit cup—she flicked a watery blue look at Lili. "Everything okay here?"

"Sure," Rachel answered for her. "And thanks, but I thought you were bringing me a scrambled egg."

Patsy's smile was sardonic. "You order what you order. I bring what I bring."

Rachel gave a dry laugh. "Guess that about covers our whole relationship."

"Guess it does at that." Patsy dredged up a fleeting

half-smile before sailing toward the register to ring up a pair of private pilots.

Tearing her eyes from her stepmother, Rachel looked back to Lili, who was fishing a five from her small purse.

"Patsy put you up to this?"

Lili looked up sharply. "*What?* Why would she—"

"Seems awfully strange"—Rachel cut into an egg with the side of her fork—"everyone being so interested in my friendships."

Lili pushed the folded five beneath her empty mug before she stood. Frowning down at Rachel, she said, "Maybe people are worried about you, that's all. On account of everything you've been through. You don't have to get all *weird* about it, Rachel. If you're dumb enough to want to saddle yourself with a loser, on top of all your other problems, go ahead and be my guest. After all, everybody knows you're the boss around here, not me."

She was so clearly upset—and so ridiculously loud about it—that every eye followed her until the door shut behind her with a furious jingle. Afterward, there were a lot of furtive glances Rachel's way, glances she ignored as she picked at a completely tasteless breakfast.

CHAPTER FOURTEEN

As if you could kill time without injuring eternity.
— Henry David Thoreau,
from Walden, I: *Economy*

With the sun-drenched afternoon winding toward its close, Zeke spoke in hushed tones, calming the mule as he rubbed antibiotic ointment into a long gash on the animal's dun-colored left shoulder. But his gentle fingers belied a molten core of fury—fury at whatever cowardly shitheel had sneaked in here during his absence two days earlier. He suspected the same son of a bitch who'd tried to shoot him at the viewing area, though he couldn't fathom any reason the man would follow him to his home. Nor could the irritatingly dismissive deputy, the many-chinned Leo Varajas, who had come to see him about his report.

"Witnesses from the viewing station figured that fella who ran off got spooked on account of how you startled him. Probably just another of those strange loner types we get around here." The deputy's look, as he'd peered through wire-rimmed glasses, said he counted Zeke himself among that number. *"Nothing to do with some kind of random pasture accident."*

"Kind of like these random bullet holes?" Zeke had asked him, with a nod toward his damaged pickup. But even after Zeke had mentioned seeing the stranger at the airfield on the day of Rachel's crash, the deputy had merely given a skeptical shrug and gone on about his business.

A mockingbird stopped singing, and then swooped off its perch in a scrubby little piñon pine. The abrupt silence gave Zeke a moment's warning before he heard approaching footsteps on the curving gravel drive.

After patting the mule—he had learned his lesson about

startling a tethered equine with an unexpected outburst—
Zeke turned, intent on *welcoming* the intruder before he
was seen. A few moments later, he snorted amusement at
Rachel's mangling of an old country standard nearly beyond recognition.

"Crazy . . . I'm crazy for climbing that locked gate,"
she sang, making up for the caliber of her performance
with sheer volume. "Crazy, crazy for bringing you steee-
www . . ."

He smiled, shaking his head even as he took note of both
the small Band-Aid on her forehead and the brown paper
sack she carried. "Damned good thing you're a photographer and not a singer."

"Who says I'm not a singer?"

When Gus the mule laid back his ears and whipsawed
through a loud bray, Zeke laughed.

Rachel fisted her free hand on a slim hip and directed her
attention to the animal, "Who asked *you*?"

"Patsy Cline, most likely," he deadpanned. "It's a known
fact that mules' hooves are sensitive to the vibrations of dead
musicians spinning in their graves."

Rachel attempted a none-too-convincing pout before
breaking into laughter.

"So how's the head?" He touched a spot above his eye-
brow.

"Hard as ever," she reported. "When I heard you'd
stopped by The Roost to use the phone on Monday, then
hadn't shown up for lunch the past couple days, I got worried maybe something had happened—or somebody'd
asked you to stay clear."

Apparently, she hadn't heard about the shooting incident. It
didn't surprise him, for Castillo himself had said he wouldn't
trouble her about it unless his investigation turned up hard
evidence to link the still-missing stranger to the crash. But
her words made the corner of Zeke's mouth twitch downward. "I've been going to The Roost for years. Why would
anyone ask me to stop?"

Rachel hesitated before saying, "Patsy doesn't seem to like the idea that we're . . . getting friendly."

"She's told me as much a couple times, but she's never made me feel unwelcome. Even if she doesn't think this is smart." He pointed from her to him, indicating their connection. "And she's right about that, Rachel." *A hell of a lot more right than I can tell you.*

Rachel looked down and idly kicked at a few pebbles, raising a puff of powdery dust from the dry ground. "And Lili Vega's warned me off, too."

"*Lili?* That doesn't make sense. I've maybe spoken six words to her in the last . . . um, *ever.*"

"I thought maybe Patsy put her up to it. Or else she's got big plans for you."

"Lili's practically a kid. And besides, every time I see her, she's hanging on some flyboy. A different one each week."

"Patsy, then," Rachel concluded, "which frankly makes me wonder why she thinks the two of us are any of her business."

"Is that why you're here, Rachel? To show your step-mama she can't tell you what to do?"

When Rachel's gaze snapped up to meet his, he could see her mulling the question. He wanted her to say no, to tell him she was here because she wanted to be more than "friendly."

But the mule lowered his head and bumped Zeke's shoulder, Gus's way of asking for a scratch. Zeke recapped the antibiotic ointment and wiped his hand on a rag before rubbing the dun neck. And in that small interruption, the answer to his question slipped away.

Instead, Rachel stepped closer, peering at the mule's cut. "Poor thing. What happened to him?"

"I'd sure as hell like to know that myself. On Monday, after I walked back from Patsy's, I found him and both the horses loose. They'd broken the gate open from the inside. Found blood spattered on the ground there." He pointed to the spot.

"Whoa." Rachel's attention snapped back to the enclosure, where both Cholla and the pinto mare were idly snuffling the dirt for wisps of hay. "Are those two all right?"

"Just spooked. Took me forever to catch the three of them, even with a bucket of sweet feed. And Gus here was a bloody mess. That's why I drove back to Patsy's. I had to call a vet from Alpine."

"You don't have a phone?" she asked.

"Not much of a talker," he said by way of explanation.

"Could there have been a fight with one of the horses? Little corral scuffle?"

"That's the first thing that came to my mind." Zeke shook his head and pointed out the six-inch gash, now stitched and crusted over. "But this is no horse bite or kick. Vet didn't think so either."

"Then what?"

"At first, I thought maybe a mountain lion. Could be that one ranged out of the foothills looking for easy pickings— maybe a younger cat trying to claim territory. That would explain why the animals were all so spooked."

"But that wasn't it, either?" She must have surmised as much from his tone.

"Doc says there'd be multiple claw marks if it had been a lion, and probably puncture wounds on Gus's neck from the fangs. Besides, the other night I—"

Rachel shuddered. "I know they hardly ever bother people, but those things still scare the heck out of me. So if it wasn't a lion, what could've hurt him like this?"

Zeke tamped down his smoldering anger and forced his mouth into a grim line. "Vet thought it looked like a stab wound. From a knife. I haven't left my animals alone since."

Rachel's eyes widened. "You mean a *person* did this? Someone sneaked in here while you were gone, and . . . Did you leave your front gate open?"

"Closed and locked, like today. But if you could climb it with some food, someone else could do it with a knife."

He went ahead and told her what had happened at the viewing area.

Rachel's face turned pale, making her few freckles stand out, and she looked in the direction of his truck, whose side window had been covered with duct tape and thick plastic— a temporary fix until he could spare the time to have it repaired correctly. "He could have *killed* you. Why didn't you say something earlier?"

"Sheriff didn't think it had anything to do with you, and I figured you have enough to worry about just lately."

Shaking her head, she said. "I know the world's a tough place sometimes. But this is Marfa, Texas. How could someone evil enough to do this live around here . . ."

Her voice trickled down to nothing as, nearby, the mockingbird trilled from the scrubby juniper it had claimed.

"No," she said, clamping down on whatever fear had gripped her. "I was thinking for a moment—but it couldn't have been my caller. For one thing, she's a woman, and the sheriff's checked all over the area. He doesn't think she's still here, if she ever was."

"I didn't think of her," he admitted.

Rachel shrugged. "No reason you should have. *I'm* the one she'd been threatening, so it doesn't make any sense that she'd randomly run around the county taking potshots and slashing people's livestock.

"Do you have any other enemies?" she went on. "Anyone you can think of who would want to hurt you through your animals? What about their previous owners? Could someone be upset with you for any reason?"

He hesitated, then dismissed the thought of the past he had outrun. If anyone from those days knew where he was, he'd be the one hurting, not his mule. "My manners might not be anything to write home about, but I can't imagine anybody caring enough to bother. Could be that fellow from the airport didn't want to be seen for some reason, and then he thought I was coming after him. I still can't figure out where the devil he went."

"The Marfa Lights do draw their share of strange souls." A smile tugged at one corner of her mouth. "Maybe he figured you were the alien leader, wanting to abduct him. You weren't humming that riff from *Close Encounters*, were you?"

When she mimicked the five tones from the old movie, he snorted. "Yeah, sure. And wearing my aluminum foil spaceman hat, too. But if he was just some random nut job, what was he doing at the airfield that day? And why'd he want to track me down and go after my animals?"

"Have you talked to Harlan about the mule?" she asked.

Zeke had hated to deepen his involvement with the law, but with his animals involved—and even the slim possibility of a connection to Rachel—he hadn't felt there was a choice. "Deputy came by. He thinks it's some sort of accident."

"I hope he's right," she said before glancing down at the bag she was still holding. "Oh, almost forgot about this. It's green chile stew. My grandma doesn't cook much anymore, but she got a wild hair this afternoon. Made a huge pot— must have put a whole pork loin and a sack of potatoes in it. Can't imagine what army she imagined she was feeding. Then I thought of you."

"It smells great," Zeke said, regretting that he'd already filled his stomach with canned soup and some slightly burned quesadillas he had slapped together using leftover chicken, cheese, and stale tortillas. "I've had dinner, but that'll make a first-class breakfast."

"Breakfast?"

He grinned at her scandalized expression. "Damned fine one on a chilly morning. Let me put it in the fridge . . . Oh, and thank your grandma for me, will you? And thank you for bringing it."

To his surprise, she followed him inside. When he pulled out a bowl, meaning to transfer the stew, she lifted a lidded plastic bucket from the sack. "Don't bother with that. Grandma's got a million of these old ice cream containers. Which sort of makes a person wonder, since she's a diabetic."

He put away the food, all the while wondering why she had climbed the gate and walked the long, curved track to get here. Wondering why she'd followed him inside. But he was afraid to ask her. Afraid to say anything that would change her mind and scare her off, regardless of what he'd told her by the corral. He hated the thought of pushing away the only person who'd ever cared enough to come and check on him here.

"Want something to drink?" he asked, staring into a white refrigerator far older than he was. "I have water, beer." A single longneck, anyway. He wasn't much of a drinker, but still, he had West Texas standards to uphold. "I need to make a grocery run. I've just been nervous about leaving."

"I could pick you up a few things."

"I appreciate that, but I can't sit at home forever. Before you got here, I was thinking of taking a short ride before the light goes."

"Sure, Zeke." She retreated toward the door, looking ill at ease. "If you have to go now—"

"Thought you might like to come along," he said, then chased the invitation with the best excuse he could think of. "I'm not leaving the other two behind. And it'll be easier leading one animal than two. So if you'd ride the pinto, if you've got the time, that is, and you want to . . ."

Her eyes brightened. "I'd love it. It's been a while, but I miss riding."

"Don't worry. We'll take it easy. Walking'll be good for Gus's shoulder."

Once outside, he was embarrassed to remember he didn't have a saddle for the new mare. He dragged out two bridles, Cholla's saddle, and a blanket, then said, "I'll try this saddle on the pinto. Not sure it'll fit her, though. She's quite a bit smaller than Cholla here."

Rachel shook her head. "I'll ride bareback, since we're just going to be walking."

"Wouldn't be as stable. And if you haven't ridden for a while—"

"Come on, Zeke. I'll be fine. I used to ride a lot back in the day. Bareback, often as not."

"Maybe you should take Cholla. He can be a handful, though, and—"

"He's the perfect size for you." She tactfully didn't point out that he was too heavy for the delicately built mare, but the implication lingered. The pinto was filling out nicely, and he'd tried her around the corral just to see how she moved. But she would never be a sturdy enough animal for a big man.

Conceding defeat, he readied both horses and tied Gus's lead line to Cholla's saddle. "You want to borrow a sweatshirt or something? It could get pretty chilly once the sun drops."

Rachel patted the sleeve of her denim jacket. "This'll be okay for now."

"Then how about a leg up?" he asked Rachel.

She stroked the mare's brown-and-white neck and checked her over appreciatively. "She's looking a lot better these days."

Zeke boosted her up onto the pinto's back, then handed her the reins. "Ought to. She's eating up a storm. She's good natured, easy as anything to handle. Be a nice horse for you to start back up with."

"Does she have a name?"

The saddle creaked as he swung up onto his buckskin. "I was thinking Yucca. Kind of goes with Cholla—desert plant."

"Yucca? Ugh, that's really awful. You might as well call her Creosote . . . or maybe Bastard Toadflax," she said, referring to two even less attractively named species.

"So do better."

"Shouldn't be hard. How 'bout . . ." She glanced back toward the ghostly letters on the side of the building. "How about Candle—short for Candelilla. That's a plant, too. And it sounds a whole lot prettier than Yucca. You like that better, don't you, Candle."

"If you say so." Zeke doubted horses cared what anybody called them. But if it pleased Rachel to name the mare, he didn't see the harm. "Candle it is, then. But if I ever get myself a dog, I've got dibs on Bastard Toadflax."

"I can think of only one dog deserving of the honor," she said as the newly christened Candle followed Cholla and the pack mule. "My grandma's Boston terrier's mad at me for spoiling his reign of terror. *And* having him neutered."

"Hell, woman. Remind me never to cross you."

A wry smile tilted across her pretty face. "That's a very good idea."

The crunch of shod hooves on the hard ground, the creak of leather, and the snorts of the animals curtailed their conversation. Cholla was more full of himself than usual, dancing and bucking as his passage startled a bright blue Mexican jay from a clump of smaller piñons.

"Looks like he wants a gallop," Rachel suggested.

"Probably needs one after being stuck in the corral," Zeke admitted as he settled the buckskin, "but I'm not risking Gus's stitches—or your seat—by letting him have his head."

As herding animals, both horse and mule would try to follow Cholla's lead.

"Your confidence in my riding ability is a real inspiration," Rachel said.

"Aren't you still getting over having your brain rattled last week?" he asked, causing her to grimace in reply.

As the pinto walked, Rachel shifted uncomfortably and said, "Bony as this horse's back is, I have a feeling it's not going to be my head that's sore once this is over."

Zeke wished he could allow Cholla a good workout. Anything to distract him from thinking of the body parts her innocent words had painted in his guilty mind.

After all this time, it was almost impossible to remain so close yet still stay quiet. Hands trembled, and the field glasses they were holding shook, too, as did the murderer brought into focus.

A murderer who smiled, even laughed. A killer out for a pleasant ride with an attractive companion. In the distance, mountains formed a scenic backdrop, while the first hints of a fiery sunset stained thin, stippled clouds. The vegetation, too, added to the beauty, the shrubs and pale, yellow grasses clothing the dry land in deceptive softness.

The image jerked as the watcher's hands spasmed at the injustice, the *fucking wrongness* of the scene. Where were the lost boy's smiles and laughter? Where were *his* twilight rides, his dates, and his enjoyment of a crisp, late winter evening? She imagined herself taking snapshots, putting them into an album.

His murderer had robbed her of that, of that and all the countless happy memories they would have made together. Had robbed her of her family, too, as she had dashed it all to pieces against the rocks of grief.

But tonight, this very night, she was going to balance the scales of those injustices in a way the legal system had been too corrupt or cowardly to do. And her way would be more satisfying, she suspected, already relishing the soothing balm of blood upon her hands.

CHAPTER FIFTEEN

I am a brother to dragons, and a companion to owls.
　　　　　　　—The Holy Bible *(King James version)*
　　　　　　　　　　　　　　　　Job 30:29

As the sun consorted with the Chinati Mountains, jackrabbits nibbled at tender new shoots, early harbingers of spring.

"Better eat quick, before those big-ass owls come calling," Rachel encouraged, thinking of the shredded-fur and picked-bone remnants left by the pair residing at The Roost. Pellets, too, when their prey were smaller creatures, whose indigestible remains were neatly packaged and coughed up.

Zeke turned to look at Rachel, amusement flickering in his pale green eyes.

"Do you always talk to the animals?" he asked.

When he looked at her like that, his smile lazy and his posture relaxed aboard the huge horse, Rachel wanted to pull out her camera and take a photo of him burnished by the amber light. She knew better than to try it, knew his ease would tighten into anger if he even guessed what she was thinking. But that didn't stop her from aching with the beauty of the moment.

"You have to admit," she answered, "the jackrabbits are only slightly less likely to answer me than you are."

"Hell, I run on at the mouth like a babbling idiot around you."

"You need to get out more if you call what you manage *babbling*, or even halfway sociable."

"Why muck up a good ride with a lot of chatter?"

The rough path they were following opened out into flat, grassy rangeland dotted with only a few small junipers and jutting clusters of spine-tipped agave, many of which sported dried stalks that rose like ships' masts from their centers. Rachel touched her heels to the mare's sides, prompting Candle to trot around Gus and come abreast of Cholla.

Rachel's heartbeat quickened as she told Zeke, "I'll tell you why. Because it's how two people get to know each other."

Instead of looking at her, Zeke's gaze tracked what appeared to be a line of mule deer trotting over a low ridge to avoid them. "Can't see why we'd need to do that, Rachel. Since things aren't going any further."

"Is there a woman somewhere?" she asked so quietly, the words were nearly trampled beneath the shuffling hooves. "Some woman with a claim on you?"

Zeke snorted. "Have to be a mighty patient woman, being as how I've lived alone in Marfa for the past fourteen years."

"That's not an answer."

"Why?" He looked at her sharply. "Why does it matter?"

"Gee, I can't imagine." The words came out sarcastic, even angry, but she couldn't seem to stop them. "Could it be because you had your damned tongue halfway down my throat and I liked the way you touched my breast? Because I'd like to feel—I'd like to feel more, *need* to feel more than the freaking stress and grief and worry I've dealt with this past year." She wanted to prove, too, that she *could* feel, that she was ignoring Dr. Thomas's and her new attorney's repeated messages only because she'd moved on with her life.

"But as much as I want that, Zeke," she continued, "want *you*, I won't have it if you're married, or if you ran out on a kid or three to stay ahead of child support. I'm not living with that sin, too."

He tugged the reins to stop dead and fix her with a flinty stare. "Is that who you think I am? Some irresponsible bastard who would leave my own—"

"I don't think it. But I've been wrong before, so badly wrong you can't imagine. I thought Kyle was harmless— maybe a little vain, a little too smooth for a kid his age. But it never occurred to me that he was interested in anything but taking pictures, maybe even making art. And instead he . . ." Her eyes snapped shut, screwing tight against the memory of the first set of pornographic images she'd been forced to look at—the images he'd sent to *everyone* he knew after his attempts to manipulate her failed.

"I've never married, never had kids." His voice was tight, controlled, belying the tension that seemed to dance beneath his skin. "But don't assume your situation gives you a free pass on the questions. Patsy's right. This can't work between us, and I've been a damned fool to imagine I could—"

She held up one palm. "Even a damned fool needs a friend from time to time. And if that's all you want, I'll accept—"

"It's sure as hell not *all* I want," he snarled, the rough edge of his voice enough to make Cholla dance sideways. "I want—I want what I have no right wanting. And what you'd have to be a fool to settle for."

Candle was a responsive mount, turning on a dime at Rachel's bidding. Turning back toward Zeke's place.

"Then I won't waste any more of your time." She must be insane, thinking there was something more between them than a foolish physical attraction. People had been right to warn her. Zeke Pike liked the prison he had made for himself, with his monklike cell and his stupid Vow of Gruffness.

"Rachel, please don't—"

Both horses and the mule swung their heads toward a clatter: the hooves of the deer rushing over the rise, bounding with their strange, stiff-legged leaps. On spotting the riders, the deer swerved to the east, yet their fear—even some thirty yards away—was infectious. Gus brayed and leaned back against the rope, Cholla tried to turn toward home, and Rachel was nearly unseated as the pinto bolted.

Remembering a decades-old riding lesson, Rachel pulled the mare's head sideways until she trotted in tight circles and then slowed to a stop.

Zeke, who had gotten the other two in hand, asked, "You all right? Thought you'd fall for sure."

"Me, too, for a moment," Rachel told him. "What do you think scared the deer like that?"

"Coyotes, maybe. Or . . . could be the vet was wrong and there's a wild cat around here after all."

Rachel's heart fluttered, and she pictured the cougar toying with them the way a cat played with its victims. "Let's go back then. The horses are all freaked out, and we're losing the light anyway. Besides, I'm—"

But Rachel never got the chance to admit she was scared out here, with the looming silence and encroaching darkness. Because as that moment, a predator topped the rise and headed straight for them.

A predator that bore no resemblance to the killer either had imagined.

CHAPTER SIXTEEN

The agony of my feelings allowed me no respite; no incident occurred from which my rage and misery could not extract its food . . .

—Mary Shelley,
from Frankenstein

At first Zeke couldn't make sense of what he was seeing, so he wasted precious seconds staring at the headlights and listening to the growl of the engine barreling toward them.

Even after he understood it was an SUV, his mind struggled for an explanation. Scofflaw hunters? Rowdy teens off-roading, chasing deer for sport or trying to catch a little air as they raced over the ridge? As he fought to keep control of his mount, Zeke bellowed "Stop" and waved an arm, certain the driver would change course the instant he realized there were riders down here. Not defenseless wildlife but *people.*

Yet the big, dark vehicle kept coming, picking up speed. Gus sat on his haunches, braying, while Cholla reared. When Zeke looked around, he saw the pinto bolting toward home, until the horse—or maybe Rachel—realized the vehicle's trajectory would cut off their escape. Wheeling around, the mare settled for second best—veering in the direction the deer had taken. Zeke had a glimpse of Rachel clinging to the mare's neck, the reins torn loose from her hands and whipping wildly around her.

The SUV was nearly on him when with a scraping thump, its front bumper hooked a thick-based double yucca. The bloody wash of sunset reflected from the windshield, allowing Zeke only a bare glimpse of the driver. As the vehicle, still stuck, reversed and spun its tires, Zeke realized he needed to get clear of this idiot and find Rachel before she fell.

After releasing Gus, who galloped toward home, Zeke took off in the direction the pinto had run. In the thunder of his mount's hooves, he nearly missed the sound of sharp cracks just behind him, casting him back in time to the incident at the viewing area. Was this the same son of a bitch, now firing from the still-stranded vehicle behind him? Somehow that didn't seem right, didn't mesh with the glimpse he'd had of what looked like a smaller driver. Was there a passenger inside as well? Maybe even more than one?

Zeke didn't wait around to get a better look. Instead, he ducked low and prayed the shooter's aim had not improved. Because as fast as Cholla moved, the horse stood not a chance in hell of outracing bullets.

Rachel was in trouble. Damned big trouble from the moment the panicked mare tore the reins from her hands. Stunned by the revving engine and the blinding headlights in a place no vehicle should be, Rachel had been momentarily distracted—giving Candle the moment she needed to render her rider all but helpless.

Helpless to control their flight. Helpless to save them—for nothing but disaster could come of this blind gallop.

Clinging to the thrusting neck, Rachel wound the fingers of one hand through the mare's thick mane. She tried to think of how to communicate—how to stop this madness—but it was all she could do to keep her balance as her mount shifted to avoid a rocky outcrop, then veered around a patch of prickly pear.

Surely, the mare couldn't keep this pace up much longer. Rachel heard her breathing hard, felt the heat rolling off her in waves. And the back she sat astride was sweating, making her perch slippery, as the mare plunged on and on.

"Don't you fall on me," Rachel begged the runaway. "You stay on your feet, and I'll stay on your back 'til you get tired."

But the newly named Candle wasn't the one who broke faith with their unholy contract. Instead, it was Rachel who—when the mare gathered herself to leap a fallen juniper—tumbled from her mount's back with a shout of horror.

A shout cut short by the hard-packed desert soil that rushed up to meet her.

CHAPTER SEVENTEEN

Light, seeking light, doth light of light beguile;
So, ere you find where light in darkness lies,
Your light grows dark by losing of your eyes.
—William Shakespeare,
Love's Labor's Lost
Act I, Scene 1

Like a vast eye, darkness closed upon the desert. As the bloody rim of twilight drifted off to plum, straight above, an obsidian dome dreamed star after brilliant star.

"Rachel!" Again and again, Zeke strained his throat to shout her name, then stopped his horse to listen. Again and again, the high plain returned only the distant howling of the clan of the coyote. From somewhat nearer came the chirping calls of tiny elf owls.

But nothing more, now that the engine noises had receded and the final echoes of the gunshots faded. No answering calls nor any hoofbeats, nothing to distract Zeke from the deepening darkness and the rapid cooling of the crisp, dry air around him.

He thought of Rachel declining his offer of a sweatshirt to augment her denim jacket. Thought about the other morning, when he'd awakened to light frost. He nudged Cholla with his boot heels, encouraging the horse to a brisk trot, though he doubted his mount could see much better than he could.

A stumble proved him right, nearly unseating Zeke and forcing him to stop. Once more, he called out Rachel's name, praying she was close enough to hear him.

Maybe she's close enough but can't hear. Me or anybody. In his mind's eye, he could see her, blood and brain matter

splattered on a rock or crushed beneath the pinto's flailing
body.

Zeke Pike trembled, though he'd begun to sweat.

"Rachel!" he roared. "Goddamn it, Rachel. *Answer.*"

Unnerved by his eruption, Cholla danced nervously and
tossed back his head. Zeke fought to master the horse's rising panic. Fought to tamp down his own terror.

Fear spilled over into fury. At the maniac—he suspected
Rachel's stalker—who'd tried to run them down and then
fired after them. At Kyle Underwood, for getting himself
killed and causing all this trouble. Even at Rachel, for in-
sisting she'd be warm enough, for volunteering to ride
bareback. . . .

For making him feel *responsible*, damn her, when he'd forgotten how to tend another person. Forgotten how it hurt
to care, how it could be so unutterably painful. . . .

Stupid, to let someone get this close. Bad enough the way
he hungered to touch her warm skin and smooth the silk of
her hair, to taste and feel and push himself inside her until his
frozen core burst into bright flame. But to let her smile get
inside him, to be infected by her conversation—it was insan-
ity. It was death—or worse yet, the realization that its opposite, as he'd experienced it for all these long years, wasn't life
at all, only a crude mockery of what existence could be.

Enraged with himself above all others, Zeke swore, tearing a shrill neigh from the horse beneath him. Cholla fought
to take the bit in his teeth, struggled to bolt home. Home,
where hay and grain were, where his pasture mates should
be, too.

Home, where the pinto bearing Rachel might have gone.

Had the mare circled around and headed—as horses
would—for the familiarity of her pen and shelter? Could
Rachel still be clinging to her, waiting and worrying about
his return?

He blew on the spark of the image, kindling it into a vision warm as fire. Rachel, whole and unharmed, only a bit
shaken. She would tend his animals, both the mare and Gus,

but every few moments, she would stop to peer into the darkness. She would cup her hands around her mouth and call the name she thought was his.

Would he hear her from here if he listened? Would her voice carry so far on the clear night air?

With a terrible effort, he forced himself to stillness, a calm as dark and measureless as the night that slept around him. As Zeke silenced terror, mastered rage, the horse that he rode quieted until the only sounds left were their breathing.

And the whinny of another animal off in the blackness.

Cholla stepped forward and trumpeted his answer. A neigh of greeting to his pasture mate.

"Rachel," Zeke called, the calm inside him splintering beneath the weight of hope.

Hooves clopped against hard soil, and Zeke recognized the shuffling off-cadence of a limping horse. The gelding beneath him shifted and stepped forward, nickering low as he stretched his neck eagerly.

Though the moon had not yet risen, the scant light of a million distant suns illuminated a dark form approaching. A horse, he saw, a pinto.

It came forth riderless.

CHAPTER EIGHTEEN

The gates of hell are open night and day;
Smooth the descent, and easy is the way:
But to return, and view the cheerful skies,
In this the task and mighty labor lies.

—*Virgil,*
from Aeneid

Cold. So cold that shivering woke her. Such hard shivering that Rachel's bones ached with it.

No, that wasn't right. Or wasn't all, at least. The fall had her left shoulder throbbing, the left side of her skull pulsing with violent bursts of light that sparked when she tried to lift her head.

Yet she had to raise her face from the hard grit, so she pushed off the uneven surface with her right hand. Pushed and strained to sit up, with the flashes blazing Morse code protests.

She waited out the pain, waited out the waves of nausea. And stared into a darkness so complete that she feared she'd been blinded. Hadn't the doctor warned her to be careful, that another blow to the head, after her recent concussion, could have dire consequences? Memory issues, mood disorders, coma, even death—and wasn't vision part of the brain's function? The part that allowed her to create a photograph, to fly a plane or glider, to see the people she loved.

Her father's face flashed through her consciousness, her grandmother's as well. Even Patsy's, and, more surprising still, Zeke Pike's.

Where was Zeke? Had his horse, too, bolted after the off-road vehicle came roaring toward them? Fear shot through her center at the idea that he could have been struck down—perhaps because of her.

She blinked back moisture, then noticed a bright streak—a meteor flashing through the dark skies. As it dimmed, she stared upward at the swath of stars that speckled the cold expanse. Stars far brighter and more numerous than those that dotted the diminished sky of the light-saturated East Coast. By the tens of millions, they flanked the Milky Way's pale swath, offering her reassurance that she could still see after all.

She sighed and shook her hands to get blood flowing into her chilled fingers. After buttoning her jacket, she rubbed her arms, then grunted with the effort of rising to her feet. Tottering for a moment, she watched the lights above blur as the canopy of night swayed. By widening her stance, she managed to stay upright, standing until the cold forced her to move.

But where could she go? Despite the bright display above, she couldn't see where she was walking, so she was forced to take small and cautious steps. And she had no idea of direction, no way to gauge whether she was moving toward or away from Zeke's place or the tiny airport, toward Marfa proper or the mountains. She pictured the area rolled out beneath her like a relief map, the miles and miles of emptiness she'd seen so often from the air. How easy it would be to miss one of the tiny outposts of civilization on this broad plain and wander off, directionless, into oblivion.

And yet she had to move to warm herself. To move and to pray that Zeke had made it back to safety, that he had gotten in his truck and gone for help.

Who could say how long she had been unconscious? Maybe searchers were already organizing parties and equipment. Maybe they were out looking with their flashlights and their lanterns. Or she might be closer to Zeke Pike than she thought.

She cupped her hands around her mouth and called, "Zeke, where are you? Zeke? *Anybody?*"

She never stopped to consider that "anybody" could include the same person who had tried to hurt her in the first
place. Never imagined she could be so unlucky until she
saw the headlights taking aim.

CHAPTER EIGHTEEN

Who is more foolish, the child afraid of the dark or the man afraid of the light?

—*Maurice Freehill*

Twin lights. Much like headlights, except they rose like a child's balloons above the desert. Rose and merged, the yellow-white left orb swallowing the right.

Silent and so lovely. The light swelled, spinning on a strangely disconnected axis. Hovering, then giving birth to gently glowing spheres.

The observer lowered the field glasses, smiled. Because the mystery lights were part of a pleasure so acute it had a sexual component. As if spent bullets and spilled blood had quenched a violent thirst.

From the farthest reaches of a nightmare memory, The Child's weeping faded, the cries morphing into the happy yips of the distant coyotes.

And as the glowing crescent moon cleared the horizon, its thin curve seemed the desert night's sadistic smile.

Hopeless. This is hopeless . . .

Yet Zeke couldn't force himself to give up, couldn't abandon the rough grid he had mapped out in his head to keep from getting completely lost out in the darkness. Leading both of the horses, he walked imaginary lines for hours, stopping every so often to call Rachel's name.

He continued long after he had given up hope of hearing any reply. If he stopped and let the horses follow their instincts to lead him back home, he would have no choice except to climb into his truck and drive to town to ask for help. The sheriff would have to be called and searchers organized, none of whom would want to begin looking before daybreak. Might as well keep looking on his own, then, on the off chance that he would stumble across her.

Or maybe he was avoiding Rachel's family. Zeke's throat tightened at the thought of facing Patsy, who might have mixed feelings about her stepdaughter but wouldn't thank him for losing her. And what of Walter Copeland, whose love for Rachel streamed behind him like a banner? No matter what the sheriff told him, Walter wouldn't be able to hold off until morning. He'd come back out here with Zeke and crawl on his hands and knees if necessary.

Maybe he had that right. God only knew Copeland had more claim to this futile effort—to Rachel herself—than Zeke ever would. Head bowed in defeat, he reached for the horn and cantle of Cholla's saddle and swung back aboard for the ride home.

From this new vantage, he sucked in a breath and stammered, "Holy shit . . ." at the bright orbs he saw floating off to his right. Floating, blending, shifting in color, and then separating.

Zeke had seen the area's mystery lights a number of times during the years he'd lived in the high desert. But he had never seen them in this area nor looming so close, perhaps only two hundred yards away. Close enough to reach, with just a short ride.

As worried as he was for Rachel, the lights beckoned. How many times had he wondered about their origin, wished for a closer look?

The pinto pulled against the lead rope, a nervous nicker telling him she was no fan of the idea. Cholla, too, side-stepped uneasily, rather than moving forward at his rider's signal.

Give up. Cold and hopeless, the words reverberated in the darkness, pointing him toward the path of least resistance, the path he knew too well. Give up on family, on the hope of clearing his name. Give up on building friendships, on making a real life using this name or any other.

Give up on Rachel Copeland, who, even when right next to him, stood so far out of reach. *Giving up is what you're best at, what you've come to know. Standing back and waiting for death to sort it all out, or to bury the problem six feet under.*

"Damned if I'm doing that tonight," he said. Because if the strange illumination had drawn him, wasn't it possible that Rachel, too, might be lured to investigate? With a prayer on his lips, he forced Cholla to move toward lights even more mysterious than the leering of the moon.

One by one, they winked out. First a yellow one, then a pink, then white. A greenish orb was last to go, an orb that vanished with a sound like weeping.

Yet the crying lingered, floating in the cold air like the faint plumes from Cholla's nostrils. Suspended in the starlight until Zeke realized it was human.

"Rachel! Rachel, is that you?"

His heart pounded, but his breath froze as he strained to hear the sobs.

"Zeke. Oh, my God. *Zeke.* Wh-where are you?"

CHAPTER NINETEEN

*The citizens of Marfa describe the lights as almost sentient
in their playfulness, as they frequently recede and disappear
when followed. The lights have even, on occasion, been rumored to somehow "communicate" with people lost and
stranded on the desert, in a few cases guiding them to safety.*
— Professor Elizabeth Farnum, PhD,
from "Curious Customs of the Lone Star State"

Thursday, March 13

Rachel laid her head against Zeke's back as they rode double, her arms winding around him for both security and
warmth. He hadn't trusted her to ride on her own in her
condition, and he'd said something, too, about Candle favoring one foot.

"Keep talking to me," he urged.

She wanted to close her eyes and savor the low vibration
of Zeke's words, to soak in the rich, deep sound of his voice
as her shivering abated.

"Are you with me, Rachel?" he persisted. "I know you're
hurting, but you have to answer."

"I'm still here." She squeezed his midsection and found
him as solid as a live oak, and just as reassuring in his real-
ness. Heat streaked from her right eye. "I didn't dream you,
did I? You won't fade like the lights did?"

Fear slashed at her, threatening to spill whatever little
calm she'd gathered since what she had first taken for headlights appeared in the darkness.

"Not planning on it," he assured her. "And pretty soon,
we'll be back at my place. Then we'll get you cleaned up,
and I'll run you on home."

"I—I brought my van," she said, her headache pulsing.

"You aren't driving, Rachel, not after you were knocked unconscious. Probably I should take you to the hospital in Alpine, get you checked out thoroughly."

"No." She spoke more sharply than she meant to, imagining yet another set of bills she couldn't afford. "I'm feeling a lot better now. Just a little sore. And cold."

"I can feel you shaking," he said. "I should have made you take another coat."

He had taken off his own and put it over her jacket in spite of her protests that he would freeze.

"Neither of us could've imagined this would happen. What *did* happen, Zeke? Was it a woman driving that thing? That crazy lady here from Philadelphia to run me down?"

"Couldn't say—I never got a real look at the driver. Too busy getting the hell away before whoever it was shot me."

"*Shot* you? There was shooting?" She thought back to her wild ride but recalled no sound save the desperate pounding of her mount's hooves against hard earth.

"Yeah, but the SUV got hung up, stuck long enough for me to move out of range. Didn't stay there long, though. I heard it driving off a few minutes later. Heading back toward town, I think."

"Did you recognize the vehicle?"

"Didn't ring any bells with me, but I didn't get a good look, either. At first, I thought it could be local kids—teenagers joyriding. Could've felt like fun to them to chase the deer."

"Some fun," she said, too exhausted to pay much attention to the doubt in his voice. "Damned jerks. But if they came on us accidentally, they would have turned around and taken off, right? Not kept coming."

"And not fired after us," Zeke added. "Although it's possible they only meant to scare us off. For all I know, the shooter could've been blasting away at the sky, not you and me. I just didn't think it was a wise move to sit around and plot bullet trajectories."

She pressed even closer to him, laid her cheek against his back, and listened to the beat, so strong and regular inside him. A rhythm she could depend on, like his strength and warmth. "Glad you didn't. I don't want you to be hurt on my account."

"We can't know for sure this has anything to do with you. For one thing, there's that fellow who shot up my truck. And didn't the sheriff say your caller's left the area?"

"I wanted to believe that, but now . . . How likely does it seem that a woman obsessed enough to come *two thousand* miles to get to me would make a single phone call, then turn right around and head home?"

"I couldn't make out the driver, but I did get the impression of someone on the small side. Could've been a woman."

She closed her eyes and sighed. "We could have been killed. Both of us. It might've taken days for anyone to find us."

"Someone would've looked for you."

"Not tonight, I'll bet. I told my grandma I was stopping by a friend's house. She's used to living on her own, and she's always in bed early. Probably went to sleep thinking I'd slip in after a while. And I never mentioned which friend I was visiting." She smiled, thinking about it before adding, "Though come to think of it, you're the only real friend I've got here."

"I can't believe that's true."

She shrugged. "I wasn't what you'd call popular in high school, and apparently, some people never move past that garbage. But even if I'd been the prom queen, who wants to buddy up to a killer? I might've been acquitted, but the whole situation was so ugly."

"I wish that asshole was alive. So I could kill him."

"Thanks, I think. That may be the most brutally chivalrous offer I've ever had. But it wouldn't be worth what it would cost you. I wouldn't wish it—" She blocked the memories, not only from that night but later, when she'd learned the DA's office was pursuing charges, that the photos Kyle had faked—lies that ravaged her soul each time she'd been forced to look at them—would be used as evidence against her. Had already been circulated until her e-mail box was crammed with messages that made her feel as though she had been raped in public, then forced to endure critiques on her "performance" as a budding porn star. "I wouldn't wish what I've been through on *anyone.*"

He had no answer, so she was left alone with the memory of her shame and horror—with the futility of hoping to ever escape it. But after a time, she must have drifted off, for the next thing Rachel knew, Zeke was squeezing her wrist and whispering, "We made it. We're back home—at my place."

Through bleary eyes, she saw a light shining through a window at the end of the candelilla factory where Zeke lived.

"Let's get down," he said. "Then I'll help you inside, where you can get warm."

Her legs felt wobbly after he helped her dismount, but a moment later, he lifted her in his strong arms.

"You don't have to carry me. I can make it on my own."

"I know you can." He pulled her closer to him, his tone surprisingly gentle for such a big man. "But you don't have to. Not now."

He carried her straight inside, opening the unlocked red door to his apartment. She thought he'd set her in one of the chairs beside his kitchen table, but instead, he walked beyond the kitchen and laid her on his bed before removing her shoes.

He smoothed her hair back from her face and tucked the blankets in around her. "Rest here and try to warm up. I'll start a fire in the woodstove. Then I have to go back out."

"Are all the animals—?"

"Cholla's fine, and Gus's found his way home safely. Stitches held, too."

"What about Candle? Will she be all right?"

Zeke crumpled old newspapers and tucked them beneath some kindling in a metal woodstove. "I'll do all I can for her. Don't worry."

Don't worry. Such simple words and yet so soothing. Rachel thought she wouldn't have needed sleeping pills, or even Dr. Thomas, if she'd had someone to say—and mean—that back in Philadelphia. If she'd had someone she knew and trusted to watch out for her interests while she rested.

She meant to wait for him to come back, but she must have dozed again. She woke to hear Zeke moving around the apartment and wood crackling as it burned in the stove. She smelled the faint, sharp scent of smoke, a heady, resinous odor that reminded her of campfires from her childhood.

From somewhere nearby, she heard running water, followed by Zeke's footsteps. Looking up through sleepy eyes, she saw him carrying a steaming basin with a couple of towels draped over his broad shoulder.

"Warmer now?" he asked and set the metal basin on a chair he must have brought out from the kitchen.

"Much," she said, suddenly aware of how comfortable she felt wrapped in the blankets, until she made the mistake of moving and hissed in sudden pain.

"Your head?" he asked.

"Mmm, yeah—but mostly my left shoulder. I think it took the brunt when I fell."

"Be right back." He returned a minute later with a glass of water and a bottle of pain reliever. "This won't hurt you, will it? It's non-prescription."

"That'll be great." She tried to push herself upright, but groaned as pain spun up like a dust devil.

When Zeke sat on its edge, the bed creaked in protest. Rachel held her breath, braced for contact.

He put down both the glass and pills, then slid a hand behind her. "Ready?"

With a tight nod, she let him help her up and rearrange

the pillows to support her. When she sighed, "That's good," he handed her the glass and a pair of oblong white pills.

She drained the water to the last drop, then used the back of her hand to wipe the excess moisture from her mouth. "I didn't know I was so thirsty."

"Want some more?"

"I'm okay. But I forgot to ask, how's Candle?"

"She threw a shoe and split the hoof. Nothing major, but I put on a protective boot, and I'll call the farrier to come tomorrow. I'm pretty sure she'll be good as new in a few days."

Rachel blew out a breath. "I'm glad. I was scared to death she'd break a leg, galloping blind like that."

"Damned lucky. For her, for you. For all of us."

His green eyes looked at her face so intently, she felt a flush rise in response.

He touched his fingertips to the still-steaming basin before saying, "Water's cool enough now. Let's get you cleaned up."

A chill danced along her nerve endings, then coiled beneath her stomach. Reminding her that she lay in his bed, that they were so close, so alone.

She swallowed hard, and spoke in a small voice. "I think I could drive home."

He dipped one of the towel's ends into the warm water. "Your face is dirty," he said. "And you've got no business driving."

"I—I should call, at least."

"It's after one." He wrung the towel and pressed its heat and moisture to her sore cheek. "Your grandmother must be sleeping."

Rachel leaned back against the pillows, allowing him to wash her face and hands. Knowing this was what she'd warned herself against, what she'd been warned against by others. Knowing and not caring, with the crackling wood fire a cold light in comparison to the flame igniting his gaze.

She arched her body forward and let him help her out of

both jackets. She didn't stop there, but pulled her arms free of the long sleeves of her T-shirt, then eased it from her torso and over her head.

The look she sent him was a wordless challenge to their previous denials, as well as to the logic that ruled their day-light hours. Because right now, it didn't matter that her past had made her future so uncertain, or that his background was a great, unknown *Here Be Dragons* on the map. To Rachel, the only thing that mattered was that she felt safe in this place, with this man, safe for the first time in so damned long. Safe and warm and utterly aroused. . . .

He didn't spoil it with words but instead let his gaze drift downward. He smiled gently as he reached around her torso and unhooked her bra.

He removed it without touching her. Stared at her so reverently, she felt like something sacred.

"So beautiful," he whispered, watching in silence as she pulled back the blankets and carefully removed both jeans and panties, then slipped off her socks.

Completely nude, she grew even warmer, but her skin felt tight and itchy, gritty with both desert sand and her de-sire. "Will you wash me?" she asked.

"God," he groaned as he dipped the cloth back into the water. Then he washed her, every inch of her, so slowly and carefully, it might have been a penance for the worst of sins.

It was when he began to blot her with the dry towel that his resolve snapped. With a groan, he fell upon her lips, one big hand spanning her breast. She sobbed into his mouth, accepting the thrust of his tongue as her back arched in a helpless spasm.

She pulled his shirttail out of his jeans, then slipped her hands beneath the chambray to run her palms along his hot flesh. Absorbing the play of muscles beneath the surface, tracing the groove that marked the column of his spine and murmuring approval as he fed upon her neck and stroked her still-damp breasts until the nipples peaked.

She shifted, then made short work of the buttons on his

shirt to bare the chest she'd studied so closely—for the sake of *art*, of course—in the photos she had taken. But she found the feel of that chest, so deep-breathing and hard-muscled and solidly male, with its scattering of coarse hairs and the hammering heart beneath its surface, a far greater aphrodisiac than any picture ever taken.

Or perhaps it was the gentle nips along her shoulder that had her gasping and then . . . Conscious thought melted away as his mouth dropped to her breasts.

She threw back her head and allowed the pleasure to spiral through all her senses, to carry her to a place beyond the crackling fire and soft blankets, beyond the aches caused by her fall. When he stopped, she nearly wept, until she saw him rise to strip off his jeans.

And if his chest had been a work of art, the whole of him was a museum. The muscles of his thighs, his taut waist, the size and strength of his erection—she felt her flesh give way to heat, to liquid, felt every last misgiving melt as her mind filled with an imperative. To touch. To taste, to open herself to all that he could offer.

Yet she saw hesitation war with the hunger in his expression. "Rachel," he said, "This isn't—You shouldn't be—".

She pulled his hand to her mouth and kissed it, then ran a single fingertip along his length.

Whatever he had been about to say dissolved into a moan of pure need. He moved over her, their bodies undulating, desperate for skin-to-skin contact and for friction, hurrying before their better judgment caught up with their need.

His fingers found her center, stroked her to a swift, explosive climax. A climax from which she had barely recovered before he ducked his head beneath her legs and laved the same spot greedily with his tongue. She was weeping with the feel of him, weeping with her pleasure as she maneuvered her body to take him into her mouth.

And what they did together did not feel wrong or dirty, not when they tasted of each other, nor when he plunged into her with deep and hungry strokes. For here, the same acts that every pornographer on the planet perverted with vile photos took on a rightness, an inevitability that felt more ancient than the desert.

This is what it should *be,* she knew as the darkness gathered tight around her, as it splintered into brilliance, into starlight, moonlight, then a joy so brilliant it cast all the rest into deep shadow.

CHAPTER TWENTY

I believe that in the heart of each human being there is something which I can only describe as a "child of darkness" who is equal and complementary to the more obvious "child of light."

—Laurens van der Post,
from The Dark Eye of Africa

Zeke couldn't recall the last time he had slept spooned against a woman. Breathing as she breathed, with his arms draped over her protectively. Sharing his body heat, his pillow, totally relaxed in a way that only came with satiation.

It ended all too soon, with his body's stirring, its recognition that a warm and willing female remained close at hand. With his mind waking to the realization that this was not just any female; it was *Rachel*. Rachel Copeland, naked in his bed.

So he spoiled everything by kissing the sleek hair behind her ear and cupping her breast with his hand. She woke with a desperate gasp, her body tensing. *"Get out, Kyle. Don't. What are you—"*

"It's Zeke, Rachel," he said into a darkness barely tempered by the woodstove's soft glow. "Just Zeke. Everything's all right."

After a delay, he heard her panting. "Oh. Oh, Lord . . . I guess—it was a nightmare. I—I'm sorry."

"You don't have anything to apologize for—" God only knew, she had a right to bad dreams. If he could, he'd kiss away each one, but he knew that couldn't be for them. That he'd been wrong to take what she had offered last night, wrong to take one more step down a path he couldn't travel.

"What time is it?" she asked, sounding wide awake now.

He saw the flash from her digital watch as she pushed a button to light its face. Saw, too, the tiny numbers reading 5:43 AM.

"Oh, no," she said. "My grandma will be up soon, and if I'm not there, she'll totally freak out."

Rachel tossed back the covers and then grunted as she tried to push herself upright. "Owww. I—I forgot."

"What is it?" he asked, sitting up and laying a hand along the side of her neck to rub the tension from her muscle.

"Shoulder, when I tried to use it. But now that I'm up, my head hurts, too."

"I should've taken you to the hospital. You could have a serious—"

"I'll be fine. Just sore. But I have to get going."

He reached for his pants. "Let me drive you."

"No." The sharpness of her voice was softened by a gentle touch to his hand. "Listen, Zeke. Last night was horrible and scary as hell, and—"

"Oh, great. Just what every man loves hearing," he said dryly.

"But the part afterward, with you—that part was *wonderful*. That's what I was about to say before your male ego interrupted."

"It was taking a hell of a beating, after all."

She stroked his jaw, then kissed him. He wanted to keep kissing her, to drown her hurry in a rising tide of passion.

She pulled away abruptly, saying, "It *was* wonderful. The only bright spot in a very dark night. A very dark *year*, really. But I'm not ready for this. Not the kind of 'this' that lasts."

"I'm not asking for that, Rachel." He swallowed hard. "I can't. But maybe we could—"

"I have to be honest with you." She began gathering her clothing, avoiding his eyes as she did so. "I'm not interested in sneaking around to scratch an itch every so often. Everywhere I look, I see trouble all around me. Threats and lawsuits—not to mention the usual array of family bullshit. It doesn't leave me a lot of energy to wall off pieces of myself and make them off limits. Like the part that gets attached and the part that falls in—I just don't have it in me to keep up the sex thing if I'm not allowed to get to know you."

He'd guessed that about her, warned himself that Rachel Copeland wasn't the kind to settle for an occasional no-strings tumble. But the problem was, the type of woman who would accept the conditions he could offer didn't interest him at all.

"And I've already caused my family so much worry." She stepped into an enticing pair of pale-pink panties. "When they hear about what happened in the desert last night, they're going to freak out. Especially my dad."

To spare her shoulder, he turned her around and hooked her bra, in spite of his body's protests. "I can understand that. After those phone calls and your glider crash, it's tough to believe our run-in with that SUV was a random accident."

"I'll call the sheriff. And he'll probably want to talk to you about it, too. Maybe he'll even find out it's connected to the man who shot at your truck."

"But you'd rather Castillo didn't know you stayed with me tonight." It hurt, having to be that kind of lover. Invisible. Quickly dismissed and forgotten. It was why he fought so hard to stick to celibacy.

She turned to face him. "I'm not ashamed of being with you. And I'm certainly not asking you to lie about it to protect my reputation."

"But if it doesn't come up . . ."

"Simpler that way, don't you think?" He heard, rather than saw, her smile. "And you won't have to worry about Patsy spitting in your lunches."

Both of them finished dressing, and Rachel pulled her tousled hair into a loose tail.

"I'm following you home," he insisted. "I need to make sure you get there safely. You have a problem with that?"

"Would it matter if I did?"

"If there's someone out to hurt you—"

"I know," she said miserably, "though sometimes I wish this woman would just step out of the shadows. Meet me face-to-face and get this over with."

"Probably she doesn't want it over with. This is her way of keeping her son, or at least her grief, alive a little longer. Once it ends, she'll have nothing."

"Except a nice, cozy prison cell if I have anything to say about it. Or a locked room in a psychiatric institution."

While Rachel stepped into the bathroom, Zeke went out into the chill morning to feed his animals. By the time she climbed into her van, he was warming up his pickup. Regret welled as he followed her taillights through the pre-dawn dimness. Regret that escalated when, after stopping to open the gate, she trotted back to him.

When he opened his door, she leaned in and threw her arms around his neck, then kissed him. Softly, sweetly, before she ran her palm over his whiskered cheek.

"Thanks," she told him. "Thanks for finding me last night—and for reminding me that sex can be—that it can be lovemaking."

Before he could think of how to answer, she hurried back to climb into her rusted gold van. And he wanted nothing more than to stop her.

Or to roll time back to that moment before he had awakened her with his kiss.

Rachel kept darting worried glances at the rearview mirror. Wondering if she'd hurt Zeke. Or if he thought she was insane for assuming that one night in her arms meant he'd necessarily want more. For all she knew, he was back there celebrating that she'd let him off the hook so easily, that he was free to move on to his next conquest.

But even though he'd tried to conceal himself from her, she knew he wasn't that type. Knew that being with her had meant more than he would say.

She refused to stew about it, to steep in guilt over something both of them had so clearly needed, especially after last night's terrifying ordeal. In spite of the way she'd been slandered in the courtroom and depicted by the tabloid media, she was a laughably long way from promiscuous. Still, she didn't buy into the notion that she had to spend the rest of her life a cloistered nun.

But that didn't mean she wanted to hear about her night with Zeke Pike from her family, so she fervently wished he would veer off once she turned into her grandmother's neighborhood. Preferably before somebody saw them and put two and two together.

She spotted Mr. Morgan's cat first, a fat orange tabby clambering up the pecan tree in his yard. The reason became clear a moment later, when a barking black-and-white blur leapt at the tree's base.

"Wake up the whole damned neighborhood, why don't you?" she grumbled at James Dean. She parked and climbed out of the van, then waved a quick good-bye to Zeke before returning her attention to the dog's noise.

As she approached, J.D. quieted to stare at her. She could swear she heard the whir of tiny circuits running computations in his round head. Figuring his odds of capture, bath, or at the very least fun spoiled.

"Don't move," she whispered to him. "Don't. You. Dare— Oh, damn it, J.D."

The Boston terrier took off running. Rather than chasing after him, Rachel decided to go in and grab her secret weapon, a beloved squeaky toy she'd held in reserve for just such an occasion.

She unlocked the side door and went in, then cringed at the sound of the TV blaring from the living room. Grandma must be awake, then. But had she noticed Rachel's absence?

Rachel tiptoed out of the kitchen and peeked into the living room. Her grandmother was lying on the sofa in her nightgown, an afghan covering her to the waist. She must have fallen asleep waiting up for her granddaughter.

Rachel sighed as she went to her, wondering whether she should simply pull up the afghan and leave her as she was or help her into her bed, where she would be more comfortable. Wondering until she saw her grandmother's face and screamed.

Zeke stood near the side door, holding J.D., who'd come right to him. Poised to knock, he heard Rachel's shrill cry. Pulse racing, he opened the unlocked door and hurried inside. After putting down the dog, he followed J.D. to the living room.

"Grandma, wake up," Rachel was pleading as she shook the woman on the sofa. "Please, Grandma."

One look at the waxy pallor and mottled purple on the underside of an exposed arm left him heartsick. Dead, and for some time now. There was no doubt in his mind. Placing his hand on Rachel's back, he said, "I'm sorry. So sorry, but your grandmother—"

"No." Rachel's voice trembled, and her gaze was desperate. "She's just gotten cold, that's all. If we warm her up and get a little sugar in her . . ."

J.D. jumped up, tail wagging, and pawed at his mistress's hip. Then whined and pawed again, until the afghan slid down, revealing the edge of a wine-red box . . .

A box of chocolates, open and half-eaten.

Zeke pulled Rachel into his embrace and let her sob. "If I'd been with her," she cried, "I never would have let her have them. If I'd been here the way I should have—"

"You couldn't have known, Rachel. You couldn't have expected—You only planned to bring me dinner last night."

Rachel shook her head and sank down on the floor beside the sofa. J.D. crawled into her lap and licked her chin.

"I'll be right back," Zeke told her.

He went to the kitchen and called 9-1-1. After reporting Benita Copeland's death, he noticed a list of phone numbers on the counter. Walter Copeland's, in large block print, was at the top. Zeke thought about the evening he'd brought

Rachel home from the hospital, how relaxed and happy the small family had seemed that night. How everything had changed in one fell swoop.

He went back to Rachel and squatted down beside her. She stared, unseeing, at a point past his shoulder, a lone tear sliding down beside her nose. He brushed away the moisture and leaned in to kiss her temple. "Would you like—do you want me to call your dad and Patsy?"

There was no change in her expression, only another tear and the stutter of her inhalation as she handed him a tiny, gold-edged rectangle. "It was—I found this on the sofa, next to the box of candy."

Dread filled Zeke as he took the gift card. *"See you soon, sweet,"* it read, and it was signed, *"All my love, Kyle."*

CHAPTER TWENTY-ONE

—Benita Copeland death—Tox screen? Blood/urine. Poss. poisoning or nat. causes? Diabetic coma?
—Candy deliv.—Check w/FedEx. Sender?
—Zeke Pike—verify tax records, bills of sale, Texas DL
—NTSB report—part failure, glider, prob. age-related. Accidental.
—Area sex offenders checked, alibied out, as per Dep. Varajas. Pike?

—Case Notes, Rachel Copeland File,
Harlan Castillo,
Presidio County Sheriff's Department

Tuesday, March 18

"She had eighty-six good years." Though Rachel's father looked uncomfortable in his charcoal suit, he repeated these words to each person who came to speak to him as the small graveside service ended. His eyes gleamed in the late morning sun. "Eighty-six good years . . ."

An elderly couple turned to leave, following Zeke as he made his way back to his old truck. Rachel was touched that he had shown up—and surprised to see him wearing both a tie and a sports jacket, a combination she suspected he had bought for the occasion.

"I only wish . . ." her father started.

Patsy grasped his hand. "Stop it, Walter. Please stop. *You* have nothing to feel guilty over."

Rachel stared at her, uncertain whether she'd imagined her stepmother's inflection—or the icy chill she'd felt when Patsy's gaze slid past her.

Patsy had made a show of kindness these past few days,

but Rachel didn't trust it. Nor did she trust whatever impulse had prompted the invitation to move into her father and stepmother's house.

After thanking her politely, Rachel had decided to stay in the spice-brown adobe with a sadly subdued J.D. Her dad and Zeke stopped by to check on her so often, she barely had the time to feel alone or nervous. Patsy, too, had called several times, and the sheriff had come by twice to update her on his investigation.

Rachel had been grateful beyond measure to learn that the chocolates had not been poisoned, that her grandmother's death had come without pain as she'd drifted from sleep into a diabetic coma. But Rachel could scarcely breathe for the regret crowded in her chest, the terrible knowledge that a cruel hoax meant to frighten her had taken someone she'd loved so dearly.

Her father's faced reddened as he looked at his wife. "You tried and tried to warn me she was slipping. But I was so damned blind. Refused to see how much she needed looking after."

Tears welled in Patsy's blue eyes. "*She* knew. Rachel knew it. But she still left her to go out and—"

"What can I say that I haven't said already?" Rachel pleaded. "How many times can I apologize? You know—you know how much I loved her. I never meant to stay out that night—never meant for that SUV to come out of nowhere or to get lost in the desert."

Emotion shimmered across Patsy's expression. "You expect us to believe that you and Zeke were running around the desert *all* night?"

Rachel looked out among the sun-bleached tombstones, unable to face her stepmother's suspicion—or to compound her sins with a lie.

"Don't do this, Patsy," Walter pleaded. "Rachel could have died, too."

"It doesn't matter," Rachel told him. Nothing mattered except the reality that she would never again be enfolded in the warm fleshiness of Benita Copeland's embraces, never be regaled with stories from the woman's half-imagined childhood or urged to drive a sporty little car or put on a few pounds to attract a man. No one would ever again mistake her for a dead great-aunt named Cora, or make up words to cheat at board games, or argue that James Dean really *meant* to be an angel.

She looked at her stepmother. "Go ahead and blame me. It's not like you can make me feel worse than I do already."

"I—I'm sorry," Patsy said quietly, not quite meeting Rachel's gaze. "I know how much you're hurting. I know."

"We all are." Rachel's father laid a hand on each of them as if he harbored hope that tragedy could forge one family indivisible out of jagged, disparate pieces.

Wednesday, March 19

The following morning, all three Copelands returned to the house's kitchen after their meeting with the Alpine attorney handling Benita Copeland's estate.

"I can't believe she didn't tell me." After stepping around J.D., Walter scooped freshly ground beans into the basket of an ancient coffeemaker. "All this time, she's been scrimping, clipping coupons and griping over every purchase— remember the fuss she put up about going to the hospital? And all this time, it turns out that Dad wanted . . . that he had made provisions."

Rachel went to him and hugged him, as overwhelmed as he was by the second shock she had received since yesterday's service. At the thought of Dr. Thomas's phone call— his insistence that she stop avoiding him and listen—the room whirled around Rachel briefly before she brought it into focus. *Not now,* she warned herself. *You can think about that later if you have to.*

Dragging her mind back to the present, she told her father, "You heard what the lawyer said. That insurance policy felt like blood money to her. She was happier and more comfortable living on your father's pension. The Grandma I knew never wanted for a thing."

Patsy sat with her elbow on the kitchen table, her hand covering her mouth and hiding her expression. Along with Rachel and Walter, she hadn't said a word during the half-hour drive back here. When she did speak, her voice quaked with emotion. "I underestimated her. I think we all did."

Rachel dredged up a smile, remembering the day her grandmother let her know she was well aware of her grand-daughter's legal problems—and mad as hell she'd been "protected." "You know what I think? I think she enjoyed having her secrets. She probably loved the idea of taking care of us once she was gone, too. But who would have imagined she'd been managing an investment portfolio like that all on her own?"

"She picked a darned good broker." Pride warmed her father's voice. "But it looks like my mama made some damned shrewd decisions of her own, too."

Or lucky ones, Rachel thought, for her grandmother had invested in a couple of ventures that had turned out to be huge winners—with every cent of profit rolling over into a trust to benefit her only living son and sole grandchild. While the final tally was by no means astronomical, each of them had netted several hundred thousand dollars and a half-interest in the house.

"I'm signing it over," Rachel told her father. "Every cent of it—"

His face flushing, he said, "Like hell you will."

Patsy looked away from them, her lips tightening in a gri-mace.

"Your grandmother wanted you to have it," he added, "and nothing would make me happier than seeing you liv-ing in the house where I grew up. There are a lot of happy memories here, and I don't know how I'd bear seeing it sold off to some rich out-of-towner who'd gut the place and make it a postmodernist getaway or a tourist rental or one more snooty gallery."

"I love living here," Rachel admitted, "but, Dad, you've spent a fortune on my defense—you and Patsy both. I have to pay it back to you. For my own sake, I *need* to."

Rachel knew the amount would eat up most of the cash portion of her inheritance, but clearing her conscience would be an even better legacy. And perhaps it would help to ease the tension between her and Patsy.

He laid a callused hand on her shoulder, his hazel eyes searching her face. "It wasn't your fault, Rusty."

"I only wish Castillo could've tracked down whoever sent those chocolates." The shipping company's records indicated that the parcel had been sent from a mailing center in Alpine, that the bill was paid in cash with a non-existent address on the shipping form. The Brewster County sheriff had sent a deputy to question the young clerk who'd been on duty, but try as she might, the high school student couldn't recall any details about the package or its sender. Since the flowers had been delivered to Rachel in Alpine, the sheriff there had also prevailed upon the floral service to cough up the credit card information on that purchase. But the number had been traced back to a prepaid Visa gift card—which had also been bought with cash.

"I'm talking about Philadelphia." Moisture rimmed her father's hazel eyes, and his color deepened. "None of it was your fault, not a damned bit."

Rachel froze, wondering what exactly he knew and how he could have possibly . . .

Her father shook his head. "I didn't mean to overhear you last night. I—I should have left as soon as I realized . . ."

Trembling too hard to keep standing, Rachel dragged out a kitchen chair and sank down on it, across from her step-mother.

"You're white as a ghost," said Patsy. "Walter, what did you—"

"I swung by yesterday evening," he said quietly, "just to check on Rachel, make sure she was all right. When she didn't answer, I let myself inside. That was when I heard her crying, talking on the bedroom extension."

Rachel's face burned as she guessed, "So you took it upon yourself to pick up, in the kitchen? You listened in on a private conversation—with my psychologist of all people?"

Patsy blinked hard. *"Walter."*

"No," he burst out. "No, I didn't. I thought—I thought I'd go tap on the bedroom door since it was open. I only meant to let you know I was here and I'd be waiting in the living room, in case you needed . . . Hell, Rusty, I never planned to stand in the hall listening, but when I heard you say . . . When I guessed what must have . . . I felt like I'd been poleaxed. I couldn't move a muscle."

Rachel was speechless. By this morning, she had managed to lock the facts into a dark vault, as coldly and dispassionately as if they belonged to someone else's history. Later, she could decide how to live with them, but not yet . . . and especially not with the pressure of coping with her family's reaction.

"I don't understand." Patsy shook her head. "What—what's happened . . . ?"

"The new photos," Rachel managed, "the—the experts think—they claim they're certain . . ."

When she couldn't force herself to go on, her father said, "That bastard gave her something—doped her that night at the restaurant—a few weeks before the shooting. Then he took her home and—"

"I was unconscious in those photos. The drug—they think it was a date-rape drug, dissolved into my soda—it relaxes a person's inhibitions . . . and causes amnesia. Then you pass out and . . . he set up cameras. *Cameras,* so the son of a bitch could have souvenirs of what he did to me. And not only me. They found two others. A girl he'd dated—and a young teacher from the prep school that expelled him."

"Oh, Rachel." Patsy touched her arm. "This is—"

"I wish those other pictures had never turned up." Rachel shot to her feet and started pacing. "Wish they'd—God, *why* did his mother have to keep pushing and pushing? And why didn't I—I should have . . ."

Should have stopped him sooner. Should have realized what had happened.

Her father captured her, enfolded her in his arms. "This should come out, Rusty, people ought to know that son of a bitch wasn't any victim. He—he raped—God, Rusty. Why couldn't you have let *me* kill him? I would have done it for you. I would've done anything—"

She turned away from him, unable to listen to him buckling under the strain of one grief too many. Or unable to bear his talk of rape, a word she hadn't allowed herself even to *think*.

That she remembered none of it should have been a blessing. But nightmares and imagination had steeped both dark and daylight hours in misery. *Lock it back away where it belongs.*

Patsy stared, her blue eyes gleaming. Unable to tolerate her scrutiny, Rachel moved to stand beside the kitchen window, her gaze carefully fixed on the Christmas tree–like Arizona cypress growing in the backyard. When she was a little girl, she used to crawl among the low boughs and lose herself inside its fragrant, blue-green embrace. She thought of hiding there now, where only birds could find her. But grief and her desire to escape were soon churned under by a rush of anger.

"So you spied on me and then took off so you wouldn't have to face me," she accused her father.

"You—after you got off the phone, I saw you curl up on Grandma's bed and—I thought maybe, if you slept a while—"

"That's an excuse," she said.

He nodded, looking as miserable as she had ever seen him. "You're right, and I'm sorry. I think—I needed some time, too. I'd just buried my mother, and after hearing that my daughter, my little girl—Can you forgive me?"

She nodded, though she felt light years removed from the child he saw in her. So far from innocence that she would never find her way back.

Again, her father hugged her. "I've been worrying about you. I don't want you to be upset, don't want you blaming yourself for any of it."

"My grandmother, your mother, died because I left her and because someone wanted to torment me," Rachel said. "How can I *not* blame myself for that?"

"Your grandmother," Patsy told her, "was sitting by the TV gorging on expensive chocolates, probably happy as a clam to be left in peace a while so she could do exactly as she pleased."

Rachel blinked back tears, remembering a woman who had lived by no one's rules except her own. The room's normally cheery yellow walls closed in on Rachel as she was overwhelmed by emotion.

Her father said, "You have to admit it, Rusty. If your grandma could've picked a way to go, this probably would have been it. She got to die in her own home, doing something she enjoyed. Sometimes I almost wonder . . ."

"Wonder what?"

"If that's the way she planned it."

Rachel shook her head. "Grandma would never do that to us. You know that."

"You're right," he said. "There's no one else to blame except whoever sent that candy—and the real Kyle Underwood."

They had all said he was guilty, that a *murdered* child had made choices that set the events leading to his death in motion.

As if someone like him could be held accountable for any decision he had made. Everyone had understood that he was different. Special. That he had to be protected from his actions, his decisions and his deficiencies. Others, who had had the good fortune to be born whole, bore the responsibility of looking out for God's chosen angels, of sparing them the fallout from actions they were incapable of comprehending.

Those who failed in this were guilty, as guilty as the one who struck the fatal blow.

And they would all be punished, to a person, even if it took her every last day, every minute, of the time she had left on this earth. Eventually, she would find her moment. Find the last one alone and unguarded.

Find the opening she needed to set the matter finally right.

Friday, March 21

Dread tightened Rachel's stomach when she ran into Terri shopping in the town's one-and-only local grocery around dinner time. Today, Terri wore her ice-blonde hair in a sleek twist and disguised her overflowing curves with a tastefully tailored duster jacket. Today, she didn't have her boss around to keep her disdain for Rachel in check.

Because it would have been considered an act of war not to address her, Rachel pasted on a bland smile and glanced down at Terri's cart, which contained wine, along with green grapes, crackers, and a tray of cubed cheeses.

"So," Rachel said, "does Antoinette have you helping her get ready for a Blank Canvas meeting?"

Terri sneered in response. "This is for my husband's birthday. Come on, Rachel. You're supposed to be one of the artsy fartsies these days. You really don't imagine those snobs would drink local wine and nibble cheddar cheese cubes? They'd have to have some unpronounceable brands flown in from God only knows where, if only to outdo each other."

This was one seriously unhappy woman. "If you can't stand the art people, why work for Gallinardi?"

Terri rolled her eyes, as she had so often back in high school. "How many jobs do you think there are for business administration majors here in Marfa? Cris won't live anywhere else—and not everyone *conveniently* inherits a house and a pile of family money."

Where the hell had Terri heard about that? Or was she merely guessing?

Rachel glowered down at her own cart, laden with such glamorous purchases as store-brand peanut butter, cereal, and toilet cleanser, and tried to get a grip on her temper.

"Hope you have fun at your party. And tell Cristo happy birthday for me," Rachel opened her mouth to say. Unfortunately, what came out was a blast of pent-up fury and frustration.

"Get bent, Terri," she snapped. "That's my grandmother you're talking about. The appropriate response would have been, 'I'm sorry for your family's loss,' or 'Sad to hear about your grandma.' Not some bullshit insinuation that's all about some stupid high school grudge. Or for all I know, maybe you're just jealous."

Terri's blue eyes bulged, and her face reddened, proving that Rachel hadn't lost her knack for saying the perfect thing to set her off.

"Jealous?" The blonde thrust her double Ds forward. "You think *I'd* be jealous of some scrawny failure who had to come running home with her tail between her legs? I have a solid marriage and two smart, adorable daughters— neither one of which I'd let within a country mile of a skank like you. So what do *you* have, Rachel Copeland, except a murder charge, online pictures of some amateur hour blow job—"

Rachel shrugged. "Not all of us can be pros, Terri—"

"—And a big, fat lawsuit pending," Terri said over her. "You might imagine you're some high-and-mighty artist, but *everybody* knows all this attention you and your stupid little snapshots have been getting is nothing but a way for the foundation to get some press. Just like everybody knows you're desperate for money. Which is why it didn't surprise me one iota that you cooked up a little Death by Choco—"

"You'd better stop right there, right now, or so help me, I will . . ." Rachel paused, fighting for the control needed not to lay the blonde out with a jumbo can of creamed corn. "Just shut up, that's all."

Terri pushed her tongue around the inside of her cheek, then cut a sly look toward a pair of elderly women with baskets and the teenaged produce clerk, all of whom were watching avidly. "Why, Rachel?" she asked, clearly enjoying playing to her audience. "What are you going to do if I don't? *Shoot* me?"

A second high-school-aged boy, a tall Hispanic kid with Groucho Marx brows, made meowing and hissing noises from the aisle, then raked the air with catfight claws—much to the amusement of the Pueblo Grocery's young clerk.

"If she does smack you"—one of the old women pointed a gnarled finger at Terri's jutting breasts—"I intend to testify that you, dear, had it comin'. Benita Copeland would've snatched you baldheaded if she heard you saying such things to her granddaughter. You just ask Tally Sue Ryan if she wouldn't have."

"The woman's barely in the ground, and here you are, disrespecting the family," sniffed the other woman, a tiny, blue-haired specimen who kept her box-shaped bag tucked close against her side. "It's hardly Christian—and don't I see your mama every Sunday at the church?"

"But she—" Clearly bewildered by the unexpected criticism, Terri looked from one to another of the gathering shoppers for support. "Her own grandmother . . ."

Rachel swooped in to steal the high ground. "I'm sorry we had to have this conversation." She threw in a sweet smile she knew Terri would consider grating. "I hope the rest of your day—and Cris's birthday—are a lot more pleasant."

But as rewarding as it was to leave Terri Parton-Zavala all but spitting in suppressed rage, Rachel was shaking as she loaded her groceries in the back of her van. Shaking with the thought that she would be the main topic of discussion at Terri's damned *whine*-and-cheese party.

Death by Chocolate. Rachel cursed under her breath.

"You okay, Rusty?" asked a voice behind her.

She turned to look, saw Bobby Bauer carrying a shopping bag. He wore a cap that bore the Soar Marfa logo, but the shadow of its brim didn't hide his flush.

His shrug was tight, his deep voice carefully controlled but unmistakably furious. "Small store—can't help overhearing things. Woman's got no right—no call to talk to you like that. If it gets back to Walt, that manure she's spreading—"

She shook her head and pleaded, "Don't go upsetting Dad with this—please, Bobby. It's just some old high school crap with Terri. Ancient history. Nothing I can't handle."

"How about I go and have a private word with her dad? I've known the man forever, back from the days both of us were on the Border Patrol."

"I'd appreciate that, thanks," she said, aware of how little Bobby liked to talk about the bad old days before he had found both AA and her dad's religion, flying. She was touched that he'd go to a Border Patrol friend on her behalf. "If it were just about me, I'd say no, but my family—"

"You've all been through enough," he said fervently, "and I'd do anything for your old man. He—he's helped me through some pretty rough times, taken a chance on me when not too many would have."

"You've long since repaid him, Bobby. He's told me a hundred times," she said, "he wished all the gambles he's made had paid off half as well."

Bobby's eyes crinkled with his smile, and in that moment, he was handsome. "I'll see what I can do to shut Terri up. I promise."

With a nod, he climbed into his old Ford pickup and left her wondering, would Bobby's decades-old connection to Terri's father be enough to silence her? And would it matter at this point, or had the spark of her malicious gossip already flamed into a wildfire far too big to stamp out?

Monday, March 24

By daylight on a fine day, a person could get away with murder in a place as tiny and unused to crime as the town of Marfa. Come nightfall, though, people got suspicious, tended to pick up a telephone or—since this was West Texas—firearms when they saw anything unusual.

But with their spirits buoyed by the bright, crisp sunshine of a spring afternoon, folks naturally gravitated toward positive assumptions. A strange vehicle parked in the driveway of an absent homeowner? Must be a contractor, or maybe someone making a delivery. Or probably just a family friend tending the dog as a favor. Visitor spotted trying various windows before going around into the fenced backyard behind the house? Couldn't be anything to worry over, considering the open smile and friendly wave—anyone that sociable clearly had nothing to hide, despite the presence of the huge and shrouded something that was unloaded and pushed through the back gate.

On a sunny day, a person could take all the time in the world to hunt around beneath the various potted plants on the back porch until the spare key finally turned up. Damned careless of Rachel Copeland, leaving something so dangerous lying around. Criminally careless. Asking for the kind of trouble she no longer had the will or weapon to stop dead in its tracks.

The little dog left inside did not prove much of a deterrent, either, especially when offered a meaty bone to keep him busy. So much for the new owner's security, thought the intruder. So much for her assumption that here in Marfa, she was safe.

CHAPTER TWENTY-TWO

But ne'er to a seductive lay
Let faith be given;
Nor deem that "light which leads astray,
Is light from Heaven."

—*William Wordsworth,*
from "To the Sons of Burns
After Visiting the Grave of Their Father"

Something was for damned sure wrong with Rachel, and as Zeke walked to the airport late that afternoon, he told himself he was going to do more than simply try to cheer her up; he was going to get to the bottom of it. For the past few days he'd held off pressing her for answers, for he was all too aware that a man who couldn't give any had a hell of a nerve pushing.

But yesterday, when he'd dropped by the brown adobe where she and her dad and Patsy had gathered for a Sunday dinner, Rachel's shoulders had been slumped, her hair uncombed, and both her eyes and nose red. As if every last drop of resilience had been drained from her.

As he reached the airport parking lot, Zeke spotted Rachel walking toward her gold van, her head down and her gait unhurried. Which told him that whatever had been bothering her of late had not eased its grip. He jogged over, intercepting her.

"How about an escort?" he offered, dust blowing around his legs. "Your dad mentioned he and Patsy were having dinner with some pilot friend and his wife in Alpine."

Rachel opened her van's door, which put her back to

Zeke. "It's not that I don't appreciate the effort, but I really don't need a babysitter anymore. I'd be glad to drop you back at your place, though."

On the western horizon, the first, soft hints of rose and coral bade farewell to a mild, early spring day.

The old Zeke, the one who had shunned complications, would have gone back to his work and horses. Would have felt fortunate to escape the ensnarement of relationship. But Rachel had gone and changed him, shone a light on him so blinding, he was powerless to find his way back to the man that he had been.

"What's going on?" he asked. "I thought we all agreed it made sense for someone to check the house each night before you went in."

But it hadn't been simply caution that had kept him at the adobe for hours every evening, sharing meals and board games, laughing at some ridiculous old movie on TV. As he grew increasingly comfortable—almost addicted to simply being with her, it became more and more difficult to keep his mind off the things they'd done together and his hands a safe distance from temptation. Even now, the thoughts stole closer, the memories of a night that had smashed down the walls of his defenses.

"You and my dad agreed," she reminded him, "and Patsy. But for how long? It's been over a week since . . . that night, and nothing else has happened. I think you must've been right that some teenager was behind that SUV's wheel—or maybe a couple of dumb drunks out joyriding. If someone's really out to get me—"

"Are you still thinking you deserve it?"

She shot him a fierce look. "Of course not. That's ridiculous. Yes, I wish—I would do anything to go back so I could've been there for my grandma, but I wasn't, and I can't now."

He ached to touch her, to recoup even a fraction of the intimacy the two of them had known that starry night after he had found her out in the desert. But he knew she wouldn't accept it, couldn't allow herself that comfort.

"What Zavala's saying in town," he blurted, "it's all bullshit. Everybody knows that."

A frown troubled her features, and sadness filmed her eyes.

"Come on, Rachel. Let's sit down and talk."

He took her arm and guided her to the same picnic tables where the two of them had shared their first kiss. Her hesitation and the look she gave him told him this bit of history wasn't lost on her—and wouldn't be repeated. But she sat on top of the table and planted the low-topped hiking boots she wore on the bench below.

"So what did you hear?" she asked once he sat beside her.

"I stopped by the post office this morning." For a lot of Marfa's residents, the daily mail run made for a friendly ritual, but Zeke limited his trips to once a week and never lingered for talk or coffee, as so many of his neighbors did. "Cristo Zavala was running his mouth, something about his wife's theory of how your grandmother got that candy. I told him to keep his damned opinions to himself."

"Thanks," she said. "But I doubt it's going to make a bit of difference, since Bobby's talk with Terri's father hasn't."

"Nobody buys that bullshit," Zeke insisted.

Sighing, she reached back to knead her neck with one hand. And in that moment, he wanted nothing more than to pull her into his lap, to run his hands along her warm neck and kiss her into forgetting, make love to her right here and now, since he saw no one else around the airfield. He knew he had no right to touch her and no right to push her on the issue when he wasn't capable of sharing his past with her. But he wished . . . he wished a lot of things, each more futile than the last.

"Antoinette Gallinardi dropped by earlier to talk," Rachel told him. "She claimed *she* doesn't believe the rumors, but there's been 'concern'—that's how she put it— among her fellow members of the Blank Canvas Society.

Concern about the 'seemliness' of showing my work—and especially putting me in a position where I'll have even the slightest connection to 'impressionable' students."

"Oh, hell, Rachel." He knew how important this exhibition was to her. "Does that mean they aren't going to let you . . . ?"

"They've voted to kick me out, can you believe it?" She looked up sharply, her eyes liquid, angry. "They thought they might be able to get folks past some case that happened back East. But Marfa's a very small town, and some people are up in arms, thinking I might've had a hand in my grandmother's death."

"But Harlan Castillo's come straight out and said there's no evidence to support such a stupid idea." Zeke respected the sheriff's attempts to corral the wild rumor. "Besides, anyone who knows you—"

"The thing is," Rachel said, "a lot of people don't. All they've heard about me is that I shot some TV woman's kid in Philadelphia. That I seduced my student."

"But it was proven that you didn't. You were never with him."

For a long while she said nothing, though he had the distinct impression there was something she wanted, needed, to say to him. As he wondered what it could be, his gut tightened with foreboding.

Finally, she managed, "People believe what they see. And those pictures—"

"Lies," he reminded her. "You proved they were all lies."

Once more, she fell silent.

He tried waiting her out, hoping she'd explain herself, but she turned her face from him. "Listen, Zeke, I appreciate the way you've stood by me since Grandma's death, but one night together doesn't obligate you. There's no reason you need to waste your time on someone who can't—"

"Do I look like the kind of man who hangs around because he feels 'obligated'? Do I act like a man who thinks he's wasting his time?" His frustration rose, as did his volume.

"Hell, Rachel, that's insulting. I'm not just trying to do right by you. I'm here because I—because I *can't* remember how to be anywhere else, with anyone else—even my own self. And that's not something I say lightly, not something I do—*ever*. So I don't appreciate you acting like I'm some loser to be blown off without any kind of explanation. You owe me that much."

"Oh, that's rich," she said dryly, "the person who won't tell me a damned thing about himself demanding that I come clean. Come on, Zeke. You have to admit you don't have much of a leg to stand on."

"So I'm a hypocrite," he admitted. "Too damned bad. That doesn't mean it wouldn't do you good to tell me."

She shook her head, lips pressed together in a thin line. When she finally spoke, pinpricks of anger pierced her words. "Why, Zeke? Why are you here? For God's sake, I killed somebody, half the perverts on the planet think they've seen me naked, and I'm getting my ass sued. Don't you have sense enough to keep away from something marked 'high voltage' when you see it?"

He managed a smile. "I'm still here."

"Why?" she pressed, a little more of the lioness resurfacing in her eyes. "I've already told you that the sex is over. Finished. And you're not going to change my mind."

It hurt to think that he might never touch her again, but he'd be damned if he would let her push him away so easily. "You listen to me, woman. There's nothing—not a damned thing—you could say about your past, nothing you can tell me that would change the way I feel about you. Because I . . ."

He swallowed back the words, instinct warning that he had no right to say them. That he might offer her acceptance, but it was the best he could ever do.

She knotted her hands together and stared out at some point beyond them. "Last week after the funeral, I spoke with my attorney. The one defending me against this civil suit."

But Zeke's ears were still ringing with those words he hadn't spoken. *Because I love you, Rachel.* Could he really have been about to say something so damned idiotic? Fantasies were one thing, as was the warmth he felt that Rachel's father and even Patsy had begun to accept his presence. But to say those words aloud, to give voice to how much he wanted to belong to someone, after he'd been on his own so many years . . . It was beyond stupid. He should go home before he completely lost it, dropped down on his knees, and started promising forever.

Rachel went on, despite his silence. "She told me the lawsuit may be dropped. New evidence has come up—"

Her voice broke, refocusing his attention.

"But isn't that good news?" he asked. "Won't that mean everything's all over and you can get on with your life?"

She gave a tight nod, yet her expression all but screamed that she hadn't yet gotten to the point. But before he could find the words to prize that truth out of her, Rachel stood abruptly.

"I promised you a flight." She smiled, though it looked forced, and pulled a thin cell phone from her pocket. "It's too late to take up a sailplane, but we could take a little joyride in Dad's Cessna. It's all gassed up and ready. I'll just let him know what we're up to. He gets a little freaked out if I light out without asking."

Without waiting for his answer, she walked off, keeping her back to him, animated as he hadn't seen her since her grandmother's death. Instead of reassuring him, the suddenness of the change concerned him. He decided not to argue, though, since she wouldn't be able to brush him off easily if the two of them were in a plane together.

Besides, he was itching to finally get his chance to go aloft. And the sooner the better, he thought, while there was still sufficient light to see.

Rachel wasted no time before taking him out to the small plane, a turquoise-and-white two-seater with a single propeller on the nose. After checking it over, she showed him how to climb into the seat beside hers and hook up his safety harness.

"Do you get airsick?" she asked once she had strapped herself in.

He shrugged, feeling both anxious and embarrassed to be nervous about a thing she took for granted. "Guess we'll find out."

Her brows rose, and she smiled. "So you're a virgin?"

He managed a grin. "You'll be gentle with me, won't you?"

Laughing, she started the engine and promised, "Okay, then. No aerobatics this time. But only because it's so revolting, hosing puke out of the cockpit."

He watched her drop into a practiced routine as she flipped switches and started the propeller spinning, then taxied the little plane onto the runway's edge. He wanted to ask her about the confusing array of controls and dials, to explain each step she was taking, but the loud thrum of the engine convinced him to save his questions for another time.

Besides, he wanted to remember every detail of what could easily be his first and last flight. He wasn't sure his ID could pass a commercial airline's scrutiny, especially with recent security precautions. And if he ever again traveled, he'd want to leave no record of his destination.

"Ready?" she asked as the engine grew louder, higher pitched, as if it, too, felt Zeke's anticipation.

At Zeke's nod, they started rolling, their speed mounting as they bumped along the runway. Though he had watched a thousand takeoffs, though he'd seen Rachel fly successfully since her one, ill-fated solo, his heart pounded out a warning that this was impossible; they'd never do it; they'd run out of runway before they . . .

He became aware that they were rising as he caught sight of the gleaming sun's edge, still visible from their increased height. Releasing the breath he hadn't known he was holding, he looked over the tops of hangars and The Roost, the fuel pumps and the aircraft and a small herd of pronghorn antelope grazing near the Border Patrol training area behind the airport.

Soon, the tops of the greenhouses of the huge hydroponics farm came into view, immense, dark rectangles that hid a jungle of tomato vines, with plump, red-orange fruits. Rachel tapped him before pointing to a spot across the highway and down a long, dirt road, where he spotted his old candelilla factory-home, its outbuildings like miniatures, the corral. He could even make out the figures of his mule and horses, living lives as far removed as the citizens of humming insect kingdoms.

His stomach rose, then dropped at the whim of unseen breezes.

"Sorry it's a little bumpy," she said, loudly enough to be heard above the engine. "We'll get to smoother air in just a minute."

As the plane gained altitude, they leveled out, and Zeke relaxed enough to look to the south, at the buildings and the lights of Marfa, so small and tenuous against the high plain. The land was wrinkled with a surprising number of undulations and bordered by the brown and violet shapes of mountains—Mount Livermore in the Davis Mountains to the north, the Chisos Mountains to the southeast, and the low line of the Chinati range to the southwest.

For the first time, he appreciated the vastness of the land he'd chosen as a hiding place so many years before—and the rugged loneliness with which he had surrounded himself. Only the most fragile, necessary bonds existed between himself and other people, only a few of whom had ever used his name.

And he'd been happy with his life, or at least resigned until the woman sitting next to him, piloting this plane so ably, had walked into his life seeking the same escape that he had.

"Look at that," she said.

The sun had finally given up its fight and was sinking in a blaze of glory that painted a cloud on the horizon in vibrant plums and scarlet.

"Gorgeous, isn't it?" she asked. "Kind of makes you forget all the people, all the tough times—everything that's come before this. Up here, we can leave it all behind us, leave all the reasons two people like us could never . . ."

The engine noise drowned out the rest of her words, but Zeke didn't want to hear them. Didn't want to dwell on impossibilities.

"So what do you think?" she asked him.

Because he couldn't find words, he found her hand and squeezed it. She flashed a smile his way, comprehension lighting her eyes.

Before them, the first, bright stars put in an appearance, heralding a vast darkness that would overtake them all too soon. But he couldn't let that happen without trying to find answers. Couldn't let her distract him from her pain with simple beauty.

"So what else did that lawyer tell you?" he asked, over the rumble of the engine. Swiftly, before he lost his nerve. He pressed on, acting more on hunch than reason. "Was there something else you wanted to tell me about those pictures?"

There was no answer save the droning buzz of the engine and the spreading darkness. Rachel kept her attention fastened to the dials and controls, the dimming land below them—everywhere but on him.

"How 'bout we circle town, then head back?" she asked before turning southward.

"You're not going to scare me off," he said. "Whatever it is, I'm not bailing on you."

"Good plan, considering our altitude." The smile she shot his way looked haunted.

"Don't you understand?" he blurted out. "It doesn't matter to me that you killed some son of a bitch who had it coming. It doesn't matter if you're sued for all the money in the world. It doesn't even matter to me, Rachel, that I've got no business falling for a woman. Just that I have."

She wheeled the plane back toward the airport so abruptly that his stomach lurched.

"I *have*," he repeated, feeling reckless with emotion, for

finally, he understood that being with Rachel had shattered his contentment with living a half-life in safety. He wanted more, much more, and he wanted at least a shot at it with Rachel.

Even if he knew that hope would burn to cinders within seconds, once he told her who—or *what*—he was. As he must, no matter how much it cost him.

"You can't possibly mean that." Rachel's voice was muffled by the buzzing. "*I* can't—not with . . . This is crazy. We hardly know each—"

"I know enough."

"You don't know."

"So *tell* me, Rachel."

As he waited for her answer, he saw more stars, by the hundreds. He felt strange hurtling through space just beneath them, disconnected from the reality below. Or from his better judgment. As the seconds ticked away, doubt crept in, then regret.

"See that lighted runway? We'll be landing in a moment."

"Rachel . . ." Maybe he should let it go, allow her to pretend that what he'd said didn't matter, that words spoken in the air were weightless, unimportant. That *he* was.

"So what did you think about your first flight?"

"Thought I was going to like it." Bitterness crept into his voice. "But it didn't turn out that way."

"Zeke, I'm—I'm sorry. What the—" By the light of the instruments' glow, he saw her pointing at the airport, where something outside the glider hangar was ablaze.

"It's your van," he shouted, "It's burning."

"Just *wonderful*," growled Rachel. "The cherry on the icing on a real crap-cake of a day."

CHAPTER
TWENTY-THREE

Only the worm of conscience consorts with the owl. Sinners and evil spirits shun the light.
> —*Johann Christoph Friedrich von Schiller,*
> Intrigue and Love, *V, I*

Distracted during her initial approach, Rachel brought the plane around and made a second attempt at landing. Zeke was relieved when she brought them to a safe stop on the runway.

He warned, "I know you're upset—*I'm* upset. But let me check this out first, make sure it's safe—"

"That's my van somebody's lit up—"

"Somebody who would probably rather burn *you*," Zeke reminded her.

Without waiting for an answer, he unstrapped himself and jumped out of the plane, then lit out in the direction of the vehicle. It was totally engulfed, its dark bulk disappearing inside the twisting, roaring monster of a conflagration. He hoped like hell that the arsonist was still close—and that it wouldn't be Rachel's female caller. Because he couldn't strike a woman—any woman, for any reason—and he badly wanted to cram some asshole's teeth down his throat.

Zeke stopped short, pressed back by blistering heat. *It could have been an accident,* he realized, *some electrical malfunction.* But quickly, he dismissed the thought. There had been too many "accidents" in Rachel's life—including the one that had killed her grandmother.

The flames were shooting twenty feet or more above his

head and lighting the night sky by the time Rachel ran up beside him, a fire extinguisher in her hands.

"Oh, hell." Gazing upward at the flames, she panted out her despair. "This won't be any use."

There was a popping noise from Rachel's van, followed by a hissing sizzle. Jumping back, she tugged at his arm. "Move back, Zeke. We'll get burned here. And the smoke—"

He retreated until they coughed their lungs clear in the cooler, cleaner air. Then he looked hopelessly around the airport. Though he'd already concluded that whoever had torched the van was long gone, he spotted no help, either. As it often was this time of day, the tiny airport was abandoned.

While he cursed in frustration, Rachel was pulling her cell phone from a pocket in her jeans. "I'll call for—oh."

Following her gaze, he spotted the flashing red lights coming their way. Someone passing by must have spotted the flames and called the fire department.

A Presidio County deputy, the jowly, middle-aged Leo Varajas, was first to arrive. The moment he spotted the two of them, he peered unhappily through his wire-rimmed glasses. "You again. I should've known. You both all right?"

When they assured him they were unhurt, he listened to their brief explanation of how they had spotted the fire from the air. With a nod of understanding, he said, "Sheriff Castillo'll have my hide if I don't call him out to investigate this personally."

The deputy folded his thick frame back into his SUV to make the call.

A half hour later, Zeke was with Rachel in her father's office, where Harlan Castillo plied them with questions as he sat behind Walter's desk. The door stood partly open, allowing Zeke to see the volunteer firefighters hanging around the puddle that surrounded the smoldering wreckage. One hawked and spat to clear his head and another nodded approval at the job they'd done, while a third had the fervent look of a man praying for one final flare-up to extinguish.

Castillo reached up with one short arm to scratch at a five o'clock shadow flecked with silver. His hat sat on the desk between them, where he'd laid it when they came inside. "So you're sure you saw no one? What about before you took off?"

Rachel shook her head. "No. Like I told you, I was the only one around before Zeke pulled up. And we didn't see another soul. Not before. Not after."

The sheriff's mouth thinned, and he darted a speculative look in Zeke's direction. "So what brought you here to see her? I know you eat at The Roost most days, but you're always home by this time, aren't you?"

Zeke's heart stumbled as he heard something in the question, some discordant note warning him that for the first time in all these years, he'd captured the interest of local law enforcement. "Rachel's dad asked me to keep an eye on her. Since I live so close by."

Castillo glanced in the direction of Zeke's place. "You've got power back there, don't you? I know I've seen a line of poles leading down your road."

"I have electricity." Zeke shrugged an answer. "Man's gotta keep a cold fridge for his longnecks. But what the hell does that have to do with whoever set this fire?"

Castillo shook his head. "Just satisfying my curiosity, that's all. You don't get the Internet, do you?"

Rachel gave the sheriff a puzzled look. "What's the point of this, Harlan? You think Zeke's been ordering remote-control incendiary devices off the Web? He didn't start that fire. He was with me, in the air."

Not daring to move a muscle, Zeke kept his eyes on the lawman's steady, blue gaze. "I care about Rachel. And I'd like to consider myself a family friend."

From the corner of his eye, he saw Rachel nodding, a simple, affirming gesture that filled him with gratitude.

But Castillo didn't back down. "Kinda interesting," he said in a phony-casual manner that set off all sorts of alarms, "you being so—I guess you could call it standoffish—before Ms. Copeland came back to town. Not at all neighborly, 'til now. . . ."

Zeke shrugged, though his pulse was pounding like a snared jackrabbit's. "So it's a crime in Presidio County to meet a pretty woman, take a little interest?" As much trouble as Castillo supposedly had keeping his zipper up, he ought to understand that.

Harlan smiled. " 'Course not, Mr. Pike. But it just seems odd, that's all. Especially in light of Ms. Copeland's recent troubles. And certain pictures that were—"

Rachel rocketed off her chair. "If you're too inept to find whoever set that fire, say so. But don't you dare bring up that garbage and sit here insinuating the one man in this town who's been there for me—"

"Pike *has* been there, hasn't he? When your glider crashed. When your grandma got killed. When you saw the fire—"

"I don't own either a phone or a computer," Zeke said flatly as he rose to loom above the sheriff. "Don't have the Internet to look at anything, including naked women. And I might not be the friendliest man in this town, but I'm sure as hell not twisted enough to set up disasters so I can 'rescue' my fair lady. You got that, Castillo? Because if you don't, you're gonna damned well find out how un-neighborly I can be."

The sheriff's hand had drifted to his sidearm, but his voice was cool, collected. "That a threat, Pike?"

"Zeke," warned Rachel.

Zeke's teeth hurt, he was clenching his jaws so hard. Finally, he backed off, saying, "Hell, no. It's not a threat." *A promise, maybe.*

Castillo relaxed his posture, but his eyes were full of caution. Turning from him—and from Rachel—Zeke stalked out into the cool night air.

Because after all these years, he felt the fabric of his second life give way, heard its fine threads popping like the seams of an old parachute. At any moment, his safety would collapse completely, plunging him straight down into blackness.

His instinct was to flee, to go back for his truck and vanish on some dark, lonesome highway before it was too late.

"Do you mind telling me what that was about?" Rachel demanded of the sheriff. "Did Patsy put you up to it?"

"Patsy? Why would she—" Castillo straightened, his expression sharpening. "Guess she knows the man about as well as anybody. So she doesn't approve of the two of you together?"

"She hasn't talked to you, then?"

"Not any more than she can help," he said, reminding Rachel of what the man had let slip earlier, something that clearly referenced his own guilt and Patsy's unrelenting anger. "My ex-wife and I—we stay out of each other's way as much as we can. Easier for both of us not to open up that old can of worms."

Rachel wanted to ask but didn't, since she had no doubt he'd shut down her questions as he had before. Instead, she peered through the door, but she couldn't spot Zeke out there. Had he been upset enough to try to walk home in the pitch black without a light?

She returned her attention to the sheriff. "Patsy's fine with Zeke now. You can ask her yourself as soon as she gets over here. When I called Dad, he told me she stayed home this evening with a migraine, but he's picking her up on his way back from Alpine."

Rachel had hated calling to tell her father about the fire. Over the past year—nearly a year and a half now—she'd done nothing but heap disaster onto his and Patsy's lives. Worry and expense, in equal measure. Grief and guilt punched through Rachel's center, along with the bone-deep knowledge that Benita Copeland would still be living if her granddaughter had remained in Philadelphia.

Rachel was on the verge of inquiring whether he was

certain that the chocolate hadn't been poisoned, whether it wasn't possible that the glider she'd gone down in hadn't been tampered with as well. But before she could, Castillo blindsided her with the last thing she expected.

"His name isn't Zeke Pike."

"What?"

"Or Ezekiel Pike or Zachariah, Zachary, or anything else I can figure."

Rachel frowned, confused. "Have you asked him about it? Maybe it's his middle name."

"He doesn't have a valid driver's license."

"Really?" Rachel asked, her mind scrambling for purchase. Had Zeke lied to her, to everyone? Had she been wrong about him as she'd been wrong about Kyle? *He's no damned Kyle,* her instincts whispered. "Maybe he just couldn't deal with going to the courthouse, being around a lot of people. He's a good man, one-on-one or around a few people if he knows them. But any more than that and . . ."

She thought of his reaction to the business her photo had sent him and added, a little desperately, "He's just a loner, that's all. Shy or something. But there's no harm in him."

"He ever mention where he lived before here? Who his people are or where he's from?"

Rachel blew out a frustrated sigh. "You're wasting your time. My time. Zeke Pike wasn't driving the SUV that tried to hit us in the desert, and he's certainly not the *woman* who's been calling me, harassing and threatening me for months and months before I ever met him. That woman— Kyle Underwood's mother—has sicced her lawyers on me with an enormous wrongful death suit. She's not letting this go, Sheriff. She won't drop it until she completely breaks me. Or, who knows? Maybe it's killing me she's after."

"I agree." He nodded. "The woman's unhinged. But as disagreeable and unfair as the lawsuit is, she's working through legal channels. And legal channels only."

"I don't—what do you mean?"

"I mean—" Castillo's gaze bored into her "—her daughter swears that Sylvia Underwood hasn't set foot outside of Pennsylvania since the night her son was killed."

CHAPTER
TWENTY-FOUR

*He discovereth deep things out of darkness, and bringeth out
to light the shadow of death.*
> —The Holy Bible *(King James Version)*,
> Job 12:22

In the darkness near the telescope, the observer crouched
with nostrils flared to capture the acrid reek of ash and smoke,
the pungency of gas fumes. Eyes closed and concentration focused on the burning imprinted behind the lids: the guttering
flare of lights more mundane, more physical than those that
spoke their secret tongue in coldly quiet pulses. Silhouetted
in remembered flame, the dark shape of a great owl flapped
silent wings. Tucking them in suddenly, it streaked down toward some unfortunate, small creature driven from its hidey-
hole by heat.

Some contemptible, weak creature that was carried limp
and bleeding to a nest of sticks atop The Roost. A creature
that was torn to gory ribbons and fed to a new-hatched pair
of owlets quite tenderly, with a mother's love.

Patsy showed up by herself. As she stared at the smoking
hulk so close to her café, she looked so pale, so ill, that Zeke
walked over from where he'd been waiting for Rachel in
the shadow of a hangar. He passed the three firefighters,
who stood by the side of their truck talking. None so much
as glanced in his direction, and Castillo's deputy had left to
handle a call on the other side of Marfa.

"Rachel's not hurt, only upset. Mostly pissed, but she'll

be all right," Zeke reassured Patsy. "Sheriff Castillo's talking to her in Walter's office."

He said this by way of warning, to give Patsy time to brace herself before facing her former husband. All these years, and she still had trouble with it, Zeke knew. Some serious bad blood there. Miss Teen West Texas bad blood, he surmised, and because he valued Patsy's undemanding friendship, he knew a moment's satisfaction that the beauty queen in question had blown up to the size of a parade float in the years since Harlan Castillo had made an honest woman of her. Had a nasty disposition, too, according to the old man who occasionally cut Zeke's hair.

Without taking her eyes off the destruction, Patsy blew out a deep breath and ran the end of her thin and graying ponytail between her fingers. It looked especially forlorn tonight, and her jeans and loose sweatshirt appeared to have been slept in. "I appreciate the heads-up. You all right?"

"Better off than that van." He glowered at what was left of it before asking, "So where's Walter? Rachel told me you'd be coming with him."

"He'll be along. Had to stop for gas in Alpine, but he thought one of us should get out here pretty quick. Would've made it sooner, except I wasn't dressed."

"I heard you had a migraine." In sympathy, he touched a spot beneath his own forelock. "Any better?"

The flashing of the remaining fire truck's light lit the deepening folds of her frown. "It's some new headache every day with that girl. Least now, she can buy herself another ride."

"So she has insurance?" he asked.

Patsy's laugh was mirthless. "Against fire, on that heap? I can't imagine. But she'll have some money from her grandmother. More'n any of us guessed."

Though he'd spent a lot of time around the Copelands lately, Zeke was surprised to hear of it. "I imagine," he said carefully, "that would be a help. With all the lawyer bills, too."

Patsy nodded. "Rachel told us right off, she's paying back everything we spent. Insisted on it, though it won't leave much for her. Walter argued, of course without consulting me, but Rachel's not taking no for an answer."

Zeke heard a measure of approval in Patsy's voice. Relief, too, that the business she had spent her adult life building would escape the expanding mushroom cloud of legal fees.

"Doesn't surprise me," he said. "It's been eating at Rachel, owing both of you, not having any way to fix things. And she told me tonight that lawsuit against her could end up getting dropped."

Patsy turned her face from him, but not before he glimpsed her troubled expression. "She told you all about that, did she?"

No, Zeke thought, Rachel hadn't. He was certain she'd been holding something back, something that had upset her more than either her debt or the threat of a ten-million-dollar civil suit. *Let her have her secrets,* he told himself. *It's not as if you're going to be around to help her deal with any of them.* Because he had to find a way out of the county before the sheriff's facts caught up with his suspicions and he learned that Rachel Copeland wasn't the only person in this county who had once been charged with murder.

But instead of admitting Rachel hadn't trusted him with whatever was upsetting her, Zeke answered Patsy's question with a noncommittal sound. Because he couldn't help wishing she would misinterpret his response and fill him in on a matter he no longer had any business knowing.

As he'd hoped, Patsy went on talking, growling, "Perverted little bastard ought to be dug up from his grave and shot and killed all over." Heat scorched the edges of her words. "Walter would for damned sure like to do it. And so would I, for all the grief and money this has cost us."

"I don't under—" he began.

"Even if that woman drops the lawsuits, this is a hell of a long way from over. Walt's so furious, he wants to go after that kid's piddly little estate for what he calls 'justice.' Rachel'll need more counseling, if she'll have it. And she'll stay just where she likes—at the center of her father's universe."

"I don't think Rachel wants—"

Patsy threw up her hands. "Of course she wants Walter's attention. He's the only real parent she has left."

Zeke heard the longing, the frustration in her voice, and it reminded him that even in a family, people could feel isolated. Even in a crowd, they could stand apart. Maybe that was what had started her talking to him at the café, one lone soul to another.

"It was hard enough when Rachel was back in Philadelphia," Patsy told him. "Now she's right here, with all her troubles, and I might as well have turned invisible. Because how do I compete with a girl who trails disasters in her damned wake? And now it turns out she was raped—"

"Raped?" Zeke echoed. "Rachel was—that son of a bitch *raped* Rachel?"

Patsy glared at him, said flatly. "She didn't tell you."

"Hell, no. And you're talking like she's done all of this on purpose just to mess up your life. That's a hell of an attitude to take about your own—"

"That's just it. Rachel *isn't* my own," Patsy shot back. "From the first day I came home with Walter, that girl's let me know in a hundred ways that she never will be. If she were mine—if I hadn't had my chance to have my own child stolen . . ."

Eyes welling, overflowing, Patsy couldn't go on. She fought her tears, and he saw rage submerged within the pain of it, a stinging scorpion forever trapped in amber.

It filled Zeke with a sickening suspicion. A suspicion about a woman who had served as his fragile lifeline for fourteen years. Could Patsy want Rachel gone from here so badly she would—

No. Hell, no. He couldn't hold the thought in his brain. Couldn't imagine that this woman—a woman who'd shown clear concern for Rachel's safety—would allow jealousy and resentment to drive her to violence.

But as much as he loathed asking her about it, as many questions as he had cascading through his brain about Rachel's rape—*Had she been ashamed to tell him? Had she kept it secret from her family, too?*—he had to push Patsy for more details, for Rachel's sake, at least. Because he couldn't leave her with a stalker on her tail, couldn't leave Marfa without knowing for certain if her own stepmother could possibly . . . "What did you mean, about your chance to have your own kid being *stolen*?"

Did she blame Rachel, somehow? Had Walter refused Patsy's request to have a baby, for his daughter's sake? Zeke wasn't good at judging women's ages, but it seemed likely that Patsy had been young enough to become pregnant when they'd first married.

"That bastard, Harlan . . ." Patsy started.

"*Harlan?* What did he do?"

"Anything that moved," she answered flatly. "Got me sick with his whoring—literally, I mean. Prostitutes. Gave me some filthy infection that scarred me up so bad inside, he stole my chance from me. But not his own—God's joke on me, that. After ruining me, the son of a bitch marries some younger woman and parades around those sons of theirs like trophies."

"Oh, Patsy. I'm sorry." He shook his head at the unfairness of it. No wonder she hated Harlan. But what about Rachel? Did Patsy despise her, too, for serving as a reminder of the one thing she wanted but could never have?

Patsy shook her head. "Harlan's sorry, too, damned guilty, for all the good that does me. Bastard."

Before Zeke's eyes, she reassembled her protective armor, rebuilt from scratch the broad, implacable face he'd known for so long.

"It's a long time back. More than twenty years ago. And there's no help for it. Now or then. Stupid of me to keep thinking on it, all these years later. You must think I'm some kind of monster, fussing about Rachel when she's the closest thing to a daughter I'm ever going to have. I do—I love the girl, in my way, the best that I know how."

Zeke weighed her words, then nodded slowly. "I believe it."

Patsy looked at the ground. "Sometimes I think maybe God knew what he was doing, turning a woman like me barren. Maybe I got no better than I had coming—"

He winced at the self-loathing he heard in her voice. "I don't believe it works that way. And I don't think you're any monster. It's just that sometimes, the present bumps up against the past. Knocks a few dirt layers off a grief we thought was dead and buried. It's happened to me more than once, just since Rachel's shown up. Before she came— I thought I was through remembering. Would've liked it better, maybe, if I had been."

"So you wish she'd never come home . . . Wish you'd listened when I warned you."

He shook his head. "I would never wish that. Because I was wrong to think I could just walk away from my past, wrong to think it wouldn't make a difference."

It had ruined everything, had left him with a blighted, withered remnant of a life. He glimpsed what he'd lost each time he was with Rachel. That possibility, that glimmer, had smashed open a locked corner of himself when they'd made love. But since he couldn't find the words to explain such a thing to Patsy, he said, "And because I love her. I love Rachel just like you do, the best that I know how." He felt beaten down by the knowledge that he couldn't stick around to help her through whatever memories she'd hidden, that he couldn't even stay to keep her safe.

As worried as he still was about the stalker, he'd at least dismissed the idea that Patsy, of all people, could have any involvement in Rachel's recent problems. Her stepdaughter's arrival might have stirred up feelings that reminded Patsy of old heartbreak, but the woman he'd known all these years would do her duty toward a family member. Maybe not cheerfully, but she would manage, for Walter's sake if not her own.

"You love her?" Patsy whispered. "I've see a lot of women throw themselves in your direction. Heck, I've nearly had to hose down Lili to keep her off you in the café."

He snorted, shaking his head at the thought of Lili, with her transparent words and gestures. If she had been a filly, she'd have lifted her tail beneath his nose. "I don't encourage little girls."

"Or anyone else I've ever seen. Until Walter's daughter walked in The Roost that first day."

He shrugged. "Nothing'll come of it. Rachel knows that."

"Does she? I've told her as much, but—"

"She said you'd warned her off me."

Patsy shrugged. "I like you well enough, but you're a man with 'life-long bachelor' stamped all over you."

Accepting the explanation—since he would have sworn to it himself even a few days earlier—Zeke nodded and asked her point-blank, "When did Rachel tell you she'd been assaulted?"

"Day after the funeral. That was the day she found out."

"Found out? I don't get it. How could she not know?"

Patsy scowled. "There's some kind of knock-out drops or pills—date-rape drugs, they call 'em. These perverts dissolve 'em into women's drinks. The thinking is that Kyle slipped her something and then took advantage later, after the rest of her students headed home. Some private investigators found pictures, different pictures that were really all her. Rachel looked unconscious in 'em—got some high-dollar experts lined up who'll swear to it in court. And it explains a lot of things that—I hate to admit this—made me wonder, why witnesses said she was acting wild that one night in public, why she says she can't remember."

"Son of a bitch." Fury burned in him like a live coal, igniting primitive instincts he'd swear he didn't possess. Archaic impulses to ride forth and wreak havoc, to avenge the woman his heart had no more sense than to claim. With the culprit dead, Zeke didn't know where to direct his anger.

So it was no surprise that some of it slopped over onto Patsy. "What do you mean she *says* she can't remember? If she'd known before, wouldn't she have told somebody? God, Patsy, they took her to that jail in Philadelphia and booked her, didn't they? Took her prints, strip-searched her—you think she would've put up with that ugliness if she'd had any idea of what went on?"

"No need to chew my liver out," Patsy snapped. "I didn't mean it that way. I know she's been getting messages from the psychologist for weeks, but she didn't ever call back that I know of. And I can't say I blame her. Who'd want to face such a thing? Easier to keep what's past out of sight if you can."

Zeke started, suddenly wondering if she had guessed something about him, if she'd known all along. Before he could think of a response, a truck's door closed behind him.

Patsy's gaze darted to look toward the arrival. Lowering her voice, she said, "That's Walter, and about time. I'd better go see to him. Then we'll talk to Rachel. Harlan, too, I guess."

Zeke was surprised when she handed him her keys.

"I see you don't have your truck here, so why don't you take my car back to your place. It's too dark to walk back there, and it's getting chilly. I could have Walter drop me by to pick it up on our way home."

Though there was logic in her suggestion, Zeke hesitated, caught between his desire to see Rachel and yet another reason to hurry home and pack to drive south, to the border.

CHAPTER
TWENTY-FIVE

Sometimes our light goes out but is blown into flame by another human being. Each of us owes deepest thanks to those who have rekindled this light.

—*Albert Schweitzer*

"I need to see him, Dad. Please." Standing beside his pickup, Rachel looked into her father's eyes. As upset and exhausted as she was after Harlan Castillo's questions, she couldn't go home quite yet. Couldn't leave without an explanation from Zeke Pike.

Or whoever the hell he was.

But her father, freshly filled in on the sheriff's suspicions, shook his head. "You're coming home now, Rusty. With us, where you'll be safe."

The fire truck pulled out onto the highway, leaving only Castillo's car and the deputy's parked beside her father's pickup. The two lawmen talked in quiet voices, standing vigil over the dripping, blackened hulk of the burned van. Twisted by the blaze, its original, boxlike shape was barely distinguishable.

Patsy touched Rachel's shoulder. "You heard what Harlan said. He's looking into the possibility that Zeke's somehow involved in the things that have happened since you've come home. And you have to understand that we're—your father's worried."

Rachel shrugged away from her. "He's your friend, isn't he? You've known Zeke for years, right? And in all that time, has he ever *once* caused anybody trouble?"

"Nobody but Mitch Whiteside about six years ago, when

he was beating the hell out of that half-starved yearling colt of his. Took a beating of his own the day Zeke caught him at it. Later on, Mitch groused around that Zeke went and stole that horse from him."

"So what really happened?"

Patsy shook her head. "Not sure."

"I heard that story," Walter said. "The deputy sent out to Zeke's place to investigate found him treating the horse's wounds—had all these cuts where he'd been whipped half to death with a leather strap or switch or something. Colt was a walking skeleton, so nervous you could hardly get near him."

"Poor Cholla," Rachel whispered, recalling the old scars she had noticed against the huge animal's now-gleaming, golden hide. "It must've been Cholla."

"Harlan himself came out to have a look, too," her father continued. "The way I heard it, after that, he had a talk with Whiteside, told the man to keep his sorry mouth shut or he'd be charged with every offense the sheriff and his boys could dream up. Whiteside moved on not long after, and that was the last anybody mentioned it."

"Have you seen that horse in the pasture?" she asked. "He's gorgeous. Strong and healthy and well fed. And Zeke has others on his place, too. A mule and this pinto mare somebody was starving. He saves them, Dad. He cares about them. And he cares about the work he's doing out there, making his furniture. He loves it the way I love taking pictures or you love flying planes." Her gaze swung to take in Patsy. "Or the way you love feeding people."

"Wouldn't exactly say I *love* it," Patsy murmured. "It's just something I can do."

"After what you've been through," her father said, "I don't see how you can trust a man who—hell, Rusty, you don't even know his right name."

"But I know *him*, Dad. I know him and . . . and I think I—"

"You're vulnerable now. That's understandable. But don't let it make you stupid. Let the sheriff do his job."

"We need to take her to Zeke, Walter," Patsy put in, an uncharacteristic gentleness in her voice. "I talked to him just this evening. Whoever—whatever—he is, he's no threat to Rachel. If I'd thought that, do you really believe I'd have loaned him my car?"

Her father stood beside the driver's side door, his hands jammed in his pockets, his expression doubtful. He looked old this evening, older than Rachel had ever seen him. In that moment, she wished she'd driven right past Marfa, wished she'd found some other place to start anew so as to spare him.

"If you drop me off at Zeke's place," she said, "then I can drive the car back to Grandma's."

Rachel still couldn't think of it as her house, filled as it was with Benita Copeland's belongings, with the essence of the woman she had loved so easily and naturally.

"I'll call you once I'm home safe, promise."

As her father rattled his keys, the look he shot her was suspicious. "You really want to go to him? To a man who could be anybody? Could be *anything*? After everything that happened with that little pervert and somebody burning your van and—"

"Hand over those keys, Walter Copeland, and settle yourself down," Patsy interrupted. "Rachel's thirty-two years old, and you're always the one telling me what good sense she has. So trust her on this. Trust her."

Bristling, he straightened. "It's not Rachel I don't trust."

"He loves her," Patsy told her husband, her voice solemn, or perhaps only astonished.

Rachel felt the words jolt through her, felt the desert night shift into a new reality. Breath held, she offered nothing, but simply ached for Patsy to offer a crumb more.

"He's in love with her. He said that." Turning to Rachel, Patsy frowned. "From the look on your face, he hasn't told you. And as tight-lipped as he is, he might never. But I promise you, Rachel, when a man like Zeke Pike parts with words, he means them. He wouldn't waste his breath lying to me or anybody."

Rachel smiled at her, understanding that they both knew the same man. And recognizing that by standing up for her against her father, by spilling this measure of truth like salt across the table, Patsy had offered her an olive branch of sorts. Fragile and tentative, but Rachel still recognized it for the chance that it was.

"Thank you," she said quietly, looking her stepmother in the eye and seeing someone she hadn't glimpsed before. Someone who had been as afraid of Rachel as Rachel herself had been over the unexpected—and unwelcome—surprise of her father's marriage, what she'd seen as his unholy rush to fill her mother's place.

Perhaps her father, too, saw what passed between them, for instead of arguing any further, he looked down at Patsy's outstretched palm. "Guess I've lost this argument," he grumbled and dropped his keys into her hand. "Just call when you get home safely. Call me, no matter what time of night it is."

When he heard the crunch of tires on gravel, Zeke was grabbing clothes, packing for a journey he should have taken years before. He'd been a damned fool, sinking such deep roots into this dry land. A fool to take on livestock and a bigger one to get involved with, even attached to, people.

He cursed, hearing a vehicle's door slam, fearing that his chance to flee had just evaporated, that whatever the interruption, he'd be a sitting duck when the other shoe dropped. As it must, and soon, for he hadn't bothered constructing the kind of identity that would hold up to law enforcement scrutiny. Hadn't bothered because some dark part of him had wanted to be caught.

Caught and punished. Tried, convicted—whatever it took to bring the truth of things to light. Because even if the guilty (or the *other* guilty parties, he amended) were never brought to justice, he would still have his chance to say in open court what had really happened the night Willie Tyler died for less than nothing.

But over the course of twenty long years, Zeke hadn't done a single thing to make it happen, had not been able to, for fear of shattering a heart too fragile to withstand his gamble.

Never try to come back, his mother had written . . . *I can't live through it again.* . . .

Couldn't live through the grief and humiliation of losing Zeke in the same way she'd lost his father. In his mind's eye, Zeke could see her as she had been, pushing him toward the door and begging him: *"Just run."*

Instead, he stepped out into the thin light of the newly risen moon, where he met Rachel as she climbed down from her father's pickup. Behind the wheel, Patsy nodded at him while Walter's expression hardened. Maybe he hadn't approved of his wife's loan of her auto. Or more likely, Zeke decided, Castillo had been talking, warning his ex-wife and her second husband about the nature of his suspicions.

But Zeke's focus was on Rachel, who stood just outside of the rectangle of light spilling from his open doorway. Rachel, who'd defended him against the sheriff's insinuations, though she was still reeling from the revelation that she'd been sexually assaulted.

And just that quickly, he knew damned well that he was going nowhere. That he was no longer the kind of person capable of abandoning the animals he cared for, of running off without a word to Rachel Copeland.

"Did you come to get the car?" he asked over the rumble of the pickup's engine.

As he pulled out Patsy's keys, Rachel reached forward. But instead of taking them, she merely laid her hand atop his. "I came to talk. Then I'll drive myself home."

Nodding his understanding, Zeke thanked Patsy for saving him a dark walk home and wished both her and Walter a good night.

"I'll be checking on her," Walter warned from the passenger seat. "And if she's not right as rain, you and I are going to have ourselves a lot of trouble."

"Da-ad," Rachel complained, sounding so like an aggrieved teenager, Zeke might have smiled under other circumstances.

After passing her the keys, Zeke stepped closer to the truck and nodded. "I'd expect as much."

He reached through the window with an offer of his right hand. Walter looked at it suspiciously, but at last he grimaced and returned the handshake.

"You have my word," Zeke promised as his grip tightened. "Right as rain."

Once Patsy and Walter drove away, Zeke said, "I ever tell you that I like your father just fine? Doesn't waste a lot of time on games. Doesn't try to hide the way he's thinking."

"It's pretty embarrassing at times," Rachel admitted with a tight smile. "But I wouldn't have him any other way."

Zeke hesitated, wanting to invite her inside where he could light a fire in the woodstove but dreading the moment when she saw the suitcase he'd left partly packed. From the corral, he heard a horse's nicker. From the dark heart of the desert, a night bird cried out, while close at hand, the Chevy's engine ticked as it cooled. Rachel, for her part, merely stood there looking at him, as if they had all the time in the world.

Because it was bothering him, not knowing whether she'd come out here to support him or accuse him, he finally forced himself to ask, "So, do you think the sheriff's going to find who set that fire—or do you think he's wasted all his time suspecting the wrong person?"

Above Rachel's head, a shooting star formed a bright flash, which quickly faded. She crossed her arms and tucked her hands beneath them. "Are we going to have to stand out here all night, freezing? Because I'd rather talk indoors."

"Come on in." Resigned, Zeke ushered her inside the kitchen. "Want me to make some coffee first or get the heat going?"

"Heat," she told him. "I can start some coffee."

They both worked in silence, Zeke kindling a good fire.

While Rachel rummaged around to find what she needed in the kitchen, he furtively shoved the still-open suitcase beneath his bed. Relief washed over him at the thought that he'd gotten away with it, but when he turned around, he saw her watching.

"Going someplace?" Her voice was like a shaft of ice, her expression suddenly as suspicious as her father's.

"Thought I might. Then it occurred to me there's no place else I want to be."

"Harlan has you nervous," she ventured, stalking toward him from the kitchen.

Nodding, he admitted, "Yes. He damned well does."

"Nervous enough to make a run for it without your horses?"

"I couldn't do it," he said. "You know I'm no animal abuser."

She took a step closer, invading his space. Pushing. "Then what are you? Or maybe the right question is *who* are you? Because I know you're not Zeke Pike."

There it was, he realized as pain pulsed at his temples. The very thing he'd spent so many years imagining and dreading. Reality, not nightmare, the cold, hard fact of it so overwhelming he could scarcely stay on his feet.

"I've been him longer than I've been anybody else," Zeke managed. "I'm not sure I'd know how to go back at this point."

"Go back to what? To where?" she challenged.

He returned her stare, not daring to blink, scarcely daring to breathe, as if the knowledge were trapped inside his lungs like stale air. He wanted fiercely to exhale, wanted to talk to her as he had talked to no one. But held too long, the secret had burrowed into him like some thorny horror, its barbed tendrils embedded too close to his heart.

A hiss and crackle marked the progress of the fire he had started. He felt its first heat and smelled its burning wood scraps. From the kitchen, his ancient coffeemaker burbled, and every detail of that moment branded itself in his memory.

Because these were the final moments, he suspected, the last, doomed seconds before she turned her back on him forever.

Rachel stood her ground and waited, her gaze expectant, unrelenting. Until the moment she surprised him by reaching up to run her fingertips along his stubbled jaw.

"Whatever it is," she said, "we'll handle it together."

He shook his head. "Not this."

"What are you running from?"

The veiled whisper of her voice cast a spell, igniting his nerve endings. When he shuddered, it was not with cold but the connection that shimmered in the air between them. That and the pressure of so many words unspoken.

Time now for that to change. Time now to trust somebody, even if it turned out to be the biggest mistake of his life. Because the pain of doing otherwise was too great. Because he didn't know if such a chance would ever come to him again.

"Twenty years ago, I was just a dumb kid. Thought I knew how the world worked, but at eighteen I . . ."

When he choked up, she flashed the briefest of smiles, encouraging him.

He took a step on shaking knees, then sat on the edge of his bed. Because he couldn't say this standing up.

"All I wanted was to run with the kids who wouldn't have me. The ones with the easy money and the fast cars. The ones whose fathers hadn't gone to prison."

She sat down beside him and laid her hand on his knee. He felt the warmth of her palm through the denim, the flow of her compassion. He drew strength from it to go on. "His only real crime was daring to speak up about some county inspectors who had a habit of extorting money from local businesses. Turned out that some of it was being funneled into the hands of law enforcement—so before my dad knew what hit him, our family's restaurant burned to the ground and he was charged, convicted, and locked up for arson. You wouldn't have believed how fast, and as for getting a fair trial . . ."

Old emotion roiled inside Zeke: resentment, grief, raw fury. And shame, too, that he had been powerless to do anything to help. "My dad didn't take it lying down, went on speaking out about it, writing state officials, even from prison. Until somebody—never heard who—knifed him in the shower. By that time, we couldn't even afford to give him a proper burial. Had to settle for an unmarked prison grave since the insurance wouldn't pay the restaurant claim and my mother had three boys to raise on her own."

"Is that why you took off?"

Zeke shook his head. "No. No, I was the oldest, and I had to help hold things together. We rebuilt the diner by hand, though this time it was more of a shack than a real restaurant. But at least Mom could sell beer and barbecue."

Remembering her struggle, he thought of Patsy running the little café all on her own for so long. Was that what had made The Roost feel so familiar?

"And I worked some odd jobs," he added, "to pay off those damned inspectors. I didn't want my mother to have to deal with the bastards, not after what they did to Dad."

She took his hand in hers. "You were a good son."

"No. I was a *stupid* son," he said bitterly, "because even after the lesson I'd had about what it meant to be a Langley in that town, I still believed the other guys—the guys from the right families—could be my friends."

"Langley," she echoed softly, trying out the name.

It felt strange hearing someone say it. Strange and oddly uplifting, for all the years he'd struggled to keep his legal identity hidden. The effect gave him the courage that he needed to continue.

"John Charles Langley," he told her, his own name breaking from him like a storm. It was the final barrier, one whose collapse presaged a reckless flood of memory. "One night I let those sons of bitches talk me into heisting beer out of the coolers in the barbecue shack. Afterward, we started drinking out near a place the locals call Bone Lake. I was showing off, acting like the big deal on account of how I'd been the one to provide the drinks for a change."

She squeezed his hand, encouraging, confessed, "I've made mistakes, too. . . ."

"I'd never really drunk much before that," Zeke went on. "Just enough to act like I was part of things. For one thing, I had responsibilities those guys didn't, you know? But the night I stole from my own family, I shotgunned one beer after another. Trying to get over feeling guilty—trying not to think about how we couldn't afford the loss or worry about how to say no the next time they got after me to do it. Still hurts like hell to think about how stupid—"

"You were just a kid," said Rachel. "Sure, you screwed up, but you can't mean to say you ran off for twenty years over something like that?"

He shook his head, wishing he could shake off the memories of that night. He remembered peering out through hooded eyes, watched an unresisting body being shaken. Face pale behind its mask of blood, one shoe untied and half off. "I—one of the jobs I had was looking after this kid named Willie Tyler."

"So you babysat?"

He frowned, then shook his head. "Willie was no baby. He was the same age as the rest of us, except he was a little slow. Well, more than a little, I suppose, but not so much that he wasn't desperate to try and fit in with the cool guys. The trouble was, he would do *anything* to be accepted."

Rachel winced.

"He was a nice kid, really, from a good family. They had a lot of money by East Texas standards."

"You're from East Texas?"

Zeke nodded and went on with his story. "The family had timber money from the old days, but they weren't assholes about it. Willie's folks heard how I stuck up for him when the jokes went too far and put a stop to it when some shit dared him to swim the length of the lake in January. So they came to me one day, told me they'd make it worth my while to be sure their boy didn't get himself into anything too serious."

"It doesn't surprise me. You don't tolerate abuse. Not toward animals or people."

"You're giving me way too much damned credit," Zeke growled, not only wanting but needing to snuff the admiration out of her eyes. "I was getting *paid* to watch out for him. And I did a piss-poor job of it that evening."

"That night? Do you mean he was with you? When you stole that beer and went out drinking?"

"When I got so *fucking* drunk I didn't pay a lick of attention to what he did." His eyes burned with self hatred. "To what any of them did—because I passed out face-first in my own damned vomit."

She blew out a long sigh. "I'm almost afraid to ask what happened."

He hung his head and squeezed his eyes shut, but now that they'd been resurrected, the ghosts of that night refused to go away. Ghosts of the sons of his hometown's movers and shakers, from Aaron Lynch, the high school team's star baseball pitcher, to Shane Drake, the junior class president, to Sam Henderson, the valedictorian and wrestling captain who had graduated a few short weeks earlier. And most especially the ghost of little Willie Tyler, with his goofy laugh and crooked teeth, the absolutely guileless way he'd asked, "You wanna be my buddy? Want to go to my house and see my baseball card collection? I'll let you pick your favorite. I'll give you any card you want if you'll come over."

There had been other bribes as well. An offer of his mother's brownies or the chance to peer through a secret peephole while one of Willie's sisters was changing her clothes. He'd made the same offer to anyone who'd listen, until all of his good cards were missing and there was hardly a senior in the class who hadn't seen the older—and more developed—of his two sisters naked. Marlene, Zeke remembered, had been the subject of a lot of fantasies.

"Willie ended up dead." His words came out a hoarse croak.

"You didn't—" Rachel's breathing rasped, audible above the final gurgles of the coffee. "You weren't so drunk you—?"

"I didn't kill him. I know that much. Or at least I wasn't the one who thought it would be funny to haul off and punch him in the face." Zeke still wasn't certain who had struck the fatal blow, only that when he had come to, head spinning, he had heard his three *friends'* panic as they'd realized Willie had stopped breathing and couldn't be revived.

"Oh, my God. So he died just like that, from a punch?"

Zeke nodded. "I don't think they meant to kill him. It was more like rough horseplay that got out of hand. But Willie was a little guy, maybe five-six and one twenty, and the punch that took him down—it must've hit him exactly wrong. Snapped his neck or made his brain bleed."

"Did anybody call for help? An ambulance, or—"

"Eventually. After the three of them hammered out their story. That was the part I heard when I came to."

Syllable for syllable, it replayed inside his head, an endless loop of *"My dad'll kill me"* and *"What about my scholarship?" "I get nailed for underage drinking again, and my folks are gonna damn sure sell my truck."*

Until finally, while the boy that Zeke had been had struggled to lift his face out of his own filth, had fought to see if there was something—anything—that could be done for Willie, one of them had said, *"Hey, I know what. Langley did it. Was Langley hit him so hard, it laid him out like that."*

They had scrambled onto the idea like drowning rats clawing their way onto a scrap of floating bark. Clinging tightly to how Zeke's dad had died in prison two years earlier, how Zeke himself had stolen from his own mom this very night. How no one expected much better from the Langleys, who lived in a peeling, tumbledown bungalow on the edge of the black part of town and associated with *that kind* far more than was considered healthy. Then of course the term *white trash* came up, and they started asking themselves why the cream of the town's crop, the kids with real futures, should go down over a one-in-a-million freak accident that had killed some little retard.

"Besides, if Langley hadn't got us beer, none of this would've happened in the first place."

Zeke told Rachel all he remembered, including how his own terror had sobered him up enough to make a run for home.

"And so it was your mother who pushed you into leaving," she said once he had recounted that last, heartbreaking conversation.

From the corner of his eye, Zeke caught the gleam of her tears. He wanted to tell her he didn't deserve them, but instead he nodded numbly, emotionally spent. "She gave me every cent she could scrape together and all but shoved me out the door. Because she already knew there would be no justice, that the way the wheels spun in that county, I'd end up in prison if I kept my mouth shut, and as dead as my old man if I didn't. And I wouldn't have—I couldn't. I would've run my mouth until it got me killed, like him."

"Twenty years ago . . ." she whispered.

"There's no statute of limitations on a charge of murder. And the last time I tried contacting my mom and sending money, she begged me not to come back—or to give them any way to find me. I still keep that letter, tucked inside one of my books. It's the only thing I have left. The only—"

"She loved you, Zeke. Loves you still, I'm sure."

He looked into Rachel's brown eyes. "She doesn't even know me. She only knows a boy who died that night, the same as Willie."

"It was a mistake, a tragedy. But you didn't kill him."

"Might as well have thrown the punch myself. I knew good and well the only reason those guys put up with Willie's presence was to make a fool of him. What I was too damned blind to see was that they hung with me for the same reason."

"Kids can be cruel sometimes. Cruel and selfish. But you can't blame yourself for that boy's death."

"I would think that, more than anybody, you would understand why I do. In spite of everything he did to you, you still blame yourself for Kyle's."

She stood abruptly and walked into the kitchen, where she rattled around a cupboard. Looking for mugs, he supposed.

"How do you take your coffee?" Over the sound of liquid pouring, she called to him, her voice as tightly strung as he felt.

"Rachel . . ." Rising, he wondered if he'd been wrong to bring up Kyle's name, especially after what Patsy had told him tonight.

She stared at him across the pass-through counter. "You know, too, don't you? I can hear it in your voice, see it in your eyes."

Instead of denying it, he nodded before going to where Rachel stood, her back now turned. He gently rotated her shoulders, then embraced her. Instead of resisting, she laid her head against his chest with a defeated sigh.

"I'm sorry," he said quietly. "I knew something was bothering you, but until Patsy told me what that bastard did—"

"My stepmother talks too much."

"She's concerned about you."

"Really?" Rachel stiffened, pushing back to look him in the eye. "Or was she just trying to warn you that I'm damaged goods?"

"C'mon, Rachel. Give her—give both of us—a little credit," Zeke said, though Rachel's doubts reminded him of his own about Patsy, earlier.

"This news," he went on to ask, "is this the reason the lawsuit might be dismissed?"

She nodded. "I can't imagine his mother wanting it to come out that her precious angel was a—that he'd do something like that to a woman. It'll be easier to keep Kyle a 'victim' if the suit's dropped now."

Zeke ran a fingertip along her cheekbone, then stroked the soft hair at her temple. He could have supplied the word she had avoided, but he didn't want to use it either. Didn't want to *think* about that bastard using her unconscious body.

She pushed his hand away from her face, but instead of turning it loose, she slid her fingers downward to interlock with his. "I didn't know," she whispered. "In the back of my mind I thought *maybe*, but I couldn't handle the thought, so I came up with excuses for why I couldn't remember that night. The flu, maybe, or . . . I had a hundred arguments for my attorney, and the psychologist I talked to. But right now, that's not important—"

"It's important, Rachel. Important that you learn to live with knowing. Maybe get some help, so you won't—"

She shook her head and backed away to look up at him. "Tonight, there's only one thing that matters."

He frowned, not understanding. "What do you mean?"

"Getting the hell away from here—both of us—before Castillo shows up to arrest you."

CHAPTER
TWENTY-SIX

She felt as if her soul had been liberated from its terrible conflict; she was no longer wrestling with her grief, but could sit down with it as a lasting companion and make it a sharer in her thoughts.

—George Eliot,
from Middlemarch

Zeke brought Rachel's hand to his mouth and pressed his lips against it, mainly to disguise the fact that her offer had left him speechless. Choked with emotion that she would offer up her life here, and a family that loved her, to run with him. That she would throw away her chance at a real future—one that wouldn't involve a lifetime of looking over her shoulder—for a chance to be with him.

He wanted to imagine it meant that she loved him as he loved her. He wanted to believe in the possibility of a future—however uncertain—in her company, an escape from the loneliness he had fought so many years to keep at bay. But when he looked into Rachel's eyes, he saw despair, defeat there. He saw a woman who was desperate to escape the things she couldn't face.

"You can't want to go with me," he told her. "Weren't you listening to what I told you? What about Willie? And what about the fact that I'm not who I've claimed to be all these years?"

"I don't know who you used to be." Rachel stared up at him, her expression as pained as it was earnest. "And I don't know who you might have been if that boy hadn't died, but

I'm in love with the man you are now. I'm in love with
Zeke Pike. Just Zeke, not John Langley."

He had to close his eyes, to let the words sink past his
own selfish need to hear them. To sink soul deep, to the understanding that Rachel, too, had been shaped by tragedy,
into the one woman who could possibly accept him—a
woman who believed she deserved no better than a fugitive.
Damaged goods, she'd said, using a term that should have
died out centuries before. Yet she saw herself as such, regardless of what anybody else thought.

"It's time for you to leave now." Emotion roughened his
voice, making it sound as gruff and unsociable as the armor
he'd worn so long. "Time for you to go home."

"Don't do this, Zeke. Don't shut me out of your life. I
know you love me, too. I *know* it."

He grimaced. "I'm starting to agree with you. About
Patsy talking too much."

Rachel looked so hurt, he couldn't let it go at that. He
wanted to pull her close, to kiss away her pain and confusion.
But he couldn't risk touching her, couldn't risk the temptation
to take—and keep forever—a woman who deserved more.

"Don't get me wrong," he said. "I'm not denying it. But
loving you means doing the right thing by you, Rachel. It
doesn't mean letting you run from the people who'd be so
hurt by your action."

"I know my dad would miss me." Her voice resonated
with the pain of her admission.

"He's already lost his mother. And if you think Patsy
would be happy if you took off, you'd better think again.
For one thing, that woman loves you. She's just been too
scared to admit it. Scared that you'll flat out reject her."

"If she does care about me, she's got a strange way of
showing it sometimes."

He couldn't argue that point. "And if you left without a
word, she'd never have your father's full attention. Because
you know damned well he'd look for you until the world's
end."

"All I've done is make trouble for them. They'd be better off without—"

"Don't say that." He shook his head. "Don't *ever* say it. Because once a person starts down that road, he never can go back. He's got to keep running and running until he's so far from the person he used to be that it hurts to think about it."

She picked up her coffee and took a sip. Steam rose from the mug, obscuring both her eyes and her thoughts. But she *was* thinking, he was certain of it. Thinking about what it would cost her to leave with him.

A selfish part of his heart prayed she would decide that he was worth it. Worth any sacrifice at all. Because he'd been alone so damned long, he felt it might kill him.

He drank from his own coffee in the hope of bolstering his willpower. But soon Rachel put her mug down and pushed her way back into his arms.

"I can't stand this, Zeke." She squeezed him hard and pressed her head to his chest. "I want you to be safe, I do— but I can't picture myself getting through this—even making it through tomorrow without you."

After putting down his own drink, Zeke wrapped his arms around her and stroked her silky hair. Would this be the last time they touched? The final memory either of them would carry of a brief, doomed romance?

"You'll be all right, Rachel," he said. "I—I know you're strong enough."

But when she tilted back her head to look at him with eyes like melting chocolate, it was his own strength that he questioned. And when she whispered, "Please, Zeke," that strength failed him completely.

He ducked his head to kiss her, to take her mouth so hungrily, his nerve endings crackled with sensation, electrical charges centering on a part of his anatomy that didn't give a damn whether his failure was born of weakness or some self-destructive impulse. As long as he could keep kissing her, keep touching, keep his mind and body focused on this moment, this last . . .

He shouldn't have reached beneath her shirt, shouldn't have allowed himself to feel the warmth of her skin, the lower curve of her breast, covered by her bra. It was suddenly intolerable to have that much of her and no more, to know that he was so close, so damned close to what he needed. They *both* needed.

When Rachel pushed back, panting, his body throbbed in protest. Until she peeled her top off and unhooked the lacy black bra and reached for the top button of his own shirt.

He fought to remember why this was such a bad idea. "Weren't you the one who said there'd be no more sex?"

"That was before you told me," she said, "before you trusted me with the truth. And besides, this won't be sex."

Though he should have been relieved, he nearly groaned aloud, until she added, "This will be *love*making, Zeke. Please . . . this one last time."

He didn't register the part about *one last time*, didn't hear anything beyond *lovemaking*. After that, he couldn't have spoken if he'd wanted to, for his mouth had slanted over hers to claim the kiss she offered. Though gooseflesh formed along her bare skin, his head filled with the heat and taste of her mouth, with the honey-lemon scent of her hair, with her fumbling hurry to unbutton his shirt, too. When he slid a hand between them to cup first one and then the other of her breasts, she moaned in need, her nipples already hard and tight with excitement.

Scooping her into his arms, he carried her toward his bed beside the woodstove, his breathing hitching as she nipped his neck.

"Ow," he murmured, an image forming of the lioness he'd seen in her, a corner of her soul yet untouched by tragedy.

Abruptly, he changed course, carrying her into his bathroom. He rearranged the welcome burden of her curves to turn on the shower. Then stood her up and knelt before her on the mat to pull off her boots and socks before slowly and methodically unbuckling her belt. After pulling down her jeans, he dipped two fingers beneath the band of her panties and kissed her softly, through the damp silk fabric.

She tilted back her head and groaned, knees weakening, when he swirled his tongue around the hollow of her navel. After stripping her completely naked, he pushed her a step backward, into the streaming—

"Ack. Th-that's c-cold," she yelped as he pulled off his own jeans and followed her inside.

"Sorry about that," he said through gritted teeth. "I wanted you hot and wet, not frozen."

When she laughed, he did, too, and it felt so good—so damned good—that relief carried them through the moment until the water warmed up. He struggled free of his wet shirt, then ducked his head to kiss her, caressing her breasts as he did so. She responded by running her short nails down his back.

With a groan, he bowed to suckle her breasts, and she moaned, "That's so much better," as she reached for something.

It must have been the soap, for the hand she wrapped around his shaft glided slick and warm until he thought he would explode with the sheer pleasure of it. Except he wasn't done yet, couldn't be done so soon, so he captured both her wrists and turned her around to face the shower wall.

He reached around between her legs to find her slippery and eager. He rubbed himself against her sweet cleft from behind, not entering but teasing, enjoying the beating stream of water, the pounding of his own heart, the driving rhythm of his body's hunger. Not allowing himself to think of past or future, he reveled in *this* time, *these* sensations, until he felt her bucking, stiffening.

"God, Zeke . . ." She cried out.

Her knees buckled, and he caught her, caught her and turned off the water, then rubbed her dry with fresh towels as she stood panting, her eyes closed as if she were as intent as he on locking this moment into the vault of memory, as fearful that it would never be repeated.

He carried her back to his bed, in spite of Rachel's murmured, "I can walk now."

He smiled at her. "Don't want to take any chances on you running."

"I'm not going anywhere." Her eyes made it a promise.

The fire had warmed the room by now, and Zeke added to its heat by lying down beside her. He slowly reawakened her body to the pleasure of unhurried kisses, kisses that teased, explored, and finally culminated in two bodies side-by-side, locked deeply in a rhythm that started oh, so slowly, rocking like a gentle sea. A rhythm that swirled into a storm of their own making, an urgent ebb and flow that went on and on until she broke into wave after wave of exultation and he finally spilled that portion of himself he'd held dammed for far too long.

The little black-and-white dog yelped as it was kicked, another ancillary victim. But this was the only one regretted, in spite of the blood its bite had drawn.

The death of the woman's grandmother had been less disturbing. Loved ones died, badly and too often, leaving weeping friends and shattered families, ruined children in their wakes. At least Benita Copeland had lived out a long, full life. And there were far worse ways to go than by fine, Swiss chocolate. It had been a sweet death, far kinder than the one that had destroyed the intruder's family. And far easier than the death waiting for the murderer.

Yet tonight, guilt corroded the raw edge of righteous hatred, guilt for booting the dog's ribs, sending it dashing out the back gate and straight into the street. Unlike an adult, the dog was, to a large extent, defenseless. And it had looked up with its brown eyes, as trusting as a child's.

So sad, that one small sin. And all too reminiscent.

Rachel Copeland would pay for it, as she would pay for all the others.

CHAPTER TWENTY-SEVEN

*The hero is the one who kindles a great light in the world,
who sets up blazing torches in the dark streets of life for men
to see by. The saint is the man who walks through the dark
paths of the world, himself a light.*

—Felix Adler

Tuesday, March 25

"So you'll go away?" Rachel asked Zeke as she finished
dressing. As much as it hurt her, she needed his assurance.
"If I promise to see to your animals, you'll go someplace
where you'll be safe? Please . . ."

He nodded, his green eyes awash with grief, and fastened
his jeans. He watched her step into her shoes.

"And then you'll let me know where you are? So I can
meet up with you?"

"No," he said. "I can't."

"But I'll talk to my father. I'll make things right with
him, I promise. I'll find the horses good homes, and Gus,
too. Really good homes."

"No, Rachel. You stay with your family—behind locked
doors. And don't give up on your career. If you came to me,
you'd lose both. And I already have enough on my conscience."

She shook her head. "Doesn't it matter that I love you?"

"More than I can tell you. But not enough to ruin your
life. Listen to me, Rachel. This woman who's stalking
you, she's gotten way too bold, coming out into the
open to burn your van. Castillo's sure to find her. Then

this will be all over, and you'll be free to go on with your life."

She swallowed hard, resisting the temptation to ask *What life, without the one person she could really talk to—the one person, other than her dad, that she could love?* Because she'd be damned if she played the poor-pitiful-me card, damned if she begged him to rethink a decision that had so clearly cost him.

He'd never promised her forever, had never done a thing except discourage the idea of their getting together. Because in the grown-up world, there were factors that trumped love.

"If you change your mind . . ." she started.

He touched her cheek with callused fingers. "You just be careful until she's caught, maybe move in for a while with Patsy and your father. Because it'd kill me if I found out you were . . ."

She leaned against him, hugging him for all she was worth. After a long hesitation, he cradled the back of her head, his fingers stroking her hair. He kissed her crown and whispered, "I'm not changing my mind, Rachel. And you'd better get going. I still have lots to do before I leave. I'll feed the horses, though, so you won't have to come out 'til tomorrow afternoon, and I'll leave you money for their upkeep, a check on the table in here—"

She pushed herself onto her tiptoes and kissed him hard on the mouth, catching his flavor and his heat. Long before she had enough, she pulled away and headed for the door.

"Good-bye, Zeke Pike," she said over her shoulder, then rushed outside to the car, hurrying so he wouldn't see her break down.

She didn't make it to the door before her tears came, but it didn't matter. Because Zeke didn't follow. She had the night—and her grief—to herself.

Ten minutes later, as she drove home, her cell phone rang. Eyes blurred with weeping, she made a desperate grab for it and prayed that Zeke had changed his mind, that he'd decided he couldn't live without her. Too late to check the caller ID, she remembered that he didn't have a phone.

"Hey, Rusty, it's your old man," her father said, his voice rough.

"I'm on my way home now," she told him, more irritated than she should be by his protectiveness.

"I decided to drive by the house, just to check things out before you got home. And I almost killed J.D."

"What's he gotten into now?" The dog had been so quiet lately, she almost welcomed a return to his usual mischief.

"No, that's not what I mean. I mean, I *really* almost killed him. He ran right out in the street. I barely saw something shooting toward my tires. If I hadn't reacted—run up a curb and taken out the neighbor's planter—I would've hit him for sure. You didn't leave him loose, did you?"

"Of course not," she said. "I left the doggy door unlatched so he could go out into the backyard, but both the fence and back gate were secure. I know it."

"Well, I found the gate standing wide open. And I'm not exactly sure, but . . ."

"What, Dad?"

"I thought I might've seen a movement in the backyard. It was dark, and maybe my imagination was still stirred up from the fire, but I could've sworn I saw somebody go over the back fence and take off running."

"Are you okay? There's no one there now, is there?" she asked.

"I'm fine, and if there was anybody, he—or she, I guess— is gone."

"And what about J.D.?"

"He's fine. He's with me inside now," her father told her. "But hurry home, Rusty. There's something here you need to see."

She wiped the dampness from her face. "What's wrong? Did someone break in?"

After the destruction of her van, almost nothing would

surprise her. But Rachel felt rage kindle at the thought of her grandmother's possessions being damaged.

"Just drive carefully," her father said. "I'll show you when you get here."

He met her at the door when she arrived a few minutes later. Frowning, he peered at her. "You've been crying. Did that son of a bitch——?"

"I'm all right," she said, not wanting to discuss Zeke. For the moment, she was holding fast to her fury, letting it keep her grief over losing him at bay. Better that than falling to pieces with her father.

J.D. jumped up against her leg, and she scooped the dog into her arms. He was shivering as if he'd had a bad scare— or maybe he was simply excited to see her home.

Looking around the house for signs of damage, she asked, "So what's wrong, Dad? What is it?"

"You'd better come and see this," he said, then led her into the house's formal dining room.

Her grandmother's old table and chairs had been neatly pushed into a corner. Where they had been, another table and a set of chairs stood. The very table Zeke had been completing when she'd photographed him in his workshop. Striated with rivers and creeks of turquoise, its red-brown surface gleamed beneath the domed droplight.

She stared, so stunned that at first, she didn't see the note lying on its surface. By the time she noticed and picked it up, Rachel was crying too hard to make out what it said.

"Let me read it for you, Rusty." Her father's voice was a low murmur as he took the paper from her, squinted, then hesitated before saying, "Oh, hell. Maybe you had better read this after all."

Rachel frowned, as a niggling doubt sparked, then flared into flame. But she pulled herself together, wiped her eyes, and scanned the page. *"That customer didn't ever come to claim his special order,"* she read aloud, her voice hoarse and unsteady. *"And now that you've got yourself a dining room, I couldn't bring myself to sell it to anybody else. I'd rather think about your family gathered all around it. You and Patsy and your dad and whatever lucky SOB you marry someday and have kids with. Just think about me now and then, and we'll call it even."*

"Anything else?" her father asked.

She shook her head, unable to get out the letter's last two words: *Just Zeke.* And unable to picture a future in which she could look at the table without seeing Zeke Pike, shirtless, flawless, laboring over its creation. Or imagining a green-eyed son, a dark-haired daughter—the laughing ghosts of children who never would be. . . .

Because if she ran back to Zeke now, he wouldn't take her. Worse yet, he might not leave either, which would expose him to a fate she refused to let him chance.

Still half-asleep, Marlene groped for her phone in the darkness. Without her glasses, she couldn't see the caller ID, but she knew the ringtone wasn't Dan's. Since she'd started searching for her mother, she'd given her number to dozens of people. Maybe one of them was finally calling her with something that would help. Maybe someone who knew what had happened to her mother.

The thought jolted through Marlene's system. Fully awake she pushed the "answer" button.

"Tell me," her mother's voice demanded, "what the *hell* is it you think you're doing?"

Shock set Marlene's heart rate soaring. She couldn't get a single word out.

"Marlene? Are you there?" the caller demanded. "Damn it—answer me."

Realization dawned, and Marlene breathed again. "Lord, Kathy. I thought you were Mother. You took ten years off my life."

"Be nice if she *did* call someone," her sister grumbled. "But you have to *care* about other people to pick up a telephone. And God knows that woman hasn't cared about a soul since—"

"I know." No need to waste time revisiting that old wound.

"If you know, why aren't you back home? With people who *do* love you. Lord, Marlene, Daddy never would have expected you to throw away your life, your marriage, just to—"

"What about my marriage?" Marlene rubbed her throbbing head. "Did Dan call you? Did he say something?"

"Dan's worried. *I'm* worried. And your boys are scared to death. We all are."

Shaking her head, Marlene said, "There's no need to be. I'm not like Mother. I'm just trying to do my duty, that's all. For Dad's sake, and for—"

"This is the reason we all pay taxes. So there will be people on the payroll, *trained* people to find loved ones who go missing. Don't you think they're better equipped to—"

"If you've just called to rehash Dan's arguments, I'm going back to sleep."

"I don't care if it costs me my job," Kathy said. "I'm coming to get you. Now where are you?"

Marlene rolled her eyes but didn't answer. "Just a few more days, Kath. A few more days and I'll find her. Because no one knows her the way I do. No one else listens when I explain that she's a serious threat to her own safety."

"It's not just *her* safety." Kathy's voice dropped to a whisper. "That's what has me so worried."

Marlene's breath hitched. What had Kathy found out?

"Do you remember Shane Drake? Remember, he was one of those guys—the ones who were there when John Langley killed our brother."

Marlene's mouth went dry as she recalled her final glimpse of Shane Drake, a pool of blood expanding near his head. If Kathy knew, how would Marlene ever convince her that their mother's "mission" was best kept in the family? That Marlene could find the woman before more harm was done?

"I—I've seen Shane." She faltered through the words,

remembering the cutting wit and easy grace of a teenaged boy who'd once seemed to have the whole world on a platter. Remembering Willie working so hard to color campaign posters when his "good friend" ran for class president, a "good friend" who'd so often mocked him behind his back.

"Before he was hurt?" asked Kathy.

"Hurt?" Marlene's surprise was genuine. The man had certainly looked dead to her.

"Yeah, he's in a coma after a hit and run," Kathy said, "outside of Albuquerque. And you know what else? Aaron's dead. Died in a carjacking a few weeks ago, near where he lived in Tulsa. Where *you* followed our mother."

"That could be a coincidence," Marlene said.

"And I could be Playmate of the Year." Kathy's voice was drier than her Arizona home. "We have to face facts, Marlene. When Dad died, Mom lost whatever scrap of restraint was keeping her from going hunting—because that's exactly what she's doing. Hunting them all down."

"She's a seventy-year-old woman," Marlene pleaded. "It's just not possi—"

"A seventy-year-old woman who's lost whatever hold on sanity she had since our dad's not there to keep her in check. I'm calling the police back home this morning to let them know what's going on."

"I can stop her, get her to a doctor."

"A doctor? Mar, she's *killing* people. Human beings with families of their own. At least two of them already. I don't know yet about Sam Henderson. Dan's trying to track down his mom to check on him."

Fear stitched its way through Marlene. The fear of what else could be learned. "She's our *mother*, Kathy. She—we can't let them—Daddy would never want us to—"

"Of course, John Langley's the one she'll really want," Kathy interrupted. "But if the authorities haven't been able to find him up to this point, I can't see how she—"

"She knows where he is." Marlene's gaze touched the seat beside her, where a section of newspaper lay folded. A travel section she'd found in the last room vacated by her mother.

"Mother knows exactly where he's hiding," she continued in a voice gone whisper-soft. "Which is why I hurried out here. So I could intercept her. So I can find our mother and bring her straight back home where she belongs."

"Marlene, you have to tell me. Where exactly are you?"

"You aren't calling the authorities. You're not having our mother locked up. Because she's not a criminal, she's sick, Kath. Can't you remember the way she was, the way she used to smile back before our brother—"

"What if I come out to *help* you?" Kathy pleaded. "Or Dan. Do you want Dan? And what about your boys, Mar? You could see them both, too."

Narrowing her eyes, Marlene considered. Then she realized it was a plot, a plan cooked up by Team Testosterone and Kathy. They'd drag her home if they could, leave her mother to the authorities, where she might be hurt or even killed during her capture. Or at best, locked in a cage and charged with murder, thrown in with the worst types of criminals while the real killer—the man who had cost her her sanity—lived free.

So instead of answering her sister, Marlene broke the connection. Then she pulled the battery out of her telephone. Where she was going, she couldn't afford to be betrayed by the sound of its ring.

And besides, she refused to take the chance that somehow either her sister, Dan, or the authorities would use it to track her down and stop her from doing what she must.

CHAPTER
TWENTY-EIGHT

Or ever the stars were made, or skies,
Grief was born, and the kinless night,
Mother of gods without form or name. . . .
                              —*Algernon Charles Swinburne*
                              from "A Lamentation," section II

In his workshop, Zeke threw tools into boxes, trying to keep too busy to think about what he was doing. To regret the things he meant to leave behind or fear the future he'd chosen—a risk he knew would horrify both Rachel and his mother. But it was a risk worth taking, he knew, especially when the alternatives, another name, another town, and another hollow shell of false existence, left him feeling as cold and lifeless as a corpse.

After twenty years, it was finally time to stop the running. He would first contact his brothers—both grown men now, not the raw-boned boys he remembered—and ask for their help. As for his mother, he'd beg her forgiveness and he'd pray for her strength, but he'd no longer be held hostage by her terror.

Instead, he intended to hire the best attorney he could find—an attorney who hailed from somewhere well beyond the corruption of the East Texas county where he'd grown up—to help guide him through this mess. And if he had to serve time, he would do it. Because he would willingly take that risk for the slightest chance that he could spend the rest of his life in honest freedom.

Freedom to figure out who *he* was, to pursue a life outside the invisible bars that had surrounded him. It would mean, too, that he could pursue Rachel, if she were both free and willing. If she hadn't by that time forgotten all about him.

He carried a box of tools outside, his muscles straining under the weight. As he set the box down on the pickup's open tailgate, he looked up sharply at the sound of some commotion from the horses.

He shoved the box back farther, then reached into his pocket to pull out the folding utility knife he often carried. Not much of a weapon against an intruder, be it human predator or big cat, but since he owned no gun, it would have to do. Recalling the way Gus had been injured, he slipped into the darkest shadows, then headed in the direction of nervous-sounding whickers and the clatter of shod hooves.

"Shhh, shush. Be quiet, it's all right," someone whispered.

Someone female, he realized. But he didn't recognize the voice, gleaned no information from it except the speaker's nervousness. He edged closer to the voice, to a moonlit silhouette that was definitely a woman's. A small woman, compact and—if he was not mistaken—curvy.

She was on the move, heading from the corral area toward the building where he'd made his home for so long. Her breathing sounded labored, as if she'd been walking for some distance. Or maybe anxiety was getting to her.

But that didn't mean she wasn't armed. For what woman would wander around such an isolated patch of private property alone, at night, without protection? And what innocent reason could she possibly have to be here, traveling with no light but the moon's?

Zeke closed in, attempting to move stealthily but crunching gravel loudly enough that the woman gasped, "Who's there?"

She sounded terrified, and when he didn't answer, she broke into a jog, still arrowing toward the candelilla factory building. In her haste, she stumbled. With a choked yelp, she pitched forward, and Zeke darted close to grab her arm with one hand and hoist her to her feet.

His free arm locked around her chest, and he pushed the flat steel of his blade against her neck. "Don't move. Don't scream," he warned. "I don't want to have to hurt you."

She struggled, shrieking, too panic-stricken to contain her terror. Zeke tightened his grip and ordered, "Quiet. Or you *will* end up hurt, and I don't need the damned trouble. All I need are answers from you, right now."

Whether it was his tone or his words, she went still and whispered, "I just—I want to warn you."

"Hang on just a minute," he said. "Hate to do this, but I have to."

"What are you *doing*?" Her voice slid up the register as he ran his hands along her sides and waistband, then slid them along her arms and hands.

"Sorry." He let go of her. "But I had to make sure you were unarmed before I turned you loose. Don't go running off, though. I have a feeling you wouldn't enjoy a flying tackle."

Especially since he suspected he outweighed her by seventy pounds or more.

"I won't run." Her voice shook as she faced him, her features obscured by the darkness. "I was just going to leave this for you. I thought I'd stick it under your truck's windshield wiper so you'd find it."

He heard a paper rattling as she pulled it from her pocket. A moment later, she handed it to him. He peered down at a folded section of newspaper, but he couldn't make out details in the weak light.

"We're both here now," he said. "So tell me, what is this? And who the hell *are* you?"

"It's a note and your picture," the woman told him. "From a newspaper travel section I found in her motel room."

"Whose room?" he asked, more confused than ever.

"My mother's. *Willie's* mother. She knows who and where you are. It's all there in the article—everything she needed to come find you."

As Zeke stared down at the illegible print, understanding detonated, unfurling in explosive waves around him. He'd been recognized as he had feared, recognized from that damned photo—which had brought more than customers to irritate him with their orders. Which had brought him this bizarre warning—but why? Why would Willie's sister care enough to risk coming here alone at night to let her brother's supposed murderer know about her mother's discovery? Why hadn't she simply called the authorities and had him arrested? A thousand questions spun into existence, twisting across the landscape of his thoughts.

Looking up again, Zeke could only spit out one single, simple query. "Marlene?" he asked. "You're Marlene Tyler?"

But his only answer was the sound of swift-retreating footsteps, for the woman had used his distraction to make a break for the dark cover of the desert night.

"Get your things together, Rachel." Her father's tone warned that he was not about to argue. "You're staying with us tonight. We've got the guest room ready."

Rachel nodded, too emotionally wrung out to care where she laid her head, as long as she could sleep. Besides, the image of her blazing van still burned in her mind, graphic evidence that her stalker was in Marfa. And Zeke, too, had begged her to stay with her father, Zeke, whom she would never see again. . . .

"Listen, Rusty," her father said as they walked toward the truck. "I think maybe you should drive tonight. My eyes—must've gotten some of this cleaning fluid I was using earlier in them. As it is, Patsy's given me hell about driving on my own tonight."

Rachel sighed, hating to call him on his white lie but unable to keep pretending. If she didn't press him, he—or someone else—was going to get hurt. "I think it's time to get those eyes checked, Dad. They're getting a lot worse, aren't they?"

"I told you—" He shook his head. "I just got something in them. And it's late, and I'm tired."

Excuses, more excuses. Like the ones he had been making for not reading. The ones leading him to rely more and more heavily on Lili, Bobby, and increasingly on Rachel herself, to handle not only the business paperwork but the flying. But he wasn't ready to let go yet. Might never be, because flying had been his life for so long.

"We'll call the ophthalmologist, the one that Grandma used. It might be something completely treatable. I'll take you, if you'd like. Or Patsy could—" She touched his hand, and tried not to react when he jerked it from her.

"I already know what the hell it is. Now are you going to drive the damned truck home or not?"

"Sure, Dad." She let the subject drop, and he gave the keys a high toss, so she had to reach to grab them. The house was only a few blocks distant, a drive filled with frail silence.

As she pulled up, she saw the lights were still on inside the white Craftsman bungalow where Rachel had grown up. A window shade flickered, and a silhouetted form peeked around its edge to watch them pull into the driveway. For a fleeting moment, Rachel saw her mother looking out at her. *Her* mother . . .

"Patsy's waited up."

Her dad spoke with forced cheer, but in Rachel's throat, a lump formed. She bowed her head, until J.D.—who had jumped into her lap for the ride—licked her chin. *How long,* she wondered, *have I been blaming Patsy for the problems in my life?* Her stepmother hadn't caused the stroke that shut down Jana Copeland's brain. Hadn't committed any crime other than rescuing Rachel's father from deep depression. And if the worst came to pass, if Walter Copeland had to give up flying, Patsy would be the one to see him through the crisis, as she'd been seeing Rachel through hers, in her way.

Rachel blinked back tears as Zeke's words sprang to her

mind. *"That woman loves you. She's just been too scared to admit it. Scared that you'll flat-out reject her."*

"You okay?" her father asked.

"I'm fine," Rachel said, willing the words to be true. For his sake and for Patsy's, for the sake of their shared future as a family.

A family that could never, for all her foolish fantasies, include the man Rachel loved.

Zeke went for a flashlight, then skimmed the ground with its beam as he searched for the woman he believed to be Marlene. He still couldn't believe she had made the trip here, a drive of ten or eleven hours from the East Texas town where both had grown up, simply to warn him that her mother knew his whereabouts.

It made no sense whatsoever, unless Willie and Marlene's mother—a well-dressed PTA mom he remembered for her kindness and her brownies—had gone off the deep end because of the discovery. Recalling Rachel's suspicions about Kyle's mother and her harassment, he wondered at the power of grief to corrupt a thing as wholesome as a mother's love, to warp its gentle nature into something terrible and violent.

From halfway down his long drive, Zeke heard an engine starting, then glimpsed a vehicle's taillights just before they disappeared from view. It must have been Marlene. She'd probably parked as close as she had dared without letting him hear her approach. But why? Why not simply drive up, issue her warning, and be on her way? Had speaking to her brother's "killer" made her feel disloyal?

Though the highway remained out of sight over a rise, he could see the faint glow of her headlights traveling south, toward town. But Zeke decided not to take the time to jump into his truck and chase her. Instead, he went back to his packing, convinced he would be long gone before Willie's mother either called the sheriff or came out here— something he could scarcely imagine—to confront him.

Inside, he gathered the essentials, from tools and clothing to those few books he had read and reread so often. He checked inside a cover to assure himself his mother's letter would come with him.

Of Rachel Copeland, he would take nothing, except the memory of her offer to come with him and the knowledge that he had done right by turning her down. It was a thin comfort, too tattered and threadbare to afford him any real warmth, but it would have to suffice . . . at least for the fore-seeable future but far more likely the remainder of his life.

At last, his preparations made, he found himself sitting for the last time at his table, where he'd written notes about the animals' care and a check covering their upkeep. Outside, the darkness of the desert night enshrouded the place like a cocoon. He thought of all the years he'd been here, his rides out into the desert, the wild things he'd had the pleasure of observing, the countless times he'd lost himself in the work that seemed to choose him as much as he chose it. How it had all felt like *enough* for so long, more than he deserved. But however lacking or complete that life was, it was time to put it behind him. Time to move on, once he rested his eyes for just a minute. . . .

Zeke awakened hours later, swearing and acutely conscious of the early morning light. What the hell kind of a fool slept through his own midnight escape?

As he made quick work of washing up, then feeding and watering Gus and the horses, the answer settled over him like fine dust. *The kind who really doesn't want to leave. The kind who's too damned attached to this life—and the woman in it—to let go.*

Praying he hadn't waited too long, Zeke finally climbed inside his old truck and headed down the road.

Marlene, too, awakened, startled to find that she'd been sleeping in her rental car and even more surprised that her cell phone was ringing; she couldn't remember replacing the battery last night. She was surprised, too, to recognize the ring tone as her husband's; he hadn't called in days. And Marlene had been afraid to call him—afraid of reigniting an argument for which she had lost heart.

She snatched up the phone to answer, an early morning surge of hope pushing past weeks' worth of guilt. Outside, pink-coral sunlight washed over a plain dotted with dew-damp grazing cattle. They were red-and-white cows, most of them with young calves by their sides. Some sort of yellow flowers had opened, brightening the grasses on which they fed.

"Dan, I'm sorry—so sorry we argued." After readjusting her seat to driving position, she shoved the tangle of her ash-blonde hair from her eyes. "You and the boys, you're my life, and as for my mom, Dad would understand that I've done my best. He'd be the first to tell me to come home and—"

"I'm sorry, too, Marlene. I have to tell you—this isn't good news."

"The boys." Her heart contracted at the stricken sound of his voice. Something was terribly wrong—she knew it. Oh, God, what if something had happened because she'd left, because she had *abandoned* her family for this hellish wild goose chase. "Are Josh and Taylor—"

"They're fine, Mar."

He's filed for divorce, she thought. No one they knew—not even her sister—would blame him.

But he said, "It's your mother."

"Have the police found her? Or was it the sheriff out here?"

"She's not in Texas, Baby. The man who called—he was from Tulsa, from the medical examiner's office."

"I don't understand. Tulsa?" Marlene's pulse thundered in her ears. Had authorities discovered the carjacking and her brother's dead friend? Had they found out about the others, too, about the chain of violent deaths? "Mom left Tulsa weeks ago."

"No, Marlene, she didn't. She never left the state of Oklahoma."

"What are you talking about? Of course she did. I followed her to Albuquerque. I spoke to people who saw her there." *I saw a man she ran down near a construction site.* Marlene kept this part to herself, still harboring a slim hope that she could get her mother help instead of involving the police. "And you saw her picture from that ATM, remember? The one where you spotted that Jeep Commander in the background."

"I told you the picture quality was pretty bad, remember? Maybe I thought it was your mother because I was looking for your mother. But it's impossible, because before that—the police in Tulsa found a body—"

"No, Dan," Marlene argued. "My mother used her debit card. To get a cash advance. Who else would've known her PIN? Not some random stranger wearing her hat."

"They've identified your mother. I'm so sorry, Marlene. There's no gentle way to say this, but she was found—they found the body stuffed inside a Dumpster near that little motel where she stayed. She—she had a gunshot wound. Through the face, into the brain. The person who called—he said it's likely death was instant, before she had the chance to feel pain." He sped on, rattling off another blow before she recovered. "It's a pretty rough area, and the police are investigating a string of robberies. They think she might have been shot when answering a knock at her room's door. In past incidents, people have seen two men running away, both of them dressed in pizza delivery uniforms."

"No." Marlene shook her head, anxiety exploding bright as fireworks in her vision. She had *been to* that old motor court, had questioned the woman at the desk herself. "My mother wouldn't have opened her door. You know how she was. Ever since my brother's death, she was so suspicious of people, especially strangers. Besides, this is all impossible. She doesn't even like pizza. And the woman I talked to at the motel never said anything about any body being found. She told me my mother paid in cash and left the key inside her room when she left."

"Maybe the body wasn't found until after you were there. Or the clerk had been warned not to talk about the shootings, since that sort of thing can't be good for business."

"Maybe . . ." Marlene allowed, but she still didn't believe it. Wouldn't.

"Did anyone you spoke with actually *see* your mother leave?" Dan asked.

Marlene opened her mouth to blurt *Of course,* but nothing came out. Because the woman she had questioned hadn't exactly said that. But Marlene had assumed . . .

"The man you talked to, the medical examiner," she said, "did you get his name and number? Because I have to call him right now, tell him they have the wrong person. If she was shot in the face, then maybe they couldn't tell—"

"They waited until they had a match with the dental records before they called us. They wanted to be sure."

"But what if her—" Marlene sucked in deep breaths, one after another, until she felt light-headed from the rush of oxygen. "—what if this *body's* teeth were damaged too much? Maybe they made a mistake. An honest mistake. Because that body can't be my mother."

"I know this is a shock, Marl. I know and I'm sorry."

"What—what about my sister? Have you called her?"

"I—uh—I talked to Bryce, but . . . Did you know they've separated again? But this time, Kathy was the one who took off."

"What?" Marlene's head was spinning. "When?"

"I don't know. I guess there was some kind of big to-do at her job. Boss accused her of embezzling. When Bryce tried to talk to her about it, she—"

"That can't be right. She would've told *me.* I spoke to her just—" A terrible suspicion formed in Marlene's mind. "Are—are you lying to me, Dan? Trying to trick me into coming home? Because if you—"

"Stephanie's coming tonight," Dan said flatly, referring to his half sister, who lived a hundred miles from their hometown. "She'll stay with the boys a few days. Because I'm flying out to get you, Marlene. I'm coming to take you to Tulsa, and then we'll bring you and your mom both home."

"But this is wrong. I know it." Marlene shook her head, as waves of dizziness broke all around her. "Because if I'm not following my mother, what on earth have I spent all this time chasing—some kind of vengeful ghost?"

CHAPTER
TWENTY-NINE

*Whenever I take up a newspaper and read it, I fancy I see
ghosts creeping between the lines. There must be ghosts all
over the world. They must be countless as the grains of the
sands, it seems to me. And we are so miserably afraid of the
light, all of us.*

—Henrik Ibsen,
from Ghosts, *act II*

A dream woke the observer, a nightmare vision of the
cramped and filthy hiding place chosen after last night's run
for cover. The evening should have ended with Rachel
Copeland gone forever, but instead, *he* had shown up, leaving no choice except to flee, to hide like an animal.

Like the scrabbling, desperate Child from long before.

Though the observer knew last night's hiding place had
been a crawlspace beneath the neighbor's wraparound porch,
its confines reeked of cat piss, a stench too like the kingdom
of spiders beneath the long-vanished trailer. (How brightly,
how fiercely it had burned once the lights guided The Child
to the gas can in the old shed and the matches left there so
carelessly. Last night's fire was no match for it, with no one
trapped and screaming in the burning van. No Others cursing, weeping, all but the one innocent dying as they struggled
to escape.) And when the wasps swarmed (had they been real
this time?) buzzing panic needled skin and soul alike.

Safe this morning, safe. The thought was as reassuring as the
familiarity of the clean bedding in a room kept carefully
sanitized, reassuring as the crimson glow of the rising sun
beyond the window shade.

Except the sun was drifting. Bobbing. Filling the observer with awe and horror as it bumped behind the shade, flattened itself like a sheet of paper, and slipped sideways to enter the bedroom. Once there, it hovered, recovering its third dimension and changing into salmon, pink, and then a nearly blinding white. The sphere, this sun-on-earth, swelled before giving birth to a host of smaller orbs which fanned out into a horseshoe shape around the bed. Thus arranged, they quivered, faster and faster until the room filled with their hum, their buzz like that of a thousand nests of angry wasps all readying their stingers.

Crying out, the observer raised an arm to ward off the brilliance. But the flashing blazed around that weak impediment and burned through the thin flesh of tight-shut eyelids. Conveyed a message impossible to ignore.

The time of hiding, striking from the shadows and then running from discovery had now ended. Petty mischief intended to isolate and drive the murderer from town would not be tolerated.

This time, this very day, only human blood could serve to slake inhuman hunger. If not, the observer's blood—all of it—would serve that purpose just as well.

With trembling fingers, Rachel dialed the number she'd been given, her lawyer's warning still ringing in her ears. *"It was my responsibility to pass along the message, but I strongly advise you not to call that woman,"* Marianne Greenberg had told her earlier that morning. *"Sylvia Underwood's been under a doctor's care since her son's death—and you said yourself you thought she might have been harassing you. You could end up making things worse, escalating this instead of helping. Besides, for all we know, this is a last-ditch effort to bait you into saying something damaging."*

Rachel saw her attorney's point. But if one call could end this lawsuit—if she and her family could be free of courtrooms and civil actions . . . Hellish as this conversation was sure to be, it couldn't be ten million dollars' worth of bad.

She hoped. As her call went through, her heart gave a hard bump in her chest and she wiped a sweaty palm against her jeans. She was glad to be sitting at the kitchen table, for her legs were shaking so hard, she doubted she could stand.

"Hello?" a woman on the other end said. "This is Sylvia."

A mute pause followed, during which J.D. trotted into the kitchen with one of Rachel's father's boots drooping from his jaws. *I should hang up and go get that,* Rachel told herself. *Those are Dad's best boots, his favorites. . . .*

"Is this—is this Rachel Copeland?"

Kyle's mother sounded nervous—and utterly unlike the anonymous female caller. Besides, Rachel reminded herself, if Sylvia Underwood had never left Pennsylvania, she couldn't possibly have called from Marfa, any more than she could have torched Rachel's van last night.

It must have been someone else. Terri Parton-Zavala's round face sprang to mind. Could the woman really hate her so much?

"This is Rachel Copeland," she heard herself saying. "My attorney passed along the message that you wanted me to call."

"Ms. Copeland." The woman's breathing sounded labored, her voice tremulous. "I—I've been waiting for this conversation for a long time."

"You would have waited a lot longer if my attorney had had anything to say about it."

"I—I understand that. I've been blaming you. Blaming you for everything that went wrong. But I know now—I've been made to see that making you a scapegoat has accomplished nothing. I've only been using you because I—I've been so, so furious. Angry with myself, with my son's doctors and his counselors, with the teachers and the principals and everyone who should have seen this coming. And all that anger—it swelled up so huge inside me, I didn't know what else to do with it except . . ."

Put me through nine kinds of hell, thought Rachel bitterly.

But after a moment, empathy kicked in. Because more than a year after the fact, the anguish in Sylvia Underwood's voice remained real and raw.

"Those things I said about you," the woman persisted. "It was wrong of me to do that, especially in public. I wasn't thinking about how some of my viewers might react. After you started getting phone calls, the police spoke to me about it, but at the time, I wasn't thinking of anything but my grief."

"That's understandable," said Rachel carefully.

"I just wanted to tell you I regret any pain I may have caused you. If I'd been more myself, perhaps—maybe I could have said something, made some statement, to try to undo the damage. But all I could think about was—" Her breath hitched and quiet sniffles followed. "—All I could see whenever I closed my eyes was your finger on that trigger. Pulling it and ending things forever."

"I wish none of it had ever happened," Rachel told her. "There's not a day that I don't wish it."

"Wishing and praying doesn't make one damned bit of difference. It doesn't bring my son, my beautiful nineteen-year-old son back, and it doesn't absolve you or anyone else of one bit of responsibility."

Wincing under the lash of her fury, Rachel swore under her breath. What on earth had possessed her to ignore her attorney? Could this woman have altered her voice somehow and made the calls, after all? But Rachel had come this far, so she gathered her resolve and tried again. "I don't presume to compare our losses, but when my grandmother died recently, I was angry, too. At myself, my family, even my grandmother herself for being—for doing something that contributed to her own death."

There was a long pause during which Rachel entertained visions of a brand-new lawsuit, this one demanding a hundred million dollars and her flayed hide. But finally, the other woman spoke.

"Sometimes I do—I get *so mad* at Kyle, I could *shake*

him." With her admission, Sylvia Underwood's voice dropped to a broken whisper that collapsed into itself, leaving only the sounds of quiet weeping.

That weeping drew some of the venom from Rachel's festering fury. "I'm very, very sorry," she said earnestly, tears hot in her own eyes. "I've wanted to say that for a long time. I'm sorry for your loss, and I know—I know you did your best with him. Whatever problems he had—whatever he did to me or anybody—he was—he was still your child. Your boy, and you loved him. And that will never change."

Sylvia Underwood only cried harder. But after a few minutes, she finally breathed, "My son . . . yes. Thank you. Thank you, Ms. Copeland—"

"It's Rachel, please."

"You mean it, don't you, Rachel? What you told me? Your lawyer didn't say for you to—"

Rachel's laugh was dry and hollow, a cicada's empty husk. "Are you kidding? My lawyer would have kittens if she heard the words 'I'm sorry' coming from my lips."

Sylvia laughed, too, and said, "*Lawyers* . . . But you're so right. Kyle's my child. He always will be. No matter how much it hurts. No matter how sorry I am for—for the things he did to you and those other women."

"I know," Rachel whispered, taking Sylvia Underwood's words as the closest thing to an acknowledgment of her rape that she would ever get. And rolling back the solid stone of anger that was part of her own grief, removing the obstruction from a road that might eventually—with time and work and patience—lead somewhere worth going.

Even though the journey hurt like hell.

By the time Zeke made it to Fort Davis, thirty minutes north of Marfa, his fuel gauge needle was dropping fast toward empty. With a long, desolate stretch between Fort Davis and the next available gas station, he decided he had better fill up.

He knew it was risky, that someone could ask about him

later, and a man his size would likely be remembered, right down to his green eyes. If he had the misfortune of encountering someone who had seen the photo Rachel had taken of him, it would make identification that much quicker. And if Castillo traced him to Fort Davis, he could make a fair guess as to the direction Zeke was taking. Especially if the sheriff managed to match him with the long-missing fugitive, John Charles Langley.

It could happen, Zeke knew. Marlene could have had a change of heart since last night's warning and decided to involve the law. But if she kept her mouth shut—whether or not she did it to protect her mother—he should get clear of West Texas sometime this afternoon. Afterward, he'd find a place to stay and look for a lawyer. Then arrangements might be made so he could turn himself in somewhere outside of Dogwood, Texas, where it was entirely possible that despite the passage of time, he'd never live to stand trial. Not when his testimony could incriminate the sons of the area's leading families, sons who, for all Zeke knew, could have remained in the area and claimed power as their birthright.

As he left the office after paying for his gas, his plans changed. There, fueling an old, dark-green Dodge pickup, was a man he recognized from both the airport and the viewing area.

Adrenaline pounding through his system, Zeke took a closer look—trying to remain as inconspicuous as possible—and warned himself to take his time, to be sure. Same brown hair, with a light frost of gray, and thin build, with a narrow, yet oddly familiar face to match. In spite of the hazard from the gas fumes, he held a cigarette in the hand not occupied with the pump. He murmured under his breath, half-singing along with the old Dire Straits tune rolling through the Dodge's open window. He seemed at ease and unguarded, as though he hadn't yet seen Zeke.

Zeke crept nearer, trying to keep out of his field of vision. At the moment, the man looked none too dangerous, with the cigarette now dangling loosely from his lips, its glowing tip bobbing to the beat of "Money for Nothing." Still, Zeke edged behind him; for all he knew the stranger might be carrying the same gun that he'd fired near the viewing area.

The gas pump clicked, prompting the man to pull the nozzle from the tank and replace it. But as the stranger turned, he spotted Zeke and dropped the nozzle, his eyes flaring with alarm, the lit cigarette dropping far too close to the expanding puddle.

Zeke moved to crush out the burning end before it could ignite the vapors. But his distraction cost him, and his quarry caught him with a roundhouse punch to the chin.

Pain shot upward as his jaws clacked hard together, and Zeke staggered a step backward before recovering. But that was all the time his attacker needed to throw open the truck's door and dive inside, across the bench seat.

Zeke saw him reach for the glove box, where he must have stashed his weapon. Grabbing the smaller man's legs, Zeke dragged him back out empty-handed. With a shout of alarm, the struggling man fell from the truck, his skull bouncing against the running board.

Moaning, he stopped fighting, reaching to rub the side of his head and murmur, "Shit, man."

"Sorry I had to do that," Zeke said, ignoring the ache of his jaw. "But I need to talk to you, and I didn't want to get shot for my trouble."

A shaky female voice blasted through the gas pump's intercom. "What's going on out there? I'm calling the law. Have a deputy out here right quick."

"It's all right," Zeke called back toward the speaker. "Just a misunderstanding. It's over now."

He helped the man up but kept a firm grip on the shaking hand. Dropping his voice, Zeke added, "Unless you'd rather go to jail than have a little talk with me, you might want to calm the lady's fears."

Dark brown eyes looked into Zeke's and narrowed, a sign the man was weighing options. Or trying to hash out a plan for his escape. A moment later, a quick nod indicated his agreement.

Speaking loudly for the intercom, the man said, "No. He's right. We're okay."

Moving the hand from his head, he looked down at the smear of blood staining his fingertips and swore. "Damn it. You didn't have to crack my head half-open."

"You didn't have to hit me either. Now give me your truck keys," Zeke said. After a hesitation, he added, "I just want to be sure you won't take off, that's all, or go after your gun. You try either, and I swear, that little bump on your head's gonna look like a love tap."

"Fine, okay. You don't have to freak out on me."

"You started it, jackass," Zeke said as he pocketed the keys. "Now I want you to get in my truck so we can discuss this in private."

"No way, man." His captive's look was sullen. "My fucking head is killing me. I need a doctor."

"You'll live," Zeke assured him, "as long as you cooperate, at least. Now get in there and try not to bleed on the upholstery."

As he looked into the man's face, the feeling of familiarity resurfaced, leaving Zeke to wonder if he knew him, or if he merely resembled someone Zeke did know. He opened the passenger door and stared expectantly until the man did as he was told.

"Sit there with your palms flat on your thighs where I can see them. And keep the hell still," Zeke warned before getting in on the driver's side and starting his pickup.

"Where are you taking me?" There was panic in the man's eyes, but he was careful not to break position. "You aren't taking me out somewhere to shoot me?"

"Wasn't in my plans." Zeke started driving, turning back in the direction he had come. "So tell me, back at the visitor's center that night, why'd you run?"

"You came at me. You're a big dude—hell of a lot bigger than me. And I hate confrontations."

"Sure," Zeke scoffed. "That's why you started shooting. Because you're such a freaking pacifist."

"I didn't shoot at you. I don't even own a damned gun. If you don't believe it, check out my truck. I had my phone stashed in the glove box. That's all I wanted, I swear."

"I didn't see another soul that night. Everyone had left, and mine was the only vehicle in the lot. So if you weren't the one firing, then who was?"

"It had to be that woman I was meeting."

"Woman? What woman?"

"She was supposed to pick me up there."

"Who? Who was she?" Zeke demanded.

"C'mon, man. I'm married, happily enough, but you know how it is. I like to get myself a little on the side from time to time. I start naming names, and all that's over."

"Who? And while you're at it, who the hell are you?" Zeke pressed. When no response came, he said, "Have it your way. But we're heading back to Presidio County, where you can do your talking to the sheriff there. And the feds, too, while you're at it. Those transportation people are really eager to hear your take on that canopy latch they found."

This last was pure speculation, the only guess Zeke could come up with that would explain why the man had so quickly disappeared after Rachel's crash landing, why he would feel the need to run when Zeke had spotted him later.

It might have been a shot in the dark, but the color immediately drained from the man's face and he stammered, "It was all her idea, I swear. I'm not taking the heat for any of that bullshit. I was just there to watch, that's all."

When Zeke's jaw clenched with rage, his captive trembled visibly. "You—you're not going to hurt me, are you? I wasn't the one who did it, I swear I wasn't. I didn't have anything to do with—"

"You're about to have way more serious trouble than your sex-on-the-side drying up. And if I find out you had one damned thing to do with hurting Rachel Copeland—"

"She's—she's your woman?" Terror filled his voice. "Shit, I'm sorry man, I had no idea."

It burned in Zeke's gut that he couldn't properly claim Rachel, but he said nothing to correct the man's mistake. "Which explains why you had best tell me the guilty party's name while you still can. Otherwise, I have to tell you, I know plenty of out-of-the-way places I could dump your body between here and the Presidio County Sheriff's office. Because I'm not a man with much to lose."

Zeke had no intention of killing anybody, but he allowed his fury to spill out in his words in the hope the threat would be enough.

Apparently it was, for the man beside him blurted, "It was Lili. Lili Vega. She wanted Rachel out of the picture so she could snatch up Walter Copeland's business once he loses his license."

The driver smiled, for she finally, *finally* had him in her sights. Alive and in the flesh, looking so much like the photo she had studied. A photo Providence had placed in her hands and Justice let her recognize.

She felt blessed for this good fortune, and for the increasing vigilance that had prompted her to buy a police scanner with some of the money she'd taken from the ATM. A nice young man—despite his long hair—working at the Carlsbad, New Mexico, Radio Shack where she'd stopped, had helpfully looked up the emergency frequencies she needed on the Internet and set the scanner for her. When he wouldn't take a tip, she'd given him a hug in thanks, since he reminded her of her son.

She'd only wanted to assure herself she had not been discovered, to gain an early warning if the Presidio County Sheriff started looking for her. She hadn't bargained on the radio leading her to the man she had been almost certain she'd lost.

Earlier this morning, when she had stopped by the pathetic little hovel where he'd hidden, she had found it stripped and emptied of his clothing. Very recently, she guessed, since he'd left animals behind. She'd shrieked with fury, thinking he had somehow been forewarned against her, that he had robbed her of her chance to finish this at last. To repay a debt of blood and torment, a sin that had destroyed lives.

For twenty years, she had been waiting, twenty years her family had been suffering. And though the first of Willie's so-called *friends* had told her everything as he had pleaded for his miserable life, right down to the name of the real killer, she wasn't letting any of them escape justice. Particularly the one who had been paid to safeguard Willie—the one whose disappearance had drawn things out for so many years.

And then, the call went out, and she smiled, knowing where to catch him. And hoping she could figure out a way to get him to pull over before the county sheriff beat her to it.

CHAPTER THIRTY

Injustice is relatively easy to bear; what stings is justice.
—Henry Louis Mencken,
from Prejudices, Third Series

Far too frightening to crawl back beneath the porch again. The thought of risking being trapped inside there, swallowing back screams to prevent discovery, set panic swirling and the pulse pounding.

But the observer had long been alert to the presence of such nests and knew of another—more certainly real—which had recently appeared in one of the hangars on the far side of the airport. Not a wasps' nest, this one, but made by some kind of bees. Someone else who'd seen them had been worried they might be of the Africanized variety and thought they ought to be exterminated before they got out of hand.

Whatever kind of bees they were, they'd been plenty pissed when, still half-stupefied by the chill of the morning, they and their nest had been unceremoniously scraped off by a long-handled shovel and dumped inside a thick brown paper bag. The observer—pounding heart in throat—quickly grasped the top and twisted it closed.

"Jesus. *Yes.*" Un-stung and dizzy with relief, the bees' captor laughed to hear the furious buzzing of the suddenly roused creatures. Trapped in a confined space, helpless—let the little bastards see how they enjoyed it.

"But don't worry. It won't be long." Not since Her Royal Highness had called earlier to check the schedule, to see if there would be a glider and someone available to give her a tow. Though her father had taken the day off for personal business, Rachel would come soon, she'd said, would be there by the time the bright sun warmed things up for better flying.

The heat would liven up the bees, too, in their thin cocoon tucked halfway beneath the glider's rudder cable. Secured in such a way that the paper would rip open soon after Rachel set off on her final flight.

After parking the pickup she had borrowed from her father, Rachel made her way toward the glider hangar.

"Hey, Lili, how's it going?" Rachel tried to mask her pain with false cheer but must have overshot the mark, considering the concern in the younger pilot's dark eyes.

"Sister, you look strung out." Lili tucked back a strand of hair—now colored neon orange instead of the hot pink she'd had previously. Behind that streak, she had another dyed bright aqua.

Rachel gestured toward Lili's head and tried to change the subject. "Kind of a tropical effect. I love it."

"Thanks." Lili's glow lasted only moments. "But seriously, what's wrong?"

With a forced smile, Rachel answered, "Nothing flying can't fix."

She only wished it could be so easy. Short on sleep and struggling not to wonder how far from Marfa Zeke had by this time traveled, she was also feeling lousy about this morning's run-in with her dad. She'd begged and finally browbeat him into letting her make an eye doctor appointment. After convincing the medical secretary to work her dad in today, Rachel had completed her "betrayal" by calling Patsy, already at The Roost despite her late night, and asking her to drive him to Alpine that afternoon.

"Glad to," her stepmother had responded. "I've been after him about it for the last six months. Now you can be the bad guy, and he'll have the whole drive to cry about your bullying on my shoulder."

"Works for me." Rachel had been glad to hear what had sounded like approval in the woman's voice. Rachel doubted she had thawed their long-running cold war in one fell swoop, but asking for Patsy's help with her dad had warmed the chill a bit.

Lili shot her a knowing look. "Man troubles, I'll bet. I'm an expert at those. Soaring's as good a cure as any. Bobby and I pulled out the Blanik for you, and the tow plane's fueled and ready. If you want, I'll tow you extra-high today. Give you a longer flight."

It was a good suggestion since, even though the day was heating up as the bright sun approached its apex, the best thermals wouldn't develop until later. The more altitude, the longer her glide back to earth. "Kind of troubles I've got, I'll take the highest tow you can dish out."

Rachel meant it, though as of this morning, she had one less worry. Her attorney had phoned to say it was official. The Underwood suit had been dropped. Her dad and stepmother would even get back a decent portion of the retainer, since Greenberg hadn't yet sunk too much time into the case.

Lili laughed. "You'd better bring your oxygen, then. Not really. But why don't you take this along to cheer you up."

Reaching into the front pocket of her flight shirt, she lifted out an MP3 player no larger than a pack of gum. After messing with the controls and unraveling the headphones, she offered it to Rachel with a grin.

"I put together a mix of songs for flying that is unbe*liev*-able. You're gonna love it, promise. I guarantee that you'll land smiling, or your money back."

"Well, okay. Sure." Rachel took it, feeling doubtful not only about Lili's taste in music—since the bar where she worked was as notorious for its blaringly loud hard rock as its rough-hewn reputation—but also her sudden burst of kindness. More than likely, the younger pilot was feeling magnanimous in victory since she figured that Rachel was no longer any obstacle to her hopelessly one-sided lust affair with Zeke.

Might as well take advantage of her good mood while I can.

Rachel could all-too-easily foresee a day when Lili would blame her for breaking Zeke's heart and "driving" him away.

Bobby Bauer drove the golf cart over from an odd-looking small plane he'd been working on in front of a nearby hangar. He looked happier than Rachel had seen him in a long time.

"Ready to go up?" he asked. "I'm sort of in the middle of something, but I can spare a few for ground crew duty."

Rachel squinted in the direction of the patriotically painted red-white-and-blue plane he'd been working on. "Great paint job. Whose is it? Or I should say, *what* is it?"

Bobby grinned. "Mine and my brother's. Isn't it great? One of those metal home-built kits. We've adapted an old Mazda rotary engine to put in it."

Rachel smiled, glad to see him so enthusiastic. Clearly, restoring contact with at least one member of his family had lifted a portion of the burden he carried.

Lili's forehead crinkled. "You're putting a *car* engine in a plane? Wouldn't it be easier just to—"

"Like I keep telling you, Lili-girl, life's not always about *easy*."

It sprang to mind that Lili's grandmother should have given her the same advice about her dating habits, but Rachel swallowed back the unkind thought and gestured toward some promising puffs of cloud. "Could be some decent thermals popping. Ready?"

She checked over the single-seat Blanik, a cross-country sailplane her father often flew. Though this glider was only a couple of years old, Rachel paid particular attention to the cockpit's hinges and closure apparatus. Such failures might be rare, but every time she thought about the accident, she felt light-headed.

But everything looked great, and the radio was working, so she swung her body down into the tiny cockpit, an act that—for everything that was so desperately wrong in her life—still sent frissons of excitement dancing up her spine.

Strapped inside this small space, she knew she could find the respite, perhaps even a measure of the peace, she needed to get through this first, worst day of letting Zeke go.

The best thing about these little sailplanes, Rusty, her father said so often, *is you can't afford the weight or space to take worries up with you.*

Not long later, she would realize how horribly wrong he'd been on that count.

By the time the emergency lights flashed in Zeke's rearview mirror, his passenger had lapsed into a stubborn silence. Though Zeke had prodded him with questions, the man refused to give his name or offer further details about his affair with Lili Vega.

The sheriff switched on his SUV's siren to get their attention. As Zeke pulled onto the shoulder, his gut knotted. With Castillo's suspicions running so high last night, would he listen to anything Zeke had to tell him?

Castillo headed his way, his short legs pumping to eat up the short distance and his expression inscrutable behind dark sunglasses. Yet from the way he moved and the angle of his head, Zeke had an idea the sheriff was seriously pissed.

Cranking down the window, Zeke tried to deflect a storm by saying, "I've brought you back a fellow here you'll want to speak with. This man's admitted his involvement in a plot by Lili Vega to bring down Rachel Copeland's glider."

The man beside him lurched into a denial. "I sure as hell didn't say *I* did it. It was Lili. Lili's idea all the way."

"Lili Vega?" Harlan flushed, obviously caught off guard, before shaking his head as if to regroup. "Get out of the truck, why don't you? Both of you."

Once they did, Castillo motioned them to the far side of the pickup, where they would be protected from the few vehicles that rushed past. This far outside of Marfa's limits, their only other witnesses were a small herd of Hereford cattle, who barely looked up from their grazing.

Harlan made a motion indicating that both of them should turn around. "Hands against the truck, boys."

Zeke's jaw tightened with frustration, but he allowed the pat down, as did the other man. When Castillo found neither armed, he grunted a request for identification.

"Mine's back in my truck," the thin man told him before nodding sullenly toward Zeke. "This asshole forced me to leave it there and go with him. That's kidnapping, right? He should be arrested."

"It was a citizen's arrest," Zeke corrected as he passed his wallet to Castillo. "And besides, he hit me first."

As the sheriff flipped it open, Zeke held his breath, recalling the day he'd bought the driver's license from an El Paso forger who did most of his business with illegal aliens.

"Not bad," Castillo conceded. "If I didn't know for a fact that you don't have a real one, I'd've bought it for sure."

Rather than denying the truth, Zeke blew a slow breath through his nostrils and waited for the lawman's next move. Castillo slid the ID free, then passed the wallet and its few remaining contents back to Zeke.

"I'll just hold on to this for now, 'til we can get things sorted out." Castillo tucked the doctored license into the pocket beneath his badge and name tag. "Had a call from over in Jeff Davis County. Convenience store clerk phoned the sheriff there, upset about a disturbance by the gas pumps. Deputy got there after you'd gone, but the witness pointed out the pickup left behind and reported you were headed this way, across the county line. And what with the description of the truck, I had a pretty good idea . . ."

"I stopped for gas and saw him standing at the next pump," Zeke said. "Couldn't very well leave him there. This bastard shot my truck. Owed me at the very least for that truck window I had replaced."

"I told you I didn't shoot at you," the stranger argued. "I don't even own a weapon. You can check it out, Sheriff."

"Be a lot easier—" Castillo's expression hardened "—if you gave me your name."

"They call me Sy," he said, "for Simonton. Gideon Simonton."

There was a long pause during which Castillo merely stared at him before speaking.

"Didn't there used to be some Simontons . . . lived way out by Shafter?" Castillo shook his head at the mention of a nearly deserted ghost town. "You aren't part of that bunch, are you?"

Simonton bristled, shot back a defensive-sounding, "I was only nine then. It's nothing to do with who I am now."

"Terrible tragedy," Castillo murmured. "That's all I meant by it. Before my time in the department, but still, you hear about such things, with so many people dying."

"What people?" Zeke asked.

"None of your damned business," Simonton growled.

"You've made your life my business. Wasn't my idea."

"There was a fire," Castillo told Zeke. "Killed five or six people in a trailer, years back. Family raisin' a bunch of rag-tag kids out there on next to nothing, and—"

"Leave them out of this." Sy's voice dropped to a plea, almost a whisper. "Almost thirty goddamned years and you'd think a man could get past—"

"It's no crime, being a survivor," Castillo put in. "And a boy can't help what kind of family he's born into."

Castillo's voice hinted at some misery that explained the sullen shame in Sy's eyes. A brand of poverty, Zeke guessed, far more desperate than the type that tainted his own past. Neglect, abuse: specters that would haunt a soul forever.

"Tell me about Lili," the sheriff said. "How'd you get started up with that girl? You meet her over at the Psychedelic Scorpion?"

Zeke might have imagined it, but he thought he heard familiarity in Castillo's voice—and not only with the bar whose fights were frequently reported in the *Big Bend Sentinel*. Was it possible he knew Lili from responding to those dustups, or did he have some more personal history with her in spite of the difference in their ages? But maybe it was neither. In a town as small as Marfa, people had all sorts of long-standing connections. People unlike Zeke, who had no one at all.

Sy shook his head, his gaze locked onto a lonely, scraggly wildflower that had bloomed along the roadside. "Hell, no. Place gets too rough for my taste. Met her at the street dance during the Marfa Lights Festival this past fall. She's a pretty little thing, that Lili. Likes men plenty. Isn't the kind to get hung up about the technicalities."

"He means she didn't care that he's married," Zeke muttered, the comment reminding him of Castillo's history with his first wife, Patsy, and the price she'd paid for his indiscretion. "But let's cut to the chase. You said earlier, she wanted Rachel gone so she could snatch up Walter Copeland's business. And you said something about him losing his license, too. You mean his pilot's license?"

Sy shrugged. "She thought he'd lose it for sure. On account of how his eyesight's failing. But since Rachel's come back, he's been grooming her to take things over."

Zeke shook his head. "And Lili thought if she could kill or scare Rachel off, Copeland would let *her* have the business?"

It didn't fit what he'd gleaned from the talk he'd picked up over the years. Walter seemed fond enough of Lili and spoke well of her flying. But Zeke had never sensed any sort of father-daughter bond—nor anything remotely improper— between the two. Certainly nothing to cause Lili to imagine herself as a substitute for Rachel. But then, Zeke had never encouraged Lili's attentions either, and according to Rachel, the younger woman had warned her away from him.

So Lili was flirtatious, probably even loose by a lot of people's standards. And she might delude herself in some respects, but would she resort to murder?

"She tried making some phone calls," Sy explained. "But Rachel just dug her damned heels in deeper."

Castillo frowned. "You mean to say that Lili's been the one harassing Rachel?"

Sy nodded.

"So what was your part in it?" the sheriff pressed.

"I didn't do a damned thing."

"And she just happened to tell you all about her plans?" Zeke challenged. "You helped her sabotage that glider, didn't you?"

"What else is she planning?" Castillo asked darkly. "She got any more ideas about taking out Rachel, since she didn't run her off the first crack?"

Shaken by the thought, Zeke looked at Simonton, who continued staring resolutely at the lonely blue flower.

But Zeke couldn't take the waiting, couldn't stand the thought that even now, Lili might be planning some way to hurt Rachel. "Answer him, goddamn you."

From the airport not far south of them, he heard the rising drone of a plane's takeoff.

CHAPTER THIRTY-ONE

O human race, born to fly upward, wherefore at a little wind dost thou so fall?

—Dante Alighieri,
from The Divine Comedy, Purgatorio, *Canto XII*

As the sailplane gained altitude, Rachel marveled. Not at the familiar landscape that fell away beneath her, nor at the eternal stretch of blue sky. What really got her was the unexpected discovery that Lili Vega had amazing taste in music.

Rachel turned up the volume, allowed the majestic strains of Aaron Copeland's "Fanfare for the Common Man" to fill the earphones. Allowed the swell of sound to illuminate the tawny desert plain, to make it new to her again.

Make it new. The thought billowed upward like a thermal, bubbled into prayer. *Make me new again and whole. Untouched and unscarred. Unbroken, clean and strong enough . . .*

Her photograph of Zeke filled her mind, the frozen image melting into recollections of his movements as he worked. The bliss burning sunlike through his clouded eyes after they'd made love.

Strong enough to let him go . . .

Satisfied with her altitude, she radioed her intention before releasing the tether of the towrope. With a click, it peeled away, and Lili curved around and started her descent. Rachel caught a fleeting glimpse of her face, its expression hidden by the shadow of her cap's bill. The last Rachel saw of her was the gleam of sunlight off a wing as the Piper Pawnee spiraled downward toward its landing. As the drone of the tow plane's engine fell away, Rachel found herself at 3,500 feet, blissfully alone save for the steady rush of wind.

The sheriff allowed Zeke to drive his pickup the short distance to the airport, *"On the condition you don't go and try some jackass move like running."*

He'd said this with a pointed look at the boxes piled in the truck's bed. But Zeke had given his word and followed Castillo's SUV, where Simonton had been placed in the backseat in cuffs.

Zeke was surprised Castillo hadn't locked him back there, too. Maybe the sheriff was granting him a little leeway because of his concern for Rachel. Or maybe—still suspicious but uncertain—he was allowing Zeke enough rope to thoroughly hang himself.

Zeke didn't give a damn about his reasons. All he wanted was to see Lili Vega locked up so he could assure Rachel she was safe. But as he and the sheriff both climbed out of their vehicles, Zeke saw no sign of any of the Copelands, though Walter's truck was parked close to the hangar. Lili's yellow hatchback was there, too, along with Bobby Bauer's big Ford, though Bobby, who was working on a small plane, was the only one in evidence.

Dread hollowed Zeke's stomach, a sick premonition that he'd caught Simonton too late.

The sheriff took off his Western hat and waved it at Bobby. "Mind coming over?" he called.

By the time Bobby drove over in the golf cart, the towplane had zipped in for a landing. Zeke craned back his neck, looking for a glider.

Bobby seemed confused and more than a little concerned. "What's going on? Is something wrong?"

"We're looking for Lili," Castillo told him. "Have some questions for her."

"Where's Rachel?" Zeke asked, unable to silence his anxiety.

"Lili's right there." Bobby pointed to the towplane, where she was climbing out. "And Rachel's flying. She just went up. You need me to radio her to come in?"

Lili trotted over, looking more curious than worried. "What's up, Harlan?"

Zeke wondered at her use of his first name. Was he still the same philandering bastard he'd been years before?

"Have to take you to my office, Lili." Regret weighed down the sheriff's voice. "Got some questions that need answering."

"Questions about *what?*" she asked, her dark gaze darting from Zeke to Bobby and then back to the sheriff. She rubbed her hands together, over and over, like a child washing. "I didn't—if somebody's wife's said anything about me—"

"It's nothing to do with anybody's wife," Castillo assured her. "More to do with Gideon Simonton—Sy, he says they call him. Got him back there in my vehicle. He's had some things to say about your involvement with the crash of Rachel Copeland's glider on March sixth."

As Lili's face went blank and drained of color, Zeke noticed a second reaction, more surprising than the first. A jerk of Bobby Bauer's head when the name Simonton was mentioned. A stepping back as he turned toward the sheriff's SUV and reached for something in his pocket.

With two steps, Zeke launched himself at the man, catching him squarely from behind and knocking a compact, flat-sided pistol out of his hand as both men tumbled down.

"It's Bauer," Zeke shouted at the sheriff. "It's Bauer. Get his gun."

Pinned facedown, Bauer ground out, "Goddammit, let Gid out of there. Let my brother go. And get *off* of me—I have to help Gid."

Zeke moved aside, still pressing down the man's hands, as Castillo cuffed him. They hauled the pilot to his feet.

"Gideon Simonton's your *brother?*" Castillo demanded.

Bauer's eyes were wild. "You can't lock him in a cage. Can't. He almost burned to death in—if I hadn't got him out through the window . . . He wasn't—he wasn't like the others. He was—He didn't—he never hurt me the way they did. He brought me food down there. And water. And he never called me Bastard."

"*Bobby?*" Emotion contorted Lili's prettiness. "What the *hell* is going on? And who's Gideon?"

"Don't lock Gid up," begged Bauer. "I'll tell you everything if you don't lock him in there. It was Gid's wife made the phone calls, and he helped me with—*I* was the one messed with the canopy. I just wanted—"

"You *sabotaged* that glider?" Lili charged forward, slapping at him until Castillo pushed her back. Even then, she thrust forward, screaming, "You could have *killed* Walt's daughter— after everything he's done for you? You ungrateful bastard. And you two schemed to *blame* me, didn't you? If somebody got caught, just blame the little wetback bar-bitch, was that how it went?"

"Back off," Castillo told her. "Back the hell off now. We've got 'im. And I didn't buy that story, Lili. I swear, I never believed you'd—"

"Go to hell, Harlan."

"Somebody call Rachel," Zeke broke in. "Somebody get her down here, make sure she's all right."

Rachel sucked in a deep breath at the sight of an unwelcome passenger. Striped with yellow-and-black warning, it bounced angrily against the clear canopy. Swallowing her discomfort, she told herself, *It's no big deal. If I don't bother it, it won't bother—*

She ripped off the headphones as she noticed a second, then a third bee zipping through the tight space. Then she heard the buzzing, loud and angry, beneath her seat.

That was when she realized that her *friend*, the suddenly-so-generous Lili Vega, had arranged for her to die.

Before anyone could call her, the squawk of Bauer's radio interrupted. From one of his pockets, static crackled and a frantic female voice cried, "Trying to land—won't make it to the airport. 'Bout a mile southwest—Bobby, come and find me. Hurry. I'm hurt and I'll need help."

While Zeke turned to scan the sky, Castillo pulled the radio from Bauer's pocket, keyed it, shouted, "Rachel? It's the sheriff. Where exactly are you?"

After a delay followed by silence, he pushed the radio toward Lili. "Did I do this right? You call her. Find out where exactly she is, what's the medical emerg—"

A roaring in Zeke's head drowned out the conversation. Instead, he grabbed Bauer. "What the hell did you do? What did you do to that sailplane?"

The man's head bobbed back and forth, as a child rocks to seek its comfort. "She didn't deserve it. Draining Walter's money, draining away his health—Didn't do a damned thing to deserve a business we'd worked to build all these years. A business Gid and I could run together like we—"

"I don't give a damn about that. Tell me, or I swear, I'm going to knock those teeth right down your—"

"Damn it, *settle down*." Castillo grabbed an arm and hauled him backward with surprising strength for a man of his height. "You're not helping. Lili—can you raise her?"

"Rachel? It's me, Lili. *Answer*."

But nothing came back except static, while Zeke, Lili, and the sheriff all stared toward the blank horizon.

CHAPTER THIRTY-TWO

But psychoanalysis has taught that the dead—a dead parent, for example—can be more alive for us, more powerful, more scary, than the living. It is the question of ghosts.
—Jacques Derrida,
quoted in the New York Times Magazine, January 23,
1994

Three stings, four. As another pierced her eyelid, Rachel filled the cockpit with her screams.

She fought the need to swat, fought to concentrate on getting down to earth alive—and out of this hell—as fast as possible. Using both dizzying spirals and her airbrakes, she dropped altitude. But disoriented by her pain and terror, she realized too late that she was well off from the airport and too low to do anything but make an emergency landing where she was.

She'd attempted calling Bobby, but another bee had nailed her—the side of her neck this time—and now the ground's upward rush made her forget the radio. *Just focus on the landing,* she ordered herself as she fought to level the wings, to slow her meteoric descent. *Do that, and you can freak out later. Do that, and there'll be a later.*

In the background, she heard Lili—that crazy bitch—calling her, but Rachel tuned out the sound, tuned out everything to reach a place beyond the pain, the rage and panic. To reach past her instinctive desire to pop the canopy to bail out and instead latch onto whatever skill and courage she could grab.

As the ground flew toward her, a last, defiant thought blasted through awareness: *I am Walter Copeland's daughter. I will not die this way.*

"Take the plane and find her," Castillo told Lili. "Circle where you see her and I'll follow."

As Lili raced back toward the towplane, he told Zeke, "You go ahead in your truck. I'll be there soon as I secure Bauer in the back with Simonton and call for help."

"An ambulance." Zeke was already climbing in his pickup as he said it. "Don't forget an ambulance for Rachel."

"Trying to land—won't make it to the airport." With her desperation screaming through his mind, he had to fight the fear that she'd come down hard enough to smash the fragile carapace that was her only protection. Instead, he forced himself to focus on the direction she had given—about a mile southwest—and think where this might put her and where he might cut over or find a vantage point to look around.

"Hurry," she'd told Bobby. *"I'm hurt and I'll need help."*

Hurt how, if she had not yet landed? Was it possible, Zeke wondered, that he'd misunderstood her, that she'd already been on the ground when she had called? He mashed the gas pedal, not caring that a box of tools in the pickup's bed had spilled, creating a clattering racket just behind him.

Much to Rachel's shock, she survived the landing, though the little glider bounced jarringly on its wheels and bumped along the weedy plain. It had barely stopped when she flipped open the canopy and dove out onto the sandy scrape.

Another sting—the damned bees clearly didn't appreciate the rough landing—had her standing to reclose the canopy and trap as many as she could inside. Apparently, she caught most by surprise, for after a few minutes, she'd either swatted (costing her another sting on the palm), outrun, or exhausted the rage of the last few.

Some twenty yards from the glider, Rachel staggered to a stop with her entire body shaking, her breath coming in ragged gasps, and pain radiating from what felt like every bit of flesh at once. God alone knew how many stings she'd suffered. Had it been a dozen? Fifteen? More?

With her right eye swollen shut already, she wondered if the allergy shots she'd taken through her twenties would save her. But as her thinking clouded, she couldn't remember whether bees had been among the problems treated. Didn't know if it would matter, if, allergy shots or not, she had taken too much venom.

Overwhelmed by the adrenaline still screaming through her veins, she wiped her bleeding nose, then dropped to curl onto her side and tremble among the yellow grasses. *Should call someone,* she thought, but a pat down of her pockets told her she had lost her cell phone—probably in the glider. And there was no way in hell she was lifting that canopy for another round with the furious bees.

At least start walking toward the airport. See if you can flag down Bobby's pickup. She remembered spotting a dirt ranch road fairly close by as she'd landed but knew that her scant directions might not be much help in finding her.

But when Rachel tried to rise, she couldn't coordinate her movements, and when she tried to lift her head, a black wave of fatigue rolled her back down.

CHAPTER THIRTY-THREE

Revenge, at first though sweet,
Bitter ere long back on itself recoils.

—*John Milton,*
Paradise Lost, *Book IX*

Light flashed in Zeke's rearview mirror as an SUV made a U-turn on the highway behind him. Ignoring it, he braked abruptly, then took the curve of a dirt ranch road so fast that he thought for one, wild second that he was sure to overturn. Recovering, he picked up speed and rattled over a cattle guard, an open grate that livestock would not cross.

Peering upward, he scanned the sky for the towplane but saw only puffs of cloud. "Find her, find her, Lili. Where the hell are you?"

He caught sight of the small plane about a quarter mile away. Had he turned in too soon? Should he have taken the next road? But he saw no indication Lili had yet found anything, so he continued on his course, frantically scanning left and right as he bumped over the rutted road.

His rearview mirror showed a puff of rising dust. Castillo must have followed, also betting that this ranch road would be the closest to the site.

The crash site. His mind conjured images from the days when he'd watched TV. Fiery wreckage, the staccato pulse of red lights, bodies being carried out on stretchers. His rational mind knew that gliders carried no fuel; there would be no smoke, no explosion. But the thought that it was Rachel out here somewhere, *his* Rachel, short-circuited all logic.

If I find you in one piece, I'll be damned if I let go.

A bright flash drew his eye—light gleaming off a turning plane's wing. Lili, circling low above a spot off to his
right. Praying his old rattletrap of a truck would make it,
he cranked the wheel and drove into the ragged grass to cut
straight toward the spot.

The first sound to penetrate was the bawling of a calf for its
mother, followed by the rumbling of a small plane's engine.
Distant sounds, receding sounds. Noise that faded into the
background static of the black void of her awareness.

Some passage of time. A few seconds? A few hours? No
way to know before another sound cut through. Hard,
metal slam—a door, perhaps? Sharp, urgent call. Familiar,
though, and reassuring.

Rachel *knew* that voice. She knew it, even if she could
not find her own to respond.

"Rachel. Rachel, answer me," he called.

Zeke was calling. Or was he? She had been dreaming, she
realized, nightmare images of Kyle. The feel of her sweat-
slick palm tight on the gun's butt. The slide of her finger
against the trigger.

And the single shot that saved her. A shot she was finished
regretting. Finished, because otherwise, what was the point
of surviving?

But as she roused, those images receded. Leaving only the
sound of Zeke's voice. No nightmare, no dream, but real
and solid. Here, by whatever miracle ordained it.

So answer him, ordered her unwieldy brain. Yet her
tongue lay so thick in her mouth, she could scarcely breathe
around it. Her limbs twitched, but purposeful movement
was beyond her.

Still, she heard his voice, his panic marking his progress as
he raced toward the sailplane, instead of the spot where she
lay, half-hidden by spring grasses. Toward the sailplane, where
bees awaited, buzzing fury as they bounced around the closed

cockpit. Panic slicing through her, she barely registered the approach of another vehicle, another door thrown open.

"Don't open it," she tried to warn Zeke, a muffled slur of sound she could barely hear herself. *Just turn around. Turn around and find me. I'm right here, if you'll only look around . . .*

"What—what the hell?" she heard him ask. "Wha— *Rachel!* Where the *hell* are you?"

"Here," she grunted, fighting to open at least one eye and putting everything she had into that one word. Still, it came out muddled. Quiet. A sound lost beneath the call of some bird, the hiss of wind blown through the scant vegetation.

"Rachel? Is that—" Zeke asked, followed by, "Who the hell are—?"

A single gunshot shattered her hopes. A detonation amplified by her remembered shock, the sickening horror of the recoil. Anticipation of the hot rain of blood and brain that would—but somehow didn't—spatter her skin.

Because this was no flashback, no memory dragged forth from the past by terror. For it was Zeke she heard yelping in astonishment and pain and thumping hard against the fragile glider. The desert breeze brought her a bitter gift of gun smoke, its acrid stench enough to jerk her free from her stupor, from her past, as it sent fresh adrenaline gushing through her.

Because someone had just shot Zeke, and if he wasn't dead, he would be if she didn't get him help.

"What the—what the hell is this?" Zeke asked, staring at the woman walking up to him, her handgun pointed at his chest, her blue eyes glassy and unfocused. Filthy and disheveled, she closed in on him, her blonde hair stiff in unwashed clumps.

It was a wonder she hadn't killed him—hadn't even hit him—with that first blast. Startled, he'd slammed backward against the glider, then fallen on his ass when his feet slipped beneath him.

Not exactly a testimony to his reflexes, but his concern

for Rachel had short-circuited all else, including the memory of the warning he'd been given last night.

Shaking his head, he stared at a woman in her late thirties maybe, slightly built, and shaking behind the raised weapon. Far too young to be Willie's mother. But she looked—could she be?

"You aren't Mrs. Tyler. You—you can't be, so then—*Marlene*?" It made no sense. Hadn't it been Marlene who'd come to warn him last night? Why do that if she'd meant to gun him down herself?

"You've destroyed my life, you know that?" Distorted with rage, her voice trembled as she closed in. "You were all she could think of, all she knew for so long. My mother stopped loving me the night Willie died. Stopped loving all of us. Forever afterward, no matter what I did, I could never—No one could ever make her look at us."

"I'm sorry," Zeke said, but she went on as though she hadn't heard.

"And my father—my poor daddy. He took good care of her. *Such* good care. Even though she could never love him. And I promised him—we promised we would take care of my mother, too. Broken or not."

Something had broken in Marlene, also, Zeke knew. Something critical.

"I was an idiot to take your brother to that party," he admitted, "a damned fool to believe those assholes cared about anything but using me or that they wouldn't hurt him—"

"They're all dead. Do you know that? All dead except for you." A smile ticked at one corner of her mouth, beneath her empty eyes. "She started it. My mother. The first she found was Sam Henderson. Lots of crime in that part of New Orleans. Just another tourist, dead."

"She killed Sam?" Icy fear swirled in Zeke's chest.

Marlene nodded. "He was part of it. You all were. In Tulsa, it was Aaron . . ."

Zeke couldn't believe it. "Aaron Lynch? She murdered Aaron, too?"

They'd conspired to destroy his life, but Zeke had long since lost the thread of his hatred toward them. They had been kids themselves. Kids who'd compounded one sin with another out of terror, then had to live with the results of their lies.

Now they'd died for them.

"That was where—where I found her, Tulsa. At that motel, and . . ." Marlene's head shook back and forth, pain sparking in her blue eyes. "I only meant to stop her, get her home for help, the way I promised. Promised Daddy before he died . . ."

"Where's your mother, Marlene?"

"I didn't mean to, but she pointed the gun right at—I have a *husband*. And two boys—her own grandchildren, for God's sake. And my own mother would have—She would have shot me like a stray dog."

"You had to kill her, didn't you?"

Marlene shook her head, mouth opened in an unvoiced cry of anguish.

"You couldn't help it," Zeke guessed. "She didn't leave you any choice."

"She *made* me," Marlene whispered as tears cut paths through the film of dirt on her face. "Made me. And even after—she kept going. Kept—when I went to sleep, she killed again. Aaron Lynch—I found his body crumpled by my bumper, and I—"

"Are you sleepwalking now, too, Marlene? Is she making you do this? Last night, you tried to warn me. Do you remember that?"

Marlene stared at him, her tear-clumped lashes accentuating the pale emptiness of her blue eyes. Shaking her head, she said, "I'm not strong enough to stop her. Not until we see it through."

Alarmed by her ominous use of the word *we*, Zeke noticed some movement from the corner of his eye. Understanding it was Rachel—that she was about to walk into a situation that could kill her—he blurted, "What I did was wrong and stupid. But I didn't kill your brother. You have to know I never raised a hand to Willie—"

"I do know that. Aaron was the one who hit him so hard. He told me. He confessed and begged for my forgiveness. Pleaded for his life before I—before *she* killed him."

"But if you know I didn't kill Willie, why come after me? Why go after any of the others?"

"Every one of you had some part in it. If you hadn't taken him with you, if you hadn't run away and kept the truth hidden, then we wouldn't have all suffered so long. We wouldn't—"

He edged closer. "Marlene, this is crazy." *You're* crazy.

"Stop it. Stop right there." Fury vibrated through her words, and lip curling, she lifted the gun a little higher. Preparing to kill him, as she had killed before.

Zeke forced his voice to gentle tones as if to quiet a dangerous but frightened horse. "What can I do for you? What would you like me to say?"

"I'm sorry," she answered, voice shuddering with rage. "I'd like you to say you're *sorry*. For every forgotten birthday. For the wedding she wouldn't come to, the sons' births she ignored. For elevating my goddamned *stupid* brother to a god in her mind. For making me break my promise to my father and putting her in my head and—"

"No," cried Rachel, off to Zeke's left. "No, please, you can't—"

The woman with the pistol spun, and Zeke leaped. Not fast enough to prevent the thunderclap—not fast enough to stop Rachel from falling with a splash of crimson at her chest.

He crashed down on Marlene, so hard he heard the breath explode from her lungs and a crunch that sounded like bone splintering—probably her ribs beneath his greater weight. In spite of what had to be horrific pain, she twisted around, still clutching the pistol, bringing it upward in a speed-blurred arc. Upward, toward his head.

Reacting on instinct, he grabbed for her wrist, not

caring if he snapped it. Not caring about anything but stopping her, disabling her so he could get to Rachel. But even hurt, Marlene was too fast, her finger squeezing off a second round.

The explosion was so damned loud, it rattled his teeth, yet before the noise of it registered in his brain, he was conscience of the heat, the wet, the stink of blood and gun smoke.

But not *his* blood. As Marlene fell limp beneath him, it sank in that, rather than submit—or deal with the murders she'd committed—Marlene Tyler, Willie's sister, had taken her own life.

Pushing himself off her—heedless of the gore dripping from him—Zeke raced toward where Rachel lay sprawled on her back. She was breathing, thank God. But her breathing was a labored rasp, her face strangely contorted.

"Rachel," he cried as he fumbled with her bloody shirt, searching for the bullet hole. "How bad is—"

"Not hit," she choked out. "Not shot. *Stung.* Stung too many times."

He followed the trail of blood that ran from her nose to her shirt, figured she must have been hurt somehow in the landing. But his relief turned to horror when he saw her swollen right eye, took in the angry red welts on her face, her neck, her arms. Which fit with the bees he'd glimpsed inside the sailplane an instant before Marlene had surprised him.

Bobby Bauer—the fucking lunatic—must have booby-trapped the sailplane. "It was Bobby," he said. "He's been arrested. He was after your dad's business."

A siren's wail caught Zeke's attention.

"That'll be Harlan," he told Rachel. "He'll get an ambulance and you'll be safe. We'll both be safe because that crazy woman's dead and—"

Rachel closed the eye that wasn't swollen shut. "Then it's over. Finally over."

He pulled her wheezing form into his arms and breathed a solemn vow into her ear. "Not by a long shot. Because everything's just starting for you, Rachel. So help me God, I mean to make sure of that."

CHAPTER
THIRTY-FOUR

In the attitude of silence the soul finds the path in a clearer light, and what is elusive and deceptive resolves itself into crystal clearness.

—Mahatma Gandhi

Wednesday, March 26

"He'll come back. I swear it," Rachel whispered as she stroked Cholla's golden neck. "He'll be back. I know it."

The big gelding nickered, a rumbling equine statement of support. Not so much for Zeke, who had been transported today—in custody—to East Texas, but for the grain that rattled around the bucket she carried.

From somewhere nearby, an owl hooted a welcome to the extravagant sunset. Could Zeke even see the sky now, or was he locked up out of sight of windows? Would he be safe where he was going, or would he be destroyed by the same past that had come gunning for him in the form of a crazed woman?

At least *she* was no further threat. Rachel felt sorry for the woman's family. But not so sorry that she wouldn't have killed Marlene herself to save Zeke.

Zeke . . .

As Rachel fumbled with the gate, she teared up, thinking of how deputies had come into her hospital room—the heartless bastards—to arrest him. Thinking of the look he'd sent her over his shoulder. Not scared, but determined as he'd told her to get back in bed. "Take care of yourself. Take care of your dad and Patsy and my horses.

Because I'm coming back for you a free man. A free man or not at all."

Cholla pawed the earth and gave another throaty rumble, supremely annoyed to be the last of the three equines fed.

"All right, all right already." Rachel put down his bucket before securing the gate. She moved slowly, weighed down more by sadness than any lingering discomfort. Sadness not only over Zeke's arrest, but the discovery that someone she had known and trusted—a man her father had done so much to help—had resented her enough to try to kill her.

"It isn't just greed and resentment," Sheriff Castillo had told her and her family. *"Something's seriously wrong with that man's head. Something that got started years ago. According to his half brother—who's got a criminal record in his own right—Bobby was the scapegoat. Father thought he was a bastard—thought his wife had a lover—so he beat nine kinds of hell out of the poor kid, and did God only knows what all to him. Whatever it was, it twisted him up so bad, he's carrying on about the damned lights sending him messages, telling him what he has to do."*

"The lights?" she'd asked.

"The Marfa Lights." Castillo's voice had been grave. *"I'm no psychologist, but I think he used the lights as an excuse to act in his own interest. Only way he felt entitled to go after what he wanted."*

Throat aching, Rachel tried to swallow. According to the confession, Bobby's campaign to drive her out of town had led to her grandmother's death. He hadn't meant to kill her, he'd told Harlan, only to frighten Rachel away by sending a package supposedly from Kyle.

"Selfish son of a bitch," she said, unable to forgive him. Abused or not, he'd been out to steal from her father—and he'd been willing to do anything, from enlisting his half brother's help to committing murder, to ensure his place as successor to Walter Copeland's business.

A business she meant to run herself, with her father by her side. Sharing his decades of knowledge, restoring old gliders for others. He would serve an important role, whether he understood that now or not. He would have a vital, satisfying life, in spite of the macular degeneration blurring the center of his field of vision.

There was a growl near her feet, and J.D. ran barking toward a silver Range Rover heading down the dirt road. In no mood for the intrusion, Rachel frowned and wondered if she could bring herself to be polite.

Looking elegant as ever, Antoinette Gallinardi slipped out of the SUV, her yapping lapdog struggling at the end of its designer leash. "Hush, Coco," she scolded.

The noise continued until J.D. strutted over, hackles raised, and growled. While the two dogs sniffed each other, Antoinette cast her a troubled look. "Your father said I'd find you here."

"So you've found me. Why? Did Terri give you some more tips on how to kick me while I'm down?" Rachel knew damned well that Gallinardi's assistant had relentlessly maneuvered to influence the Blank Canvas Society to kick her out of the showing. All because of petty jealousy—and a high school grudge over a band director who had long since been sent packing.

"Terri Zavala is no longer my employee." Antoinette glanced down at the dogs but appeared reassured by wagging tails. "I'm only sorry I allowed her . . . prejudices to influence the board's vote—and mine as well, I'm embarrassed to admit. I'm coming to ask, can you ever possibly forgive me?"

Rachel looked at her, considering. She let her squirm before giving an answer. "I can forgive you. Because it isn't worth my energy to stay pissed."

If Gallinardi didn't like the language, she could take a hike. Because Rachel's emotions were far too raw to pretty up for Art Deco Woman's delicate sensibilities.

"I'm so glad." Antoinette sounded as earnest as a schoolgirl. "Because I think I can convince them to reinstate you, to publicize the event more widely than ever, invite art critics from all over the country, the world, even—"

"With my *work* as the focus, mine and all the other Marfa artists?"

"Oh, absolutely. The one thing we all do agree on is that at this point, any further mention of that . . . that ugliness in your past would reflect poorly on the residents' perception of the foundation. We need to keep the focus on your talent, which, believe me, is more than capable of standing on its own."

Rachel tried to resurrect the warm glow such praise had once kindled. But Zeke's absence cast a shadow, especially here, where she half expected to see him every moment.

"I believe—" Gallinardi pursed her lips, then went on "—that if we can steer clear of any additional . . . unpleasantness or any association with . . . undesirable elements, I can convince them to proceed."

"By 'undesirable elements,'" said Rachel, "you're referring to what—or whom—exactly?"

"To a fugitive charged with criminal wrongdoing," Antoinette said flatly. "I know this may be difficult, but I think if you were to . . . let's say *distance* yourself from this Mr. Pike—or is it Langley—the board would feel far more secure supporting you. Especially considering our commitment to community education."

Rachel stared in disbelief. "So you're saying . . . ?"

"I have a great many connections, Rachel. Connections I am only too happy to use to promote a person of talent and integrity. I'm sure you realize this could be your chance to move beyond the realm of part-time dabbling and develop the gift you've been blessed with. It would be my pleasure and my privilege to do it . . . but I'm afraid my hands are tied if you insist on continuing your involvement with a man who's surely bound for prison."

Rachel pictured herself paraded around the foundation's showing, the jeweled collar around her neck connected to Art Deco Woman's leash. Rachel had already seen evidence of the scope of Antoinette's influence. Pleased, the woman could be the key to realizing all of Rachel's aspirations; rankled, however, Gallinardi might use those same powerful connections to blackball her "ungrateful" protégé within the fine art world. To a lesser extent, she could also damage the business Walter Copeland had spent decades building. A business Rachel's entire family was counting on for income.

Rachel weighed these factors carefully, weighed them against the contents of her heart. As the scale tipped, a lump formed in her throat.

A lump of regret that everything of value had its price. And sometimes, heaven help her, that price was a love led trusting to the altar, its throat slashed in a bloody sacrifice.

Wednesday, April 2

"What the hell do you mean?" Zeke stared puzzled at his younger brother, who sat across from him in a small room near the cell block, one reserved for attorneys to meet with their clients. Painted institutional green and furnished with dented metal castoffs, the room was kept ice cold for the "comfort" of its users.

Jason broke into a broad smile that reminded Zeke of their late father. Who would roll over in his grave if he'd learned his second son had become a Preston County prosecutor, complete with shark-gray suit and tie. *Somebody has to ride herd on the justice system in this county,* Jason had explained, *at least try to keep these assholes honest.*

"I mean," Jason told him, "that you're a free man. With Shane Drake out of his coma and willing to testify that Aaron Lynch killed Willie and then threatened the other two to stop them from talking—"

"He didn't threaten them. Didn't have to. They were all more than willing to pin that murder on a Langley if it would keep them out of trouble."

"He doesn't want that to come out in court."

Zeke shook his head, confused. "*Who* doesn't?"

"The district attorney. My boss." Jason leaned over the

table, a shrewd expression on his leanly handsome face. "Who happens to be Shane Drake's mother's brother."

"Oh, I get it," Zeke said. "Uncle DA would rather let a Langley walk than expose his nephew to criminal charges."

"There *is* that," Jason told him, "along with the election this fall. First time in Herb-the-Nerve's tenure he hasn't been running unopposed. Believe me, this is one can of worms he doesn't want anybody opening."

"So that's *it*? After all these years, I'm free if I can keep my mouth shut."

"You're free," said Jason, "and you *will* keep your mouth shut, if Nate and I have to use massive quantities of duct tape to enforce it. For our mom's sake, of course."

Zeke thought of the brief, private meeting his brother had pulled strings to arrange, of how his eyes had misted— all right, *more* than misted, at the sight of his mother looking older, yes, but strong and vital as she'd wept throughout their bittersweet reunion.

"For Mom's sake," Zeke agreed. "And because I figure that fractures to Shane's skull and spine are punishment enough. At least since he finally spoke up for me."

"So what now?" Jason asked him as, after he was processed out, the two of them walked into the green, pine-filtered light of a warm East Texas morning. Beneath the needled canopy that overarched the courthouse lawn, a few of the town's namesake dogwoods raised myriad white flags, as if in surrender to the area's lingering corruption.

"Breakfast, I guess. Didn't have much appetite after picking the first dozen weevils out of the jail's corn bread." As the two of them walked, Zeke stared out at the town's square, a prosperous-looking downtown lined with quaint antique shops and cafés, a bookstore and a gift shop. Over the past twenty years, progress of a sort had come to this place. Enough that it no longer felt like home.

Would anywhere, now that the world had shifted and he was no longer either Zeke Pike or John Langley, but this strange, new man? *A free man*, free of everything except the knowledge of the tragedy he had once set in motion, a tragedy that sent shock waves of destruction through Willie Tyler's family. Deep in thought, Zeke didn't hear the car until it was almost on him.

"John," his brother warned, shouldering him clear of the bright red sports car that slipped around a corner and accelerated, its engine growling like a hunting cat.

Growling and then squealing as the tires grabbed the pavement and the car jerked to a stop. A woman leaped out of it, a woman who raced to throw her arms around him and kiss him until East Texas fell away. As a vision of his true home filled him, Rachel Copeland pulled his spirit like a tethered glider to soar among the clouds.

EPILOGUE

Love is not consolation. It is light.

—*Friedrich Nietzsche*

Eight months later

"There's one thing I regret," Zeke said as they maneuvered toward where a pair of raptors hinted at the presence of a thermal. With the sun fast dropping toward the horizon, this might well be the day's last.

Rachel turned her head to look back over her shoulder. "I know you're sorry about Willie. Sorry about Marlene, too, and her poor family, all those families touched by what she did. But you have to let them go, Zeke, the same way I've let go of the things I can't change."

He smiled, thinking she was starting to sound like the counselor both of them saw in Alpine. Though he wouldn't admit it under threat of torture, Zeke knew the sessions had helped him as well as her.

"I'm not talking about that," he explained. "What I meant to say is I'm sorry I wasn't there to hear you to tell Gallinardi to get bent."

"Oh, that." Rachel laughed. "I didn't put it that crudely. Not quite, anyway."

The altimeter spun upward as Zeke turned to catch the column of warm air. He felt a surge of joy—and pride in the still-novel achievement.

"Steady," Rachel urged him as they spiraled upward. "That's it. That's right—you've got a really good feel for this."

"I'm an expert in good feels." He leaned forward and tip-toed fingertips along her shoulder, though he couldn't reach the good stuff.

Rachel smacked his hand. "I keep telling you, this is a cockpit in name only. So let's keep the correct head in the game so you'll be ready for your solo."

After a time the lift died, and he turned toward home. As he glimpsed the first pink flush of sunset, he sobered. "Do *you* have regrets, Rachel?"

"I wish I'd stuck to my guns and insisted on the lemon cake for our reception. Patsy's a real sweetheart, but that strawberry nightmare . . ." She made a gagging sound.

He shook his head, remembering their attempts to eat her creation to spare Patsy's feelings. And Patsy's white-faced horror when she realized she'd been so nervous about baking her first wedding cake, she'd somehow managed to put in more salt than sugar. It had taken them months to get her to laugh about what they'd teasingly dubbed her "Freudian slip of the spoon."

"I meant about turning down Gallinardi and the Foundation," he said. Since Rachel's dis-invitation to the showing, she'd been given the cold shoulder by art snobs far and wide.

"Heck, no," Rachel answered without a moment's hesitation. "Business might be off a little, but I'm loving the flying more all the time, and my dad seems a lot happier. Besides, they can only keep me away from the showings and the art mags. They can't keep me from shooting."

"You'd better not let Gallinardi hear you say that, or there'll be a restraining order for sure."

She laughed again. "You know what I mean. Because shooting the photos is what makes me happy, not the accolades. And thanks to you, I'm selling plenty of framed prints to people who'll enjoy them. Regular people who come by our workshop to look at your stuff."

"Word's getting around, Rachel. More and more of the tourists show up looking for your stuff and not mine. And it seems to me at least a few of 'em are serious collectors looking for the next big thing."

"Or are they looking for a certain beefcake shot of my

dear husband?" she teased, reminding Zeke of the one photo he felt too self-conscious to keep around the workshop. Though the original was hanging in their bedroom at the cinnamon adobe, he studiously avoided looking at it.

As he descended toward the airstrip, he changed the subject. "So, you think I'll ever make a decent pilot? Or at least a safe one?"

Rachel hesitated before answering. "I think you'll make a more-than-decent pilot. And if I didn't—if I didn't think you'd be a safe one, do you think I'd risk our lives—all three of our lives—letting you fly?"

Zeke thought it must have been the wind's noise that had made him hear the words *all three*. But after he regrouped, he asked, "J.D. didn't stow away, did he?"

She shot a smile over her shoulder. "Nope," she said, eyes glowing, "but someone else did. About six weeks back, according to the doc."

"The doctor?" Zeke echoed, then broke into a broad grin as her meaning came clear to him.

Dead ahead and just below them, a solitary light ascended from the rose-washed desert. But it couldn't hold a candle to the brilliance of the future just coming into view.

SARAH ABBOT

Destiny Bay

Someone is watching...someone who knows what Abrielle Lancaster wants to know: what caused her mother to leave the tiny, picturesque St. Cecilia Island a broken woman.

Abby has fallen in love with the island's dangerous beauty, with its quirky customs and warm-hearted inhabitants. But most of all, she's fallen in love with enigmatic, charismatic Ryan Brannigan, the one man who has every reason in the world to hate her.

Is he the one who's been lurking outside her bedroom window in the dark? Is he the one who's painstakingly plotted every move to recreate a relationship so twisted and terrifying it will never, ever die?

ISBN 13: 978-0-505-52744-5

FIRST TO KILL

Nathan McBride was retired. The former Marine sniper and covert CIA operative had put the violence of his former life behind him.

But not anymore.

A deep-cover FBI agent has disappeared, along with one ton of powerful Semtex explosive, enough to unleash a disaster of international proportions. The U.S. government has no choice but to coax Nathan out of retirement. He's the only man with the skills necessary to get the job done.

On the one side is a ruthless adversary with a blood-chilling plan—and on the other are agents who will stop at nothing to see their own brand of justice done.

ANDREW PETERSON

Coming September 2008   ISBN 13: 978-0-8439-6144-7

JUDITH E. FRENCH

SUPER KILLERS

Human monsters. They torture and terrify, then terminate innocent lives. For pleasure. And always there is a pattern, a signature that sets their crimes apart.

BLOOD SPORT

Agent Jillian Maxwell is sure she's identified one of the worst ever. Twenty-three unsolved murders in two years. A trail of bodies with slashed throats, dumped by the sea. Her distractingly hot new partner disputes her theory, but Jillian's instincts tell her she's closing in on her quarry. The postcards she's received before each strike hold the key; she knows the scene of the next murder—Ocean City, Maryland. Despite "Cowboy" Reed Donovan's objections, she'll go undercover to draw out the perp. Only too late, she realizes there's more than one player in this deadly game, and she's been set up to be the latest loser.

ISBN 13: 978-0-505-52757-8

□ **YES!**

Sign me up for the Love Spell Book Club and send my FREE BOOKS! If I choose to stay in the club, I will pay only $8.50* each month, a savings of $6.48!

NAME: _____

ADDRESS: _____

TELEPHONE: _____

EMAIL: _____

□ I want to pay by credit card.

□ VISA   □ MasterCard.   □ DISCOVER

ACCOUNT #: _____

EXPIRATION DATE: _____

SIGNATURE: _____

Mail this page along with $2.00 shipping and handling to:
Love Spell Book Club
PO Box 6640
Wayne, PA 19087
Or fax (must include credit card information) to:
610-995-9274

You can also sign up online at **www.dorchesterpub.com**.

*Plus $2.00 for shipping. Offer open to residents of the U.S. and Canada only. Canadian residents please call 1-800-481-9191 for pricing information.

If under 18, a parent or guardian must sign. Terms, prices and conditions subject to change. Subscription subject to acceptance. Dorchester Publishing reserves the right to reject any order or cancel any subscription.